DAVID MARK

Cruel Mercy

MULHOLLAND
BOOKS

HODDER

First published Great Britain in 2017 by Mulholland Books
An imprint of Hodder & Stoughton
An Hachette UK company

1

First published in paperback in 2017

A CIP catalogue record for this title is
available from the British Library

Paperback ISBN 978 1 444 79815 9
eBook ISBN 978 1 444 79812 8

Typeset in Plantin Light by Hewer Text UK Ltd, Edinburgh

Printed and bound by Clays Ltd, St Ives plc

Hodder & Stoughton policy is to use papers that are
natural, renewable and recyclable products and made
from wood grown in sustainable forests. The logging and
manufacturing processes are expected to conform to the
environmental regulations of the country of origin.

Hodder & Stoughton Ltd
Carmelite House
50 Victoria Embankment
London EC4Y 0DZ

www.hodder.co.uk

For Roisin and Pharaoh,
with love and awe.
You know who you are.

'And here, shipmates, is true and faithful repentance; not clamorous for pardon, but grateful for punishment.'

Herman Melville, *Moby-Dick*

Then . . .

The first girl was still alive when he poured the cement into the cavity between the floorboards and the earth. He decanted it tenderly, like wine from a chalice. She managed to raise her hand above the level of the setting liquid and over the course of the next two days the cement-coated limb turned to stone. He watched the transformation without interval. Viewed it dispassionately. Viewed it the same way he had watched her die.

At length, the sight of the stone hand began to unsettle him. Even when he closed his eyes he could still see that arm and wrist, that palm and halted pulse; fingers curled inwards, rising up from the floor as if reaching out for him. Eventually he had to hack it off with a spade. The hand sits on his bedside table now. He uses it to hold his ring, watch and crucifix as he sleeps. The flesh inside the stone shell has started to corrupt but he does not mind the odour of the rotting claw. It is a comforting smell, like baking bread or mown grass.

With the second and third girls he made sure their hearts had stopped beating before he began to pour.

By the time he entombed the eighth girl he had begun to know, almost to the exact hour, when their pulses would give out through lack of food and water. He had begun to know on what day their cries would stop.

This girl is different. She is still alive two days after he expected her to expire. She still has some lustre in her eyes.

It is almost as if she believes there is still hope . . .

* * *

I

Though she can no longer feel her legs, the girl senses they are drawn up, baby-like; pressed against the swell of her gut.

In these moments she fancies that this place, with its wooden roof and bare earth and its dead-animal smell, is a womb. She is an unborn child, protected and embraced by the walls of the cavity in which she squirms.

At other times, she feels that the chamber has the properties of a cocoon. She will be reborn as something magnificent; all effortless grace and dazzling wings.

In such moments, she does not despise her confinement but sees it as the man wishes, as a place where she is safe. She can almost forget the reek of piss and blood and the sensation of scuttling beasts that scamper, multi-legged, like disembodied hands, across her unwashed skin.

The man is right, after a fashion. She is safe, down here. Her prison is impregnable. She knows the ceiling to be sturdy and immobile, having banged upon it with fists and knees until both were bloodied and numb. She knows that she can only burrow down a few inches into the cold soil before she strikes rock. At first, she had believed herself capable of turning onto her belly; perhaps finding a softer patch of ground where she could begin to tunnel out. But the wooden timbers are only a few inches above her face and the size of her stomach makes it impossible to rotate. So she lies in the dark and the cold, sticking out her tongue and trying to catch the water that drips through the cracks between the wooden panels. She savours the tastes of mud and brick; of spilled gas and old leaves.

It has been several hours since she last lapped at the chemical-tasting water that her captor gently drizzles through the tiny fissures above her face. She has begun to yearn for the pleasant numbness that she has come to associate with its presence upon her tongue. Her thoughts are becoming less fuzzy and the pain in her stomach is turning from a vague ache into something that seems to be tying her intestines to her spine. She realises that she is choking. Her tongue has rolled to the back of the dark, wet cave of her mouth. For an instant she imagines rolls of fifty-dollar bills, wrapped with a band and pushed down her gullet. And then the image is gone; replaced by flashes of gold that stab into the blackness of her vision with each dry, punishing cough.

She can hear movement up there, the rhythmic *thrump-thrump-thrump* of the rocking chair as it moves forward and back, forward and back, disturbing the dirt and the dust and the chalky grey powder that carpets the floor and which billows down onto her filth-streaked face.

Please, talk to me. Please, don't give up. I'll listen. I promise I'll listen . . .

The sound of the rocking chair stops abruptly. Icy panic fills the girl's chest and throat.

Footsteps reverberate softly on the floor above her face. A sprinkling of dirt tumbles through the cracks and into her open mouth. She begins to cough again and closes her eyes, instinctively, as she begins to retch and heave.

She opens her eyes as the hinges creak. Light floods the six-foot-by-six-foot pit in which she has lain these past weeks. It is not a harsh light. It makes her think of old-fashioned photos and oil paintings. It speaks to a part of her that she only half remembers but the voice is strong. She finds her eyes brimming over, emotion pushing on her chest. She finds herself reaching up. She wants to be picked up, like a child, wishes for warm, strong fingers to close upon her wrists and to lift her, effortlessly, from this pit of filth and despair. Through the blurring swirls of her vision, she fancies that she can see her father, with his straight back and his curly hair; his gold cross and colourful shirts. Tries to smell him, to lose herself in the sweat and soap powder and tobacco and rum. She cannot find it. There's only the stench of herself.

And then him.

Him, with his pale eyes and pale skin and his empty mouth.

She opens her eyes into the thin, sunken face of her captor. He looks like a dead thing. Looks as if he has begun to decompose, only to open his dead eyes and worm his way back into the light.

'Please,' she begs, and it sounds as though there is a foot on her throat. 'Talk to me. Please. You can. I'll never tell. I'll never say . . .'

She sees herself in the blackness of his irises. And then she sees, for a moment, the person she was. She has a name. A family. A home. She used to be called Alejandra, but these past years she has answered to Ali. *More American,* her father said, in an accent thick with the sounds of home.

Her head feels like it is exploding. Memories collide and smash and splinter. She was running through the place her family called Alphabet City. Counting the streets, the way she always did. The early-evening sky was silvery-blue; like the blue around St John's severed head in the jigsaw-puzzle picture that glared down behind the priest as he smiled and twinkled through Mass. Blue, like the man's watch, scratching her wrists as he pushed her down and covered her body with his own. His *associate.* That was the word he used, that warm night when she looked upon the handsome devil who did things to her that she did not understand and which, at first, she did not want to stop. Regret came later. Regret and pain, followed by those long months of not knowing what to do or what to say and watching her body change while praying over and over again that nobody else would see the truth of her.

A sudden rasp, almost masked by the casters of the chair. A sudden mechanical noise, and then it feels as though her ears are filling with water as the tomb reverberates around her.

'Forgive me, Father, for I have sinned. It has been eight months since my last confession. I have allowed the devil to seduce me on four occasions when I was unable to stop myself from touching my skin in a way that would displease the Lord. I have harboured many impure thoughts. I have thought disrespectfully about the man who calls himself my father. I am grateful for his kindness and yet when he speaks to me I feel a great rage inside me – a hunger for something I can't describe. I have imagined myself stealing into his room at night and smashing his brains in with a hammer – perhaps driving a nail into his skull as if it were the wrists or feet of our Lord. I do sincerely repent . . . *Shush, please, no more* . . . I repent of these sins and ask for the strength not to repeat such offences. Forgive me, Father, for my actions in making this confession. The girl I took had kind eyes and spoke kindly to

4

me. Please allow her torture to cease. She suffers and screams and cries and her skin has begun to repel me. Father, please intercede with our Lord and pray for her agonies to cease so she may rest with Jesus and her sinful flesh can be consumed by this sacred earth. Bless me, Father. Amen.'

Ali pictures the other girl and knows, with an intuition she cannot comprehend, that she too was, is, in this tomb. She sees the girl as a mirror image of herself, beneath the ground, growing weak, fading with each flimsy tick of her heart. She wonders whether the girl still lies next to her. Whether her head is near her own feet so that they sleep top-to-tail, as her mother used to call it. She wonders whether there was pain in her final moments, or if she flew to heaven as softly as falling asleep.

Ali suddenly remembers a sensation of . . . hollowness. Of being an empty thing; a vessel, to be filled. More than that. Exhaustion. Her knees and back ached. She was scrubbing floorboards. Floorboards that were almost golden. Floorboards in which she could see her face. Mama had been skinning poblano peppers that morning. The apartment would smell of *sofrito verde*. There was homework to be done but nothing she did not enjoy. History. English. But then it rolls over her again; that memory of *wrongness*. That sensation of unease, like a patch of dampness on her clothes or a stone in her shoe. She remembers pain. Remembers sitting alone in the bathroom and weeping into her hands. Her mind fills with traffic and neon. That night. *That night* . . . running down the alley off Avenue C; four streets from home, safe in Alphabet City; in these streets of guns and dealers which her father still called *Loisaida*, and where she never felt afraid.

In the mirrors of his eyes, she sees herself clearly. She lies on her back, face twisted upwards, bare legs drawn up to her belly. She is dressed in rags and she senses that her black curly hair looks like the hide of a long-dead bear.

Strong hands close around the bare skin of her wrists. She makes little noise but for a strangled gasp as she is pulled upwards, jerked into a sitting position and lolling in this unfinished grave like a puppet.

For an instant, she sees the room. Brick fireplace. Wooden walls. A solitary wooden chair and a table with a tape recorder. A three-seater sofa, covered in magazines. Empty food cartons and discarded clothes. A wall, crammed with books. And mirrors. So many mirrors . . .

He pulls her upwards and suddenly the pain is not in her arms. The whole lower half of her body seems to contort in agony and the sensation gives her strength. She resists the tugging on her limbs. Instead she gives in to the crippling pain encircling her whole lower half. And then she is free, slumping back into the hole in the ground as her captor steps back; staring in horror as the thing in her belly rotates, straining at her thin flesh, like so many pythons in a bag.

'My baby,' she says, as memories flood her like daylight. 'Please . . . !'

The light is snatched away as the lid of her prison slams shut. Her scream bounces back and forth between the wood and the earth until she is lost in an echoing tomb of her own cries.

PART ONE

Thirteen Nights Ago

The branches reach out for him like the grasping limbs of dead souls. Withered, rotting things that cling to his cuffs and his hands and his hair like the forsaken. He thanks God that he cannot see their faces and that they cannot see his. He has sent a lot of people to hell and he does not doubt they take it personally . . .

He brushes the thoughts away, crashes past the branches and the spindly leaves, pushing onwards; his boots thumping down through the thick snow and striking the hard earth beneath. He can hear his own blood banging in his ears. The sound of the gunshots is still echoing in his skull and the torch in his hand jerks up and down with each urgent step.

'Here, you old fuck,' comes a voice filled with laughter. 'I see you. Follow the light.'

Claudio curses and raises a hand to his face as the glare of the flashlight skewers him. He is still wincing when the younger man emerges from the tangled pocket of evergreens and walks slowly towards him. He still has his gun in his right hand. Claudio holds a knife, its hilt thick with blood, in his left.

'You catch him?' asks Claudio breathlessly.

'Fuck no. Prick was fast.'

'Faster than a bullet?' he asks irritably, and wipes the sweat from his forehead, leaving a smear of crimson upon his skin.

'What you wanna do now?' comes the reply. 'His accent was Russian. Somebody's fucking us around. This is a set-up. There might be more of them . . .'

Temper overwhelms Claudio. None of this was supposed to happen.

Crisp.

Efficient.

Clinical.

That is how he made his name and kept himself alive these past forty years. The younger man is all bravado and front, with his soft calfskin coat and his sweatpants, his white trainers and his gold chains. His name is Luca and he may have just got them both killed. Claudio chews on his lower lip with his one remaining incisor.

'Stop that, man.' Luca laughs. 'You're like a fucking vampire. And these woods are creepy.'

Claudio makes a fist then takes a deep breath, trying to reign in his temper. He was supposed to be pretending to be a traffic cop, for fuck's sake. And he'd arrived in sneakers and sweatpants! All he had to do was keep them quiet until Claudio arrived. But he couldn't help himself. Had to show off. Had to show he was a man who mattered . . .

'I'm sure I clipped him,' says Luca. 'You hear all that bullshit? Did he look important to you?'

'You know the Russians – everybody says they're somebody important,' says Claudio quietly. 'I know that accent though.'

'Doesn't mean he mattered.'

'Something's gone wrong here,' whispers Claudio, suddenly aware of the absolute silence of the woods. 'This wasn't the job. I smell lies. And now there's nobody to ask because they're fucking dead.'

Luca shrugs. He doesn't much care. He's enjoyed himself tonight. He's had a chance to hurt somebody. There's a light in his eyes as bright as the blood upon the snow.

Claudio shakes his head again. 'There'll be repercussions. I don't like repercussions.'

Luca rolls his eyes like a petulant teenager. He turns his back on Claudio and starts walking back to where he left his car.

Claudio stands still. It could have all gone perfectly. It was a good plan. A perfect pincer movement, followed by enough layers of rumour and speculation to ensure that nobody ever guessed at the truth.

He watches the younger man trudging away through the crow-black woods. He's struggling through the thick snow and cursing the cold. His gun is hanging loosely from the hand he is using for balance as he totters precariously in front of an old oak with a long, splintered branch . . .

Claudio has stayed alive far longer than he has any right to expect. His longevity has given him a curious kind of sixth sense; a skill for reading situations and staying a step ahead. Perhaps it is his many years in the shadows that have taught him how to read darkness. He does not care to overthink it. But when he feels the air behind him change shape and texture, some primal force takes over and he drops to his knees. Instead of slamming into the back of his head, the branch merely clips him on the top of the skull. He does not make a sound as he topples forward: collapsing onto the tree roots and the hard snow with his arms outstretched and his legs out straight behind him. Christ-like, he lies immobile, only half seeing out of one eye as the man from the trunk, the man who fled into the woods, steps over him and runs lightly towards Luca. Claudio tries to speak but cannot seem to make his lips move. He feels wetness upon the back of his neck.

'Come on, old man, we've got to get busy . . .'

Luca is a few feet away, struggling through the snow. Claudio's world is black and white; a photographic negative; a snowstorm of newspaper print. In its centre a silhouette, an inky blob that crosses between himself and his companion in purposeful, efficient strides.

Helpless, feeble, he watches as the man who attacked him darts ahead quickly, silently, and without another word he grabs Luca by the collar of his stupid calfskin jacket and pushes him forward. The branch goes into his chest just below his ribcage and exits between his shoulder blades. There is a sound like somebody has snapped a dozen small branches and then the soft hiss as the air in his lungs gurgles upwards through bloodied lips and into the cold night air.

On the ground, Claudio breathes out, slowly. He tries to become a part of the forest floor. He does not want the man to come back and finish him off. He knows that were the roles reversed, it is what he would do. He is a killer. He takes no pleasure in it but it is his life's work to stop human hearts. He came here, to this lonely place on the road to Crow, to kill two men. He has done what he was paid to do. He wasn't expecting the third, who took off into the darkness as soon as Luca pulled the trigger and the big dark Irishman fell forward onto the snow-covered earth.

Claudio watches as the man who killed Luca disappears into the trees. After a moment he begins to move. Slowly, soundlessly, he checks himself over. There is a gash to the top of his skull and blood in his mouth, but apart from a ringing sensation in his ears he is unharmed. Damp and cold, he pulls himself upright and leans against a tree. He reaches into his pocket and finds his cigarettes. Lights up, and breathes out a cloud.

'Fuck,' he whispers to himself. It covers the majority of his feelings.

Pissed off and sore, Claudio consoles himself with the thought that it is not his fault. Luca fucked up, not him. And nobody told them about the Chechen. He did his job right and then other forces got in the way. Even as he thinks it, he finds himself shaking his head. He has seen men killed for so much less. He has killed men who had perfectly good excuses for their screw-ups. He closes his eyes and searches for comfort. Finds it in Belle. The little girl is the only light in the blackness inside him, but she is a light that grows brighter every time she holds his hand and looks at him as if he were something other than a monster. For her, he would stop all this. For her, he would try to be a better man. But neither she nor her mother knows how he earns the money that sustains them and he never intends for them to find out. He lives on borrowed time. For forty years he has been waiting for it all to stop.

As he stares at the body of the young man impaled on the tree, Claudio feels a shiver of premonition. He suddenly fears that he is at the start of something that could lead to his end.

I

Now . . .

There's a chunk of plastic cat shit in Detective Ronald Alto's Zen garden. It's just sitting there, next to the little rake, forming a gruesome mouth beneath three shiny pebbles.

Alto fights back a smile as he wordlessly picks up the offending addition and deposits it in his top drawer. It clatters down among the other pieces of artwork that the detectives of New York's Seventh Precinct have seen fit to place in the little bamboo and sand construction that sits in the in-tray on top of his age-blackened desk. He presumes this evening's contribution was made by Detective Hugh Redding. Reviewed critically, the cat shit lacks subtlety but has a certain potency. The same could be said for the man himself. It certainly doesn't possess the creative genius displayed by Sergeant Kendricks, who last week recreated a beach homicide out of Lego figures in the ten minutes that Alto was away from his desk.

'B minus,' announces Alto, without looking at the trio of detectives at the far end of the long room, who sit shovelling Chinese food into their mouths with plastic knives and forks.

'Objection,' shouts Redding, beginning to rise. There is rice on the front of his off-white shirt and the seams of his grey trousers strain under the pressure of his flesh.

'Overruled,' says Alto, waving Redding back into his chair.

'It's a litter box,' shouts Redding, picking a shrimp off the rolled-up cuff of his shirt sleeve and popping it in his mouth. 'I want the shit back. Belongs to my stepson.'

'Early Christmas present, was it?'

'Little prick left it in my shoe.'

'And you thought of me?'

'I always think of you, Ronny,' says Redding, puckering up and blowing a kiss. 'Can't sleep unless I'm spooning you in my mind.'

Alto decides to end the conversation with a grin and a raised mid-finger. He is a veteran of the Seventh and well versed in the foul-mouthed sexual banter that is as much a part of the squad room as the black linoleum, the beige walls, the battered silver filing cabinets and an aroma that would make a perfumer's head cave in. It's a pungent cocktail of perspiration, ethnic food and clothes dried out in a too-small room; marbled with coffee and stale cigarettes. Alto associates the smell with home. He missed it when he spent his year on temporary assignment with Homicide South. That was a hard time. He made the right contacts, put away some bad people but it was a difficult few months for his soul. He had to stand by while deals were made that turned his stomach. He found himself changing. He found himself starting to see the advantages, the opportunity for manipulation, rather than seeing the victims and the villains. His time with Homicide came to an end through a combination of failing to kiss the right asses, and becoming too fond of the bottle. He knows himself to be tenacious but in drink he becomes obsessive.

For the last few months of his time in Homicide he was doggedly pursuing a money-launderer who had links to Paulie Pugliesca's crime family. Loose lips alerted him to the crooked lawyer's existence and he became convinced that if he could put a face to the legend he would have a useful lever to use against Pugliesca. The old man's soldiers were responsible for a half-dozen hits during his time on Homicide and he had fought tooth and claw to keep the murder investigations under his remit instead of being folded up into the larger Federal investigation into organised crime. Instead he found endless layers of bureau-cracy and legal red tape and became so entangled in who owned what and which company belonged to what offshore account, he found himself drowning. He returned to the Seventh as a borderline alcoholic. The file he collected on the lawyer still sits in his desk; the smug, round-faced bastard grinning up through the sheets of arrest reports, requests for information and legal documentation. He doesn't know why he keeps it other than a feeling, deep in his core, that it matters.

Adjusting his glasses, Alto sits down in his swivel chair and slaps his hand down on the keyboard of the chunky computer. The machine is all but useless and he prefers to use his own slimline laptop for his casework, but when the screen desktop is dark he can see the reflection of the squad room in all its grey misery, and at this hour, on an evening this grim, he is far too short on self-loathing to put himself through it.

Ronald Alto is forty-two years old. He's tall and slim and is one of the few detectives in the Seventh who worries about how much exercise he is getting, how much he drinks, and whether he has consumed enough portions of fresh fruit and vegetables each day. His colleagues have stopped inviting him to join in their nightly banquets of cultural cuisine, though tonight the smell of chicken chow-mein is so strong that he could well be passively consuming a share of their artery-hardening calories. It took Alto a year of hard work to lose the sixty pounds he packed on after Lisa walked out on him and he is obsessive in his desire not to let a single ounce of fat slip back onto his middleweight boxer's torso. Lisa would consider this typical of him. If he had been less obsessive about his work, perhaps she would never have left. Alto would disagree. She was always going to leave him. Obsession had nothing to do with it. He considers himself neither more nor less devoted to his work than any of his colleagues. He simply struggles with going home to watch shitty TV and eat dinners off a tray when he could be taking steps towards catching killers. He presumes he would be the same in whatever profession he chose. Were he a carpenter, like his father, he would not be able to stop sanding or varnishing simply because his shift had finished. He would need to see the job through to completion. He told Lisa that long before they were married and continued to mutter it, sullenly, in the face of her tears and tantrums through the course of their three-year marriage. She was already gone a week by the time Alto realised she had made good on her threat. It was not the absence of Lisa that plunged him into misery – more the fulfilment of the gloomy prophesies made by friends, family and colleagues when he announced his intention to wed. Cops' marriages don't last, they said. Marry another cop or marry nobody. He ignored their grim predictions, confident that he would be the exception to the rule. Nobody was pleased when he was proved wrong.

Alto opens his laptop and, in the few seconds it takes for the machine to come to life, turns to look out of the dirty windows at a view he knows better than his reflection. The detective room is on the second floor of the utilitarian Seventh Precinct, which shares its home with the handsome heroes of the Fire Department. It overlooks a dreary, blustery corridor of the Lower East Side. The constant wind seems to have picked up a vast chunk of Manhattan's most uninspiring constructions and deposited them at the edge of the East River. The Seventh, housed at the pleasingly exact address of 19½ Pitt Street, looks out on a scene almost Soviet in its bleakness. This is a place of housing projects, bridge ramps and squat brick buildings, rattled almost insensible by the constant rumble of vehicles crossing the bridge overhead. Nobody would put this view on a Christmas card, despite the hard, frozen snow that is piled up on the sidewalks like garbage bags. Fresh snow hasn't fallen for three nights but the temperature has yet to get above zero and the flurries that did fall have turned to jagged white stone. The emergency rooms are overrun with people who slipped and hurt themselves. Alto heard a story yesterday that a Vietnamese shopkeeper had been assaulted by the son of an elderly lady who fell outside his store. The dutiful son had blamed the shopkeeper for not shovelling the snow away from his building. The shopkeeper had suggested that it wasn't his responsibility. Devoid of further rational argument, the son made his point by kicking the shopkeeper unconscious. It has been years since such anecdotes shocked Alto. He no longer questions what people will do to one another. He just tries to tidy up afterwards as best he can.

A buzz from his cell phone reminds him to take one of his vitamin tablets. His hooded, military-issue coat hangs on the back of a nearby chair and he searches its pockets for the correct bottle. He takes two green tablets with a swig of electrolyte-rich water, and then slides himself back over to his computer.

'Dinner-time, George?' shouts Redding, with his mouth full.

'Just an hors d'oeuvre,' replies Alto, grinning. The men and women of the Seventh have two nicknames for him. One is George Jetson, a reference to his diet of spaceman pills. The other is Bono, in tribute to the amber-tinted spectacles he wears to combat the migraines he suffers when he spends too much time beneath bright lights. Both nicknames are remarkably affectionate. The Seventh is full of police officers with handles like Boner, Stinkz and Ball-sack. To Alto, Ball-sack seems particularly unfair. After all, her mother named her Deborah.

Alto's fingers move over his keyboard and he pulls up the relevant case file. He sends it to the printer and sits back, waiting for the ancient machine to start rattling and spitting like some steam-powered beast. His eyes flick up to the clock above the filing cabinets. It's 10.18 p.m. He probably has a few minutes . . .

A moment later, Alto's posture tenses as he looks at the mugshot filling his screen. The man's name is Murray Ellison and if Alto doesn't find a way to put him in prison there is a very good chance he will kill him. Last summer, Ellison drugged an NYU philosophy student he met in a bar off East Broadway. She had been out drinking cocktails with friends and the handsome investment banker had taken a shine to the petite nineteen-year-old with her bubblegum-pink hair, her hippy dress and her little boy's body. He said hello. Charmed her. Bought her drinks and another round for her friends. Whispered in her ear until she goose-pimpled and blushed. High on new experience, lost in drink, she let him near enough to stir Rohypnol into her sangrias blancas. As the drug loosened her inhibitions, she told her buddies she was going to stay with her new friend. They were thrilled at her daring; excited that she was going to do something so delightfully brazen. He promised them he would ensure she got a taxi

17

home. Instead, he took her to his East Village apartment and raped her near-unconscious body. He went to bed and left her on his living-room floor. The combination of alcohol and Rohypnol caused her to choke to death on her own vomit.

Alto cannot prove what happened next but has no doubts about the sequence of events. Alto has traced the calls made from Ellison's cell phone and knows that he rang an unregistered cell phone forty minutes before a stolen Volvo was dropped off at the kerbside outside his building by a stocky man in a woollen hat and a ski jacket. He has never been traced. A short while later, a man who looked a lot like Ellison was spotted by a neighbour placing a suitcase in the trunk of the car. He then got into the vehicle and drove away. The vehicle was picked up by surveillance cameras on a residential street in Red Hook. The driver covered his face as he left and did not lock the door. Instead, he left the keys in the ignition. It was stolen four hours later. Whoever took it seems to have abandoned the vehicle a short while afterwards. Alto has a feeling they looked in the trunk. Not long after, it was stolen again. By the time the contents were reported to the police, making a case against Ellison seemed damn near impossible. The District Attorney said there were too many gaps in the timeline. Once the neighbour began to have doubts about who it was they had seen, and with so many opportunities for other parties to have put the case in the trunk, the whole thing became too difficult to proceed with. There were no usable forensics, and Ellison had good lawyers. He stuck to his story. The girl came home with him, they had sex, and she left. The suit his lawyer was wearing cost more than Alto's car. Ellison smirked his way through his interviews and even had the balls to wink now and again at the officers watching from behind the mirrored glass of the interview room. Alto managed to track down the petty thief who sold Ellison the vehicle but he refused to testify and left the city before Alto could secure a subpoena. The District Attorney's office was impressed with the work Alto had done to demonstrate the victim's last movements, but did not have sufficient belief in a conviction to prosecute. Ellison was set free. Alto, who had been present at the victim's autopsy, had to be physically held back as Ellison stepped onto Pitt Street and climbed inside a sleek black limo. He was in the process of pulling his gun.

After the outburst, his sergeant bought him the Zen garden. Told him to let it go, to be a bit more Buddhist about the whole affair. Karma was a bitch, and Ellison would eventually get what was coming to him. Alto heeded his sergeant's words. He just wanted to make sure that karma knew exactly what was required.

Alto is staring into Ellison's green eyes when the phone on his desk begins to ring. His eyes flick to the clock: 10.30 p.m. The visitor is bang on time.

After telling the desk sergeant he will be straight down, Alto crosses to the printer and collects his sheaf of papers. He pauses for a moment and decides that it will be too cold without his coat. He returns to his desk, pulls on the great grey garment that makes him look like a member of the KGB, and walks briskly down the stairs to the reception area. He does not need to be told which of the people waiting in the small reception area is here for him. He performed a Google search on his visitor the moment he was told who was coming. And the man standing reading the noticeboard is unmistakably Detective Sergeant Aector McAvoy of Humberside Police in Merrie Old England.

'Sergeant McAvoy,' says Alto, swiping his card on the security scanner and pushing through the plastic barrier. 'A pleasure.'

The big man turns from the noticeboard like a teenager who has been caught looking at a skin magazine. He looks startled. Embarrassed. His big face is red and his tousled hair is damp at the temples. There is grey beneath his eyes, as if an artist started drawing him in charcoal then switched to pastels halfway through. He has a ginger goatee, running to grey and the big brown eyes of a Disney animal. There are scars running from his eyelid to his jawline. They are angry, painful-looking wounds, at odds with the gentleness of the rest of his face. He's wearing hiking boots and dark trousers that disappear into the hem of a long, dark blue woollen coat. His right hand, when he extends it, is pink and broken and solid as rock.

'Detective Alto?' asks McAvoy. 'I'm Sergeant McAvoy. Oh, sorry, you already said . . .'

Alto fights not to do a double-take as he spots a blush creeping onto the bigger man's cheeks. On his computer are the reports he requested detailing this man's part in the successful detection of two different serial killers on his home turf in Yorkshire. One of those men ended up dead. The other is serving multiple life sentences. In both cases, McAvoy had bled in pursuit of his quarry. In both cases he was praised for his insight and bravery. Alto has been looking forward to meeting him.

'Good flight?' asks Alto.

'No delays,' says McAvoy. 'Humberside to Amsterdam, then Amsterdam to here.'

'Amsterdam, eh? Any time to enjoy yourself?'

'I was only there two hours,' says McAvoy, not appearing to understand the reference.

'When did you get in?' asks Alto, his tone breezy.

'Into JFK a couple of hours ago. Taxi to the hotel, then I walked here.'

'So there's no point asking you what you think of our fair city?'

'I'm sure it's lovely,' says McAvoy, apparently apologising for not being able to give a better researched answer.

'First time in New York?'

'Near enough,' he says, pushing his hand through his hair and giving a twitchy little smile. 'Flew through here years ago. Changed for a flight to Texas. Rugby team. I was still a student then.'

'Texas, eh?' asks Alto, and tries to win McAvoy's affection. 'They say everything's bigger there. Doubt they said that when they saw you.'

McAvoy's blush turns scarlet and Alto realises he is dealing with a man whose shyness could well be a fatal affliction. He feels embarrassed by McAvoy's discomfort and gestures towards the door so the bigger man has time to recover himself. Out on the street the cold hits Alto immediately and he winces in greeting to the uniformed cops leaning against the front wall, drinking coffee and speculating on the parentage of the firefighters with whom they are engaged in a bitter fight for parking lot supremacy.

'Sorry we couldn't lay on some better weather for you,' says Alto, as he leads McAvoy down the sidewalk away from the precinct. 'There's a little place up here we can grab a quiet corner and something that actually tastes better than the plate it's served on. I can't promise you the same in the detectives' room.'

McAvoy gives a nod of agreement. He walks comfortably enough on the snow. Doesn't hunch inside his jacket the way that most people do. His big strides seem to devour the sidewalk. Alto is no small man and is well used to the company of men whose general size and shape would be best equated to kitchen appliances, but next to McAvoy he feels like he is walking beside a suddenly mobile building.

'Cab driver give you his life story?' asks Alto.

'His name was Jack,' says McAvoy, looking across the street at an ugly housing project. 'Been here since he was seven. Runs a limo firm but still drives cabs. Hasn't been back to Hong Kong since he was nineteen but hopes to get there next year. Likes the Knicks. Has a cousin in London and wanted to know if it's true that we all carry umbrellas.'

Alto laughs. 'Cab drivers like that where you're from?'

'Depends whom you get,' says McAvoy, and Alto finds himself oddly pleased by McAvoy's use of the word 'whom'. 'The stand-up comedians would have you believe that every taxi driver is a racist chatterbox with the social graces of a barnyard animal. I wouldn't like to say. Cabs are expensive. I usually drive.'

Alto notices that McAvoy has slowed his pace a little and seems mesmerised by the tall buildings across the street.

'Not exactly pretty,' says Alto, nodding. 'It gets more hipster the further we go.'

'It looks like Snakes and Ladders,' says McAvoy. He turns to Alto, his brow furrowing. 'Do you have that here? The game with the ladders? And the snakes? All the fire escapes. We just need some huge dice.'

Alto considers the building that McAvoy is looking at. He has never thought of it before but suddenly finds himself seeing it the way his new acquaintance does. 'We say Chutes and Ladders, but I'll tell that to the boys,' he says, nodding appreciatively. 'You must have an artistic soul.'

'My boss would make a joke about being an arsehole,' says McAvoy.

'Asshole, you mean?'

'She wouldn't say that. Wouldn't sound right.'

'She? You got a lady boss?'

McAvoy nods. 'She wouldn't call herself a lady either. Tougher than any of us. Best police officer you'll ever meet.'

'Can't be easy when you don't hate the boss,' says Alto, stepping around some garbage bags and feeling his feet slide on the hard snow. 'Hating the boss is what gets a lot of cops through the day.'

McAvoy considers this, while mumbling a 'good evening' to two black youths in baggy sweatpants and puffer coats standing outside the liquor store and watching their curse words turn to clouds on the cold night air.

'Nothing to hate,' he says. 'And it helps that she saved my life.'

'I Googled you,' says Alto tactfully. 'You've seen some action, eh?'

McAvoy turns his head away. He seems to be at last feeling the cold. He draws himself a little closer into his coat.

'Where is it you're taking me?' asks McAvoy, and his voice is a little colder too.

Alto points at the dark glass of an Irish bar. They are only a couple of blocks from the Seventh but already the buildings seem cleaner and the shops and restaurants more inviting. The cold weather has thinned out the normal night-time crowd but there are still huddles of students, office-workers and intoxicated diners milling around. Alto pushes open the door and his glasses mist up as they approach the long, copper-topped bar of Lucky Jack's.

'Nice,' says McAvoy appreciatively, looking at the dozens of whiskey bottles and the gleaming silver bar-taps. It's dark and atmospheric and the lights dance pleasantly in the shapely bottles stacked up behind the bar.

'You drink, I presume,' says Alto, saying hello to a large man with a green Mohawk who is drinking Guinness and reading the *Tribune*.

'A bit,' says McAvoy. He's studying the specials written in chalk on the blackboard by the toilets. 'I'm intrigued by the hot buttered rum. And there's a mucky hot chocolate sounds good. Would you think the worse of me?'

Alto wonders if the big man is joking. He works with men and women who drink beer and Bushmills. He gives a smile and turns to the young, handsome barman, who gives himself away as Australian with his opening 'G'day'.

'Mucky hot chocolate for the big man and a Brooklyn for me,' he says brightly, and turns around to find McAvoy looking out of the window at the bum wrapped in a sleeping bag in the doorway across the street. Alto barely noticed him. He was just a shape among the piles of hard snow and the uncollected garbage.

'Thanks,' says McAvoy, taking the hot chocolate. Without another word, he goes to the door and walks out, crossing the street in six strides. Alto watches McAvoy deposit the drink beside the homeless man and gently place a hand on his shoulder. He talks to the man for no more than a minute, then makes his way back to the bar.

'A lemonade for me,' says McAvoy, slipping out of his coat. His cheeks are burning.

'And a lemonade,' says Alto to the barman. He smiles. Gives a little shake of his head. 'You looked like a massive Jesus, healing the sick.'

'A massive Jesus,' says McAvoy, and gives what seems to be his first proper smile in an age. 'Don't say that near my boss.'

'You seem to love that woman.' Alto laughs.

'And don't say that near my wife.'

The two chink glasses and hunch forward in their stools, elbows on the bar.

'Copper to copper,' says McAvoy, indicating the bar-top.

'You're fucking weird,' says Alto, and grins, suddenly enjoying himself. 'Seems a shame to spoil the mood.'

McAvoy's smile fades. He gives a little nod, as if preparing himself. 'You've been told why I'm here,' he says.

Alto takes another sip of his Brooklyn and pulls the papers out of his coat pocket. 'You want to know whether we've caught the people who shot the Miracle Man,' says Alto, in a way that suggests the news is not going to be good.

McAvoy puts his head on one side. Sucks his cheek as if weighing up whether to lay down playing cards that he has no faith in.

'No,' he says at last. 'I want to help you find the other victims.'

'There're more?' asks Alto. 'Just what we need.'

'There's one more, at least,' says McAvoy.

'And what makes you think that?' asks Alto conversationally.

McAvoy looks at the ice chinking in his glass and breathes out, as if from his toes.

'Because he's family. And he either pulled the trigger, or you just haven't found his body yet.'

. . . feeling any better today, handsome? You've got a bit of colour in your skin. We'll have these curtains closed, what do you say? I was right to let the sun work its magic. I always say you should grab the sunshine in both hands and rub it all over your face when you get the chance. There's more snow coming so you enjoy Mr Sun while he shines. Beautiful blue sky too – though there are black clouds rolling in. My brothers and me, we used to purse our lips and blow when the clouds came; trying to push the rains and the snows back out to sea. Let them have it back in Nantucket, that's what Mother would say. They've got the clothes for it. Anyways, I'll leave you to it. You need your rest. I'll be back to clean you up but don't be clock-watching now. I hope your friend comes in again. I know you enjoy his visits. You just keep it calm, though, y'hear? Your pulse rate went too high last time. You need things steady and safe. Get yourself back to strength. We've been betting on whether your eyes are blue or brown. I've said brown. Fionnula from Ward C swore blind you had blue. Said she heard it from the anaesthetist's lady friend. Blue, and unresponsive, though you don't want to hear that, I'm sure. I don't want to cheat. I want you to open your eyes and show me those twinkly brown peepers while you smile and praise Jesus for the miracle that you are. God bless now. I'll be along in a while . . .

Never fucking shuts up, this one. Well intentioned, but Christ, it's like living with a children's TV presenter. Don't know who she is. Just a noise. A sort of rainbow noise, like looking through a crystal. Not like Holy Joe. He's beige. Parchment, maybe. Voice like crinkling paper. Typical fucking Bible-basher. Prayer after fucking prayer, psalm after bloody psalm. I'm the miracle, that's what they say. A miracle. Bollocks. I can't fucking move. Can't open me bastard eyes. Can't do a thing but listen and smell. Decent food, by the whiff of it. No flowers, but there's something like Christmas trees and cinnamon wafting up what's left of me nose. Shouldn't have said that out loud, Dr Grey. Don't distress the patient. Poor bastard doesn't know his own name but he knows he's had his nose sliced off and a bullet put in the back of his head. Should be pushing up daisies. But he survived. Miracle Man. Modern Lazarus, though Lazarus didn't spend the next two weeks in a hospital bed in a fucking coma, did he? But Lazarus didn't come out swinging, and this one fucking will. He's fecking strong, is this one. Doesn't die easy. Doesn't go down, even when his legs are telling him to fall. He's a fighter. Doesn't know his name, but he knows that much. Knows he doesn't give up. Knows he can take a beating and come back stronger. Knows that some-body is going to pay for this. Somebody is going to fecking bleed. Just remember. Try to remember, son. Think now. There was snow. Snow like icing on a cake. Some greasy prick in sweatpants trying to make you squirm. Trees like sticks of charcoal. And then he ran and you watched him go; told him to run till his lungs burst. There were shouts, and then the shadow was falling forward and there was a bang and it was all fucking dark until Nurse Rainbow started telling you how lucky you were to be alive and that you needed to get your strength but she was praying for you, and so was this nice man who wanted to read to you from his Bible and said he was family . . . remember. Get better. Start swinging. Make somebody fucking bleed . . .

3

McAvoy is aching. His whole body hurts. On the plane he felt as though somebody were staging an elaborate record attempt, or answering some difficult metaphysical conundrum about how many people of Celtic origin could be crammed into a standard-class discount flight from Humberside Airport to JFK. He had never seen so many red-haired people in his life and had half wondered whether he had accidentally stumbled into a convention. Had there been a mix-up? Was he guest speaker? It was the large lady with the Cork accent who put him right. It was always like this around Christmas, she said. The Irish loved the Americans, so they did. Vice versa, and all that. They were going to New York for the parade. They were going to see family. They were going to see aunts and uncles and distant cousins who had extended the offer of free accommodation during the festive period. They'd booked months ago for less than the price of a train ticket to London and they were planning to show the city how to enjoy itself. There were eighteen of them in all. McAvoy counted. As they took their seats around and about him, McAvoy had the distinct impression he was watching some sort of display team.

It wasn't a comfortable journey. Here, now, he wants to stretch out, like a cat in front of a fire, but he fears that if he did so his skeleton would make a noise like a machine gun and he knows enough about America to be concerned that such a commotion would lead to people leaping for cover and returning fire. He hasn't slept in twenty-four hours and would be the first to admit that he is entering the exhausted and manic state that only the parents of young children can truly comprehend.

He sits forward on the uncomfortable chair and tells his half-hearted hallucinations that he has no time for any nonsense.

27

Instead he focuses on his new companion, studying the smaller man's face for any clues to his thoughts. He finds himself unexpectedly optimistic. He expected the worst on his interminable cab ride from JFK. Some gruff New York cop who would treat him with disdain and tell him that he had no authority here and should get himself back to England before he got himself into trouble. In Ronald Alto, he seems to have found the complete opposite. He's warm, welcoming and surprisingly pleasant company. McAvoy just hopes he hasn't used up his annual quota of good fortune on this one small bit of luck. He fancies he will need a lot more in the days ahead.

'Your wife's brother?' asks Alto, raising his eyebrows. 'There was no mention of that when I got the call.'

'I don't want to lie to you,' says McAvoy quietly. 'Maybe whoever called you had less trouble with deceit.'

'It was my colonel who called me,' says Alto, and he appears to be making connections in his head. 'Said he'd been asked for a favour. Said I was to share what we had with a detective from England who had some knowledge of our victims. Told me to use my judgement but not to let you get yourself in trouble or in the way. Same colonel who landed me with the Miracle Man case in the first place. Body wasn't found here so it shouldn't have been mine but the hicks upstate were out of their depth and the victims had been staying in the Comfort Inn five minutes from the Seventh so he threw it my way. I still haven't said thanks.'

'That's where I'm staying,' says McAvoy, looking at the back of his hands. 'It made sense when I booked it.'

Alto shrugs. 'Colonel was a bit evasive, now I think on it.'

'I'm not 100 per cent sure that I mentioned my own family connections,' says McAvoy, as if confessing to smashing an expensive vase in a friend's house. 'My boss knows. She called some associates who owe her a favour. They must have contacted your colonel.'

'Less trouble with deceit?' asks Alto, seeming to wonder whether or not he has been tricked or treated unfairly. After a moment he shrugs. 'If you tell the boss the truth in some precincts you have to buy everybody else's drinks for a month. I'm not going to get testy about it. And thanks for being honest. Shall we compare notes or would it be easier if you just told me what you know?'

McAvoy shakes his head. 'I know next to nothing. If you could tell me what you've got, I'll see if I can contribute anything.'

Alto finishes his Brooklyn and calls for a sparkling water. 'One beer a day,' he says to McAvoy, by way of explanation. 'I try to live right.'

'Wife's rules?' asks McAvoy.

'Ex-wife's,' says Alto. 'Every pound I put on is a victory for her.'

'Wish I had your resolve,' says McAvoy. 'I have a sweet tooth. There are times when I'm around 90 per cent cake.'

'Your wife's a good cook?'

McAvoy screws up his eyes. He nods, momentarily unable to speak.

Alto removes his glasses, cleans them, and puts them back on, while McAvoy struggles with the ball of gristle in his throat.

'You want another?' asks Alto, pointing at his lemonade.

McAvoy shakes his head. He suddenly needs to feel like a policeman, and not like a damn fool far from home on an investigation he has no right to be involved with, and which, however it plays out, will break Roisin's heart. His smile fades. He nods, as if preparing himself.

'Let's hear it,' he says, in a voice that should belong to a smaller man.

'Tuesday, November 26th,' says Alto, pulling his phone from his pocket and looking at notes. 'Fourteen days ago, if my math is right. The flight from Dublin arrived at JFK at 8.20 p.m. On board were Shay Helden and Brishen Ayres.'

McAvoy nods in confirmation of the names. On the flight over he has familiarised himself with the backgrounds of both men, though in truth he had long known the name of Brishen Ayres. In the Travelling community the man is something of a legend. Raised with a traditional Gypsy family, Ayres showed talent as a boxer in his youth. Trained at first by relatives, he soon surpassed their standards and joined a legitimate boxing gym in Galway, where he came under the tutelage of a coach who had trained a dozen champions. In

Ayres, he saw somebody with the talent to go all the way. It was not just his natural technique or his southpaw stance that set him apart: there was a killer instinct present in the youngster that put a primal fear into anybody who stepped between the ropes with him. By seventeen, he was a member of Ireland's Olympic squad. He never made it to the Games. He was knocked down in a hit-and-run incident a month before the tournament. Both his legs were shattered and pelvis all but crushed. Though he recovered, his career was over.

In his rehabilitation, Ayres showed the same fighting spirit that had made him a contender. And when he got himself fit enough to stand, he decided to use his skills. Though unable to fight, he knew he had something that he could pass on to others. He started training other Traveller boys and girls. Before long, Gypsy families on the mainland were sending their children to Ayres for month-long training camps. Remarkably, non-Travellers started to seek Ayres out. At the age of twenty-six, Ayres bought the boxing gym where he used to train. Within a year, he was coaching champions. A decade on, Ayres was one of the best-known faces in Galway and had become an advocate on Travellers' rights. He was liked and admired in his own community and beyond. There were many who called for him to be made head coach of the Irish Amateur Boxing Association and solely responsible for the Olympic team. Whether Brishen ever sought the job was open to speculation but when a Sunday tabloid printed the details of his many criminal convictions as a younger man, it was obvious he was never going to get the nod. Instead, he concentrated on identifying potential professional fighters.

In Shay Helden, he found one. The Traveller boy did not take up boxing until he was fifteen, when his exasperated father contacted Brishen and begged for help in controlling his wayward son. Brishen put him in the ring and instructed three of his best prospects to take a round with him. Helden put them down in moments. Brishen had identified somebody with a right hand that could buckle a car hood. Brishen started to train him in earnest and within a year Helden was catching the eye. The kid was good. He could win medals. But Helden sought a different kind of gold. He wanted to go straight into the professional ranks and there was no shortage of promoters and managers who whispered in his ear. In a bid to keep Helden on the right path, Brishen agreed to act as his manager. He arranged his fights, helped his reputation grow and nurtured him like a son. Two weeks ago, he brought Helden to America to meet with a boxing coach whose name was synonymous with the best of the best. Dezzie Estrada was willing to take a look at Helden with a view to taking him into his stable of fighters. And Brishen was not going to stand in his way. They flew to America in the hope of making both of their dreams come true.

Three days later, their bodies were found in a shallow grave in a patch of woodland off Silver Spur Road, two miles outside the tiny town of Cairo in upstate New York. Helden had been shot in the back and then stabbed through the base of his skull. Ayres had been shot in the head from point-blank range. Both men had been mutilated. The two rural police officers who found the bodies were already in a state of shock at their grisly discovery when Brishen Ayres coughed up a mouthful of dirt and began clawing his way through the earth. The local papers called him the Miracle Man. He has been in a medically induced coma at the specialist brain injury unit at the Wade-Christie Presbyterian Hospital ever since.

'You have a list of their known movements?' asks McAvoy, noticing, with a touch of satisfaction, that the homeless man across the street has brought the mug back to the bar and that the barman is fixing him another, free of charge.

'It's all in the file,' says Alto, nodding at the documents. 'I can walk you through it. Let's just say there are a lot of bars on there. Those Irish boys know how to drink.'

McAvoy nods. A lot of the information was sent on via email when Trish Pharaoh started pulling the strings that would allow him to the periphery of the investigation. Pharaoh is the only one who knows what failure will cost him and his family. Were he to try to tell Alto the truth, he doubts he would have the vocabulary to make him understand just what is at stake.

'This family connection of yours,' says Alto, scratching at the hair by his ear. 'This suspect we seem to have missed. What can you tell me?'

McAvoy pauses, gathering himself. 'Valentine Teague,' he says, forcing himself to meet Alto's eyes. 'Twenty years old. Flew into JFK the following day. Also from Dublin Airport.'

'And?' asks Alto, sitting forward a little.

'Valentine Teague's family is a rival to Shay Helden's family,' says McAvoy, with a hint of a sigh. 'I don't know how much you know about the Traveller community but rivalries go back decades. If two clans are at war, there're no limits to what they'll do to one another. The Heldens and the Teagues have been fighting for years. Once in a while, a member of one family calls out a member of the other one. A "straightener", they call it. It's a matter of honour. Valentine called out Shay Helden just when Shay was starting to get noticed. Valentine's a tough little brute but Helden flattened him. The video's on YouTube. Brishen was furious that Shay had fought a bare-knuckle bout. Said it risked his chances of getting licensed. Told him if he fought outside the ring again he would cut all ties with him. Shay respected that. Brishen ordered the two families to bury the hatchet and because of the esteem he was held in, they called a truce. Seriously, in Traveller terms it was like an armistice. Valentine had showed enough skills to attract Brishen's interest and Brishen started training him too. He's a prospect. Could go all the way.'

Alto looks down at his empty glass and signals to the barman, who is busy untangling Christmas lights at the far end of the bar. He orders a large Canadian Club. McAvoy decides he has earned a treat and asks for a Baileys. He waits until they both have their drinks before continuing, giving a moment's concern to the notion of who will pay for the drinks. He hasn't had a chance to get any dollars yet.

'So this Valentine kid flew out a day later?' prompts Alto. 'That's news to me.'

'There were problems with his visa,' explains McAvoy. 'Neither he nor Helden had a passport and there were endless questions bouncing back and forth with the authorities. Shay's paperwork came through on time and he and Brishen flew out together. It took a letter from the Bishop of Galway to get Valentine's visa approved.'

'The Bishop of Galway? Friends in high places.'

'There's a priest in the parish of Oughtermore who's a big supporter of what Brishen is trying to do for the Traveller lads, apparently. He called in a favour with the bishop, who wrote a letter explaining that Brishen's trip was of the utmost value to his community and that Valentine was a crucial part of his team. The paperwork came through a day later and Valentine flew out alone.'

Alto clinks the ice cubes in his glass. McAvoy can see him putting the pieces together.

'And then his old rival is found dead on Silver Spur Road East – the ass-end of nowhere on the road to Cairo.'

McAvoy takes a swig of his sticky drink. Savours the flavour. Wishes he had a bar of chocolate to dunk in it. 'The Heldens want blood,' he says. 'As far as they're concerned, Valentine did this.'

'And you?' asks Alto, cocking his head.

'I don't know what to think,' says McAvoy, realising he means it. 'Valentine is a bad-tempered little so-and-so but he's all about his fists. I can't see him using a gun and even for a resourceful lad I can't imagine he could just walk into a bar and buy one from the first rough-looking fellow he saw. And besides, he idolised Brishen.'

'The wounds are unusual,' says Alto, and as he shifts on his bar stool his knees touch McAvoy's. Neither man seems to notice. Their energies are all in their heads. They are two detectives: questioning, querying, ruminating; untangling the riddles of an ugly death.

'Tell me,' says McAvoy.

'Shay Helden was shot with a .38 semi-automatic Ruger hand-gun. The bullet travelled an estimated distance of thirty yards. The wounds to his lower legs suggest he fell while running. A short, sharp blade was then inserted at the base of his skull. He'd been given a good beating.'

McAvoy swallows his drink. It tastes of nothing.

'And Brishen?'

'Shot in the head while kneeling. The bullet entered his head just behind his left ear. It travelled beneath the skin, shaving a trench in the bones of the skull, and exited behind his right ear, taking with it a chunk of ear-lobe.'

'It curved?' asks McAvoy.

'Our ballistics guy says he's only ever seen it once before. It's dumb luck. Brishen must have been turning his head as the gun fired. Chance in a billion, though that's not an expert estimation, just mine. Different gun to the one used to shoot Shay.'

'And the other wound?' asks McAvoy, rubbing at his beard and pulling a face. 'And does that mean Valentine bought two guns? Why would he?'

Alto shrugs. 'Brishen's nose was cut off and put in his shirt pocket. Different knife to the one used to finish off Shay.'

McAvoy digests the information, nodding to himself as if in agreement with a contention.

'Two guns. Two knives. Two killers,' says McAvoy. 'At least. Shay tries to run and Brishen turns to watch him go. Brishen is shot in the head and Shay makes a run for it. Or Shay runs and Brishen turns to watch him go and that's how the bullet missed the best of his brain. Either way, it's a lot of work for one man – least of all Valentine Teague.'

'You think?' asks Alto, looking wistfully at his empty glass.

McAvoy screws up his face. 'It's possible,' he says. 'What about the car they were travelling in?'

'It was stolen from outside a bar on Mulberry. Expertly hot-wired. Wherever they were going, they were going there in a hurry.'

'Running to something, or away from something?' muses McAvoy. 'It was found at the scene, yes?'

'Yes. The only prints are theirs and the owners. From the position of the seats and the placement of the prints, it's clear Brishen Ayres was driving. Nobody in the back so far as we can tell.'

'Would that road lead anywhere significant?'

'The road where they left the car is a dead-end. If they were going to Cairo they should have stayed on the main road. The road where they died goes nowhere.'

'So perhaps they were diverted down there by whoever did this,' says McAvoy.

'We've worked on pretty much that same scenario,' says Alto, in a way that suggests he does not want to rain on McAvoy's parade.

'The trouble is that it snowed so it's damn near impossible to get bootprints or make sense of how many people were there. All we know is that for whatever reason, their vehicle left the Interstate at around 4 a.m. We don't know why, or where they were going. Next day, a hiker and his dog found Helden's body in a half-hearted grave. Called the officer in charge at Cairo. A couple of officers came to the scene. It didn't take them long to find Brishen. His body was slumped in a trench, half covered in dirt and snow. The temperature was well below zero and that's what saved him. That burst of adrenalin that kicked in when they moved him – that's as much of a miracle as his survival. He died in the helicopter but the paramedics brought him back. Hasn't woken up since.'

McAvoy looks longingly at the last dregs of his Baileys. Wonders if it would be frowned upon to run his finger around the glass and suck it like a lollipop.

'The nose,' he says, frowning. 'This is a lot more your area than mine but doesn't that have some sort of Mafia connection?'

Alto laughs. 'Everything has a Mafia connection,' he says. 'The Mob these days – it gets its ideas from movies about the Mob. If you're thinking that having his nose sliced off was a message that he had been sticking it in where it wasn't welcome, then tell me – where had he been sticking it? He'd been in New York not much over two days. He and Shay spent most of that time in bars, at the gym, or at church. I'm sure they're fast workers but you can't piss off the Mob sufficiently to get whacked in that time.'

McAvoy sucks his cheek. 'They went to church?'

'St Colman's,' says Alto. 'It's all in the timeline in your folder.'

'Thank you,' says McAvoy, draining his Baileys. He's suddenly tired to his bones.

'You've gone a funny colour,' says Alto, taking off his glasses. 'How long since you slept?'

McAvoy manages a smile. 'Couple of days. I'll get a few hours as soon as I get back to the hotel. I'll be okay.'

'And your plans tomorrow?' asks Alto cautiously.

'I'll know better once I've familiarised myself with their movements. I may talk to a couple of people, if that isn't treading on your toes.'

Alto shakes his head. 'Don't make waves and don't pretend you've got more authority than you have and you will be fine. It's not illegal for a man on holiday to ask questions.'

'Thank you,' says McAvoy, and means it. He slides off his stool and stretches. His hands are in the air as Alto settles their bar tab and he is momentarily afraid that it looks as though he were trying to keep his fingers as far away from his pockets as possible.

'Have a great night,' says the barman as they head for the exit, and McAvoy feels oddly warm at the ease with which the words slip from the young man's mouth. At home, McAvoy considers himself to have enjoyed good customer service if nobody tells him to go fuck himself.

McAvoy and Alto part at the corner of Ludlow and Rivington. Alto offers another handshake. As their hands touch, Alto asks his question, taking McAvoy by surprise.

'Your family connection,' he says, looking up, half smiling. 'You never elaborated.'

McAvoy refuses to look away or let any embarrassment colour his cheeks.

'My wife,' he says. 'Before she was a McAvoy, she was a Teague.'

'Her brother,' says Alto, raising his eyebrows. 'So you're out here to prove him innocent and stop the family back home going to war? Christ.'

'I'm not trying to find him innocent,' says McAvoy earnestly. 'I'm just trying to find him.'

'And you think he's either a killer or a corpse?'

McAvoy takes his hand back. Rubs it over his face and marvels for a moment at the sheer absurdity of his presence here. Though he hates to be so inarticulate, he shrugs. He doesn't really know what he's doing here or what he hopes to find. He wants his family and his own bed. Wants Trish Pharaoh to tell him what to do. He's alone, in a strange country, where cops step over the homeless like bags of rubbish. *Garbage*, he corrects himself, and feels Hull and home slip even further away.

'I wouldn't want to be you,' says Alto, not unkindly.

'No,' says McAvoy, turning away. 'Nor would I.'

4

McAvoy kicks the dirt and snow off his boots, hoofing the brick frontage of the Comfort Inn with sufficient force to risk an avalanche. He pulls open the glass double doors and nods a weary hello to the smiling Asian twenty-something who mans the front desk. His name-tag says he is called 'Tiz' and McAvoy is too tired to ask what peculiar name he has shortened in order to make his name more amenable to tourists.

'Back so soon?' asks Tiz. He has a paperback splayed open, pages down, on the desk in front of him. The cover shows lurid red text on a black background and three monochrome faces stare up, menacingly. 'Mafia's greatest hits,' explains Tiz, following McAvoy's gaze. 'Bit of a break from college work.'

'You're a student?' asks McAvoy, and makes an effort at conversation. Tiz was only too happy to give McAvoy the same room that Brishen Ayres and Shay Helden had been staying in before they were shot and left for dead. McAvoy also asked to see their luggage but that had long since been taken to the Seventh. It proved nothing more illuminating than the fact that the duo travelled light.

'Macro-economics,' says Tiz brightly. 'I wanted to do photography but there's not much money in that.'

'You don't have to decide what you want to be at your age,' says McAvoy, trying to dispense something vaguely useful to the younger man. 'Do what matters to you.'

'Money matters to all of us,' says Tiz solemnly, in a way that suggests he thinks he has said something profound. 'Everything okay with your room?'

'Great, thanks,' says McAvoy, though in truth he barely took in its features while dumping his bag an hour ago. 'Nice big bed.'

Tiz coughs and glances down and McAvoy suddenly suffers the horrifying thought that he might think he has been propositioned. 'My wife would love it here,' he adds, colouring. 'She's never been here before. Can't wait to bring her. My kids too.'

'Well, you be sure to give them my best wishes,' says Tiz, in the guileless, good-natured way McAvoy finds so endearing. 'Have yourself a great night.'

McAvoy splutters out a thank you then decides he will spend the rest of the night worrying about it if he doesn't salvage something from the conversation. Looking around for inspiration, his gaze falls back on the young man's book.

'You're really into this stuff?' he asks, trying to sound encouraging. 'I try to turn away from all that, if I can. I've seen films and read books, of course, but when it's real it just makes me shudder.'

'This is macro-economics at work,' Tiz says, brandishing the book. 'You want to see how to stay ahead in a changing marketplace, ask the Mob. They're lessons in longevity and diversification. I was going to write a thesis on it until Dad told me not to.'

McAvoy looks confused and Tiz leans on the desk, warming to his subject.

'They adapt,' he says, as if explaining to a small child. 'You know about the history of the Mob? How this obscure code from a little island kicked into the sea off Italy ended up as one of the biggest economic forces in America? Man, there's more to the Mafia than racketeering and drugs and killing people off. Their structure is the basic model used by some of the most successful businesses in America.'

McAvoy continues to look blank and Tiz throws up his hands, exasperated. Looking around him he finds a copy of a free newspaper on top of some glossy magazines beneath his desk.

'Take the Pugliesca family,' he says, pointing at a small article in the bottom right-hand corner. 'Boss of the family will be doing time until he's about 500 years old but the company, the family, is more profitable than ever before. They hide their profits, see. No different to any big company that wants to get away with paying half a cent in tax on billion-dollar reserves. This case here,' he says, pointing at the paper, 'it's a failed RICO attempt on the acting head. They're trying to get old Paulie's assets but on paper he's worth less than the cost of a slice of apple pie. Every company they try to link to him turns out to be a dead-end, or registered to somebody who died and left his assets to some benevolent fund that nobody seems able to take credit for. They're technical wizards and their accountants and lawyers would be enjoying corner offices and six-figure salaries at blue-chip companies if they weren't already making twice that working for the Mob.'

McAvoy raises his eyebrows. He isn't sure what response is required but he gives an encouraging smile. 'Oh,' he says. 'That's better than killing people, I suppose.'

'They do that too,' says Tiz, beaming. 'You want to hear about Sally-Boy in '81? They found half of one leg and the rest hit a parked car two streets away . . . ?'

McAvoy nods a polite goodnight and hurries his way down the short corridor to the elevator. His room is on the seventh floor, and moments later he is pushing open the white door to a room not much longer and taller than he is. A mirrored wardrobe and a dressing table take up one wall and the rest of the room is covered by the bulk of the king-size bed. The rectangular window offers him a view only of his own reflection, but when he presses his forehead to the cool glass he can see the backs of towering buildings and the roofs of apartment blocks; all covered with the same hard snow. On the top of one building, he can make out the shape of a boat, part covered in a sagging tarpaulin. McAvoy starts to speculate on precisely how its owner intends to get it to the water, and then decides that in this hipster area, the environmentally conscious owner may well be preparing for environmental disaster and the sudden swelling of the Hudson River.

A small bathroom containing toilet, sink and shower completes the tour of the room. McAvoy wonders if Brishen and Shay experienced the same mild sense of disappointment upon opening the door. He wonders too whether they expected the room to come with twin beds rather than one large double. He files the question away for later.

Sighing, he sits down on the bed and starts unpicking the damp laces of his boots. He has one boot on and another off when a wave of homesickness and bewilderment seems to rise out of the floor and soak him to the bone. He feels as though everything he knows and loves is a million miles away. He lies back on the bed and fumbles in his coat for his phone. It's a little before midnight. It may only be 5 a.m. back home but McAvoy knows from painful experience that Roisin and the children will be wide awake and desperate for some words from Daddy. He wishes he had something to tell them. He wants to hear their voices so badly that it feels like a physical pain. He tries to picture them, but the images that flood his mind threaten to make his eyes spill over and he screws up his face, wishing to God he could reach out and stroke Roisin's soft, dark skin. He is here for her. Here for his children. Here because the Heldens turned up at Roisin's little sister's confirmation and threatened Papa Teague with all the torments of hell in payment for Valentine's crimes.

Lying back on the warm, soft sheets, McAvoy lets his mind drift. Was it only four days ago? He feels as though he has been carrying this pain inside him for an age. But there is no mistake. He got the call on Saturday. Shay Helden had already been dead more than a week. Roisin had spent the previous couple of days in Galway, unaware of what was brewing across the Atlantic or how much trouble her little brother was in. The children had gone with her. Fin's school had been unusually understanding about the fact he had gone to Ireland in term time but Roisin had explained that there was a family bereavement. McAvoy had bitten back his objections when Roisin had put her hand on his cheek and told him to shush, and that all the boy would miss would be some colouring-in and another fecking lesson about the Tudors. McAvoy had found himself silently hoping that nobody at the school ever got round to counting up how many grandmothers Finlay has lost during his school career.

McAvoy was decorating the living room in preparation for their return when the call came. He'd been invited to Sinead's confirmation but Roisin had spared him the agony of coming up with an excuse when she said that she'd rather he got on with the decorating. She'd known that the presence of a policeman at an occasion for Travellers would have been awkward for all concerned. She had only recently started mending bridges with her family, who had all but disowned her eight years before. Her crime was marrying the Scottish detective who loved her to his bones.

Roisin is a strong enough person not to give a damn about other people's opinions but she had been unable to disguise her delight at being invited to Sinead's big day. Roisin is the second oldest of eight children, and Sinead had only been three years old when Roisin left the family home. But family is family, and the event had been important to both factions. McAvoy had been pleased that Roisin was happy, though in truth he had felt some disquiet at the idea of her taking the children across to what he knew would be a raucous affair near the family's home turf in Galway. Roisin had settled his nerves. She'd told him that it was only for a couple of days and that all she wanted was to show off her children. She promised that anybody who tried to get Fin drunk would feel the back of her hand, and McAvoy had no doubts she was sincere when she said it. He gave her his credit card and said she should buy the children new outfits for the occasion. She came back with a three-piece tweed suit and matching flat-cap for seven-year-old Fin, and an ocean of sapphire taffeta and silk for two-year-old Lilah. It was going to be a Big Fat Gypsy Confirmation, and Roisin was keen to show she had not lost sight of her roots. She might live with a policeman in a battered house by the sea, but she had never been ashamed of her origins and her family.

McAvoy had been holding up a strip of gaudily patterned wallpaper when his mobile rang. He was halfway up a ladder, bare-chested and paint-spattered, sticky with wallpaper paste and with half a Mars bar sticking out of his mouth, as if he were smoking a cigar. He answered the phone to Roisin's tears. Ten minutes later he was on the road to Trish Pharaoh's house, his knuckles white around the steering wheel as he crossed the Humber Bridge; a soft, sideways rain blowing in from the east and jewelling the glass of the cursedly slow people-carrier he had bought for its safety record.

He called his boss Pharoah en route. Chewed on his bleeding cheek as he spat out the details Roisin had cried into his ear. She had her front door open the moment McAvoy's car pulled into the drive of her semi-detached home on the Scartho estate in Grimsby. She had sent her four daughters into town. They had the place to themselves. Nobody would hear if he decided to break down. And by Christ that's what he wanted to do. Wanted to sob with frustration and fear. Wanted her to pull him into the safe folds of her curvy body and lose himself for a moment in the smell of her perfume and cigarettes. She was his boss and his best friend and, aside from his family, the person he cared most about in the world. Instead, he kept her at arm's length. Paced the living room, repeating himself, pushing his hands through his damp hair until he looked clownish and ill; asking questions, questions, questions . . .

'You've heard of him, yes? Brishen Ayres. Great boxer. Got hurt. Hit and run. Real shame. I was boxing myself in those days and he was the one everybody feared. Great coach too. Bad lad in his youth but doing great things for Irish boxing. He's made peace between the Heldens and the Teagues, Trish, I swear it. Valentine was so excited about going over to America. It was his big chance. He said he hoped to be back for the confirmation. Family hadn't heard from him in days. Then the news started filtering through. Roisin's family heard about what happened around the same time as the Heldens. Papa Teague said the confirmation had to go ahead. He had some of his boys on the lookout, just in case. Nothing happened at the church but once they got to the reception, that was when it all kicked off. Papa Helden was tooled up. Toting a shotgun, he was. Had half the lads with him. Roisin swears she thought her father was going to get shot dead right then and there. It was only the priest who calmed things down. He was there as a guest, representing Brishen. He put himself between Helden and Teague. Managed to get them to hold off on killing each other. He said he would make enquiries, that he had friends in America who would get to the bottom of what was happening. They've agreed a ceasefire – for now. But it looks like Papa Teague thinks the worst of his son because as soon as he had Roisin alone he begged her to use her connections – that's what he called our marriage, a damn connection! – to make sense of it all. And she agreed! Told her daddy that her husband would fly out there and fix everything. Find Valentine, or, at the very least, save him from what the Heldens will do if they get hold of him. Trish, I'm just a Yorkshire copper. She doesn't understand. She and the kids – they think I'm some sort of superhero who can make the bad stuff all go away. And now word has got to the Heldens that I'm going out there and that means Roisin has put herself directly in harm's way because if I find out that Valentine did it, they'll expect me to help him run, and if he didn't, they'll think I'm lying! I don't know what to do!'

He wailed for an age, half to himself, half to his boss. She smoked her black cigarettes and drank her wine and untangled her hair from her big hooped earrings and plucked the dropped ash from her cleavage. Her brain was turning over so fast he expected her eyes to spin. But she knew what to do, who to call. And she waited until he ran out of breath before she delivered her lecture.

'Your family think you're Superman and you're complaining? Do you know what most people think of their loved ones, Hector? They think they're thick, or weak, or so fucking boring they may as well be a brown loaf. Your problem is that your family has faith in you. Well boo-fucking-hoo. Hector, do you know what sort of a person you have to be to deserve optimism? Do you know how vastly better than everybody else you need to be for people to presume that you will win? You are the only man I've ever met who deserves to be thought of in entirely glowing terms, and I say this as somebody who spends a good portion of every day wanting to kick you in the teeth for being so fucking wholesome. Now stop snivelling, be quiet, and go get me another bottle from the cupboard. I've got some calls to make. And if you want me to take you seriously, you'll wipe the chocolate off your lower lip. Now, bloody move.'

McAvoy finds himself smiling as he begins to doze off. If nothing else, he is here. He's spoken to a real New York City detective.

He has drunk spirits in a Manhattan bar. He's closing his eyes in a king-size bed in a cheap hotel on the Lower East Side. He has a list of times, places and people. Tomorrow, he will take comfort in the simple act of procedure. He does not truly expect to find Valentine Teague, but he can at least prove himself worthy of his family's belief in him. If he does happen to find him, he wonders whether the little sod will even be grateful. McAvoy has had little to do with him these past years. He has memories of him as a child, with his red hair and freckles and tramlines shaved into the back of his head. He was always up to mischief. Could get McAvoy's wallet from his back pocket and be busy emptying his account while his prey was still sitting down. And as a grown man he has been little better. Fighting, stealing, ripping the lead from abandoned buildings or stealing the scaffolding from construction sites. Even so, it's hard to dislike him. He's a charismatic soul, with his twinkly eyes and his easy charm. He gave McAvoy all kinds of gentle abuse when they were invited to the sit-down intended to mend the bridges between Roisin and her parents, but something told McAvoy his brother-in-law, on some level, didn't completely hate him. That felt like a result.

In this spirit of uncertainty, McAvoy drifts off to sleep, one boot on and the other one off; sprawled in the bed where Brishen Ayres and Shay Helden slept for a night before they sped out of New York as if hell were chasing them; on their way to damnation down a quiet road in the midst of a snow-covered forest.

As the blackness takes hold, McAvoy reaches out in his mind. Brushes his fingertips against the soft skin of a woman with dark hair and kind, blue eyes. He does not know whose flesh he touches, but it brings him comfort, and keeps him safe inside his dreams.

5

This is a grey place; a sketch in pencil smudged with a licked thumb.

It is a cavern of flickering darkness and weak firelight, made into an ethereal, shapeless space by the wraiths of smoke that drift up from the candles which have burned down to the base.

It is a place that smells of man and earth, of pig and plant: as though hot animal fat has been poured upon fresh-cut lilies.

There is a figure at the centre of this smear of smoke and dust. Naked and corpulent, a scarred mess of jellied flesh. He calls himself the Penitent, and were he presented with an image of how he appears at this time and in this place, he would not recognise the figure who stands in front of the perfect white altar cloth and holds the short, bone-handled knife in his right hand.

The Penitent stands upon the sacred ground and allows himself the faintest moment of idle, human thought. He considers his feet, and enjoys them.

The Penitent wonders whether his face is as pale and fleshy as his toes. They are the part of himself he considers most often. His hands, though clean and unlined, have always felt like sinful things so he has never truly examined them for fear he will see his suspicions confirmed and be forced into an act of atonement. His toes, however, are sinless things. He has never utilised them as implements of his own debasement or pleasure. They are tools. They are beneficial to his work.

Here, now, he finds himself questioning the goodness of his feet for the first time. In studying them, he is allowing himself to open the door to vanity. The Penitent does not know what he looks like. He does not allow himself the luxury of a reflection. He is aware of his appearance only in the way others respond to it. He is not repulsive enough to warrant a second glance but he has never been looked at in a way that suggests he is attractive. The parts of himself that he can see are pinkish and plump, as though he were made up of uncooked meatloaf. There is a curious mottling around his hips. The blemishes are the only ones upon his skin that were not put there by a human hand, though he does not truly believe them to be God's work. He presumes they are a sign of advancing age. He has never seen the naked form of a man of his own years so would not be able to say with any certainty whether he looks as he should.

There are moments, sinful moments, when he would like to consider himself in the clear liquid loveliness of a full-length mirror. He would like to strip himself of all clothing and ornament and consider himself in his entirety. He feels like a painter who has spent years working on a masterpiece, only to have his eyes put out before being able to see it completed. To blind the artist would be no sin. The Penitent would have no regrets in sliding needles into Michelangelo's eyes before ever allowing him to marvel at his own creations. The works should be for the glory of God and not for human vanity. He sees his own work in the same way. He has transformed his appearance into something that rejoices in celebration of the creator. To step back and look upon it would be to give in to pride and he knows this sin to be almost irredeemable.

Naked, he stands upon the earth and feels cold brown soil tickle the bare soles of his feet. In the light of the candles he sees his own shadow cast upon the far wall. It is a bulbous, misshapen thing. He turns away from the shadow before it can look back at him. Watches the flame dance on the mosaic of brass leaves. They form the shape of a tree. Each leaf carries a name. Each name represents a life taken and a soul transformed. They flow outwards from a carving of a rose; a simple engraving of a perfect bloom, folding in upon itself; white lines against gold.

He has begun cutting himself before he realises it. Only the warm trickle of blood running over his penis and thighs to puddle upon his perfect fleshy toes alerts him to the damage he is doing to his skin.

The man leans down and takes a pinch of ash from the urn that stands upon the altar cloth laid out on the mound of earth. He opens the inch-long wound he has carved into his breastbone and places the ash inside as if he were seasoning meat. The pain is a sharp, precise thing, and he allows himself a hiss of ecstatic agony. He reaches out and takes the fat church candle from the altar cloth and drips hot wax upon the lesion. When healed, the nugget of scar tissue will blend seamlessly with the concentric circles of similarly blackened skin that spin outwards from the centre of his sternum to cover much of his torso and upper arms. He would like to continue the work upon his back but he knows that the skin there is already too abraded to serve as a canvas for such an offering.

Unsteadily, the Penitent reaches forward and takes the clay chalice in his right hand. He pours its contents upon his skin, washing away the blood and dirt and allowing the blessed water to trickle down over his skin to pool with the sacred earth beneath his toes.

Only when he has finished his ritual does he pick up the leather-bound book that sits upon the altar cloth. He opens its pages at random and begins to read aloud.

'. . . *I know what I do is wrong. You are more innocent than I am. You have committed fewer sins and broken no covenants. But my soul will burn for evermore if I do not empty myself of sin and through these acts I am washed clean. You will find glory for your part in this atonement. You will be praised for your sacrifice and exulted among the angels for helping this sinner through the gates of heaven . . .*'

The Penitent closes the book and caresses the soft leather as if it were flesh.

It has not always been thus. The Penitent was once a sinner. He desired flesh other than his own. Such desires cost him his dreams but brought him the peace and absolution he dared not think he deserved. Through his crimes, he met the priest. And the priest became his friend. He guided him. Gave him a chance to become

47

a good man. Absolved him of all sin, past and future, and allowed him to pass on such blessings to others.

Only when the thudding dizziness ceases does he sink to his knees and, from there, he slithers forward until his naked body is touching the carpet of dirt and ash, water and blood.

He presses his face into the ground.

He only stops digging when his lips touch the familiar cold kiss of fragmented bone.

6

McAvoy is feeling that peculiar pride enjoyed by all visitors to a foreign land when they have achieved some minor success like buying a stamp in a shop where the owner speaks no English. In the hour since he woke up, he has managed to draw money from an ATM, and secure directions to Thomas Street, off West Broadway, from the Latina maid who was depositing a dispiriting breakfast outside his bedroom when he emerged. She told him it was complimentary, though it had looked quite the opposite. He now sits in a diner eating blueberry pancakes and syrup, with a separate plate of sausages and home fries. As a nod to Roisin's efforts to improve his diet, he is drinking green tea and a glass of fresh orange juice, though there was a malted milkshake on the menu that caught his eye. He has secured a spot by the window and is watching the city come to life. A procession of schoolchildren, younger than Fin, pass by the glass two-by-two, led by a figure wearing so many layers they could survive a collision with a bus. The children's smiles are hidden beneath colourful waterproofs but their pink cheeks and bright eyes seem oddly pleasing, when contrasted with the grey and yellow sky hanging low over the city and obscuring the tops of the tall buildings across the street. There was no more snow during the night, but slush and dirt still form small mountain ranges on either side of the sidewalk and he has seen several people slip and fall while walking too quickly across the wide road. As he cleans his second plate, he finds himself admiring the sensible wardrobes of the New Yorkers. They are dressed for the conditions, buttoned up inside large coats, hats and scarves. At home, in such conditions, probably half of the commuters hurrying through Hull would be coatless and any man wearing a hat would find his masculinity sorely questioned.

'Can I ask you what that's all about?' asks McAvoy, as the Hispanic waiter takes his plates and gives him the nod of a professional who likes his food to be appreciated.

'I'm sorry, sir?'

McAvoy points in the direction of a man in Lycra and fleece jogging down the opposite side of the road beside a husky who appears to be wearing matching running shoes. 'The slippers that the dogs wear. That's the third one I've seen.'

The waiter smiles. 'The city puts down salt to melt the ice. It's not good for the paws. Some people love their animals too much, yes?'

McAvoy finds himself laughing. 'My kids would love to see that. They'll never believe me.'

'You have many children, sir?'

'Two. A boy and a girl.'

'Beautiful, my friend. I have six children. All under ten years old. My wife, she gets pregnant if we share bath water.'

McAvoy coughs, feeling like a Victorian English gentleman, unsure of the etiquette of the conversation.

'You could try showers,' he says, hoping this is appropriate.

The waiter roars a laugh, throwing back his head to display bright white teeth. The other diners in the small, gaudily coloured deli turn to look and McAvoy catches the eye of a student-looking girl with purple hair and glasses and a ring through her nose. She smiles at him in a way that makes him feel instantly guilty, and he lowers his head. The waiter moves away, still laughing, and McAvoy busies himself with his phone. Last night he took photographs of the pages in the report that Alto had given him. As he considers them, his vision blurs. His chest feels tight and he has to fight to control his breathing. Below the table, his hands become fists. These moments have been coming more frequently; these sudden attacks of clarity. For an instant he is aware of himself. Sees the huge, blundering fool who sits in a coffee shop pretending to be something other than a coward and a fraud. He wants to bite down on something to stop his teeth from chattering. Just as quickly, the tremor in his soul subsides, and he is sitting, forcing out his breath through pursed lips, his hair damp at the temples.

'Concentrate,' he whispers to himself. 'Do the job. Focus. Work.'

He is scrolling through the witness statements given by staff members at Dezzie's Boxing Gym when his phone rings and startles him. The number on the display screen has unfamiliar digits at the start, and every sensation of unworthiness evaporates. She has come to his rescue in response to his unspoken prayer.

'Good afternoon, my love,' he says quietly into the phone.

'It's morning for you, isn't it, babe? Have I done the maths wrong?'

'Just before 8 a.m.,' says McAvoy, smiling at the sound of Roisin's voice. 'And you have to say "math", not "maths", if we're going to be all American.'

'So I suppose you're drinking coffee?' asks Roisin, and her Irish accent transforms into a New York drawl as she says the word.

'Green tea and orange juice, I swear.'

'With doughnuts,' says Roisin. 'You're a cop in New York. There have to be donuts involved.'

'Do you think we're running the risk of getting all our information on America from the movies?'

'When you get home you can tell us the truth about the place,' says Roisin. 'I'm sure it's half the size it pretends to be and the skyscrapers are no taller than a bus. Have you seen anybody famous?'

'Not yet,' says McAvoy, disappointed not to be able to impress her. 'But the dogs wear little slippers over here. It's to keep their paws safe.'

'That's sweet,' says Roisin, and McAvoy hears the soft crackle of her cigarette as she sucks on the filter with lips that he knows will be covered in pink lip-gloss that tastes of strawberries.

'I thought we were going to keep the calls to a minimum,' says McAvoy, trying not to sound reproachful. In truth, he would sell his shoes and walk barefoot through the snow in order to speak to his wife.

'I know,' she says. 'But I was missing you. We all are.'

'Are they there?'

'Fin's playing. He says to tell you that in New York, a sandwich is called a submarine.'

'I didn't know that,' says McAvoy, grinning.

'He might have meant subway. I prefer it his way.'

'Anything from Lilah?'

'She threw a ball at a picture of you last night,' says Roisin. 'I think she wanted to play catch. That, or she's pissed off at you for leaving.'

'Did you tell her I'm only here for her mammy?'

'Time and again. I think she forgives you. I do too.'

'Forgive me for what?'

'For not being clever enough to build a machine that will split you in two. That way you could leave yourself with me and still go and find Valentine.'

'I'm sorry, my love. I'll get working on that once I get home.'

'I'll pimp it for you once it's finished. Diamanté crystals and a leopard-print seat.'

'You're a visionary,' says McAvoy, glancing up. The girl with the purple hair is smiling at him again as she stirs her coffee. He looks away.

'You caught anybody's eye yet?' asks Roisin playfully. 'Made anybody fall desperately in love with you? Got some little New York tart hanging off your arm?'

'The cleaning lady was nice,' says McAvoy, colouring. 'I think she was in her sixties but you could tell she was game.'

'I hate her,' says Roisin, with an audible pout.

'And there's a girl looking at me now,' he whispers. 'She has purple hair. She looks a bit like a thistle. She keeps smiling.'

Roisin is silent for a moment. 'Hand her the phone,' she says, in a voice he knows to be only mockingly cross.

'You're maple syrup and she's a glass of water, my love,' says McAvoy, and hopes it sounds romantic rather than lame.

'Thank you. You realise she's only looking at you because you're a big sexy galoot, don't you? She just wants your body.'

'She can't have it. It's broken.'

'Flight was a killer, was it?'

'I needed a massage when I got here. I don't think Detective Alto was quite ready for that kind of hello.'

'You said in your text he was Scandinavian. They're into that, over there.'

'I think we run the risk of cultural stereotyping.'

Roisin gives a little laugh and then her voice grows more serious. 'You'll be careful, yes? I know you're only there for me and I know you'll be okay but just promise me you'll be careful.'

'I've promised before. I'll promise again.'

'Mammy and Daddy have put a lot of faith in us, babe. I swore you'd find Valentine. I don't want to think about what will happen if you can't.'

'It will be okay,' says McAvoy, and he suddenly feels as cold inside himself as the air beyond the glass. 'I'm going to speak to the owner of the gym where they spent some time. I've got calls in. There are irons in the fire. I'll do all I can.'

'I love you, Aector,' she says, and there is a mixture of pride and sadness in her voice. 'You can have sex with the girl with purple hair if you like. I won't make a fuss.'

McAvoy laughs, wanting to reach into the phone and wrap his arms around his wife. 'If she makes the offer I'll politely decline. I'll tell her I'm married to the woman of my dreams.'

'Lorraine Kelly?'

'You make me laugh, my love.'

'You make me whole. Stay safe.'

'And you.'

McAvoy ends the call and looks at the photo that serves as the screensaver on his phone. He strokes Roisin's face with his thumb. He wishes he could have told her how unlikely it is that he will have anything like success. Wishes she had told him that, deep down, she knows that his best will not be good enough this time. When he raises his head from the phone, the girl with the purple hair has gone.

★   ★   ★

53

Dezzie's Boxing Gym squats in the basement of a four-storey building on a quiet tree-lined street running between the bustle of West Broadway and Church Street. The building is an ornate affair, with an elaborate frontage; all big, church-sized windows and intricately carved, ornamented sills. While the majority of the building is given over to offices, the basement is a place of pain and triumph and McAvoy feels very much at home as he leans against the counter by the door and waits for Dezzie Estrada to come and give him five minutes of his time. For all that McAvoy is uncomfortable in the macho world of banter and boasting, he has always felt comfortable in a boxing gym. He learned the art of pugilism at boarding school in his teens and would have received a scholarship to university on his boxing prowess alone had he not also achieved straight A grades in his exams. He boxed through-out his two years at university and briefly considered a career in the fight game, before his coach pointed out that to be a true champion McAvoy would have to hurt his opponents so badly that they risked never getting up again. McAvoy, who had never thrown a punch without worrying about the consequences, did not have the necessary killer instinct. He turned his attentions to rugby instead, and when he quit university, a year shy of his degree, it was rugby that offered him the best chance of a career. He spent two years coaching fitness at a succession of small clubs and academies, before he gave in to the inner voice telling him to become a policeman. Though he has not worn boxing gloves for almost fifteen years, McAvoy still feels at ease here. He likes the smell. It's a place of perspiration and liniment; leather and metal. Were Trish Pharaoh beside him, she would doubtless say that it reminded her of her bedroom. The walls are lined with old boxing posters and photographs of Dezzie with his arms around a succes-sion of champions; some household names and others only recognisable to true fans. A boxing ring with a blue floor and white ropes takes up a large space on the pitted wooden floor and patched-up heavy bags hang from metal chains. Gunmetal-grey lockers run along one wall; some bearing dents and creases that show Dezzie's charges possess no shortage of killer instinct.

'Here he is,' says Marcel, who mans the front desk of the gym and is so enormous that McAvoy presumed he was standing on a raised platform. His shoulders are broad enough to impair the view of the merchandise cabinet to his rear, with its collection of hoodies, T-shirts and sweatbands bearing the legend 'Fighting Beats Crying'.

McAvoy turns and follows Marcel's gaze. Dezzie Estrada is making his way across his gym, nimbly side-stepping a large, red-faced man who is pounding a heavy bag with powerful, if avoidable shots. The other two men availing themselves of the gym's facilities at this hour are lithe, olive-skinned and dark-haired lightweights shadow-boxing near the free-weights, beneath a large cut-out poster of Sugar Ray Leonard. McAvoy has not had a chance to examine all the posters but he has already identified an image of Dezzie with his arm around the shoulders of a Hollywood star, getting in training for a film role and looking mildly intimidated by his mentor.

Dezzie Estrada is in his late forties and McAvoy knows from the magazine articles he read online that he is of Cuban heritage. He grew up in Brooklyn and had a decent enough amateur boxing record but lacked the punching power to get far in the professional game. Despite his lack of an explosive right hand, Dezzie was a student of the sport and showed himself to have a coach's eye for detail when he began offering heartfelt tips to friends and opponents alike. Spotting an opportunity to do something vaguely useful with his life, he went to night school and trained in sports physiotherapy, while studying for various coaching certificates. After a spell in Brooklyn, he opened the Thomas Street Boxing Gym in 1994. His star rose when he coached a young Costa Rican to the WBO Lightweight title, and by the turn of the millennium he had a stable of quality fighters. His star has shone brightly ever since.

McAvoy considers him. He's probably about 180 pounds and his hair is shaved down to a grey stubble. His nose and left ear show the signs of having taken too many blows but he is still a good-looking, if battle-scarred individual, and he walks with the cat-like gait of a fighter who knows how to slip and jab. He's dressed in a T-shirt that shows off well-defined arms, and sweat-pants that taper into white socks and battered sneakers.

'I'm Dezzie,' he says, in an accent that is all attitude and street. 'You're the English cop?'

McAvoy extends a hand and squeezes Estrada's palm in his. He is unable to resist putting a little power into the shake and he senses Estrada doing the same. If each man were holding a walnut there would be pieces of shell all over the floor.

'Scottish, actually,' says McAvoy, releasing his grip. 'But I help solve crimes in England.'

'You sound like Shrek,' says Estrada, smiling widely to show Hollywood teeth.

'I can live with that,' says McAvoy, busy thanking his lucky stars that Pharaoh is not here to tell Estrada he sounds like Scarface. 'Fabulous place. I've read a lot about it. About you, too. Incredible to be standing here.'

'Thanks,' says Estrada, and seems to mean it. 'You fight?'

'Used to. Lacked the cutting edge.'

Estrada nods. 'You don't have to fight angry, but you have to know how to access your hate.'

'That was my problem.' McAvoy smiles. 'Not enough hate.'

'We could train that out of you,' says Estrada, bringing Marcel into the conversation. 'I've got fighters who only beat their oppo-nent because they're imagining they're beating the crap out of me. I can make people hate.'

'Is that another T-shirt slogan?'

'I'll keep that one for my autobiography,' Estrada says. 'Now, you said you had some questions about Brishen and Shay? Shit, it shook me up to hear what happened. Can't help feeling guilty, y'know?'

McAvoy angles his head, indicating that Estrada could proba-bly elaborate.

'They were here at my request,' says Estrada, and rubs his palms together as if trying to start a fire. The gleam in his bright brown eyes seems to fade along with his smile. 'I've spoken with Brish a hundred times on the phone and Skype, man. He's a good guy. The best. We

56

had a mutual respect thing going, if you follow me. There ain't many coaches who I'd give a dime for but Brish knows the game.'

McAvoy makes a show of consulting the notes in his phone. 'Their flight arrived on the Tuesday night. Can you tell me when you met them in the flesh for the first time?'

'Sure,' says Estrada, his eyes unwavering. 'They were here for 7 a.m. on the Wednesday morning. Brish wanted to keep Shay to his routine, despite the flight and the beers they sank the night before. They wanted to train.'

'Am I right in thinking that if things went well, there was a chance you would take over from Brishen as Shay's trainer?'

Estrada balls up one cheek, pulling a face that indicates the situation was not so clear-cut.

'You gotta understand, a lot of people want me training them,' he says, and the words do not sound like bragging. 'I got a dozen kids a week coming in for try-outs, wanting to show me what they can do. Most times I tell them they're not ready. Sometimes I tell them to join the gym and I find them a coach from my staff and tell them I'll oversee but it won't be a day-to-day thing. I ain't got a lot of room on my team. I train four different world champions and another four who have title fights coming up inside twelve months. Brish had never asked me to take a look at anybody before. I took him at his word that he wasn't going to waste my time. I made no promises, but yeah, if he'd been good enough I would have sponsored his application to spend a few months in the States and I'd have trained him, no question.'

'If he'd been good enough?' asks McAvoy. 'You weren't impressed?'

Estrada pulls a face. 'The kid could punch, no doubt about that. And man, he had stamina. He trained like he was trying to generate enough power to keep the city alight. It was his footwork. He was a year off ready, I think. Needed a rope tying to his legs, to watch the ballet or keep a thumbtack in the heel of his shoes. He was too flat-footed. I think Brishen knew it, but he wanted a second opinion.'

'Could you tell me the exact sequence of events?' asks McAvoy, trying to make it sound like Estrada would be doing him the biggest favour imaginable.

'No problem,' says Estrada. 'The cops came by when they found the bodies. Asked much the same questions you're asking. You sure they're cool with me talking to you?'

'I'm here as their guest,' says McAvoy, as blithely as he can. 'I was having a drink or two with Detective Alto last night.'

'Alto, yeah, he was the guy. If he's cool, I'm cool. So, yeah, what you wanna know?'

'The chain of events,' says McAvoy, and subtly starts recording the conversation with his phone.

'Well, they were here for a few hours on the Wednesday morning. Worked the bag, some light cardio, sparred with a couple of my boys. Around noon, they said they were going to see the sights. I had another fighter in Shay's weight division I wanted to see him in the ring with so I said they should come back for around 6.30 p.m. It didn't go the way Shay wanted it to. Brishen neither. That was that, y'know. No hard feelings. We shook hands and they went off. Next thing I heard was that they'd been found upstate. Shay dead, Brish dying. Fuck, man, I don't know who they pissed off but I had to sit down when I heard.'

McAvoy puts a hand out and finds himself giving Estrada a manly rub on the shoulder. Estrada gives a little smile in thanks at the gesture.

'Brishen's phone records indicate he called you late on Wednesday evening. You spoke for one minute and fifty-four seconds. Can I ask you what that was in connection with?'

Estrada looks confused. He pauses, and for a moment all McAvoy can hear is the squeak of rubber-soled sneakers on the hard floor. 'My cell phone or the gym phone?' he asks. 'The detective didn't ask me nothing about that.'

'I'd already told him, boss,' says Marcel, listening in. 'The detective, I mean. It was the gym phone. The Irishman was asking about his friend.'

'Shay?' asks McAvoy, puzzled.

'No, the little fucking weasel,' says Marcel, scowling. 'Valentine.'

McAvoy swallows. Tries not to let his emotions show in his face. 'Valentine?'

'Oh, the other one,' says Estrada, nodding. 'Sorry, man, he

didn't seem to matter. Showed up here late on the Wednesday night. Maybe 10 p.m.? Brishen and Shay were done by then and I was looking to close up. Said he was Brish's brightest prospect and wanted a try-out, like he'd been promised. I didn't like the kid's attitude.'

'You weren't expecting him?'

'Hell no,' says Estrada. 'Brish hadn't mentioned him. There was no way I was giving him the time of day, man. I told him to come back when he'd sobered up.'

'He'd been drinking?'

'I'd hate to think he was sober.'

'He left?'

'He didn't want to but Marcel here can be persuasive.'

'You threw him out?' asks McAvoy, turning to the huge man.

'Didn't need to. He called us a few names in a language that sounded like it was from *Lord of the Rings* and then he punched a couple of the lockers and left. I tried to call Brish to tell him some kid had been using his name but his phone was off.'

'You left a message?'

'Nah, man, I don't leave messages.'

'But Brishen called you back asking about Valentine?'

'He sounded a bit liquored up himself,' says Marcel, in a conspiratorial whisper that puts McAvoy in mind of old ladies gossiping at a bus stop. 'He wanted to know if one of his other prospects had come by. Told him he must have a sixth sense. I said he'd been in and made a bit of a dick of himself. Brish swore a bit, but more to himself than to me. He said thanks and told me to call if he came in again. Said bye and hung up.'

'And you told this to Detective Alto?' asks McAvoy, wondering why it hadn't appeared in his report.

'Shit, man, I didn't put it together,' says Marcel apologetically. 'Cop was asking me about Brishen and Shay so that's what I told him about.'

'Me too,' says Estrada, shrugging. 'Cop asked about the two who got shot. Didn't think nothing of some kid using Brish's name. It matter?'

McAvoy gives a little nod. Estrada is looking at Marcel and McAvoy wonders if something unspoken is passing between them.

'Is this the person who came by?' asks McAvoy, and he calls up a photograph of Valentine on his phone. It is a copy of a snap that sits in a frame atop the fireplace of Papa Teague's caravan. It shows a pale, freckly youth with a pointed face and hair that hangs long at the back and short at the front, with tramlines shaved above his left ear.

'That's the little weasel.' Estrada nods, and Marcel concurs. 'Eyes looked like he had raw ginger up his ass. I swear, Brishen never vouched for anybody but Shay.'

'Was there anybody else in the gym when he showed up?'

'Just Marcel and me,' says Estrada. 'Marcel left and I wasn't far behind.'

'And you didn't see him again?'

'No, didn't pay him no mind until you brought it up.'

McAvoy nods. Pockets his phone. 'You should probably contact Detective Alto,' he says. 'I'm here only as an observer. It's his case.'

'Damn strange,' says Estrada, scratching his jaw. 'Should be Homicide South or the County Mounties. The Seventh only get seventy-two hours, and that's only if the body's in their precinct.'

McAvoy frowns. 'Yes?'

'Hell, they change the boundaries often enough, what do I know?' says Estrada, back-pedalling a little. 'Like you say, I'll call him.'

McAvoy smiles in thanks and shakes Estrada's hand. The grip is less crushing this time.

'You wanna hit the bag?' asks Estrada playfully. 'Can teach you a little hate, you Shrek-looking Limey motherfucker.'

'Limey?' asks McAvoy, smiling.

'I don't know the curse word for a Scottisher,' says Estrada. 'But whatever it is, you're it.'

He raises his hands and slips out a couple of jabs that fall well short of where McAvoy stands. Behind the counter, Marcel grins.

'I'll just go home and cry,' says McAvoy. 'Crying Beats Fighting, if you ask me.'

Estrada shakes his head and gives a little salute, before turning his back and moving to where a man in a red tracksuit is twisting at the waist while holding a heavy ball. McAvoy feels pain in his arms just looking at him.

'I think I need to own a Thomas Street T-shirt,' says McAvoy companionably, leaning on the desk. 'Am I an XL?'

'Not here, brother.' Marcel laughs, and turns to the cabinet behind him. 'Not much more than a medium.'

'Excellent,' says McAvoy. 'My wife will be delighted I've gone down two sizes while I've been away.'

Marcel puts the shirt in a clear bag and then frowns as McAvoy offers him a fifty-dollar bill. 'Nothing smaller? I ain't got much change.'

McAvoy raises his hands in apology and Marcel pulls out his wallet. He hands McAvoy a twenty-dollar bill and McAvoy glances at the assorted bills, receipts and paperwork spilling out of the battered leather.

McAvoy gives his best smile as he moves back from the counter. 'Thanks again,' he says and waves a hand, vaguely, in Estrada's direction.

He is halfway up the stairs when he raises his phone to his mouth and records his own voice asking the question rubbing at his frontal lobes like sandpaper.

'Why is the witness statement from a Marcel Costa, when the big guy's driving licence says his surname is Aguilar?'

As he emerges back into the cold, grey air of Thomas Street, McAvoy ends the recording and starts making a call. He is so engrossed that he does not notice the girl with purple hair and glasses in the coffee shop opposite; her endearing smile replaced with a cold, dead-eyed scowl.

7

. . . against everyone who shall wish me ill, afar and near. I summon today all these powers between me and those evils, against every cruel and merciless power that may oppose my body and soul, against incantations of false prophets, against black laws of pagandom, against false laws of heretics, against craft of idolatry, against spells of witches and smiths and wizards, against every knowledge that corrupts man's body and soul . . .

He's at it again. Holy Fucking Joe. Our Father, Our Father, Our Fucking Father. Jaysus, but give it a rest. He hears you. He gets the point, man. Pick another bloody book. Put the radio back on. Sing me a fucking song. Or speak up. It's just mumbling. The same dull monotone, day after bloody day. Asking for forgiveness. For himself. For me. I know those words. Know them to my bones, whoever's bones they may so be. I can taste His body; His blood. I can feel the glass beads between finger and thumb and see the light through the coloured glass. I just don't know my fucking name. I tell you something for nothing, my friend, whatever sins I've committed, I'm serving my sentence for them. This is purgatory. This is the place between. Trapped here, not something nor nothing; not feeling, not knowing, only half remembering, waiting for an alien body to decide if it wants to live or die. I know that prayer. I recognise it just from the words I can pick out. Idolatry. That's what you're apologising for. Jaysus, there are worse sins. God in heaven, He understands. The Bible's centuries behind the times and He's in no rush to come and update it. Can you blame Him? Who would look at this world and think of it as somewhere worth visiting? Hang about, those words are familiar too. I remember them in a voice of purple silk. Not like this beige bastard,

62

droning on, saying his pleases and his thank yous every time the orange nurse offers him coffee and tells him he's doing the Lord's work. Fuck it, Sister, I don't know the man. Don't know myself. But whoever the fuck I am, I know that I can only take so much prayer. He's interrupting. Breaking my concentration. Every time I think I've got hold of the memory he stutters out another 'Amen' and it pops like a soap bubble. But I'm nearly there, I tell you. It's all just ripped-up pictures and swirled smells right now but I'll unpick it, by God I will. I see a man. Beard like a bear. The sort of man who can blunt a razor in one shave. Angry eyes and big fists. And the little lad. Ratty eyes and red hair and temper like a ferret. The kid in the gold tracksuit. Gaffer tape and bruises. The fat man. Bald as a worm; glasses and blue stones. Snow hitting the windscreen like I'm driving through static. Lights on the road then cold on my skin; shouts and bangs and a mouth full of blood and stones. Eleanor Rigby; my face in my fucking pocket. Christ, don't listen to the beige man. Hear this. Hear me. Help me find the strength to wake, Lord. Help me remember. And let me have my vengeance.

8

'Tuck your chin in. Right to your chest. That's it. Good girl. Now, one, two . . . three!'

There is a splash as the seven-year-old girl with the mass of curly black hair and the soft mocha skin hits the water with the grace of an elephant falling from a plane. The water has not yet rolled back when she emerges; her goggles on her cheeks like a second pair of eyes and screwing up her features in the way that people do in the moment before they are shot in the face.

'Getting better,' says Claudio, as the little girl doggy-paddles over to him, wiping her hand over her face and coughing through her giggles. 'Better than a mermaid.'

'Mermaids can't dive. How would they stand on the side?' asks Belle between splutters.

'There are two types of mermaid,' says Claudio softly. 'Some have fish-tails and human bodies. Others the other way around.'

Belle considers this. 'Like, a massive fish head and skinny human legs?'

Claudio nods. 'They're not as popular as the other type.'

'No,' says Belle, considering the picture in her head. 'Do they wear trousers? Because if they didn't, they'd have their butts out.'

Claudio sucks his cheek in. It's the closest he gets to a grin.

'Did she see me?' asks Belle, scanning the spectators who sit in ones and twos in the blue and yellow plastic chairs that overlook this heated swimming pool on Society Hill, Philadelphia. Belle is revelling in this unexpected day off from school. A special treat, Claudio had said. A *secret*. 'Momma. Did she see?'

'I'm sure she did,' says Claudio, treading water and enjoying his stepdaughter's weight around his neck. He looks at the spectators and fails to see Mia. He refuses to let his disappointment show on his face. 'I bet she's just popped out to phone her friends and tell them how good you're getting.'

'It's cold out there,' says Belle, concerned.

'She has her coat.'

'But her tummy is bare.'

'That's because she has a nice tummy.'

'Will it snow again?'

'Her tummy?'

'No, silly. The sky.'

'Do you want it to?'

'Yes.'

'Then yes, it will.'

'You think I'll get the dive right next time?' asks Belle, looking into his eyes in the way that makes him feel like the only man in the world.

'I think you'll be the greatest diver in history,' says Claudio.

Belle pauses a moment, looking at his face. 'You should smile when you say a nice thing,' she confides, like wisdom. 'You have a nice smile.'

Claudio twitches his lips. 'Like that?'

'It's a start. But you should show your teeth more.'

'I don't have nice teeth,' says Claudio. 'If I smile in here, people will think I'm a shark.'

Belle giggles. 'Be a shark!' she says. 'I'll be a mermaid. You can chase me and I'll hit you with my tail.'

Claudio nods. 'I doubt I'll catch you,' he says. 'I'm old and slow and you're young and gorgeous and the best swimmer in this whole pool.'

Belle considers this. There are no more than a dozen people in the twenty-five-metre swimming pool but she sizes them all up as if preparing for a contest. 'Maybe,' she says. 'That old man isn't fast but he has stamina.'

'That's a good word,' says Claudio. 'When I was your age, I wouldn't have known that word.'

'How many years ago were you my age?'

Claudio does the math on his fingers. 'Fifty-seven years ago,' he says. 'And I wasn't so pretty.'

'You're not very pretty now either,' says Belle, giggling.

Claudio is in no position to disagree. He's out of shape and his skin is pale and malleable, like a bowl of oatmeal left out since yesterday. There is a mess of ruined skin on his left bicep and he lacks all his teeth save two in the lower set. There is a redness across his cheeks and his nose is crooked. His short grey hair is thinning on top. He looks every one of his years. His is a face that has witnessed violence, and though some of the other swimmers may be wondering what his relationship is with the brown-skinned little girl, nobody looks at him long enough to risk catching his attention. He looks like a man capable of causing harm.

'Are you going to be a shark or not?' asks Belle, kicking away from the man who has been sharing her mother's bed for the last couple of years and who has brought a little stability into a life that previously lacked much structure.

Claudio is about to do as he is asked when the older man who impressed Belle with his stamina breast-strokes between them.

'You practise your front crawl,' says Claudio. 'I won't be far behind.'

Belle pulls a face and glances at the older man, who is now treading water next to Claudio. 'You might have stamina but I'm faster,' she says confrontationally.

'I don't doubt it, sweet-pea,' says the older man, grinning to expose a full set of perfect white teeth. 'You show me what you can do.'

Belle turns and does a good impression of a motor-boat: churning through the water in a whirl of foam, her dark head popping up and disappearing again like an otter.

'She ain't elegant but she's motivated,' says the elderly man companionably. 'Take after her momma?'

Claudio looks at the older man and, with the subtlest of nods, they move to the side of the pool. They each place an elbow on the wet tiles and bob there; water up to their throats.

'Where is Momma?' asks the old man, his lower lip dipping below the water.

'Supposed to be watching,' says Claudio. 'Think she's gone for a cigarette.'

'You sure that's all?' asks the man.

'Sure enough,' says Claudio.

They consider one another for a moment. The older man is tall and loose-limbed, and though the water obscures it, Claudio knows he has a pot-belly that makes him look pregnant, and a scythe-shaped scar on his lower back where his kidney was removed a decade ago. His hair is dyed black and he squints when he talks. The squinting is a habit. Two years ago he underwent laser surgery on one eye and had a replacement cornea in the other. His vision is now perfect. But he still wears his thick glasses when doing business; albeit with non-prescription lenses. The FBI don't know that he now has 20/20 vision. He plays this to his advantage. At his last prosecution for racketeering, the jury were shown him in conversation with a known Mafia boss. In it, he was pictured without his glasses. His defence attorneys demonstrated he had no idea to whom he was talking. Here, now, neither he nor Claudio can be sure they are not being observed. But they know nobody is recording them. The Feds are not allowed video surveillance in an environment where children are in a state of near undress. The old man now conducts most of his important meetings here. He knows nobody is wearing a wire, and with his mouth below the waterline, nobody can read his lips. His name is Giulio Pagano, and he is consigliere to the boss of the Philadelphia Mob. The boss is in a jail cell, on the same landing where Pagano spent twenty years. For two decades, Pagano was not allowed to swim. Since his release eight years ago, he has made it his business to swim every day.

'She still on the blow?' asks Pagano.

'She says not.'

'We can find out for certain.'

'I don't need that. I trust her.'

'Keep an eye on it.'

'I will.'

Claudio floats in the water, waiting for Pagano to speak again. They have much to discuss.

'New York's not happy,' says the old man at last. His green eyes catch the movement of the water and briefly sparkle. For a moment, he looks intelligent, as though he were working things out and making calculations a dozen moves ahead of everybody else. Claudio knows it to be an optical illusion. He has known Pagano for the better part of half a century and he's a dumb fuck who has survived at the top of the Mob because he is no threat to anybody more important. He's also a vicious bastard, whose paranoia is becoming a cause for concern.

'No?' asks Claudio.

'Not happy at all,' says Pagano.

Claudio waits for more. When nothing comes, he gives a shake of the head. 'Don't treat me like one of your punks, Giulio. I know this routine. I learned it from the same men you did. Talk to me.'

Pagano considers for a moment then smiles, widely. 'Still a ball-breaker, eh Claudio?'

'I'm whatever you need me to be. Always have been.'

Pagano purses his lips, as though thinking. He rubs a hand over his face. 'They like you,' he says, his mouth below the waterline and his words bubbling on the surface. 'That's why they asked for you. It was important.'

'So you said.'

'And it went wrong,' says Pagano, without accusation.

'How was I to know there was a fucking guy in the trunk?' asks Claudio quietly. 'Luca only opened it up to see if there was a tyre iron in there to hit the big man with. Some angry Russian jumps out shouting curses. What were we to do? Luca tried to get him on his knees with the others but he wasn't having any of it. Luca wanted to show what he could do. Took a knife to one of them. That wasn't what we were there to do. Next thing Luca's started shooting, the the Irish are dead, the Russian's somewhere in the woods. We went looking. The Russian knocked me down. Did what he did to Luca. Whole thing was a damn mess. I didn't know the Irishman was alive until I read the papers.'

'Did he tell you who he was?' asks Pagano coldly. 'Tell you how important he was to our new friendships? There are lots of unhappy people, Claudio. It's going to be expensive. It's going to cost somebody dear to smooth things over. We need to know what he was doing there. Need to know if the person who's going to pay for this is one of ours, or one of theirs. I spoke up for you.'

Claudio considers him. Pagano is a crook and a killer. He's a liar who would sell what is left of his soul if it helped add a few more feathers to his already comfortable nest. Despite their history, he knows Pagano would sell him out in a moment.

'I bet you did,' says Claudio. 'What was the decision?'

Pagano looks at Claudio like a mechanic about to tell a naïve motorist how much it will cost to repair the damage under the hood.

'Like I said, it needs cleaning up, Claudio. It's a mess. There's even a cop over from England. It was meant to be clean. They wanted the best. They asked for you.'

Claudio controls his breathing. His fingers are twitching and he forces himself to stop them.

'Why was I even there, Giuli? Somebody asks me to do a job, I do it. But somebody's been lying to me. I want a chance to find out who. That's why I came to you. That's why I didn't run.'

'You know what would have happened if you ran,' says Pagano.

'Do I?' asks Claudio, putting his face in the water and rubbing a hand over it. 'I know who you send after the people who run. You send me. So who would you send, eh? Who you got who can do what I do?'

The older man considers this. Claudio can almost hear his thoughts. He knows that nobody is irreplaceable, but for decades he has been one of the Philly Mob's biggest assets. He has never run a crew or risen above street level in the organisation's hierarchy. But he was a made man by the time he was in his mid-twenties and is the most lethal of his organisation's enforcers. For the Philly Mob, he has killed twenty-nine men. For their associates in New York, he was involved in a further sixteen murders. During a brief spell on the run in Italy, he put bullets in six members of the Camorra crime syndicate during a month of bloodshed on the streets of Naples. He is a stone-cold killer. And now, however gently, he is being threatened with the consequences of a failure that was not of his making.

'There'll be money spent over all this,' says Pagano, his face full of regret. 'There has to be blood too. People are asking questions.'

'Maybe I should have done the same,' says Claudio, narrowing his eyes. 'Asked questions, I mean.'

'You've never asked before.'

'I've never felt I was being lied to before. Those boys from Ireland? They'd only just arrived. How much harm could they have done? How much of a threat? That wasn't a hit, it was a fucking murder.'

Pagano concedes the point with a wave of his free hand. Behind him, Belle is standing on the edge of the pool, palms together, head tucked in, preparing to dive. The light comes in through the high windows and seems to make her glow. Pagano follows his gaze.

'She's a beauty,' he says, then gives a salacious wink. 'Gonna be hard to keep her off the pole when she's a teen, eh? Gonna have hips like her momma.'

Claudio refuses to rise to it. 'She's going to be fine. It's all going to be fine.'

'You're well liked, Claudio. You're respected. You're a neat worker and the people who know your name know you're to be feared. You're the guy we send when somebody's really fucked up. You've never been thought of as a risk.'

'And now?'

Pagano shrugs ruefully. 'There are loose ends, you know that. The way it looks . . . Luca's dad wants blood. The Chechens will want it too. If one of theirs killed one of ours, you know what has to happen – deal or not. Chechens or Russians or whatever you want to call your new friends – they killed Luca. Accident or set-up, that's the bit that's eating me. And I'll bet a dime to a dollar it's what's eating New York too. Go do your thing,' says Pagano, with the slightest of nods. 'Luca's old man needs answers. He deserves them. And you need to hand him somebody to hate that isn't you.'

Claudio licks his lips. 'What if what I find upsets the new deal?'

'Don't start asking questions like that.' Pagano smiles. 'They're not for you to think about. Worry about what went down in the woods.'

Claudio closes his eyes. He knows better than to argue. There is so much he could throw in the other man's face but it would be like slamming his fist into a wall. Pagano will never acknowledge what they both know to be true. Will never talk about that night in 1981 when they were forced to choose a side in the Mob wars that were ripping New York and Philadelphia apart.

'Just find out why he was there,' says Pagano. 'Find out who skewered Luca. Don't let this English cop or any fucking angry Irishmen slow you down. Do what you do best.'

Claudio nods. He expected nothing less. He is not a man who spends a lot of time worrying about what he cannot change, but these past days have taken their toll upon him. He had not even known whether to go home, whether he should expose Mia and Belle to the consequences of what went on upstate. In the end he came home purely to find out whether he was to be allowed to live. He is still unsure whether he has been reprieved, or sentenced afresh.

'Two days,' says Pagano, looking at him hard. He turns away. He swims a dozen strokes, his eyes fixed on Mia. When he pulls his tall, pot-bellied frame from the water, a broad-shouldered man in a tracksuit emerges from the changing rooms and wraps a fluffy white bathrobe around his shoulders.

Belle swims to her stepfather. 'Was that one any better?' she asks. 'The dive?'

Claudio pulls her close and enjoys the sensation of her wet, curly hair against his cheek. He has already lived more years than he expected to and never believed himself capable of the feelings that Belle has filled him with. Were he to consider it properly, he would admit to only staying with the girl's mother because he loves the child.

'You're going to be a champion,' he says.

'Your eyes look sad,' she says, considering him. 'Do you want to be a shark?'

71

'I'm too tired to be a shark, Belle.'

The little girl looks at him thoughtfully. 'Who was the old man?'

'He thinks he's a shark,' says Claudio. 'Really, he's a jellyfish.'

She giggles at this. 'He looked like a jellyfish who had lost some legs.'

'He's lost more than that,' says Claudio. 'Will you be okay for a day or two if I go away?'

Belle pulls a face. 'You just got back.'

'I'll bring you a present.'

'From somewhere good?'

'New York,' he says.

'That's not very exciting,' says Belle. 'I've got snow-globes from there already. Could you go to Japan?'

'Maybe next time,' says Claudio.

She takes him at his word, confident that he will never lie to her. She has no reason to doubt him. He has made good on every promise he has made her. He'll even make sure she becomes a diving champion, and if that means shooting every competitor, so be it.

'Your brain looks busy,' says Belle, holding him by the chin and angling his head this way and that. 'What are you thinking about?'

Claudio wonders if she will ever be old enough to hear the truth. Wonders how her eyes would change if he spoke of the gunshots in the snow and the man who kept a veil of delicate skin in a leather bag in his pocket the way the superstitious fishermen used to when he was a boy. He knows she will never be old enough. Knows that he will go to his grave before he would allow this bright, precocious child to glimpse the images his mind is spitting out like a broken printer; handing him memories he neither wants to see, nor has ever truly understood. For a moment he is a young man again, sitting in the front seat of the nondescript Buick and waiting for Salvatore Pugliesca to open the door of his home on South Broad Street and pay the price for his deceit. For a moment he is standing over what remains of him. He is remembering the mute prick with the fish eyes and gasping mouth; watching as he hacked at his own trapped limb with a kitchen knife as his lips moved, soundlessly, in forlorn prayer.

But Claudio is a man who has spent forty years trying not to let his nightmares take control of his life, and he would not wish such pain upon the child.

'I'll watch Momma while you're gone,' says Belle solemnly.

Claudio pulls her close and pushes a tendril of hair behind her ear. Suddenly, Belle takes his hand and examines it like a fortune-teller.

'You have nice hands,' says Belle. 'Skinny fingers.'

Claudio examines them. Gives a little laugh. Realises he has never paid them much attention. Here, now, he feels an absurd dislike for his fingers; fingers built to hold the handle of a gun or detonate the bomb that blew a boss's son to pieces.

'I didn't like that man,' says Belle, scowling, pointing at the door to the changing rooms.

'No?'

'What does he do?'

Claudio considers this. 'He makes decisions.'

'Good decisions?'

Claudio closes his eyes. 'We'll know in a day or so.'

PART TWO

1972: The First Absolution

The boys and girls look like figures in a faded lithograph. Their skin is almost translucent from lack of sunshine. Their gums, ruptured by rotten teeth, bleed as they chew for comfort on arms through which the bones are clearly visible and which are patterned with the scabs left by the hypodermics that puncture their parchment flesh.

Were he still the boy from Queen's, Jimmy Whelan would find the nearest nurse and slam their head into the nearest wall. He wants to burn this place down, to watch the flames rise high over the treetops in this dark corner of Staten Island: an inferno visible from every window in Manhattan.

But Jimmy Whelan is no longer a boy from Queen's. He is a priest. He is a servant of God. He knows temper to be the pathway to hate and he knows hate, alongside temptation, to be the fuel of all true sin. He tries hard to be Father James Whelan. But right now he truly wants to be Jimmy.

'I told you,' says Dr Piechowiak under his breath. He has his hand to his nose.

'No,' says Jimmy. 'No, you said it was bad. This is evil.'

The two men stand in the shadows of the dormitory and look upon a scene of biblical suffering. Boys and girls, their ages impossible to gauge, are scattered like stones around the square room with its drawn drapes and its single bulb. Their heads have been shaved to prevent infection. Their fingers and chins are covered with oatmeal and drool. Some are little more than corpses;

77

withered arms and atrophied legs, cuddling themselves in puddles of urine and coated in their own filth.

'And they know?' asks Jimmy, refusing to make any attempt to protect himself from the smell. If these poor boys and girls can endure it, so can he. 'The people in charge? The authorities?'

'The authorities have been told time and again,' hisses Dr Piechowiak. He has a mouthful of strong mints and they clatter off his teeth as he talks. With his flat features and his sharp teeth and mop of uncombed hair, the doctor looks like a frightened cat.

'And?' asks Jimmy, casting anxious glances around.

'Senator Kennedy even demanded answers and nothing changed,' says the doctor. 'I had no choice. I'm bringing the TV reporter, the guy with the big moustache. Something has to change. I can't be a part of this any more.'

Jimmy wants to shout. He wants to bellow and bang his hands on the metal cots and their threadbare mattresses. He knows he cannot. He and Dr Piechowiak are trespassers. The doctor handed in his notice weeks ago, appalled at being part of such a regime. He needs the help of the earnest young priest if he is to raise awareness of this place and have it shut down. Jimmy wants to do some good. He's only young but already has a reputation for getting things done. He is still unsure whether to accept the offer of a transfer out of his Hell's Kitchen parish and into the splendour of St Colman's on the Lower East Side. He's good with the neighbourhood kids. He organises the basketball leagues and referees the boxing matches and is not above banging on the door of a neighbourhood punk who has been knocking their wife and kids about and promising to show them what hell looks like if they don't mend their ways. He doesn't want to be tempted by the splendidness of St Colman's. He knows there to be many ways to praise the Lord and does not want to be the kind of Catholic who believes that God is all about the gold brocade and stained glass.

'Almost every patient has hepatitis,' says Dr Piechowiak in Jimmy's ear. 'One member of staff for every eighty patients. They put on a good show when the parents come but any parent who makes too much of a fuss gets told that this is what is best for their children. Some of them aren't even retarded. They just have problems, or they're a little slow. Some can't express themselves the way they want, or move as good as other kids . . .'

Dr Piechowiak stops talking as one of the figures detaches itself from a space by the wall. He's perhaps in his mid-teens. He wears a nightshirt. His skin is as pale as milk and his eyes have the pinkish tinge of a cornered rat.

'Come on,' says Piechowiak.

Jimmy waits for the boy to come close. He squints into his face. There is a sudden moment of recognition. He cannot place the boy but he knows he has seen him before.

'Hello, my son. What's your name?'

The boy cocks his head. He opens his mouth but all that emerges is an ugly, rasping gulp. He has no teeth and his gums are black.

'He can't speak,' says Dr Piechowiak. 'Physically he's fine but he can't make a sound. He saw bad things when he was younger. His guardian placed him here three years ago.'

Jimmy considers him. 'Tony,' he says, at length, and something flickers in the young man's eyes. Jimmy puts his hand to his chest and tries not to let his thoughts show in his expression. 'Your godfather,' he says. 'I know you. Your family. Why are you here, my son?'

'He's strong,' interrupts Dr Piechowiak. 'Half strangled one of the orderlies who found him playing with a dead mouse. Be careful.'

'Are you strong?' asks Jimmy, and he puts a hand on the boy's bare arm. Tony flinches, as though brushing up against hot iron.

'We have to go,' hisses the doctor urgently.

Jimmy looks at the boy's arms. They carry scars and bruises; yellow and blue discolourations in the shape of forefingers and thumbs. Jimmy grinds his teeth. He knows this kid. They used to call him the dummy, back in the neighbourhood. Tony, whose guardian wouldn't let the poor bastard even take the family surname. 'Leave it blank,' said Paulie Pugliesca, when asked to fill in the name for the baptism. That had stuck. Tony Blank. Sal

Pugliesca's little brother. Didn't speak. Strong. Crazy, if you pushed the right buttons . . .

'Do you want to leave this place?' asks Jimmy, without looking away. 'I can help you. I can talk to Paulie . . .'

The boy stands immobile for a moment, then gives a quick nod.

'Trust in the Lord,' says Jimmy, and blesses the boy. 'I'll talk to your guardian. Get you out. Get you somewhere else. Close this whole thing down . . .'

'Father Whelan!' protests the doctor urgently. 'We must go.'

'Believe in me. I'll believe in you.'

Dr Piechowiak pulls the priest by the arm and they disappear into the darkness, hurrying to the open window in the doctor's old study where they gained entry.

The boy stares at the space where they stood for a long time after they have gone.

Then he blesses himself and sits down cross-legged on the floor.

He whispers to the dying mouse that he holds, like rotten fruit, in the palm of his hand.

'Believe in me, I'll believe in you. Amen.'

9

McAvoy sits in the cool, still air of the church and feels as if he is pressing his face against stone. He is comfortable here, in this chilly, peaceful space, with its smells of furniture polish and incense. It has always puzzled him that air made up of so many prayers should create such a gentle embrace. He pictures prayers as urgent, skittish things; spectres born behind locked teeth. Instead, he feels himself strangely comforted. The temples of his youth were the joyless and functional kirks of the Free Presbyterian Church of Scotland. He has always enjoyed the gaudy splendour favoured by the Catholic Church. Though he has never made up his mind on the existence of a higher being, McAvoy is always quick to marvel at the ingenuity and creativity of human beings and within St Colman's he feels he has discovered a magnificent example of man's potential.

The pew on which McAvoy sits is to the rear of the church. There is not much light coming through the tall, arched windows but enough to illuminate the face of Jesus, resplendent in white robes and golden halo, smiling benignly upon a kneeling woman with covered head; herself encircled by men with clasped hands. The light shines through the elaborate panes of yellow and blue glass that serve as ornate canvas for the scene and McAvoy enjoys the flickering pattern that the coloured glass throws upon the grey and white stone tiles of the church floor. A more human Jesus is depicted in oil paints behind the cross. His face hangs down, streaked with dirt and blood, and the bones of his shoulder joints strain under his weight. It is a brutal, angry image and McAvoy, who has seen more horror than most, recognises it as the portrait of a dying man. It strikes a more personal note than any of the benevolent-faced statues or angelic cherubs that look down from the high walls.

McAvoy pushes himself back in his seat and his knee cracks with a sound like a stick breaking. He has been sitting here for almost an hour. It is a little before 6 p.m. According to the schedule in the atrium to his rear, there should have been a Mass at 5.30 p.m. but a few minutes ago, a short, twitchy man with white hair came and whispered in the ears of two parishioners in the front pews and they left moments later, telling the other gathered communicants that Father Alatriste had been called away. There are now only half a dozen parishioners left inside St Colman's, and McAvoy has yet to find the nerve to go and talk to any of them. He feels like an imposter here. He was confirmed Catholic in his teenage years for no more divine reason than it helped his application to the exclusive boarding school his stepfather wanted him to attend. As an adult, he is an infrequent visitor to church and has not attended confession since his early twenties. Roisin, too, is only a lukewarm Catholic, though she wears a crucifix and blesses herself whenever confronted with bad news.

'No Mass tonight,' comes a voice in McAvoy's ear. He spins in his seat. Leaning forward, her face inches away, is an elderly lady. 'Father Alatriste is attending a parishioner who will be with God before the morning. You're welcome to follow me down to St Brigit's.'

McAvoy takes her in. She's probably in her mid-seventies. Her white hair is cut into a sensible bob and there is no dust on her bifocal spectacles. She's wearing a pale blue jumper, woollen skirt, thick tights and flat shoes and is holding a damp overcoat and pink scarf over one arm.

'I think I'll just sit here a while,' says McAvoy, leaning forward so he can whisper into her ear. He catches a smell. Face cream and some delicate floral perfume.

'There's no better place for it,' she says, nodding, and McAvoy hears a trace of Connemara in her accent.

'Beautiful church,' says McAvoy, when it appears that the lady is in no rush to walk away.

'We like it,' she says. 'Not as splendid as old St Patrick's but it has the feel of God about it, wouldn't you say?'

McAvoy considers this. 'I'm sure the parishioners at most churches say that.'

'True, but I'm not sure how many of them mean it in their heart. I've always felt that if Jesus came to New York, this is where he would go and talk to His Father.'

McAvoy finds himself smiling. He puts out a hand. 'I'm Aector,' he says, and as he shakes the old lady's hand he feels the lumps and swollen knuckles of arthritis.

'Mary,' comes the reply. 'One of eleven Marys in my class year, before you say anything. It's a popular name.'

McAvoy is about to speak when Mary ushers him along the pew. 'I'll take the weight off,' she says, and lowers herself onto the pew next to him. Her damp coat touches his legs.

'You're a tourist, then,' says Mary, in that guileless, gently probing tone that McAvoy fondly associates with Irishwomen of a certain age.

'I am indeed,' he replies.

'And you'll be Scottish.'

'I am. Was it the hair or the accent that gave me away?'

Mary smiles, showing teeth too perfect to be real. 'You couldn't look more Scottish if you were wearing a kilt and eating shortbread from a tartan tin.'

'We were Irish originally,' confides McAvoy. 'My ancestors obviously thought that Ireland wasn't rainy enough and went looking for pastures new.'

'The whole world was Irish originally,' says Mary, and her voice drops the reverential tone with which she had first whispered in his ear. Now he has made her smile, she has clearly decided they are friends. 'St Patrick's Day in New York – you need to get out of the city. Everybody starts telling you their life story and claiming that their great-great-grandfather came over on the *Star of the Sea*. If they're all telling the truth the blasted ship would have sunk under the weight. I don't know what St Patrick would make of the way he's remembered. The Paddy's day before last, I had to shoo out a load of Mexicans who were dressed as leprechauns. That's not the sort of thing you expect when you wake up in the morning.'

McAvoy chuckles in his seat. The more Mary talks, the more Irish she sounds. He decides to confide.

'My wife's Irish,' he says proudly.

'The real thing?' asks Mary.

'We're pretty sure,' he says. 'She's Traveller.'

Mary eyes him and makes a noise in the back of her throat. She's intrigued. 'And you're a gauja, then,' she says. 'Bet that went down well.'

'I didn't expect to hear that word while I was here,' says McAvoy. He has grown familiar with the term employed by Gypsies for non-Gypsies.

'I've no problem with the itinerants myself,' says Mary graciously. 'What do her family make of you?'

The question is too large for McAvoy to begin grappling with so he just smiles ruefully. 'I'm a policeman, too,' he says.

Mary winces and gives a little laugh. 'I bet they've got one caravan to entertain you in and another parked somewhere out of sight, full of all the stuff they don't want you to see.'

McAvoy finds himself enjoying Mary's company. He settles back in the pew.

'You been a New Yorker for long?' he asks, turning away from the altar to give her his full attention.

'Came here in '65,' she says. 'I was twenty-three.'

'Seeking a new life, were you?'

'More that I was bored to tears with the old one. A man swept me off my feet. Men can do that, when you're young.'

'An American man?'

'No, he was somebody I'd known all my life.'

'School friend?'

Mary laughs and gives him a playful slap on the arm. 'You're not much of a policeman. It was God.'

McAvoy catches sight of the pin on her coat. He screws up his eyes, aware he has missed the obvious.

'I've been a nun for more than fifty years,' she says. 'Nice to know I can still shock a handsome young man.'

McAvoy gives in to a fit of coughing. 'You're part of this parish?'

84

he asks, trying to remember if he has said anything controversial since Sister Mary came and joined him.

'My order works all over Manhattan,' she says, waving a knobbly hand. 'There aren't as many of us as there once were but we try to have a presence in every church.'

McAvoy thinks back to what his new friend said about houses of worship and her words take on a deeper significance.

'So you have a bit of expertise on which churches are worth my time?' he asks.

'All churches are worth your time but some were built to glory God and others to glory the men who were paying for it.'

McAvoy likes her words. 'And this place?'

'Built for God, although there are times I wonder if He's grateful.'

McAvoy isn't sure what she means. 'I'm sorry?'

'That lady.' Sister Mary nods. Beneath a stained-glass window showing St John the Baptist holding his own severed head, an elderly, dark-skinned woman is leaning over a row of candles. She is stick-thin and the coat that dangles off her shoulders looks as though it is still on the hanger. She has her back to McAvoy, but her body language speaks of cold bones and heavy burdens.

'She looks cold,' says McAvoy.

'She could light a million candles and it wouldn't warm her,' says Sister Mary, and she crosses herself, tutting at the world in general. 'It's no small miracle she has the strength to stand.'

As McAvoy watches, the woman by the candles lowers herself to her knees. She starts praying, completely motionless, face turned upwards as if she is hypnotised by the flame.

'She lights one every morning and night,' says Sister Mary, and her voice drops again. 'I admire her.'

'Who's she praying for?' asks McAvoy.

Sister Mary tucks her lips back over her teeth, as if demonstrating an unwillingness to gossip. Then she leans forward, and McAvoy puts his ear closer to her lips. He catches that same smell, and wonders whether nuns of a certain age know God well enough to tell Him they are going to start wearing a little bit of perfume now and again.

'Her daughter,' whispers Sister Mary, blessing herself. 'Must be not far off forty years she's been praying for her to come home.'

'She ran away?' asks McAvoy.

'Taken,' says Sister Mary, with another genuflection.

'You don't have to talk about it if it's painful,' says McAvoy, who wonders if he really wants to hear another sad story when he already knows so many off by heart.

'If she can stand to live I can stand to tell her tale,' says Sister Mary, and the brightness in her tone sounds forced. 'That lady is Magdalena. The family are Puerto Rican. Local to here. Loisaida Avenue. Years ago, she and her husband lost their youngest daughter. I forget her name, God forgive me. She was only a girl. Fourteen or fifteen. Magdalena used to be a cleaner here, as well as working two other jobs. Her husband, God rest him, worked every hour the Lord sent. Good people.'

'What happened?'

Sister Mary gives a polite little shrug. 'Somebody took her. She didn't come home one night after school. They never heard from her again.'

McAvoy shakes his head as the full weight of such a loss floods through him.

'She crops up in the newspapers now and again, every time there's a body found or an anniversary passes. Her husband died without ever knowing the truth. Magdalena lives on her own now. Same little apartment she used to share with her family. I think she's older than I am. She's been in my prayers for forty years and I hope she'll be in yours too.'

McAvoy lowers his head. Instinctively, he wants to run to her and place his arms around her. Wants to promise her answers. He wonders how many other policemen have done the same over the years.

'We're all tested,' says Sister Mary thoughtfully. 'God only sends the tests He knows we are capable of passing.'

McAvoy can't keep the look of uncertainty off his face. 'You really think that?'

Sister Mary's smile is a tight, sad affair. 'I have to. Fifty years of prayers – I have to hope they've been going somewhere.'

'I'm sure you've done amazing things,' says McAvoy, and he has to drag his gaze away from the small, still figure by the candles.

'I hope so, in God's name,' says Sister Mary. 'There are always new fights.'

'From your accent I'd say you're Connemara,' says McAvoy, and makes himself look at Sister Mary. 'I doubt you're short of fight.'

'My father used to say he'd made more people hear bells than the Angelus,' says Sister Mary warmly. 'You know Galway?'

'My wife's there,' he says. 'Went home for a confirmation. Mending bridges with her family.'

'That's why she's not with you?' asks Sister Mary. 'You're here for work?'

'I'm here for her,' says McAvoy, looking down at his boots.

'And I'll be guessing you weren't welcome at the confirmation.'

'Not particularly. It was last week, in Tuam. Am I saying that right? With a "ch"? St Anthony's. We'll hopefully both get home to Yorkshire about the same time,' says McAvoy, and he realises his words are a prayer.

'I know St Anthony's.' She smiles. 'Pretty place. There's a retreat in the saint's name upstate, so I hear. You might benefit from a rest.'

McAvoy smiles. 'If I retreat any further I'll disappear,' he says.

Sister Mary considers him. 'I don't think you're one for retreating,' she muses. 'I reckon you're going into battle even when you're sitting still.' She seems to be considering something, sucking on her lower lip like a sweetie. She looks into McAvoy in a way that reminds him, absurdly, of his wife. She gives the tiniest of nods, making up her mind. She has weighed him, and found him worthy.

'I had a grand old chinwag with a Galwegian not two weeks ago,' says Sister Mary. 'He was lighting a candle for his mother and father. I recognised the accent in his prayers.'

McAvoy sniffs and scratches at his hair, keeping his tone light. 'You get many people from the Old Country coming to this church?'

'With a name like St Colman's?' scoffs Sister Mary. 'We should be serving Guinness at communion. I know more about what's

87

going on back in Ireland than I do Manhattan. There's always somebody to chat to. These boys were full of the craic.'

McAvoy wonders if he should just come straight out and ask, but Sister Mary saves him the trouble.

'Grand big fella, the young lad was,' says Sister Mary. 'I thought they might be father and son but I didn't see much similarity in their features. You don't like to ask, do you? But he said he were the young lad's trainer. They were after a blessing for a fight he was going to be having. I don't like the thought of people knocking lumps off one another but better in a boxing ring than in the pub, that's what I say. And with their accents what they were I had no doubt Father Alatriste would have said yes if he were about the place. As it was, Mr Molony came and said he would point them in the direction of St Brigit's.'

If Sister Mary were allowed to play poker, McAvoy fancies she would face heavy losses. She audibly sniffs as she mentions Mr Molony. McAvoy finds himself unsure what to ask next. He knew that Brishen and Shay had visited this church. He came here hoping to speak to parishioners who saw them here. He believes that from the way Sister Mary is talking she is completely unaware that the two men with whom she chatted were found – one maimed, one murdered – not long after. McAvoy does not want to tell her.

'Is that where they went?' asks McAvoy. 'St Brigit's?'

'They went off with Mr Molony,' she says, and the same look passes across her face.

'He's part of the church?' asks McAvoy.

Sister Mary gives a harsh little laugh. 'Thinks he owns this one,' she whispers conspiratorially. 'He's a lawyer, or so we're told. God forgive me but he's a hard man to get along with. I nearly had a coronary when he offered to show them the way to St Brigit's. The last time I saw him doing something for somebody else he had his stopwatch out so he could check how much of his time he was giving away for free.'

McAvoy laughs at the idea. 'What's his role?' he asks.

'Sacristan,' says Sister Mary. 'You know what that means? Lighting candles, wiping the communion cup, blowing out the candles and lighting them again. An honour. Too old for it if you ask me. He's been doing it the best part of forty years. It's an important job but he's one of those people who think they're doing something nobody else could do half so well. It's not pride, it's pomposity.'

'You've had some run-ins?'

'He holds the purse strings,' says Sister Mary. 'Even Father Alatriste can't get a bean out of him without making a ding-dong. Mr Molony's part of the furniture here. Been coming since he was a boy. And because his firm looks after all the legal side of things, the archdiocese put up with him. He and I have had some cross words but you can imagine who came out on top. Money talks and there's no doubting that he's made a lot of it. I'm sure he's very good at what he does. But do you remember what I was saying about people who build churches for God and people who build them for themselves? I'm sure you can guess which category Mr Molony falls into.'

'Molony,' says McAvoy. 'Irish family.'

'So he says, though I think he would have said he was from anywhere if it got him into Jimmy Whelan's good graces. You'll know him, no doubt.'

McAvoy opens his palms, unable to contribute. 'Jimmy Whelan?'

'Priest in Galway,' says Sister Mary, as if addressing an idiot. 'He was here for a short spell early in his ministry. Native of the Old Country but raised in a bad part of the Bronx. He was a great priest in his youth. I'm sure he is now too. You might think I'd be all fire and brimstone but in truth, I like a progressive priest and he was that, sure enough. He's been a grand servant, both here and back home. We have good links with the churches in Galway and he's a lot to do with that. It's a joy when he comes back to visit, though the visits are too few and far between. You wouldn't pick Mr Molony as being a friend for him but they've got memories in common and having a patron like that is no hindrance for Mr Molony. He's made a habit of making himself some powerful friends.'

McAvoy sifts the words for a deeper meaning but decides that the kindly nun has simply started to drift from the point. He tries to turn Sister Mary's attention back to the conversation she had with Brishen and Shay.

'There were only two men from Galway, were there?'

Sister Mary looks at him quizzically. 'Is there something you're not telling me, Mr Policeman?' she asks.

McAvoy pauses then pulls the picture of Valentine from his pocket. 'Do you recognise this man?'

'And who might he be?'

'My brother-in-law,' says McAvoy.

'He'll be why you're here, I'm guessing.' Sister Mary peers at the picture. 'I don't recognise him, though I'd take a guess at his character from the picture alone. God loves us all, though I don't think He can be held accountable for that boy's hairstyle. You able to tell me why you want to know?'

McAvoy shakes his head apologetically and Sister Mary gives him a smile that says she's not offended. He puts the photo away. He suddenly feels a chill across his back and neck, as though a window has been left open. In the corner of his vision he sees the candle flames stretching out, almost to breaking point, on a sudden breeze. He looks round to see that Magdalena is pulling herself up, still staring at the candles.

'I can't imagine carrying that kind of pain,' says McAvoy, and as he says it Sister Mary puts her cold, arthritis-riddled hand on the back of his huge hand. It sits there, cool and soothing, like the air inside the church she loves.

'You can,' she says. 'I see it in your eyes. You can imagine it all too clearly.'

McAvoy watches the old lady shuffle past and wishes he could do something to make it better.

'Say your prayers. That's all you can do.'

And McAvoy knows, to his very bones, that she is wrong.

1972: The Second Absolution

The trees in the churchyard are swaying as if their leaves and branches conceal some kind of great, shimmying beast, rustling with a noise like brown paper. They're evergreens. European. They're home to pigeons and squirrels and the occasional robin. Jimmy Whelan tells himself these things as he walks between the headstones. He finds it easiest to focus on mundanity. Other priests whisper prayers or touch their rosary beads but Father Whelan does not wish to draw God's eye to his actions. He has always been cautious. His prayers mention nobody by name. He does not profess to understand God's will but he understands His erratic approach to pain and mercy and does not trust himself to offer up any individual to God's surveillance. His prayers are opaque, unfathomable things: vague requests for forgiveness; for strength – food for the poor and peace for the troubled. He has not shared these secrets with his brother priests. The prayers he speaks aloud during Mass are different to those he says at his bedside. In church, his sermons are thoughtful studies, relevant to the congregation and the times. The God he speaks of to his congregation is just and loving; a benevolent father who asks only that His flock behave with love in their hearts and do Him honour with action, thought and deed. The God of Father Whelan's private moments is a different deity – a brutal patrician as liable to stop a baby's heart as regard a barren woman's prayers for a child.

As he walks between the headstones it occurs to Father Whelan that when he pictures his Lord, he does not see the pale-skinned, beatific figure of the Bible whose likeness adorns the walls and windows of the church. He sees a man in a black leather coat. Black, curly hair and stubble on his jaw. Wing-tipped shoes and slender fingers; gold necklace and chunky rings. He sees the men from the neighbourhood. He knows the image to be a sin and yet he cannot shake it. He personifies his God as a local crook, dispensing death and mercy with clear-eyed dispassion.

'You fucking roller-skate here, Father?' asks Paulie, through a cloud of cigarette smoke. 'I'm freezing my balls off.'

Father Whelan considers the man before him. Paulie Pugliesca is in his late thirties. He's a made man – a capo with one of the Five Families that run most of the organised crime on the eastern coast. He's a handsome, charismatic man. His pink and purple shirt is open to his breastbone and his collar protrudes over the black leather. The medal on his gold cross shows St Christopher.

Paulie grins at him and takes his hand. He kisses him on both cheeks. He smells of red wine and basil.

'Good to see you, Paulie,' says Father Whelan. He is a little younger than the man before him. He has heard the rumours about Paulie's capacity for violence. His son, young Sal, is said to have inherited it.

'You need all this cloak-and-dagger shit?' asks Paulie, putting his hands in his pockets. 'A priest hasn't got enough quiet places, huh? Needs to drag my sorry ass over here?'

Father Whelan looks around him. They are in the quiet, over-grown cemetery that stands in the grounds of the little Dutch church in this soft pocket of Syracuse. It is a peaceful place, far away from prying eyes. Father Whelan does not want to be seen talking to Paulie but nor does he wish to stray far from consecrated ground. Though he fears God, he yearns for His proximity.

'You gonna ask, Father? Your message said you had a proposi-tion for me. Ain't been propositioned by a priest since I was an altar boy and I don't think that sick old fuck ever did much prop-ositioning after that.' Paulie smiles at the memory. 'You enjoying St Colman's? Beautiful church. We give handsome, y'know that, right? Ain't cheap saving souls.'

Father Whelan says nothing for a moment. Listens to the trees and concentrates on breathing. It has taken him several weeks of careful thought and prayer to persuade himself that he is right to ask this man for help. He has exhausted the other avenues open to him. He is a man of much fight but insufficient influence. The same could not be said for Pugliesca.

'You spitting it out, Father?'

Eventually, Jimmy lets himself speak. He barely recognises his own voice as he does so.

'There's a place on Staten Island,' he says quietly. 'You know about it because you allowed your godson to be placed there. Tony. The boy you promised to care for.'

'I do right,' says Pugliesca, and he lounges back against the lichen-covered gravestone of a young Irishwoman who died two centuries before.

'It's a terrible place, Paulie. I've been inside. It's hell. The suffering those poor children endure.'

'It ain't no picnic.' Paulie shrugs. 'But hell, the kid didn't belong nowhere else. You saw him in the neighbourhood, Jimmy. Staring with those bug-eyes, gasping like a fish when he tried to talk; sitting on the sidewalk scratching at his privates like a fucking monkey. He needed a hospital and they say that place will fix him.'

'It isn't fixing him,' says Jimmy. 'Not at all. Not anyone. It's an ugly, horrible abomination of a place.'

'If it were all that bad it would be shut down,' says Paulie. He looks at his watch and seems disappointed that he has made this trip for such trivialities.

'Senator Kennedy wants it closed. The doctors want it closed. But the state won't close the doors. I've written letters. I've begged the bishops. The TV interviewed me and I've called every reporter who owes me a favour. No difference. It's still open.'

Paulie cocks his head. 'And what do you want me to do about it?' he asks.

Jimmy closes his eyes. He wants to pray but forces himself not to attract God's glance.

'I want you to take Tony home,' he says. 'Bring him into your family. Treat him with love. Care for him. Make his life a happy one.'

Paulie laughs and grinds out the cigarette on the headstone. 'You want me to bring that crazy fuck back into my house? Back to where my wife and daughters sleep?'

'Sal always cared for him,' says Father Whelan. 'I saw them together often enough. Tony used to follow him and Sal would help him fit in. I saw affection there.'

Paulie rubs his jaw. 'Sal's got a soft spot for dumb animals. He always bitches at me for letting him go into that place.'

'So you'll take him home?' asks Father Whelan.

Paulie shrugs. 'You want more. I know you want more.'

'That place can't be allowed to continue,' says Father Whelan. 'It has to be stopped. I don't know how to make that happen. But maybe you do.'

Paulie runs a long, thin finger across his lower lip. 'That'd be the Church's work, would it? That'd be me serving God? Because I tell you, Father, I need some currency with the man upstairs. The Church don't like me and mine one little bit. You hear we ain't allowed to bury our dead no more? Priests in the city won't say a Mass for the poor bastards who die for our thing.'

'Your thing, as you call it, is the Mafia.'

'Ain't no Mafia,' says Paulie. 'Just men trying to make a living.'

They both fall silent, considering one another. The wheels in Pugliesca's mind turn swifter than Father Whelan's.

'I'm a reader,' says Pugliesca suddenly. 'I like old books – the ones thick like a sandwich. Old stories. Heroes. Villains. Damsels in distress. They tell stories from a time I understand, when men did what they could to get by and God understood that.'

'God understands all,' says Father Whelan reflexively.

'But the things I do – they'll have me sent to hell,' says Pugliesca.

'God forgives all,' says Whelan.

'He do if you confess,' says Pugliesca. 'But you think I'm gonna walk into confession and tell Father Patrizio that I just spent the night fucking two Chinese whores in the back of a meat store? You think I'm going to tell him that I put my gun up the ass of a loan shark from Long Island and shot him in his guts and that me and my son went back to where we had him every second day to see how much closer to death he had drifted? You think I'm going to tell that old Italian fuck that I beat a man with golf clubs and raped his wife because they were skimming off the take? You think that?'

Father Whelan closes his eyes. He already understands.

'God forgives all,' he says quietly.

'And you're God, ain't that right? You're his consigliere. You say who gets in and who goes the other way. You can forgive me, that right, Father? For this and for anything else.'

'If you are truly sorry,' begins Whelan.

Paulie smiles. It's an attractive sight but there is an ugliness that lurks just underneath.

'There were men like you back home,' he says, lighting a new cigarette. 'Specialist priests who looked after the souls of the old Sicilians. Listened to their confessions and kept them pure.'

Whelan clings to what he believes. 'That place has to close. Tony deserves love. I'll help you. I'll assist in any way I can . . .'

'Forgiveness,' says Paulie. 'For now and always. For me. For my son. You keep our souls safe and I'll have that place closed. All those poor suffering bastards will get clean bedsheets and loving hugs wherever the fuck you want them putting. But you become my friend, Father. You listen to whatever I tell you and you get me through to heaven. You say the words at my men's funerals. You keep us good, yes? Keep us fucking holy.'

Father Whelan finds his breath catching in his chest. He knew today would cost him part of himself. He did not know it would be his soul.

'Bless me, Father,' says Pugliesca, and he drops to his knees before Whelan, who steps back in fright. His shoe crushes a small blue flower that pushes up through the cold, hard ground.

Whelan fights with himself for a moment, and then places his hand on the killer's head.

'I absolve thee,' he says, in a voice that shakes. 'Of all now, and future sin . . .'

10

'Show me the whiskies. Have they got Jura Superstition? It's big at the top and big at the bottom and if you make any comments or start to blush or say a single solitary word in response to that sentence, I will set fire to your legs . . .'

McAvoy drops his head in a gesture of defeat. He picks the silver laptop computer off the top of the wooden beer barrel and carries it back over to the bar. He shakes his head apologetically at the barmaid, who grins and gives a thumbs-up. Then he leans over the bar and slowly moves the laptop from left to right so that Trish Pharaoh can see which whiskies are on offer. After a moment, he withdraws and places her on the bar in front of him. He often feels foolish, but Pharaoh always manages to put him in situations where he feels that, intellectually, he is one rung up the evolutionary ladder from a grapefruit.

'Satisfied?' he asks.

'I like the Monkey Shoulder but I think I'd probably try a bourbon. When in Rome, and all that. Are you still on bloody hot chocolate or have you decided to treat yourself to a shandy? Honestly, you've spent all day walking from bar to bar and church to church and I doubt you've drunk enough to get a wasp pissed. That was some bloody hike back from St Brigit's. I got tired just tracking you on Google Maps. Let your hair down. Have a Baileys.'

McAvoy is grateful that there are only two other customers in this dark, low-ceilinged bar on Queen Street. Pharaoh has not made any attempt to change her personality in deference to the fact that she is, to all extents and purposes, a disembodied head being carried around in the arms of a blushing giant.

'I've got a Guinness,' says McAvoy, a touch petulantly. 'I'm joining in.'

On the screen, Pharaoh pulls a face. 'I can't handle Guinness,' she confides. 'Does things to my insides.'

'Really?' asks McAvoy, unsure whether he wants to know.

'Yes. Makes them become outsides. Not a pretty picture.'

McAvoy carries the notebook back to his table. He's sitting in the window, perched on a high stool. A giant barrel has been turned into a table and his barely touched Guinness is serving as a paperweight on his sheaf of notes. From here, he looks out through scaffolding and tarpaulin at a surprisingly quiet street. He expected something from the movies: steam rising from subway grates and nose-to-tail yellow cabs. Instead, the traffic is sporadic and pedestrians come by in ones and twos. Even this atmospheric Irish theme pub is unexpectedly deserted. He was in here earlier today, checking for any inconsistencies in Alto's time-line, but found none. He identified it as a bar worthy of further enjoyment; not least because it serves the kind of home-cooked Irish food that reminds him of Roisin. He has already devoured a huge bowl of stew and soda bread, though he is unsure whether the accompanying wedge of Oreo cheesecake originated in Donegal. Still, as Irish bars go, this one is more authentic than most. The walls are decorated with signed posters of Ireland's football, rugby and hurling stars and there is so much Guinness paraphernalia draped around the bottles, barrels and pumps that McAvoy isn't sure where Alyson, the brassy, gap-toothed and totally authentic Dublin barmaid, is going to put the Christmas lights when she finishes untangling them down at the end of the bar. Occasionally, the noise of her cursing can be heard over the sound of Van Morrison, and the accented swearwords make McAvoy feel almost as homesick as the stew did. He can imagine Roisin being similarly fulsome in her descriptions of the 'fecking twinkly bastard-shites'.

'She's got massive boobs,' says Pharaoh, as McAvoy puts the laptop down. 'Huge, I mean. Employed for her conversational skills, was she?'

'You know you're on loudspeaker, don't you? People can actually hear you. You're saying this stuff out loud.'

'What's she going to do? Fly over and slap me? I'm thousands of miles away.'

'But I'm not,' says McAvoy, a note of exasperation creeping into his voice.

'That fat bloke on the stool,' says Pharaoh, peering over McAvoy's shoulder. 'He looks like he's been carved out of ham.'

'If you're not quiet I'm going to shut the lid,' says McAvoy warningly.

Pharaoh grins. She's got a blanket around her shoulders and is wearing a pair of blue flannelette pyjamas that gape a little between the buttons. She's wearing a touch of eyeliner and lip-gloss and her long black hair is mussed up around the crown, as though she has been wriggling on her back. It's around 3 a.m. in England and she is sitting in the kitchen in her house in Scartho, Grimsby, drinking wine and smoking. She is leading a raid on the house of a suspected double murderer at daybreak and had every intention of getting a few decent hours before the fun started. She never made it to sleep – preferring to obsess over what McAvoy has been up to since she waved him goodbye at the airport. McAvoy would have been happy to talk to her on the telephone but her eldest daughter has recently shown her how to use Skype and she was anxious to see whether McAvoy looked okay. He likes that she worries about him, though in fairness the majority of things that cause him grief stem directly from her.

'You should be grateful I care,' says Pharaoh through a cloud of smoke. 'Some people would feel a little hurt not to have been asked to tag along on some jolly to America.'

McAvoy's mouth drops open. 'I asked you!' he says.

'But you didn't sound like you meant it,' says Pharaoh, pouting. 'Besides, some of us have a job to do. Some of us don't have understanding superiors who can cover for them while they're gallivanting on the far side of the world.'

'I do appreciate it,' says McAvoy. 'You know I do.'

'Stop looking like a kicked puppy, Hector. If I was with you in

New York, Roisin would burn my house down. We both know this.'

McAvoy nods. 'She's grateful for your help, honest. You've got me here – got me help . . .'

'You can make it up to me when you get back. A shoulder rub, a box of Maltesers and you have to punch Shaz Archer in the solar plexus.'

McAvoy grins, enjoying the fire that comes into Pharaoh's eyes when she mentions the stunningly attractive but morally bankrupt head of the Drugs Squad. 'Done.'

Pharaoh takes another swig of red wine and looks down at her notes. She leans forward and McAvoy picks up one of the ear-buds from the table and inserts it. Before she got the volume levels right, Pharaoh's voice had been loud enough to risk tinnitus, but he fancies that when she is talking about confidential police files, she will be less inclined to shout.

'I've got what you wanted, anyhow,' says Pharaoh. 'A very nice sergeant in the Guards was happy to cooperate. He said nobody from the States had requested the information and wanted to know whether anybody in New York actually knew their arses from their elbows. I didn't offer an answer, though I did point out that it should be "asses". What do you think? Is this Alto character lazy or crap?'

McAvoy takes a swig of Guinness. Remembers what it cost and lets half of his gulp flow back into the glass.

'I didn't get the impression he was either,' he muses. 'Remember, I only know that Valentine was here because of my connections to the family. Estrada mentioned him purely in passing. It was dumb luck. What we've got to remember is that if two people were found in a ditch with bullet wounds back home, that would be kind of a big deal. Over here, it's just a Thursday. We'd have eighty officers on it. Here, they've got Alto.'

Pharaoh purses her lips, thinking it over. She seems prepared to give Alto the benefit of the doubt.

'Well, he'll be delighted with what you've got gift-wrapped for him,' says Pharaoh, smiling. 'I tell you something, Hector, you've married into a lovely family.'

McAvoy tries not to let himself look upset. He refuses to be ashamed of Roisin's clan. He knows the majority of them to be good people, if a little rough around the edges. Valentine is the blackest sheep, and were it not for his bond of blood to Roisin, McAvoy doubts he would be trying so hard to say something vaguely laudable about the lad.

'Her parents are kind,' says McAvoy defensively. 'Sisters too. They're wary of me but they're not unwelcoming. They just don't know what to make of me.'

'Who does?' asks Pharaoh, finishing her wine. 'Anyway, Valentine is a bad sort, there's no doubting that.'

'What have you got?'

'More than Alto. Valentine's got convictions for assault, burglary, handling stolen goods, benefit fraud and being involved in illegal bookkeeping. Longest sentence was for the burglary – fourteen months. He served five. Not a desirable lad. You can see why the authorities were a bit twitchy about giving him a visa.'

'That's where the bishop stepped in.'

'Indeed. His letter was about as close to being a ringing endorsement as it's possible to get.'

'You've seen it?'

'I have friends in low places. It was a nice letter. Explained that Valentine had a chance to turn his life around helping disadvantaged Catholic youngsters learn how to box. Said that one of his most esteemed priests – a former New Yorker, no less – had known Valentine all his life and personally vouched for his intentions.'

'That's unusual,' says McAvoy, taking another swallow of his drink. 'Isn't it?'

'I don't know.' Pharaoh shrugs. 'Maybe bishops vouch for Gypsy criminals all the time. But it struck me as odd. Know what else struck me as odd? The letter to the authorities doesn't mention Brishen or Shay.'

'But Valentine told his parents they were going as a trio,' says McAvoy.

'I know. But do we have any other sources to back that up?'

McAvoy considers it. He has been assuming that Valentine had been telling the truth. But what if he came to America for entirely different reasons to those he confided to his family? Perhaps the boxing was merely a cover story? But then why would he show up at Dezzie Estrada's gym? Suddenly, the phone call made by Brishen to the gym takes on a more sinister tone. Was he checking up to see if he and his protégé were in danger from the young Teague?

'Don't get ahead of yourself,' warns Pharaoh. 'The Guard in Galway reckons the NBCI—'

'NBCI? Remind me.'

'National Bureau of Criminal Investigation. They're basically us, but in Ireland. Ask me to say it in Gaelic, I dare you. Anyways, he says they're getting more interested in this situation by the day and they were good enough to do a little trawl of Valentine's internet history. Can you look stuff up on the web while still talking to me on this thing?'

McAvoy gives a tiny laugh and minimises the image of Pharaoh. He pulls up a search engine and hears Pharaoh's voice telling him what to look for. In moments, he is reading the sixth page in a lengthy thread of arguments underneath a video of a bare-knuckle boxing match.

'Remember when YouTube was used for pictures of dogs slipping over on shiny floors?' asks Pharaoh. 'World's moved on a bit.'

McAvoy watches the first few moments of the bout. It shows a huge, bear-like man, stripped to the waist but covered in so much body hair that it is initially hard to tell. His face is little more than eyes and nose peeping out through a wall of black fur. In the video, he is relentlessly pummelling a tall black man, who is struggling to stay on his feet. Both men have taped hands and they are surrounded by a jostling crowd of onlookers who roar encouragement. It is a barbaric encounter and McAvoy knows that if he continues to watch, he will see the black man get truly hurt.

'Read the comments,' says Pharaoh. 'Starts with TravellerVal81.'

McAvoy does as he is told. In the first posting, the contributor labels the big bearded man a pussy and says that he wouldn't last five minutes with the fighters of true Gypsy stock. The comment gains attention in moments and soon contributors the world over are pitching in on whether or not the Irish bare-knuckle fighters are the best in the world or overrated. The debate becomes fierce. TravellerVal81 names men he reckons could knock the hairy boxer on his arse. He counts himself among their number. The argument continues over three pages. Then a contributor called Boxguy12 appears. Their post is simple: I CAN MAKE THIS HAPPEN. MSG ME DIRECT.

After that, there are no more postings from either man and the discussion fizzles out.

'The massive bloke in the video is known as Byki, which is a Mob term for "bull" or "bodyguard" or "massive beardy bastard who eats live rabbits",' says Pharaoh, reading the name from her notes. 'He's a bare-knuckle fighter, in case you didn't realise it. The NBCI has run his details. American-born but his parents were Chechen. Lives in New York. This video is one of about a hundred in circulation, all showing him pummelling local hard cases. Turns out he used to box professionally but lost his licence when he took part in an MMA bout and gouged somebody's eye out. Lovely chap. Linked to a suspected heroin importer by the name of Sergey Volotov but he's not served any time. Volotov has, but not in the States. He's done proper hard time – the kind of prisons where rape is pretty much timetabled.'

McAvoy closes the search engine and enlarges the image of Pharaoh. Her eyes are particularly blue tonight and there is a tiny curl of red wine at the corner of each lip, so it looks as though she is smiling. She's not.

'Who is Boxguy12?' asks McAvoy.

'Traced to an email account of a similar name, set up on a computer that was using the Wi-Fi connection of a café on Church Street.'

'I don't think I'm far from there,' says McAvoy. 'I could go . . .'

'No need. I had NBCI run the other name you gave me, just because I'm, y'know, good at this shit. There's a reason your new friend Marcel from the gym didn't give Alto his real name. Only took a couple of phone calls to the States to learn he was fined a thousand dollars three years ago for his involvement in an underground fight club in Wilmington, Delaware. Violations of the "combative fighting" laws.'

McAvoy rubs his forehead. 'Valentine said he came here to fight . . .'

'The question is whether or not Brishen knew,' says Pharaoh. 'Whether he was involved. You think he was?'

McAvoy shakes his head. 'From what I know of him he wants boxing to get away from that image. He's cut boxers loose for fighting in underground bouts. I can't see Dezzie risking his reputation for the underground scene. But if Marcel was sourcing fighters . . .'

On the screen, Pharaoh nods. 'I'll do a bit more digging. See what we can find out about Brishen and whether he's as squeaky-clean as you reckon. I'd love to chat to the priest too, but NBCI are urging me to be a little tactful on that one.'

McAvoy cocks his head, knowing that Pharaoh will already have come up with a way to respect the NBCI's wishes and still get what she wants.

'I've contacted his office in Galway,' she says, suddenly looking prim and deferential. 'Told his secretary I'm an English policewoman with questions to ask him about a boy in America. I don't think it will be long before he calls back.'

'That was tactful?' asks McAvoy. 'You might be best just going straight to Father Whelan. Jimmy. He's the real connection here. And from what I've heard of him, he's a good man.'

Pharaoh shrugs. She is not a fan of religious organisations and thinks of the priesthood as a loose collection of weirdoes, oddballs and degenerates.

'This nun of yours,' says Pharaoh, musing. 'She said Brishen wanted a blessing for a boxing match. What do you make of that?'

'I think we're making big jumps,' says McAvoy. 'Remember, I'm here to find Valentine, not run a whole murder investigation with one laptop and a phone.'

Pharaoh laughs, though it is not a particularly happy sound. 'If you find something you'll run with it, whatever happens.'

McAvoy says nothing. His mind is speeding up. He finds himself making connections and drawing lines in his imagination. He wants to talk to Alto, to share this information with him and ask him for names and places. If Valentine came here to fight the colossal man in the video, the reason he has not been in touch with his family may be because he has been beaten to death. And if Brishen and Shay were witnesses, they could have been put in the ground to stop them talking.

'Father Whelan,' says Pharaoh, chewing her lip in the way that makes McAvoy want to slap her on the nose like a cat who won't stop grooming itself. 'I asked NBCI if he was a character worthy of further investigation and they gave me pretty short shrift.'

'All he did was ask his bishop to write a letter,' says McAvoy placatingly.

'And Brishen and Shay visited the church where he started out,' says Pharaoh.

'If they know Father Whelan, that's a normal thing to do,' says McAvoy. 'Say a prayer, light a candle . . .'

Pharaoh waves a hand, as if this religious stuff could be filed under the word 'bollocks'. 'RTE News has been running the story on every bulletin,' says Pharaoh. 'I've seen some of the footage. Lots of shots of Brishen at his gym, and interviews with a load of people saying how terrible it is what's happened. They had Barry McGuigan on the evening bulletin, saying what a loss this was to Irish boxing. I think the Guards will have to send somebody out before too long, if only to show they're involved.'

McAvoy feels like shuddering at the thought of again being involved in a case that garners so much attention. He finds himself marvelling at the contrast between the furore in Ireland and the inactivity of Alto over here.

'You were telling me about Whelan . . .'

'He was on the same bulletin,' says Pharaoh, curling her lip. 'Saying what a good man Brishen is and how he hopes to travel over to be at his bedside. Urged his flock to say their prayers.'

McAvoy waits for more. When nothing comes, he opens his hands.

'I asked the sergeant in the Guards about Whelan and he talked about him like he was the second coming, or something. I find that disconcerting.'

'You're biased,' says McAvoy, without taking the time to find a more tactful way to say it.

'Probably,' concedes Pharaoh. She pauses, as if ordering her thoughts. 'I've no doubt there are great priests who make a real difference to their communities and help people live good lives. I get all that. I also know that they spent so long being pretty much infallible they got very good at doing evil deeds. I'm not saying your Father Whelan is anything other than a great guy. But he found a way to allow Valentine Teague to go to America and I don't know why he did that and I would like to know more. I'd like that a lot.'

McAvoy smiles. He wishes she were here, sitting opposite him, waving her hands as she talks and spilling her drinks on his notes; making him blush with crude innuendo and telling him he's a bloody idiot and a good cop. More than that, he wishes she were in Galway, close enough to Roisin to keep her safe.

'One more thing,' says Pharaoh, looking through the last page of her notes. 'Mr Molony. The bloke the nun told you about. That's the only gap in Alto's timeline. Some time between leaving St Colman's and turning up at the next bar, there are about three hours unaccounted for. Now, Alto has clearly presumed they were drinking and just didn't keep the receipts from that particular bar. We only know they were at St Colman's because Brishen had one of their leaflets in his pocket when he was found. Now, after you met your lovely nun, you went to St Brigit's and asked around and nobody remembered them. That suggests they weren't there. That might not mean anything in the slightest but it makes Molony somebody worth talking to, and Alto doesn't have a statement from him, which means he's on your agenda. And you might want to know a little bit about him before you track him down.'

'And you have something that helps?' asks McAvoy hopefully.

'Momma loves you,' says Pharaoh, grinning. 'I did a little digging. Or at least, Ben did.'

'Ben?' asks McAvoy, startled. 'Does he know . . . ?'

'About your connection or whereabouts? No, of course not. He does as he's told and doesn't ask questions, unlike some great lumbering sergeants of my acquaintance.'

McAvoy relaxes a little. DC Ben Neilsen is a good cop, with a silver tongue and an uncanny ability with databases and technology.

'He's found mentions of Molony online. Going back years. Newspaper articles all about charity work and the history of the church and the different appeals he's involved in. Even ran a charity back in the late eighties that collected money for political causes in Ireland.' Pharaoh pauses. Shrugs. 'I'm not going to jump to conclusions there but I am going to underline his name in big red letters on the whiteboard in my head.'

McAvoy waits. Starts making connections of his own. His head suddenly feels too full. He just wants to find Valentine and get home and already he feels as though he knows too much, and nowhere near enough.

'I'm going to send you some articles,' says Pharaoh. 'Ben's got electronic copies of some of the more important clippings. I don't know how much of it is relevant but I know you like things to be as complicated as fucking possible, so I'm obliging. I'm also getting seriously drowsy, so if there's nothing else, I'm going to go and fall asleep on the sofa for the next three hours and have a good hard think about Gérard Depardieu.'

McAvoy pulls a face. 'Seriously?'

'I like big, peculiar men,' says Pharaoh with a smile. Her face softens, transforming her into the motherly, tactile woman who matters so much to him. 'Be careful. They have guns.'

'I don't want to be here,' he says, and the confession feels like release. 'I'm so out of my depth, Trish.'

'She'll be proud of you no matter what happens,' says Pharaoh, and it looks a struggle for her to keep the scowl off her face. 'She'll never forget that you went. You tried. You jumped on a plane and went to do something when nobody else did. You're a good man, Hector. Now, stop flirting with nuns, and go show Alto how to be a cop.'

McAvoy is about to reply when he sees her blow him a kiss and cut the connection. He sits and stares at the blank screen, suddenly full of his own reflection. His phone and laptop light up simultaneously as the emails start pinging through. He pulls out his phone, wondering if he should send Roisin another trio of kisses. He sees that among the emails from Trish, he has a text from Alto. It contains an address, and four words: **I need your help**.

McAvoy looks at his watch. It's a little after 10 p.m. He has spent the day retracing Brishen's footsteps and growing steadily more frustrated. A couple of hours back he gave in to his growling stomach and ordered a large pizza in a sports bar off Times Square. The dish that arrived was the size of his patio furniture at home but he still managed a brownie and Oreo milkshake and straw fries. So far, he fancies that polishing off the meal has been his biggest achievement to date.

He drains his drink, waves at the bar staff, and heads out into the cold and the dark of Queen Street. He has a cab inside two minutes, and texts Alto to tell him he will be there soon. Eyes on his phone, he does not see the Lexus that pulls away from the kerb and begins to tail him; two men in the front, and a girl with purple hair in the rear.

She no longer looks so much like a student. There is a gun in her left hand, and a picture of Aector McAvoy in her right. Her eyes are focused on the rear of the cab.

She in turn does not see the short, bald man in the nondescript Proton as he pulls out of his own parking space and begins to follow both vehicles.

She will not see him until the bullets start to fly.

II

Alto knows he should not have had the extra drink last night. He has spent these past months on the strictest of regimes but in the easy company of the Scottish detective, he allowed himself the extra measure. That drink led to another on his way back to Pitt Street. By 3 a.m. he was in the all-night liquor store and by breakfast time he had drunk three-quarters of a bottle of Wild Turkey. He slept it off on a cot bed in one of the empty rooms on the top floor of the station. He woke with a headache so powerful it seemed to spill out of his skull and leave agony in the air. He dry-heaved his way through an energy shake and a fruit salad, popping ibuprofen as if he were eating peanuts. By mid-afternoon, his headache had subsided sufficiently for him to begin considering a beer. He started on the Heineken just before his evening meal of leftover Chinese food and as he sits in his car in the parking lot at the rear of Norfolk Street, his belches taste of bourbon and Szechuan sauce. He is barely recognisable as the elegant, well-presented man who greeted McAvoy just last evening. His amber-tinted glasses are perched on his head and the front of his checked shirt is open almost to his navel. The T-shirt beneath is dirty with spilled food and drops of whiskey. There is mud on the knees of his dark jeans and the knuckles of two fingers on his right hand are swollen. When the drink eases off, he knows he faces a lot of pain.

On the passenger seat, Alto's cell phone lights up. His first thought is that it will be his ex-wife. He left her enough messages last night. They started with apology and progressed through maudlin expressions of self-loathing to angry, bitter stabs of recrimination. He doubts she will reply, or even if he still has the correct number for her. He only told her how much he hated himself because it would have been too pitiful to leave such a diatribe on his own voicemail service. He knows last night's drinking was an act of self-abuse. He can already feel the tentacles of depression start to drag him down. He wants to lose himself in food and alcohol, cigarettes and women. He knows, too, that he will not stop feeling this way until the man who haunts his thoughts is behind bars or in the ground.

'Alto,' he says, answering the call without looking at the name or number on the screen.

'This is Aector McAvoy,' comes the voice. 'You texted me. I texted you to say I'm on my way but I didn't hear back. Is everything okay? How can I help?'

Alto holds the phone away from his ear. The big man's accent is a pleasing sound: lyrical and poetic. He remembers sending the message, typing it out with one quavering thumb while swigging from the bottle of Wild Turkey. He thinks he may have fallen asleep since then. He checks the display and sees how many calls and texts he has missed. It's coming up on midnight. He's been here for more than two hours. The last thing he remembers is making a decision that he knows he will feel guilty about for a very long time. He needs to use the Scotsman. Needs to play the poor sap like a fiddle.

'Hello? Detective Alto?' comes the voice.

Alto coughs, wincing at the foul taste in his throat. He shakes his face. Rubs his hands through his hair and finds his glasses, which he pulls on. The headache is pulsing at his temples. His stomach feels acidic and he has an overwhelming desire to start growling in a low, whimpering expression of displeasure.

'Sergeant,' he says, looking at the bottle on the seat and hating himself. 'I'm sorry it took so long to get back in touch. How are you finding New York?'

'Fine, fine,' says McAvoy, and Alto can tell from the whistling through the phone that the big man is outside. 'I came to the address you gave me. What's the situation? We've got a lot to talk about.'

Alto coughs again and his mouth fills with bile. He half chokes on it before opening the car door and spitting onto the hard snow of the parking lot. He tries to get a hold of himself. Memories are coming back to him. He was following Murray Ellison again. He watched the slimy prick move from one bar to the next, surrounded by cronies dressed in the same uniform of blue suit, expensive shirt, silk tie and cashmere coat. In each bar, Alto drank. What started as surveillance became something more. With each drink, the hatred he felt for Ellison became more potent. By the time Ellison made it to the Toytown Speakeasy, he was with just two of his associates and had drunk nothing stronger than sparkling water. Alto, on the other hand, was drunk almost insensible. When he tried to follow Ellison into the club, bouncers blocked his path. He told them he was a cop trying to save a life and they laughed at him. He swung a punch and took one for his troubles. Somebody stepped on his hand. He dragged himself back to his car. Found his phone and tried to concentrate on what the hell he was here for and who he could ask for help. Everybody from the Seventh would do time for Alto but he could not in good conscience ask anybody close to him to risk their careers.

The image of the big Scotsman filled his head.

Alto sent him a message, asking for his help.

As he wipes his mouth, Alto feels a moment's disquiet at bringing the visiting detective into his personal vendetta but he quickly tells himself that the end will justify the means and that if McAvoy knew the truth, he would volunteer his services. Alto is simply sparing him the burden of that conversation.

'Detective,' he says, trying to sound as sober as he can. 'You're here? Nearby? What can you see?'

'Apartments. Offices. A little alley with a sign for a toy company. Where are you?'

'Surveillance vehicle, not far away,' says Alto, eyes closed. 'This is a big operation so I'm doing you a major favour letting you near the scene. When the arrests go down, things may get messy. We have officers inside but if they move early, they'll blow their cover.'

'What's happening?' asks McAvoy, sounding nervous. 'Is this to do with Brishen?'

'Look, I can't say much,' whispers Alto, improvising quickly. 'There's a man inside. Good-looking. Expensive clothes. Answers to the name of Murray Ellison. He's one of ours. But the girl he's with is a civilian and we want her out of there. We can't risk warning her so it's up to you.'

'Me? I've got no authority . . .'

'We're all cops, Sergeant,' says Alto, feeling bad but knowing he has little choice if he is to ensure that Ellison does not leave the club with another girl. 'You simply have to go inside and double-check that he's in there. If there's a girl with him, we need to get her away from him. There's an agreed code. You simply approach the table where they're sitting and you explain that the police know all about him and that she should get herself away from him before he slips something in her drink. I'd do it myself but my face is known . . .'

There is silence from the other end of the phone. Then McAvoy's voice comes back on, stern and strong. 'Detective Alto, I might be new in town but I'm not a complete fool. Whether it's a joke or an initiation or simply something to pass the time, I want you to know that it's not appreciated. I'm tired and I have information to share with you and when I've shown it to you, I want you to share with me. Now, tell me your location or I'm going back to my hotel.'

Alto starts to protest then runs out of steam. 'He's a date rapist,' he says, his voice wheedling. 'This is what I do. I follow him. I warn people not to go near him. I try to stop them becoming the next victim. But the bouncers won't let me in and I'm in no state to be believed. I know he's got himself a target in there. You just need to warn them. Tell them who he is. What he does.' Alto hears how feeble he sounds and tries to regain control. 'Look, Sergeant, if you don't help me you can forget having any more help. You'll go home to your wife without getting another word from me and your brother-in-law's case will go to the very bottom of the missing persons list – if anybody ever gets around to filing a complaint. You do this, or you may as well go home now.'

For a moment, there is only the sound of whistling and the wind. Then Alto jumps in his seat as the passenger door opens and the big, open face of the Scottish detective peers down at him; face half in shadow and half in light.

'Lie to me again and we'll fall out,' says McAvoy softly. 'Now, tell me who this bastard is and how we stop him.'

The man to McAvoy's left is dressed in a way that he presumed had gone out of fashion around the time of the Cuban Missile Crisis. He is a vision in beret, round spectacles and fawn trenchcoat. He's not smoking a Gauloise but he looks as though he would dearly love to be. He's sipping from a china cup that sits on a floral saucer and the small, lank-haired woman he is talking to seems to be urging her internal organs to start shutting down out of sheer boredom.

On the street, the man would appear remarkable, but inside the bar he does not provoke comment. McAvoy would hate to label somebody with the word 'hipster' or 'beatnik' but his vocabulary is offering him no alternatives. This is a club for the ultra-cool; the painfully sophisticated. The Toytown has been styled as a 1920s speakeasy – the kind of place where Lucky Luciano and Meyer Lansky would sip bootleg whiskey in the company of goodtime girls while discussing who would live and who would die. It is styled true to the period, with crushed velvet chaises-longues, opulent candlesticks and chandeliers; wooden floors and soft red lights. The cocktails are served in cups and saucers and there is even a proper old-school telephone booth next to the toilets and a cigarette machine on the wall. McAvoy was tempted to take photographs to show Roisin but the light is too low and he fancies that the image would come out looking like a whore's boudoir. Instead, he tries to take a mental picture of the rest of the clientele. The majority are under thirty and McAvoy could make a fair guess at the social status of the women who sprawl around the circular table or lounge in sumptuous armchairs. These are people for whom money is not a problem. They are the sort of people who could use the word 'zeitgeist' without irony and who think they're performing an act of benevolent largesse when they give away last year's designer dresses to thrift shops. It is an almost exclusively white crowd and while McAvoy is no more familiar with their accents than any visitor to American shores, there is something about them that makes his brain fill with words like 'Ivy League' and 'Weekend in the Hamptons'. He does not feel comfortable here. Feels even less so since he spotted Murray Ellison.

McAvoy is not letting himself think too hard about the implications of what he is about to do. He can imagine all too clearly how his actions would sound if repeated . . .

Yes, sir, I was called to the scene by a detective I have only met once before who asked me to go and warn a girl I had never met before that if she stayed with Mr Ellison, her life might be in danger. No, sir, I have never met the man before.

Ellison perfectly fits the description offered by Alto. He is sitting on a wooden stool, one leg angled across the other to form a number '4'. His shoes look more expensive than McAvoy's house. He is sipping from a cup and listening, head cocked, to a blonde girl who kneels at his feet. She is rolling thin cigarettes on the varnished wood and her movements suggest she has had too much to drink. Whoever Ellison arrived with, he seems to be without any other company now. The girl's own cup and saucer is a little off to one side. McAvoy wonders whether Ellison has spiked it yet and realises he is in no position to ask. He knows nothing about this man. All he has is the word of a New York detective whose speech is slurred with alcohol. Were he to articulate his thought processes, McAvoy would say that he is doing this because, above all things, he needs Alto on his side. Whether or not Ellison is guilty of the crimes Alto accuses him of is not for McAvoy to say. If he is, McAvoy intends to prevent it happening again. If he is innocent, the worst that happens is that Ellison will find his chances of seducing this girl sorely impeded.

'Another?' asks the barman. He's wearing a flat cap, braces, a stripy shirt and has an apron around his waist.

'Ginger ale,' says McAvoy, reaching into his pocket and depositing his last ten-dollar bill on the bar.

'Meeting someone?' asks the barman, pouring his drink and doing complicated things with a stirrer and straw.

'Not sure,' says McAvoy, ad-libbing. 'I've got bad eyes. That chap over there, with the blonde . . . I think he's a friend of a friend but I don't want to make a fool of myself. Do you know him?'

The barman looks over McAvoy's shoulder at the mezzanine area. He shakes his head. 'Not somebody I've seen before. Not much of a drinker. He's on sparkling water. Got a White Russian for his lady friend there, though she'd already had a few before her friends left.'

McAvoy nods, accepting his drink and the pittance in change. He gives a little sigh of resignation then turns from the bar and crosses through the throng of drinkers and up the stairs to the main lounge. He looks up at the artwork that comes into focus as he approaches Ellison. Finds himself surveyed by the soft-focus eyes of voluptuous nymphs in voluminous satin, staring out from behind dusty glass and gaudy golden frames. The walls are coated in textured purple wallpaper, embossed with flowers and swirls. For a moment, McAvoy truly feels as though he is approaching a Luciano or a Lansky figure and feels himself start to sweat, as though he is about to pull a gun. Instead, it is his phone he retrieves from his pocket.

Murray Ellison looks up as McAvoy looms above him. The girl raises her head from the job of rolling cigarettes as his shadow falls across her. Up close, he reckons she is probably no more than twenty-one. He peers at her eyes. They are glassy.

'You're Murray Ellison,' says McAvoy chattily. 'I've read all about you. In the papers, wasn't it?'

The man looks untroubled by the sudden interruption. He could not look more languorous if he were wearing a towel and a soap-on-a-rope.

'You are. You were in the papers. You got away with raping that girl. The one who died.'

McAvoy starts to colour as he says it. Forces himself not to. The girl is looking up at him, confused.

'You're brave,' says McAvoy, turning his attention to her. 'Last girl who went home with this guy ended up dead. He had to spend a lot of money to get away with it. You've got some serious courage.'

Ellison smiles, showing Hollywood teeth. 'Friend of Alto's, are you? That man's going to get himself in trouble.'

'Alto? Not sure I know the name. I just know that you're not taking this girl home tonight. That's final. So enjoy the rest of your water. Have a sip of your lady friend's tipple if you reckon you can stay awake afterwards. Then get yourself on home.'

Ellison does not look at the girl. He keeps his eyes fixed on McAvoy's. McAvoy does not want to look away first but he senses movement and has no choice. He realises that the noise of the bar has dropped to a hush. People are looking at him. Instantly, he feels himself shrink. He cannot stand the thought of being an object of such scrutiny, but he also knows that this is his chance.

'Do you know Murray?' he asks, raising his voice and addressing the room without turning away from the grinning man. He knows he is terrible at things like this but also knows what Pharaoh would do if she were here and finds himself channelling her for the crowd. 'Keep a beermat over your teacups, ladies. Take a good look at his face. Got away with rape and murder, did this one. I don't think I like that kind of luck. I reckon that nice, liberal, law-abiding people like yourselves probably don't want to drink with a man like this. So when I'm gone, I'd love it if you helped him feel unwelcome.'

McAvoy finally takes his eyes off Ellison and addresses the young girl, whose eyes are starting to look like they belong to a doll. 'Can I take you home?' he asks her.

'Who do you think you are?' asks Ellison. 'I'll find out your name and finish you, whoever the hell you are. Alto's a psychopath. He's got a vendetta against me. This is harassment and I swear, it will cost you both.'

McAvoy ignores him and has to fight not to breathe a sigh of relief as the girl gathers her things and starts to stand. She seems unsteady on her feet and McAvoy has to stop her stumbling as she reaches out for him. He feels her wrap an arm around him and the act feels like that of a child. She weighs next to nothing. She smells of sweet liquor and cigarettes; perfume and expensive shampoo. He holds her as gently as he can and then moves them both away from the table. He keeps his eyes on Ellison until they are at the stairs and then turns, manoeuvring himself and the girl towards the door. The other drinkers part as he moves through them. At the door, the two bouncers step aside without a word.

'Christ,' says McAvoy, breathing out as the cold air hits him. In his arms, the girl shivers. He turns her to him and gently raises her face with one hand while cradling her, child-like, in the other. Her eyes are heavy and her mouth seems slack. McAvoy no longer has any doubt that she has been drugged. He picks her up like a child and hurries down the wrought-iron steps into the alley. It's a drab, grey space and the images of Golden Age Hollywood stars that have been daubed onto the concrete walls do nothing to make it seem like anything other than the back entrance to a Soviet Gulag. McAvoy walks quickly down the passageway and then up the stairs, emerging onto the street with the girl still in his arms. Alto's Proton is waiting by the kerb. Alto has the window down and his eyes look more alert. He sticks his head out as McAvoy approaches.

'Shit, had he spiked her? Had the bastard already done it . . . ?'

'Can you drive?' asks McAvoy, approaching the car. 'I know you've had a few to drink but she needs a hospital. Call for a patrol car or an ambulance if you think that's better. I don't know what's right and wrong right now. But she needs help and—'

The words are cut off as Ellison appears from the alleyway and strikes him across the back of the head with a china cup. McAvoy's first thought is for the girl in his arms and he does not allow himself to turn and face his attacker for fear of hurting her. Three more blows strike the back of his head and he hears Ellison swearing and cursing him over the sudden ringing in his ears.

Everything seems to slow down. To McAvoy's left there is a sudden movement. McAvoy looks up and sees Alto's face appearing over the top of the vehicle like a rising sun. He sees him extend his arm, black gun in his fist.

'No. Alto, no!'

McAvoy swings the unconscious girl over his shoulder like a sack of coal and twists where he stands; placing himself in Alto's line of fire. Ellison starts to swing a punch at McAvoy's face.

McAvoy has his right hand free. Though Ellison is tall and fit, McAvoy's fist is the size of a skull. Were he to punch this murderer and rapist, Ellison might not get back up again. So the blow that McAvoy connects with is open-handed. The sound of the slap echoes off the tall buildings. So too does the strange, guttural bellow that Ellison emits as his feet give way and he starts sliding into unconsciousness from the knees up.

'Christ!' roars Alto. 'Christ, I could have shot you!'

McAvoy slides the girl back into a more comfortable position and checks her face. Her eyes are closed and when he opens them with a gentle thumb and finger, she does not seem to see him.

'Take her,' says McAvoy, in a voice that brooks no argument. He hands the girl to Alto and bends down to where Ellison lies limp on the snow. McAvoy checks his pulse. He's breathing. There is a red palm print on his left cheek that makes him look as though he has pressed his face against hot stone.

'Do what you must,' says McAvoy, checking Ellison's pockets. With grim satisfaction, he retrieves a small packet of white pills.

'He holding?' asks Alto, opening the back of his car and sliding the girl onto the back seat.

'Very much so. This might get a little chaotic. I think I should go.'

McAvoy stands and looks at Alto, who looks back at him as if seeing him for the first time.

'We need to talk properly,' says McAvoy. 'Valentine. This matters, Alto. We need to do things properly.'

Alto nods, and his glasses slip down his nose. As he struggles to right them, McAvoy turns and begins to walk away, back in the direction of Ludlow.

McAvoy makes sure he is out of sight before he presses himself against the brick wall of a high-rise and lets his breath come out in one long, low stream. His heart is thudding and he feels an urge to throw up. Stars are dancing in his vision. He closes his eyes and waits for it to subside, barely registering the soft whisper of tyres on the wet road.

When he opens his eyes, there is a black Lexus idling in the road. He wonders if he is about to be asked directions and tries to remember whether he has a map in his bag. Then he remembers that the bag is in Alto's car . . .

'Get in,' comes a female voice, and McAvoy squints, trying to focus. The back window of the car is open and a girl is grinning at him. She seems familiar, like a picture of somebody he once met.

'I'm sorry . . .'

This time, she pushes the gun all the way out of the window and the streetlights bounce off the shiny black metal of the barrel.

'I said, "get in".'

McAvoy is too dumbfounded to speak. He is torn between asking whether this is serious, and the urge to run. Instead, he does nothing. Just looks at the gun, and the girl; barely registering the large man who smells of garlic and pickle who gets out of the passenger side of the car and takes him by the forearm.

Within moments, he is inside the car and the girl has her gun beneath his chin.

'Put this on,' she says, and hands him a bag for a bowling ball.

'I think you've made a mistake,' begins McAvoy, finding his voice.

The girl hits him in the windpipe with the handle of the gun. For an instant he cannot breathe. He feels as though his eyes will pop. Feels as though he is drowning.

The next time she tells him to put his head in the bag, he acquiesces without a word.

Only when McAvoy's eyes are obscured, his mouth and nose full of the smell of leather and sweat, does the girl sit back in her own seat. She pulls out a cell phone and sends a simple message: **We have him. Get ready.**

As she watches the lights of New York flash by her window, she allows herself a blush of pride. This man is strong. He slapped that other man to the ground like a child. She did well to take him so simply. It will score her points and further cement her growing reputation. She is becoming important. Trustworthy. A good soldier.

She considers her prize. He is big and strong and scarred and handsome, in a broken sort of way.

It is a shame, she thinks. *He will not look so fearsome come the morning.*

12

There is a pleasing sterility to the room in which the Penitent now stands. It is a space of white sheets and straight lines – the air marbled with antiseptic and fresh paint. Were it not for the milky foulness of his own suppurating skin, he would be pleased to stand here and take deep cleansing breaths. Such pleasure is denied him. He is never free of his own odour. It has grown stronger these past days. He reminds himself of out-of-date food. He is cloaked in an intrusive, cloying stench that serves, as God wills it, to remind him of his own advancing mortality.

The smell has grown worse since his talisman was taken. For a long time, the Penitent believed his sin was in keeping the idol; a pagan, superstitious act that cheapened him in the eyes of his God. Now he believes that the true sin was in allowing it to be taken. He was right to venerate the token. It was a thing of purity; a relic to be cherished. And he gave it away as if it were a trinket.

The Penitent allows himself a moment's contemplation. He would like to open the curtains and consider the city beyond the glass but to do so would be to risk seeing his own reflection and such vanity is not permitted. Instead, he puts his plump, pink hands upon the crisp white sheets and adjusts his posture so that, for a blessed moment, his shirt no longer sticks to the bloodied ruin of his back. He genuflects as he does so, thanking the Lord for allowing him this one small act of mercy.

He prays; lips moving soundlessly, words tumbling over one another in his head.

'Behold me at Thy feet, O Jesus of Nazareth, behold the most wretched of creatures, who comes into Thy presence humbled and penitent! Have mercy on me, O Lord, according to Thy great mercy! I have sinned and my sins are always before Thee. Yet my soul belongs to Thee, for Thou hast created it, and redeemed it with Thy Precious Blood.'

It is a favourite prayer, taught to him parrot-fashion by his mother. It was she who showed him the loving God with whom he has been enraptured for so many years. His father's God was a stern, unpleasable patriarch; unquenchable in His thirst for praise and unyielding in His commandments. His father's God was created in his father's likeness. The Penitent's father was a brutal, joyless stoic who did not even seem to take any pleasure in the beatings he rained upon his son. He beat the Penitent so he would become a better man. Only through his mother's God did he find love. Only through his mother's God did he find a deity to adore instead of fear.

The Penitent straightens and feels the cloth of his shirt touch the open wounds upon his skin. The hiss of pain causes him to cough and the cough becomes a wet and ghastly succession of retches and gasps. Blood sprays upon his chin. He knows his insides are bleeding. But he has so much to atone for and he does not know if it is God's will that he should be healed by the medicine of man, or to place his fate in his saviour's Almighty hands.

The Penitent is aware of the lightness at his sternum; the absence of a familiar weight. For many years, a small leather pouch hung there, made of the same dark substance as the surface of his Bible. Inside the pouch was his talisman. He took it from the faceless child; the miracle infant. And he kept it about his person through his own transformation from sinner to redeemer. He feels the absence of the talisman the way others would experience the loss of a loved one. Everything has begun to unravel since it was taken away. He believed the act to be a kind one; a noble and decent thing. But he was deceived. The Penitent allowed himself to stray from the path. He betrayed the guidance of his intercessor. He made a terrible, terrible mistake. He acted more as man than angel and invited a demon into his home. And there is not enough holy water or blessed earth to undo his foolishness.

The Penitent knows himself to be a sinner. He also knows himself to be absolved. He will not burn for his indiscretions. And yet his sins weigh upon him like a cross. The Penitent has two lives that should never have bled together. He is skilled in presenting the correct face to the correct witness.

Here, now, he feels as though the two sides of his nature are mixing, like different coloured candle-wax squashed together in a fleshy hand. His mistake has undone a miracle. His humanity is a fissure in the earth into which good men have tumbled.

Limping slightly, taking his weight upon his better leg, the Penitent leaves the pristine sanctuary of the white-painted room.

He walks gently down the corridor and returns to the bedside.

He leans over Brishen Ayres, and waits for the miracle to awake.

The Penitent wants to see how his eyes look when he pulls himself out of hell.

13

McAvoy feels as though he is being baked alive: cooked in the oven of his own hot breath. The bag presses in tight on nose and mouth and the pain in his throat makes every inhalation agony. He tries to force his breath to come out softly, gently, through gritted teeth, but the action pains him and threatens to make him give in to another burst of coughing. He no longer knows whether the rumbling he can hear is from the car tyres on asphalt or the sound of blood in his head. He can feel himself beginning to panic. He wants to lash out. His hands are free, held in fists at his side, and it takes all his resolve not to wrench the bag from his face and start swinging blindly at the people who have taken him. Instead, he forces himself to stay calm. Talks to himself. Tries to focus on being a policeman. In his mind he attempts to put together a physical description of his abductors, but his thoughts are becoming blurry and he finds his memories morphing, blending, until the man driving the car becomes some ghastly hybrid of men who have hurt McAvoy before. He conjures up memories of a man with blue eyes; his scarred features ripping apart as the blast from an exploding car tore through his skin. He feels the sudden impact of a blade and sees the fury in the face of the man who hacked down at his bleeding features. Each of McAvoy's scars sting afresh as his mind dissolves in a swirl of past agonies and fears. Instinctively, he reaches out for Roisin. Tries to imagine her face pressed against his own; her cool fingers stroking the sweat at his temples and her gentle voice shushing him as she does when she eases him from his nightmares. He tries to remember her songs. The greasy lining of the leather bag becomes her cheek and he softly rubs his damp beard against it.

He jerks to the right, suddenly and instinctively, as he feels hands in his pockets. He raises his hands but a sharp tap of the gun barrel against his throat makes him force them down. Nimble, dextrous fingers remove phone, wallet, ID and his reading glasses. He wonders if he should speak, or whether the effort of doing so would simply fill his cramped prison with more hot, desperate air.

He loses sense of time. At first he had thought he would be able to remember lefts and rights or intuit whether the vehicle was heading north or over water. Now he does not know whether he has been in the car for minutes or hours.

Sweat begins to pool at the base of his throat. Across his back and shoulders his clothing sticks to him. It feels as though he is drowning . . .

The car slows and abruptly comes to a halt. McAvoy twitches. This is an expensive vehicle and it made little noise as it purred through the quiet New York streets. Even so, McAvoy can sense the difference in the vibrations. This is not a stop-light. Wherever they were heading, they have arrived.

A blessed blast of cool air billows up and over McAvoy's face. He catches the faintest whisper of perfume and realises the girl has given him a moment's respite. Perhaps she has been in a similar prison and pities his pain. Perhaps she simply does not want him to die before they get whatever it is they need.

'You breathing, big man? Here.'

Cold water dribbles over his lips and the plastic bottle lifts the bag just enough for him to catch a glimpse of her features. She is almost completely in shadow, the interior of the vehicle illuminated only by the soft blue lights of the dashboard. Wherever they are, there is no street lighting. Greedily, he swallows down two great gulps of water, then gives in to a fit of coughing as he tries to drink in too much cold air.

'Careful, careful,' says the girl, withdrawing the bottle. She is silent for a moment, then: 'Close your eyes. If you open them I'll hurt you.'

McAvoy nods and does as he is told, screwing up his face like a child presented with an unpleasant mouthful of food. He feels the bag being removed. Moments later, a softer material is wrapped around his head and face. He can smell perfume. The faint trace of cigarettes and sweat. She has removed an item of her own clothing and masked him with it.

'Can you hear me? He's coming. You sit quietly and you nod, and you behave yourself. You try anything else, you will be very badly hurt.'

McAvoy nods. Already the soft wool of the mask is beginning to grow damp with the sweat from his forehead and cheeks but at least he can hear better. He opens his eyes. He can still see nothing through the material of the mask.

He hears doors opening. Senses the shifting weight in the vehicle. The door to his right is pulled open and a sudden swell of cold air encircles him. He finds himself beginning to shiver.

He hears voices. Low, mumbled, male voices. Then the girl. Has she got out? He can feel his hands twitch. He feels as though he is losing control. He feels as though he should sit on his hands for fear of tearing off the blindfold.

'This is him?'

The voice is precise; the syllables neat. McAvoy senses the closeness of a newcomer. He can feel himself being inspected. Is not sure whether to thrust his head forward in defiance or push himself back in his seat.

'He's a big man,' comes the voice, appraising him. McAvoy feels a hand squeeze the muscles in his forearm. 'Strong, too.'

'I'm sorry, I don't know who you are . . .' blurts McAvoy, and his words are muffled by the cloth around his lips.

'Shush. Spare your lungs. We know how you are feeling and I promise you, your breath could be better served. I have never been fond of those who plead.'

Inside the mask, McAvoy realises he can no longer hear his own ragged breaths. The man's words have slowed his lungs. Despite his fear, he finds his temper prickling.

'I'm not pleading,' he says, with a note of irritation. 'I'm talking.'

There is a soft laugh at his ear and then the weight of the vehicle shifts again as somebody heavy-set climbs inside. McAvoy feels the figure's big, muscly limbs brush his knees as he manoeuvres past him and into the back of the vehicle. There is silence for a moment and then the rasp of a match being struck. McAvoy smells burning, then the pungent aroma of expensive tobacco.

'This badge of yours,' comes the voice, and McAvoy wonders if the man is holding it in his hand for inspection. 'This real?'

'Of course. I'm a sergeant with Humberside Police . . .'

'Shush,' says the voice, more sternly this time. 'I had my doubts, you see. The hair. The scars. I figured that was just your story. Brishen swore vengeance and I know his people do not make such threats without having men at their disposal to back it up. It had occurred to me that you were that man. But you are Scottish, not Irish. Perhaps I am becoming paranoid.'

McAvoy catches the faintest whiff of an Eastern European accent. He wants to speak. To tell his captors who he is and what he is here for. But some inner sense counsels him simply to listen.

'If you had been this implement of vengeance, I would have known what to do with you,' muses the man by McAvoy's ear. 'But my darling girl has been reading your telephone and it seems you are a policeman of some reputation. I do not envy your situation. Families can be burdensome things.'

McAvoy locks his jaw. He feels violated at the thought of these people probing through his personal life. He remembers the messages that Trish was sending. Remembers how much of his investigative notes have been saved onto his cell phone.

'I am not good with the technology but my darling here can open a locked cell phone the way you or I would unscrew a jar of pickles. And she has found things inside that make me wonder if perhaps it would not be best just to end your little investigation in a manner that has proven effective in the past.'

McAvoy braces himself, fighting down the urge to raise his hands.

'Perhaps once, I would have ordered such an action,' says the man thoughtfully. 'Today I am reluctant to insist upon such measures. Executions are a young man's luxury. I have reached an age where I believe life to be valuable. Yours, in particular, seems to have worth. Your children are beautiful. Your wife loves you. Even your boss seems to think you are a soul that matters. I do not feel I can extinguish all of this as punishment for trying to do your job.'

Cautiously, McAvoy unclenches his fists. He concentrates on his breathing.

'I see from your phone that you have discovered how Marcel makes his side money,' comes the voice ruefully. 'You should be aware, Marcel is not what you would think of as a bad man. People like violence. They like blood. In the fights he arranges, people get to see that and almost nobody ends up dead. It is no different from the boxing we see on television but instead of the millions of dollars going to promoters and TV companies, a few thousand dollars go to fighters who truly need the money. And yes, there are people like myself who take a little cut to make sure all goes well, but there is nothing evil about what we do. Men have always wanted to know who is the toughest kid in the playground. We give them an opportunity to find out.'

McAvoy cannot help himself. 'Brishen hated bare-knuckle bouts,' he says.

'He did, he did,' agrees the man. 'But principles are expensive and Brishen had run out of credit. I would so dearly love to tell you that your Irish boy died because of a falling-out at a bare-knuckle boxing match. That would be so very neat and it would send you home. But I think we both know that you would not believe me and, in truth, I am as mystified as you are about what happened to the Irishmen after they left the company of my associates.'

McAvoy hears himself snort; a sound of disbelief. 'Who did they fight? Who won? Where were the bouts? How many men were with Brishen?'

'So many questions, Detective,' says the man. 'And I have so few answers. But you should know that the question of which nation breeds the superior fighters remains unresolved. The Irish hit hard. But so do my boys.'

There is silence in the car and McAvoy hears the man to his left sigh.

'I understand New York cops,' he says. 'They work hard. They understand death. They see bad things and they have pressures that I can help them with. I do not know how to persuade you to do what I want and for that reason there are people in my employ who believe it would be best to kill you.' He breathes out wearily. 'You cannot comprehend how much has been undone in just a few days. The Irishmen stumbled into something and we are only beginning to see how the pebbles they dropped in the ocean became a tidal wave. People with whom we wished to do business fear that we have broken our word. And despite many efforts, it is proving difficult to persuade them of the truth. The man you say you came for – it would do you well to forget him.'

McAvoy's eyes slide shut. 'Valentine.'

'He is an extraordinarily difficult person to like,' says the man, almost in wonder. 'He was in my city for under forty-eight hours. Now we have bodies, missing people, cops from the far side of the world. The boy knows how to make an impression. I have no doubt his whole family are of the same mould. Your wife, perhaps, is the exception. If it transpires that Valentine has told lies, if he has his own agenda, the Teagues will be made to pay. Out of respect for your efforts, I will try to avoid any injury to your wife. But for her, there are threats closer to home. The Heldens want blood. They will get the wrong blood, but it will satisfy them nevertheless.'

McAvoy's mouth opens and he finds himself about to warn his captor what will happen if any harm should come to his family. He realises the futility of such words. The man already knows everything he needs to about how McAvoy feels about his family.

'You have no reason to believe me, but I promise you, this was not my people. Things went wrong, but what happened to Brishen and Shay was unforgivable. I am as motivated as you are in discovering who did this thing. Focus your gaze elsewhere, Detective. Looking at me and mine will get you hurt.'

The far door opens and McAvoy feels another gust of cold air. A moment later, he can smell the closeness of the girl. She puts his ID, wallet, spectacles and phone back in his pocket.

'Nice family,' she says. 'Your boss . . . is she always like that?'

McAvoy drops his head back, trying not to let the relief make him tremble. 'I just came here to help,' he says, not knowing why. 'I didn't want any of this . . .'

'You seem okay, for a policeman,' says the girl. 'I'm sorry this had to happen. Things get complicated sometimes. We're searching for the same thing. I saw you slap that man outside the club and it made me sad to think that we would have to hurt you. But you are what you say you are. Even so, you're a long way from home and you will find that New York is a very lonely place for the friendless.'

The rest of the journey passes in silence. Half an hour later, gentle hands remove the mask from McAvoy's face. The door to his right is already open. He clambers out, unsteady on his feet, and the girl gives him a curt, professional nod. In her hands, she holds a purple cardigan and a gun.

'You can find your way from here,' she says. 'I hope if we meet again, it is for the right reasons.'

The vehicle moves away even as the girl continues to talk. McAvoy memorises the licence plate and watches the car until it turns right and disappears. Only then does he drop to his knees and start retching, bringing up spit and bile and blood. He stands as though he were testing out his muscles after a car crash and looks around him. He sniffs the air and begins to stagger in the direction of the river; feet unsteady on the hard snow, looking for something he might recognise.

From his pocket comes a vibration. He pulls out his cell phone. Roisin and the children have woken up. They love him, and are very proud. They wish he was here.

McAvoy manages to convince himself that the tears that sting his cheeks are from the retching, and not the cold, hateful loneliness in his belly.

Claudio follows the Lexus for another hour. He was surprised that the Chechens let McAvoy go. He watched the whole thing from the shadows and barely disturbed the snow beneath his feet. He was waiting for a gunshot. Had expected them to put a bullet in his forehead then cut off his hands, face and feet and dump him somewhere off Staten Island. The Scotsman must have some cards up his sleeve, he reckons. That, or a silver tongue.

He decides to act before they reach Brighton Beach. That is their turf, not his. And he needs seclusion and privacy. At one time in his career, he would have scouted out locations and learned all he could about his targets before embarking on a piece of work. But this situation is unique. He does not have the luxury of time.

He waits until they are on a quiet stretch of road, bordered on one side by car lots and the dark shape of an empty mall on the other. Then he reaches into the back seat and finds the blue light. He stretches his arm out of the window and sticks the magnetic light to the battered roof of his car. The rig on his dashboard contains several different types of siren. He gives the short, two-note burst of a cop car and watches with satisfaction as the vehicle in front rolls to a stop on the deserted street.

Claudio gets out of his car. He is dressed like a detective, in rumpled suit and comfortable shoes. He keeps his face in shadow, scratching at his hairline as he approaches the car. Automatically, the windows slide down in the driver's door. Claudio turns his face away from the glass and reaches, gently, into his coat.

'What was I doing?' asks the big, hairy man at the wheel.

'Licence and registration,' says Claudio, still half turned away from the car.

The hairy man scowls. 'You're not a patrol car. You a Narc? This is fucking harassment, man. You a faggot or something?'

'No,' says Claudio. 'But I'll let you suck my dick if you ask nicely.'

The driver's temper blazes through his caution and he grabs for the handle of the door. Claudio's gun has been in his hand since he pulled up. He raises it and there is a soft pop as he puts a bullet in the driver's shoulder and another in his knee. Round the far side of the vehicle he hears a shout and looks up to see a man fumbling with a semi-automatic weapon. Claudio shoots him in the hand before he has a chance to start firing. He puts another bullet in his knee.

Claudio turns as the rear door of the car opens. He stares into the face of a girl who seems too young to be playing with such terrible people. She does not look afraid of him.

'I don't want to have to shoot you,' says the girl. 'I can't see your face. I don't know who you are. Just go. This can be the end of it.'

Claudio knows he could shoot her through the glass of the rear door before she has a chance to pull the trigger. But he is proud that the only woman he has ever killed was by accident. The groaning men in the front of the vehicle will be able to provide him with what he needs.

'Your friends are going to help me find out what I came for. But it pays to be thorough. Did you copy his cell phone?' asks Claudio.

'The Scotsman?' Her face creases and she looks taken aback by the unexpected question. 'Of course. Why? What is it to you?'

'Do you have it?'

'No.'

'Disappointing.'

'I have it on my email account. Give me your name and address and I'll send it straight away. But you have to back off. Things aren't what you think . . .'

Claudio gives a half-smile. She has a confidence that feels familiar.

'I'm getting a tingling feeling,' says Claudio. 'I get like that when people tell lies. And I feel like every fucker has their own agenda right now. I feel like I'm snorkelling through bullshit. There's a stink coming off you . . .'

He stops talking as a thought occurs to him. Without betraying his intentions in his body language, he unleashes a kick at the car door. It slams back into the girl's body and she stumbles backwards. In two swift strides he is upon her, pushing the car door against her torso. He sees her face up close. *Now* she's scared.

'Good night, Officer,' says Claudio and his voice is that of a lover.

He strikes her on the side of the head with the barrel of his gun. Her eyes roll back and her body slumps, still pinned between the door and the rest of the vehicle. He releases the pressure and she slides to the hard ground. There is a clatter as her gun hits the road.

Claudio bends down and lifts up her shirt. On her pale, flat belly is a tattoo of a skull skewered by an orthodox crucifix. Taped in the space between her breasts is a small, black transmitter. He leans in and speaks directly into the tiny microphone.

'I could kill your agent. But I won't. I hope you appreciate this.'

Out of decency, Claudio pulls down the undercover agent's shirt. He grabs her by the cuff of her jeans and drags her to the other side of the street. He checks his watch. Probably under a minute until they get here. He crosses back to the car. The driver of the vehicle is hissing and bubbling through the pain and the blood loss so Claudio hits him, hard, in the temple, and his head falls forward as though he has been shot. Then he grabs the driver by the lapels of his leather jacket and drags him onto the floor. The icy surface makes it easy to slide him the fifteen feet back to Claudio's car, though he notices that it takes more effort than it used to do to get him into the trunk. By the time Claudio has repeated the routine with the passenger, he is almost out of breath.

For the sake of completeness, Claudio checks the back seat of the car. Slipped underneath the passenger seat is the laptop that the girl had been working on when Claudio pulled them over. He retrieves it and slides a finger across the screen.

Claudio's face changes and the light of the screen seems to seek out the abrasions and hollows of his countenance. The agent was going through the information she had taken from McAvoy's phone.

Something changes inside Claudio as he sees a face he remembers. A face from then. From before. From that time of bullets and bombs, when he carved out his own conscience and cooked it on the flame of a church candle. He feels as though pieces of shattered glass are forming a shape in his mind. He senses a set-up. Senses that all roads are leading him to one door. Claudio takes the laptop. He nods to himself, like a boxer who knows the next round will hurt.

Emerging from the back of the car, Claudio takes a revolver from his pocket and slips a special, fat-headed bullet into the chamber. Then, with practised precision, he shoots a hole in the side of the car. The fuel tank explodes a second later.

Claudio climbs back behind the wheel and drives away, just as the first burning chunks of metal rain down, slamming into the compacted snow like meteors into the earth.

14

'Never say a word, chavva. Not so long as you breathe. You'll have honey poured in your ear and whiskey in your mouth but this place, this secret, you carry to the grave . . .'

I was a boy, I think. I remember that feeling; that sensation of doing something that belonged to a world I wasn't a part of and that was so fecking exciting I might just piss myself. It was just me and Da. Full moon and the feel of silver between finger and thumb. That cold, glaring light of a moon made of the same stuff as the still, looming statues that stood to our left. There wasn't a sound, except the scrape of Da's big strong fingers scratching through the roots and the earth.

'Ye want to scare yerself, imagine your great-great-grandfather. He were here, chavva. Here just like we are now. Same tree, same earth, same stones. Picture yer da, no older than you are now, shivering . . .'

There wasn't much of a ceremony but it felt like one. He found the pouch in moments. Dug it out of the ground and held it up like he'd unearthed a diamond. Wasn't much bigger than a pebble and it didn't shine. But it was gold.

'Yer great-great-grandfather took a coin from every member of the clan and he melted it down and buried it beneath this tree on the night of a full moon. Only the oldest sons in the Ayres line have known about this place, or the secret of our good fortune. There'll be those who tell you it was dark magic but that's bollocks. It was hard work and the knowledge of a good shuvani that meant we didn't suffer like most. Now, kiss the rock, put it back, and don't expect to see it again until you're a father yerself.'

I did as I was told. Felt the thrill of it. Tasted the soil of my people. Felt the shower of loose earth as he ruffled my hair.

'You're my boy, Brishen. You're my blood, no matter what.'

Brishen Ayres. Fecking hell, I remember it. Jaysus, keep hold, man. Don't let it go. You're Brishen Ayres. You're a Traveller. Your father was Roddy, your Ma was Fionnula. You were a fighter. You got hurt. Fuck, you did! Metal and bright lights and the hard road against your face. But you fought back. You kept swinging. Became someone. A teacher. And the boys came from fecking miles around and you made them into men. The big lad – he could be something. Someone. The little gobshite too . . .

I see it now. Brishen Ayres. You made a bad call. Backed the wrong horse. You made a mistake and you had to put it right . . .

On the monitor that sits next to Brishen Ayres's bed, the display registers a sudden spike. Above the crisp, clean sheets, two of his fingers begin to twitch.

The Penitent looks up from his Bible. He sits in the floral, hard-backed chair and drifts in and out of sleep as his concentration permits. He reads aloud when the mood takes him and wafts lazily through the rooms in his mind when he does not care to speak.

He wonders what Brishen can see; trapped in that place between life and death. Wonders whether he can see His face, and whether it is as glorious as the one that he carved from the baby boy as he lay in a dead girl's arms and suckled upon a brown breast: inches from her unbeating heart.

1973: The Third Absolution

'He asked for you by name, Father. Said you were his friend. Doesn't want a lawyer. Won't talk to anybody else. We wouldn't have called at all but the duty sergeant's a Catholic and he suffered a bout of guilt and compassion. Lethal brew. I hope you don't mind but we couldn't leave him like this and we sure couldn't walk away. Poor bastard – he's taken the beating of a lifetime but he won't point the finger.'

Father Whelan likes the earnestness in the tall, handsome detective's eyes. He looks like he's of German ancestry. He has pale skin and blue eyes and he parts his hair neatly just above his left ear. He's wearing a smart beige suit, which looks too flimsy to provide much protection against the bitter autumn chill.

'I'll do what I can,' says Father Whelan, and reminds himself how many times he has told his flock that this, along with trusting in the Lord, is all that can be asked of anyone. He wonders whether he believes it.

Father Whelan and Lieutenant Lofgren are whispering together in the corridor of the emergency room at St Clare's Hospital. It makes Father Whelan feel strangely discomfited to be back in Hell's Kitchen, where half the people still call him 'Jimmy' and the other look disappointed in him for leaving to go to swanky St Colman's. He doesn't begrudge them their displeasure. He has made a lot of poor decisions in past months. He has listened to confessions that made his blood turn to water. He has absolved bad men of terrible deeds.

'You ready, Father? I'll leave you with him. If he wants to file a report, you got my number.'

Father Whelan nods a curt thanks. He finds it harder to smile than he used to. He finds good manners wearisome. When he raises his hands to bless people he looks as though he is lazily swatting flies. His soul is beginning to weigh him down.

The curtain offers no resistance as he swishes it aside.

It is all he can do not to gasp at the sight that greets him.

The man in the hospital bed has been beaten purple. His face is a mass of swellings and discolouration that make Father Whelan think of trampled grapes. He is bare-chested, and upon his skin has been carved the words 'SICK FUCK'.

A smile splits the battered features of the plump young man. Tears leak from his eyes and he winces in pain as he tries to pull the blankets over the wounds on his torso.

'Father,' he says, through broken teeth. 'Jimmy. Oh thank you. Thank you . . .'

Whelan looks again at the man. Through the bruises he sees a face he half recalls.

'Peter?' he asks. 'Sweet Jesus, what happened to you?'

Father Whelan's mind fills with a jumble of images. Peter was younger than him and by the time he entered the seminary, Whelan had left. Despite that, he went back regularly and he had found the young man to be one of the most attentive theologians at the worldly lectures he occasionally gave within the cloistered walls of the seminary. Whelan had made the effort to seek him out. He was bookish. Clever. He could recall perfect passages of Scripture. Could name chapter and verse. But there was something unappealing about him. He was not popular with the other trainees. His Catholicism was different to Whelan's. Peter served God dutifully but it was without the compassion that Whelan hoped to bring to his own ministries. Peter searched for the Lord in books while Whelan sought him out in the hearts of others. Peter nodded sagely at the acts of self-sacrifice and martyrdom in the Gospels. Whelan pitied the poor men and women for their agonies. For all that they shared a seminary, Whelan could not remember more than a half-dozen conversations between himself and the younger man. Why had he asked for him? What had happened to bring him here?

'Do I call you Brother? Father? James? Please, bless me. Forgive . . .' His features crumple in a wave of weeping.

Whelan crosses to the bedside and takes a plump, purplish hand in his own. It is clammy and Whelan remembers what they called him when he was not around. 'Sweatball'. Suddenly Whelan recalls why Sweatball left. He looks at the words on Peter's chest and lets the question show in his face.

'You swore,' says Whelan coldly. 'Swore in front of the bishop that you would turn from that path. You were helped, Peter. You could have gone to prison but they came to your aid. You could not be a priest but you could be a good man. What did you do?'

'I tried,' sobs Peter. 'I'm so alone, Jimmy. You were always kind to me. Do you remember what you said, when I begged you for answers? Do you remember telling me that God had a plan for all of us? That He would forgive me. That I was loved beyond my imagining. You saved me with those words, Jimmy.'

Whelan tries hard to recall. He was something of a big brother to the younger seminarians. He doled out kind words and motivational chastisements as he saw fit. He was popular and knew how to bring the best out of people. For all that, he recalls feeling little for Peter that could be considered a source of salvation.

'I was watching,' says Peter. 'They were so full of life. So perfect. The light in their eyes was the light of God. That was all I sought – to be closer to Him through their perfection and innocence. I tried to talk to them and they ran away. I stayed, hoping they would return to the park where I had seen them. But when they came back they were with men. And those men hurt me, Jimmy. They did this to me. And I did nothing to stop them. Their every lash brought me closer to God. Every moment of pain helped my redemption.'

Whelan wants to drag his hand away from the fat man's. And yet he cannot. He is a priest because he wants to heal and to save. He wants to bring his fellows into God's kingdom and he believes, truly, in the forgiveness of sins and the intercession of saints.

'I cannot be the man I am any longer,' whispers Peter. 'Tell me, if you forgave my body, could my soul still enter heaven? If I sought out my death at the hand of another, would that be suicide? I search for the words in the Book but my soul cannot fathom answers . . .'

Whelan closes his eyes. These past months he has seen the cold, empty blackness that can reside within a man's heart. He has heard Paulie Pugliesca gloat as he recounted the deaths of those who'd wronged him and has granted absolution in the face of his own revulsion. In Peter he sees a sinner but he also sees a man in search of redemption. He sees a chance to buy back a little of his own soul.

'Peter, God has not forsaken you. Nor does He wish for you to suffer. Jesus died for our sins and through His suffering we were born anew. Your suffering is a sin against God, not an act of reverence. Peter, will you pray with me? If I become as brother to you, will you trust your goodness to me?'

Something wondrous and perfect flares in Peter's eyes. Whelan witnesses the birth of hope.

'You were always a fine scholar. You have a good mind. I can help you. There are charities that can use a man such as you. I recall you saying you had read legal textbooks. Could you consider studying for such a profession? There is much you could do to help the Church. And I could be there beside you. I could help you overcome your temptations and in so doing you could help me towards my own salvation. I believe in you, as does the Lord. Tell me, Peter – will you allow me to bring you back to God's path?'

For a moment there is silence. And then Peter gives in to sobs of pure joy – tears trickling down his cheeks like a baptism from within.

And as he prays at the bedside, Whelan waits for the warmth of God's love to fill him. Waits for the slightest flicker of reflected peace to enter him.

He is still cold as he whispers his final 'Amen'.

15

It feels as though there is a drawing pin in McAvoy's throat. Every time he swallows he pulls a face and looks momentarily like a cat throwing up a fur-ball. The action makes his eyes water. He quite understands why he is sitting alone. As he left the hotel this morning, he waved a vague hello to the young girl on reception and her smile deserted her completely. He looks like a man who has been up all night drinking and sounds as though he smokes his cigarettes the wrong way around. He is now the only customer in the gelateria on First Avenue though the owners are unlikely to see a dip in profits. He is spending plenty on ensuring he does not run out of lemon and mint sorbet. He is hopeful that the next bowl will finally succeed in numbing his throat, though it is his sinuses and forehead that the sorbet seems to be targeting. He has to keep stopping to grab the bridge of his nose and wince in the face of an attack of brain-freeze.

McAvoy slept for three hours last night. When he made it back to his hotel room he showered and drank four glasses of water. He called Roisin and told her that he was making progress and hoped to have more for her soon. He called Pharaoh and told her he was fine, just tired, and that no, he hadn't been crying. Then he called Alto and left a message. He kept it brief. Something had happened. He thought he might need some help. He'd keep his phone on and would look forward to his call. And he hoped he remembered that he owed him.

It was still dark when McAvoy woke; his phone lying on his chest and still open on the image he had been staring at as he fell asleep. He had not made much headway on the documents that Pharaoh had sent him but seeing that his every piece of information was in the hands of the men and woman who took him last night, he intended to find out why it was so damn important. He fell asleep before he succeeded.

The room seemed too small, suddenly. He needed food and different colours; different lights. He slipped into the same clothes as yesterday and left the hotel, noting as he emerged that there was a smell of snow in the air. He started walking and did not stop until he found somewhere he could imagine spending the next few hours of his life. A small part of him had been inclined to send a text to Roisin, informing her that New York was the sort of place where one could get an ice-cream sundae at 6 a.m. but he failed to find sufficient motivation.

Here, now, McAvoy sits at a small plastic table and drinks his iced tea and takes small, painful mouthfuls of his sorbet, and tries to digest the information he has read and reread over the past hour. He knows himself well enough to be aware that there is panic hiding somewhere inside him. He is distracting himself right now. He has witnessed such things before, seen husbands, wives, mothers and fathers show no emotion upon being told of the horrific death of a loved one. They simply put the information in a locked place inside so they can focus on practicalities. Tears only come when the cage is unlocked. McAvoy knows that somewhere inside him lurks a complete loss of control. But he can keep the creature at bay for as long as he is working, thinking and trying to make sense of a picture made up of so many ripped-up pieces, and so many missing ones.

McAvoy gives a little cough that threatens to become a bigger one, and stifles it with a slurp of his drink. Again, he considers the document open on his phone. Ben Neilsen had deemed it important enough to add to the bundle that Pharaoh forwarded to him. It is a newspaper clipping from early 1981. The image is of a slim, dark-haired priest in simple black shirt and gleaming white dog-collar, staring beseechingly into the camera with sorrow in his eyes. He has one arm around the shoulders of a short, dark-haired woman, who is weeping into his chest. McAvoy reads the article again.

PLEASE PRAY FOR OUR MISSING ANGEL

Fr James Whelan has urged the people of the Lower East Side to unite in their prayers for missing schoolgirl, Alejandra Mota Valverda.

A special candlelit Mass was held last night at St Colman's Church – just five minutes from the absent girl's home.

'Ali was a friend to all who knew her,' said Fr Whelan, 29. 'There is good in all people but Ali's goodness simply shone. She is in our prayers and all that matters is that she comes home. She is not the sort of girl to run away and I have personally told the investigators to discount that very idea. Her family are good, hard-working people who are crumbling under the weight of this. Their faith will sustain them and I urge New Yorkers of all faiths and backgrounds to unite in sending them their prayers and words of support as they go through this dreadful time.'

Alejandra disappeared three weeks ago. The teen had been assisting her mother, Magdalena, with her duties as a cleaner at St Colman's. She left the church at a little after 8 p.m. but did not return home.

The diocese has begun a collection to sustain the family. It is being administered by sacristan and parishioner Peter Molony, 28.

Mr Molony said: 'The family are struggling because they are investing all of their efforts in the search for their missing girl. Any financial assistance that can be offered would spare them one burden at such a difficult time. For this reason the parish has set up a fund in her name and we know that the good people of New York will assist in any way they can. Prayers are enough, but dollars can make a difference.'

McAvoy finds his lip curling but does not fully understand why. He feels disconnected from things. He cannot decide whether the connections between the players are easily explained or unfathomable. Father Whelan is offering support to the families of Brishen and Shay. He secured a letter of recommendation for

Valentine Teague's visa. More than three decades ago, he was pastor at St Colman's, where he worked closely with sacristan Peter Molony. Brishen and Shay visited St Colman's and met Molony the day before they were attacked.

Were he standing in front of the murder wall at Courtland Road Police Station back home, McAvoy would be drawing a great circle of red ink around Molony's face. But Alto has not even questioned him. McAvoy needs to meet this man. He seems to be a connection of sorts, though he cannot see how the sacristan could be linked to organised crime and underground boxing.

McAvoy looks up at the sound of the door opening and jerks back in his seat as the girl enters the bar. She looks tired. Pale. She is no longer wearing her spectacles and her purple hair looks incongruous against the smart blue pantsuit and furry scarf she is wearing.

'Relax,' she says, crossing to where he sits and sitting down hard in a plastic chair. 'Half the world's still asleep and the half that's awake couldn't give a damn. Enjoy your breakfast. You've earned it.'

McAvoy sits perfectly still. This close, she smells different too. She's suddenly all body lotion and medicated shampoo. As she sits, McAvoy sees fresh bruising at her hairline. She waves at the young Italian girl behind the counter and mouths the word 'coffee'. A moment later, a cup of strong black liquid is set down in front of her. She takes a sugar cube from the bowl and places it between her teeth. As she sips the coffee through the sugar, she eyes McAvoy, who has not moved since she walked in.

'Give yourself a moment, Sergeant,' she says curtly. 'You'll work it out.'

McAvoy pushes the bowl of sorbet away. He coughs, in case his voice comes out as a squeak.

'You're a police officer,' he says, and it sounds as though his voice is coming from far away.

'Very good,' she says, not taking her eyes off him.

McAvoy rubs his throat. 'You hit me in the larynx with a gun,' he says, with a hint of rebuke.

She shrugs. 'I spent a lot of time becoming that girl. It's what she would do.'

McAvoy is about to speak when the door jangles again. The street outside is still dark and deserted and against the backdrop, Alto looks almost ghostly. He looks ill; the lines in his face cadaverous.

'I see you two have made your introductions,' says Alto, joining them.

The girl barely registers the newcomer's presence. She seems transfixed by McAvoy. Her glare is making him uncomfortable.

'I'm Polina,' says the girl, placing another sugar cube between her teeth. 'Polina Tymoshchuk. I've spent the past ten months getting close to Sergey Volotov's organisation. I even had the skull of a zev, a thief and soldier, tattooed on my stomach and the devil on my ass. I spent seven months in Rikers as part of that cover. And there's a very good chance I'm burned. My legend's fucked. It's all been for nothing.'

McAvoy returns her gaze. 'You make it sound like I'm to blame,' he says. 'You took me. You threatened me. You half crushed my larynx. I'm sorry your operation's had a hiccup but I don't think you can point the finger at me.'

For the first time, Tymoshchuk turns to Alto. 'His accent's charming, don't you think?'

Alto stares down at the tabletop. He has not met McAvoy's eye.

'What happened to your head?' asks McAvoy, indicating the bruising at Tymoshchuk's temple.

'I met an interesting man,' she says. 'The two men who helped me take you away? He shot them, took them, and blew up our car.'

'He didn't shoot you,' says McAvoy pointedly.

'No,' says Tymoshchuk. 'And thank you for your concern. He made me as a Fed. I don't know how, but the bastard spoke straight into my wire and said he hoped they appreciated him leaving me alive.'

Beside her, Alto shakes his head. McAvoy turns to him.

'I don't understand,' says McAvoy. 'Have you been helping me or trying to hold me back? I thought we were on the same team.'

Alto looks up, his amber glasses smeared with grime and steam. 'There were jurisdictional conflicts,' he says. 'The murder of Shay Helden has links to a large, ongoing, pre-existing investigation and there were fears that operational integrity could be compromised.'

Alto is clearly regurgitating something he himself has been told. It sounds like manager-level jargon to McAvoy, who is fluent in the language.

'What does any of that mean?' he asks, growing frustrated. 'I just want to find Valentine and go home.'

Tymoshchuk runs a hand through her hair, giving the tiniest wince as her fingers appear to touch something tender. She slides her satchel off her shoulder and retrieves a fat, pinkish file. She puts it on the table in front of her and holds it shut with a hand that shows the tiny faded marks of jewellery now discarded.

'Did you book him?' asks McAvoy, suddenly turning to Alto. 'Ellison? The man with the girl? Was she okay? Did she get to hospital?' A hard look comes over his face. 'Was that all about operational integrity too, or did he really pose a threat? How many lies have you told me?'

Alto gives a chastened little nod. 'That was a real one,' he says. 'Most of what I told you was real. I just couldn't give you it all. We're mounting a case against Ellison. You saved that girl's life. You're here today because I owe you for that and because I think you deserve to know more than you do.'

McAvoy shifts in his seat. He takes his phone from the tabletop and nervously plays with it as he waits for more.

'After this conversation, I think it would be best to curtail your visit to the Big Apple,' says Tymoshchuk. 'We tolerated you as a favour to our allies across the Atlantic, who said you had skills to offer and were extremely biddable. Alto is a team player. He gave you enough to keep you out of the way. If you'd known about the Pugliescas, I dread to think how many pieces you'd have ended up in.'

McAvoy takes a breath. 'Pugliesca?' he asks, and he locks his teeth around the word as he trawls his memory for anything connected to the name. He shakes his head.

'Pick a page,' says Alto lightly, and pushes the file across the tabletop.

Cautiously, McAvoy opens the folder. It opens on a newspaper clipping: a story about a court appearance by one Salvatore Pugliesca on racketeering charges. The accompanying image

143

shows a swarthy, curly-haired young man sneering at the camera amid a tapestry of microphones, notepads and flashing cameras.

'Dropped for lack of evidence,' says Tymoshchuk. 'His daddy had a lot of powerful friends. Still does. Knows how the game is played. Who to play, and how.' She looks at Alto as she says this, and her lip curls.

McAvoy scowls. He pushes the folder away. 'I'm just here to find out who hurt Brishen and Shay and to see if Valentine was involved and whether he's dead or alive. The rest is nothing to do with me.'

Tymoshchuk finishes her coffee. Sighing, she opens the folder and pulls out a photograph, which she hands to McAvoy. It shows a youngish man with dark hair. He wears an expensive jacket with sweatshirt and jeans and were it not for the slack-jawed agony on his face, he would be handsome. A tree branch has entered his torso just below his ribcage and exited from the small of his back. There is snow in his hair and upon his shoulders and he is arched backwards, one hand on the branch that killed him, as if trying to push himself free.

'That's Luca Savoca,' says Tymoshchuk, and her finger pushes down on his face as if she's squashing a bug. 'I'm a firm believer that in this life, there are no absolutes, but I make allowances for this kid. He's an absolute piece of shit. He's the son of Nicky "Bathtub" Savoca. Savoca is number two to the acting NYC boss, Paulie Pugliesca. He has been for years. On paper the family belongs to Andrea Benzano, but he's not due out of prison until a week before his 189th birthday. I wouldn't set aside money for a cake.'

McAvoy's head is spinning. The names flow over him like water. His confusion shows in his face.

'And you think Salvatore Pugliesca is involved?'

Tymoshchuk looks at him as if he's an idiot. 'Salvatore died in 1981 about three months after that picture was taken. He opened his front door and a nail bomb turned him into ravioli.'

'Why?' asks McAvoy.

'There are no shortage of theories – give it five minutes and there'll probably be a documentary come on somewhere offering different ideas. We're pretty damn sure it was the same old story.

Power struggle. Sal was whacked to send a message to his old man, Paulie. It was a good hit. Expert.'

'Right,' says McAvoy, keeping up. 'So . . . Luca Savoca? The man with the tree branch in his midriff . . . ?'

'This picture was taken last week at woods off Silver Spur Road,' says Tymoshchuk, as if talking to a child. 'This spot,' she adds, tapping the trees and snow, 'is about a quarter-mile from where Brishen and Shay were attacked.'

'He was found later?' asks McAvoy, grasping for something to hold onto.

'Not by much,' says Alto.

'But this information wasn't made public. It wasn't shared. You didn't tell me.'

'No,' says Tymoshchuk. 'That's because there are jurisdictional challenges, like Ronny here said. The challenges in this case are the huge operations we've been running for the past two years and which we've sunk millions of dollars of taxpayers' money into. We have indictments coming down soon on senior figures in both the Chechen and Italian Mobs and a big part of that is the testimony of various low-level members of Pugliesca's crew.'

'Including this boy?' asks McAvoy, indicating the photograph.

'Afraid not,' says Alto, with a glance at Tymoshchuk. 'The Feds couldn't flip Luca. He takes the whole loyalty shit seriously. But he knows more about his daddy's business than anybody and for that reason he was a prime target. To keep him out of harm's way during what he knows to be a tricky time, Daddy Savoca sent his son to look after some of the family's interests upstate. He's been keeping his head down, staying out of trouble.'

'And?'

'And we've had a wire on his cell phone for the past three months,' says Tymoshchuk, with a hint of pride. 'Last week he took a call from somebody we didn't recognise but which we've since tracked down to a neighbourhood in Philadelphia. There was a piece of work to be done. Luca was invited to participate. Luca couldn't have been more excited if you'd told him he was throwing out the first pitch at a Yankees game.'

'And?' says McAvoy again.

'Luca was told to switch to another phone and we couldn't hear any more. But less than twenty-four hours later, Brishen and Shay had been shot and Luca was impaled on a tree.'

McAvoy looks again at the picture. 'There has to be more.'

'We recovered Luca's gun,' says Alto. 'He put the first bullet into Shay Helden but not the second.'

'And what did he do to Brishen?' asks McAvoy, unsure he really wants to know.

Tymoshchuk sucks her teeth. 'There was a switchblade recovered from the scene. It had been used to cut off Brishen's nose. But the bullet in his head came from a different weapon. What's more, the knife belonging to Luca wasn't used to finish off Helden.'

McAvoy realises he has closed his eyes; shutting down his other functions so as to make better sense of what he is reading. His face flushes as he realises the bit that matters most.

'So, this whole thing may be nothing to do with Valentine,' he says brusquely.

'We never thought it was,' says Alto. 'It might seem that I wasn't doing much to follow that line of enquiry but that was because we knew from the beginning this was a gang hit gone wrong.'

McAvoy screws up his face as questions line up like soldiers. 'But how did Brishen and Shay become targets in the first place? Where were they going? Who had they upset?'

There is a moment's silence before Alto speaks again, apologetically. 'The Italians and the Chechens have been getting closer. Working in tandem, you might say. Your Irish boys upset the Chechens somehow. God only knows how but they found themselves in the middle of something and now we're getting word that both the Italians and the Chechens are blaming one another and treating it like a prelude to a fucking war. We're hearing that the repercussions are going to be biblical.'

'Why?' asks McAvoy. 'How?'

Tymoshchuk shrugs. 'Ninety per cent of my job is sifting through bullshit and bragging. We've got some ideas but the truth is, we don't know what has upset the relationship or what the hell Luca was doing up there. What we do know is that the night after they arrived in New York, Brishen and Shay managed to get themselves involved in a bare-knuckle boxing match. We're sweating informants and we're looking for key witnesses, but whether Shay won or lost, it went bad.'

McAvoy looks at Tymoshchuk. He tries to calm his thoughts. Dredges up a name. 'You've been undercover with Sergey Volotov's crew for a long time?'

'I've been getting closer,' she says. 'His boys are all muscle and they needed somebody with a brain. I found one of his cyber team on a chatroom on the dark net. Got through his security in under thirty seconds. Told him I'd spread the word unless he vouched for me with his bosses. Got a foot in the door, so to speak.'

'But you don't know about the fight?' asks McAvoy, looking incredulous. 'Who won, what went wrong?'

'He keeps me away from the street stuff,' she says. 'You were my first chance to prove myself. I told him I'd been monitoring communications at the FBI. Some big guy was coming over from Scotland or Ireland or who the hell knew where and it would be best to check him out. There was some fear that you were connected to the Heldens or the Teagues. I figured you wouldn't mind being used as a tool.'

McAvoy looks at Alto. 'You both used me.'

Tymoshchuk shrugs. 'You should be pleased. We don't want Valentine for murder. I'm sure he'll turn up. You can tell your wife that the Feds have assured you he wasn't involved.'

McAvoy scratches at his head, wondering if this woman can possibly be for real. 'You expect that to end things? They won't accept that. I won't accept that.'

'You don't have a choice,' says Tymoshchuk. 'Maybe Brishen will wake up soon and he can make a call home and everything will be sweet. Maybe not. We've indulged you and we're grateful for your cooperation. Ronny here will drink your health with the boys from the Seventh. They've all heard about the way you slapped that bitch Ellison down and that's the reason I found a half-hour to thank you, and to tell you that you can relax now, your work is done. Ronny here reckons we owe you more than that but he's not the one calling the shots. He shouldn't have asked you to help him out with Murray Ellison either but that's for him and his conscience. Now go get yourself another ice cream.'

Tymoshchuk stands up, and McAvoy reaches across to take the file before she can. She shakes her head and he lets go of it like a well-trained dog with a Frisbee.

'Your wife's a lucky lady,' says Tymoshchuk, and she looks momentarily genuine. 'I like the way you operate. But you're going to get hurt. Leave this alone. Ronny, come on. You can run me back.'

Alto's lips are pressed together in a tight line. He seems about to offer a handshake but resists. 'I've had your bag dropped off at the hotel. What you did last night . . . I shouldn't have asked, but it mattered.'

They leave without another word.

For a full thirty seconds after they have departed, McAvoy sits staring into the sticky swirls of his melted sorbet. Then a small, tinny voice makes him jump.

'Well, she was a fucking bitch,' says Pharaoh, from the phone on the tabletop. 'Is she bigger than me? Could I take her? I bet she's one of those fit people – the sort who go upstairs to have sex because they can handle the climb. What a bell-end.'

McAvoy lifts the phone and feels as though he is coming to after a bout of unconsciousness brought on by repeated kicks to the head.

'Did you believe any of that?' asks McAvoy, who called Pharaoh the second that the two officers walked in.

'Some,' says Pharaoh grudgingly. 'But if you don't talk to Molony then I'm going to fly out and do it myself, and then Roisin will get all cross, and I hate the thought of that.'

'You can't afford the flight,' says McAvoy, around a tired smile.

'Nor can you. Now, go and do something that pisses people off. You're good at that. Who knows, they may end up thanking you for it.'

'You think?'

'Not a chance. Now, I've got to get off. I'm about to charge an arsehole with murder. We've got you on speakerphone. I think this anecdote may keep him entertained in the cells.'

'Thanks, Trish.'

'No bother.'

PART THREE

1975: The Fourth Absolution

Father Whelan sits in the back of the black Cadillac and watches the man in the driving seat ignite his cigarette with a gold-plated Ronson that flames red and gold in the darkness. He breathes out a plume of smoke and gives the priest a smile that accentuates his delicate features. He's pretty, this Sicilian. Has delicate fingers too. Thick black hair and pleasant brown eyes. He looks harmless enough. But Father Whelan has been taking his confession for the past three years and knows the man who drives the car is anything but.

'He'll listen to you. You've got the juice. Tell him it will look good for him on Judgement Day. That'll mean a lot to him, because if he don't play ball, Judgement Day's going to come a lot faster than he thinks. We can make a donation to one of your good causes,' continues Paulie Pugliesca softly. 'You know how this can go. Whatever you like. Just tell this prick he's a lost sheep. He's a good boy. Just made a mistake. The girl will be okay. We'll buy her something expensive.'

Father Whelan wishes he could better explain to this man why he cannot simply walk into the Sixteenth Precinct and demand they release the young man they picked up tonight for grabbing a thirteen-year-old girl as she walked home from school. He drove around with her for an hour. Dropped her off two blocks from home: scratch marks on her face and bloody down to her bare feet.

'He's a ball-breaker, this one,' says the driver to the large, silent man in the passenger seat. 'I do everything he asks and he denies me this courtesy. I move the dummy to a nice place upstate. I pay for his therapy. I let him come home. I give him a job and a family. I give money to the Church, to the poor, I have my guys digging gardens and painting windows each feast day. And he won't even show me some love on this one. What's with this guy?'

Father Whelan casts around for the right words. He hopes he is a good priest. He loves his flock. Loves his church, with its great pillars and columns and its beautiful blue glass. He never wanted to get to know these men. But circumstances brought him into their lives. He begged a favour from the guardian of a scared boy in a filthy hospital and the cost is higher than he ever imagined. He gives the man in the driving seat absolution for his sins and carries around the knowledge of his misdeeds. It weighs heavily upon him.

'Supposing it's not a misunderstanding,' says Father Whelan. 'She was just a girl.'

Paulie gives him a knowing look. He's growing tired of having to be persuasive. Both men know that Whelan will acquiesce. He'll do what Pugliesca asks because Pugliesca owns a part of him now. He has already done far worse for this bright, ambitious man who has risen to become underboss of a New York crime family before the age of forty-five. His son, now twenty-two years old, is expected to become even more successful. Whelan had always known him to have a mean streak but he did not expect the young man's tastes to run to such excess. The things he did to that poor young girl. At the hospital they said she would never be able to have children . . .

'Some of these girls ain't no girls,' says Paulie. 'Some of these girls are women. They're tramps. They lead you on and then bitch when you try to give them what they've asked for. He's young. He'll learn. I'll beat him till he knows how to behave but he ain't gonna do time for this.'

Father Whelan clutches the tumbler of whiskey between his knees. 'She was thirteen,' he mutters.

'He didn't know that. She led him on.'

'He may not listen,' protests Whelan. 'This policeman, I mean.'

'You're a priest, Father. A good man. And this prick is one

devout motherfucker. You vouch for the boy and I swear, I'll keep him on the right path.'

'His brother . . .' begins Whelan.

'Tony ain't no goddamn brother,' says Paulie, anger flashing in his eyes.

'He was there, wasn't he? Watching. Helping.'

'Sal was showing him the ropes.' Paulie shrugs. 'How to be a man. How to take control.' He smirks. 'Y'know, like a big brother should.'

'I want Tony away from his influence,' says Whelan, his voice shaking. 'A nice place. A place of his own.'

'My home not good enough, huh? You weren't so high and mighty when you was begging, Father.' Paulie twists his jaw then forces himself to relax. 'I understand, Jimmy. I'm fine with whatever you say. Sal's got plans anyway. A nice house for Tony. Pretty place, upstate, where he can watch the birds fly and the flowers grow and roll about in his own shit like a fucking lord.'

Whelan thinks quickly. Tries to turn this situation into something positive. 'And one of my flock – a man working so hard to become a better person. He's bright. Creative. I want a job for him. Something with a future. Something he can feel proud over.'

'You hear this guy?' asks the driver. 'The Church don't like blackmail.'

'This isn't blackmail. It's a contract.'

'Whatever you say, Father. Just get him out of there. He's not a bad boy. He just made a mistake.'

Father Whelan climbs from the car. It's a cold night but sweat makes his dog-collar stick to his neck.

As he walks towards the lights of the station house, he finds himself genuflecting.

Despite his bargain, he knows there is no such thing as a moral calculus. There is no equation or algorithm that can bring him comfort for tonight's work.

16

'Wave now. Wave to Daddy. Good girl!'

On the screen, Lilah is smiling her huge, gummy, gap-toothed grin, trying to grab the image of her father's face as it looms at her from thousands of miles away.

'Are you being good, my sweet?' asks McAvoy quietly, focusing all his attention on his daughter. 'Are you pretending you like those clothes?'

Roisin's face fills the screen as she pouts at her husband. 'She looks adorable!' She lifts up Lilah for closer inspection and examines the leopard-print dungarees and furry gilet that the two-year-old is currently sporting. 'I don't know what you're moaning about – she looks sensational, so she does.'

In the back of the taxi, McAvoy finds himself grinning. His notebook sits on his lap and Roisin and Lilah have been taking turns to try to lift his spirits. The snow has not yet begun to fall but it is only a matter of time. Not long ago, a commuter who wanted to get to the office before the blizzard began made the mistake of stepping out in front of a delivery van. McAvoy's cab is stuck in the resulting traffic jam. He is doing better than the commuter, who is stuck beneath the wheels, and exceptionally dead.

'The hair?' asks McAvoy, shaking his head.

'She's amazing,' says Roisin, and kisses her daughter's neck, which prompts a fit of giggles.

'She looks like Pebbles from the Flintstones,' says McAvoy, gesturing lamely at the solitary pigtail that sprouts from the top of his daughter's crown.

'Never seen it,' says Roisin dismissively. 'I'm a lot younger than you, remember.'

McAvoy feels better just looking at his wife. She's wearing a velour tracksuit top over a low-cut black vest and there is fake tan and glitter across her chest. She has done her make-up the way she does it when he's not around: thick lashes and lots of sparkle. Sometimes she leaves so much glitter in their bed that it looks to McAvoy like the kind of crime scene he would find following the murder of a pixie.

'Run and play,' says Roisin to her daughter. She puts Lilah on the floor of the caravan that she and the children have been staying in for the past few days. Lilah blows her father a kiss. 'She's loving it. Wants to go home, but still loving it.'

McAvoy feels suddenly cold. It's a little after 9 a.m. but it feels like twilight. The air is the blue-black colour of a fresh bruise and the shivers of the pedestrians who hurry past the cab windows seem strangely contagious. He feels as though he has been wrapped in wet blankets.

'The Heldens were here again,' says Roisin quietly, leaning in. 'I don't know how long they'll wait.'

McAvoy tries to keep the panic from his face. 'I swear, not half an hour ago the FBI told me that Valentine is not a suspect. He didn't do this.'

'Then where is he?' asks Roisin, and immediately softens her features in apology for snapping. 'What's happened to him?'

McAvoy bites his lip. He wants to ask her something but fears the answer. She reads his face like a large-print book and her eyes grow large as she speaks straight into his soul.

'I didn't know,' she says. 'Swear to God, I never. If Valentine went there for a fight he kept it quiet. Same with Brishen. And Father Whelan would surely never have written Valentine a letter if he'd known it was for fighting.'

McAvoy says nothing. Hopes she'll speak again.

'I told Dad what you've found out. I don't think he was surprised.'

'Can I speak to him?'

'Dad?' asks Roisin, surprised. 'He's drunk a gallon of poteen, near enough. Him and the men are tooling up – calling in favours. He's not here.'

McAvoy frowns, annoyed at the world's failure to cooperate. 'I have questions about Father Whelan,' he says dejectedly. 'How well does your dad know him? How did Brishen persuade him to write a letter for Valentine?'

'Valentine went to church sometimes,' says Roisin, looking around for an explanation. 'And Father Whelan and Brishen are really close. You should see the poor priest. He's carrying such a weight on him, so he is. I think he wants to go over there to be at Brishen's side but he's doing so much good work here. You should see the parish priests! They're scuttling around making us all cups of tea and bringing sandwiches and trying their damnedest to look like they haven't been treating our kind like scum for centuries. Father Whelan's been here almost constantly for the past forty-eight hours. He's taking confession, leading the prayers. I swear, if it weren't for him staying at the site I think the Heldens would have already started shooting.'

McAvoy nods. He doesn't know what advice to give.

'He's a good man,' says Roisin. 'I know bad men and he's not one, and that's nothing to do with the robes or the faith. He's kind. He took me to one side and said he understood how hard this must be for me. He gave me a blessing. Gave me one for you.'

'For me?'

'Da told him you were out there helping. Father Whelan said it meant the world to him, knowing Brishen wasn't alone out there. How is he? How does he look?'

The taxi moves forward a few feet and McAvoy allows himself to hope they are about to make some headway. A moment later the car stops and the Indian driver gives vent to a torrent of abuse.

'I'm on my way to the hospital now. I want to see Brishen for myself. See how he is. Get my mind around what I'm actually here to do. And then I'll have some questions for the man he left St Colman's Church with – Mr Molony.'

'Do you want me to ask Father Whelan about him? You said they were old friends . . .'

'Not yet,' says McAvoy. 'I need to work some things out. If

Father Whelan does get talking about his time in New York, text me. I'd love to have a listen.'

'Would I be your partner in crime?' asks Roisin impishly. 'That would be exciting. I've got his number, if it's helpful. His mobile. Told me to ring if things were getting too much.'

McAvoy nods appreciatively, looking out of the window at the front of a large museum dedicated to the history of the tenement building. If things were different, he would like to go inside. Would like to poke around and fill his head with new knowledge. He wonders if he will ever get the chance.

'On Sunday they'll be collecting for the families,' says Roisin. 'Da will be going to Mass, come what may. I want you home, Aector, but if we don't get some answers I don't know what you'll come home to.'

McAvoy closes his eyes. He doesn't want his wife to see his fear and hopelessness.

'I have to go,' he says, and puts his hand to the screen. On a halting site in Galway, Roisin does the same. Both feel the cold, flat surface of the computer screen but in the moment, they feel a familiar caress. McAvoy holds his hand there for several moments, his big fingers dwarfing those of his wife. As he finally lowers his hand, he sees the blue ink on her palm. He is about to question it when the car lurches forward and in a shower of Urdu swear-words, the driver performs a hard turn in the middle of the road. The notebook slips off McAvoy's knees and as he grabs for it, he severs the connection. As he looks at the blank screen, he sees nothing but his own face, and the desire to punch it to fragments threatens to consume him.

He hides inside himself for the forty-minute journey; does not give a damn about the changing neighbourhoods or the swelling darkness or the shifting tone beneath the tyres. When they arrive at the hospital, he does not question the exorbitant price of the ride. He climbs out into air cold enough to take his breath away and passes a handful of notes to the driver, who fails to thank him for the handsome tip. The cab pulls away even as McAvoy is retrieving his bag and trying to close the back door.

He turns from the parking lot to look at the hulking mass of the specialist neurological hospital where Brishen Ayres is a patient. He does not want to go inside, to look at the ruination of a decent man's face and be forced into apologising for his inadequacies.

Steeling himself, huddling into his coat, McAvoy approaches the large sliding door of the reception area. He stops in front of it, needing a moment's pause to make a decision. Then with a nod to himself he enters the large, warm atrium and gives his best smile to the pretty Filipina woman behind the desk. She does not have much interest in his warrant card but when he explains that he is family and has come all the way from Ireland, she makes a call. Ten minutes later, a large black woman who smells extraordinarily floral is all but linking arms with McAvoy as she leads him to the elevator and rides with him to the sixth floor.

'Down there, third room on the right. He's going to wake up soon, I tell you that much, and there are a lot of people in this hospital who would give their left leg to know the colour of his eyes. I'm sure you'll already know, being family, but I won't cheat.'

The nurse is a force of nature and keeps grabbing McAvoy by the forearms to tell him what a good man he is. As she clasps him to herself, she raises a finger skywards and says, 'Praise Jesus.' McAvoy does not know if it is an instruction or a suggestion so decides to leave Him out of it altogether.

Gathering himself, straightening his clothes, McAvoy moves down the pristine corridor. He closes his eyes and steps into Brishen's room.

A small, round man is sitting on a hard-backed chair. A Bible is open in his lap; the words blurred and indistinct on tissue-thin pages. The man is perhaps five feet tall, though he is quite round at the middle and his head is completely spherical. The bald patch on the top of his head and the glasses he wears are both perfectly round. He looks as though he is entirely composed of circles.

His name is Mr Molony.

And as he looks at McAvoy, his prayers die on his tongue.

★   ★   ★

Detective Ronald Alto should be feeling good. Sure, he feels as though he's wearing somebody else's skin and is belching a medley of bourbon, antacid tablets and ibuprofen, but most of the detectives in the Seventh feel this way at mid-morning on a weekday and would still look favourably on any suggestions that involve spicy food, a round of shots and a topless bar.

Alto's had so many slaps on the back this morning his shoulder is starting to hurt. It seems that everybody from his colonel to the guy sweeping the snow from the front porch has heard about the collar last night and he will not have to buy himself a drink for a long time. Ellison is about to be charged. In the next few minutes, Alto will stand beside Colonel Deane and the Deputy Director of Operations and tell the assembled news teams that a dangerous predator has been arrested. It looks as though Ellison is ready to cough to a string of date rapes and despite the desperate attempts of his lawyers to shut him up, he has already put his hands up to slipping the fatal dose into the dead girl's drink last summer. The fight has gone out of him. McAvoy slapped the smarm right out of his mouth. He's sitting in a holding cell, bubbling and snotting and saying he's so very sorry. Alto's getting the credit for the whole damn thing, as if it were a subtle, clever piece of police work. In truth, he got himself so drunk he could barely see and then sent a good man into a lion's den, armed with nothing more than half-truths and a conscience. That he left McAvoy sitting forlornly in an ice-cream parlour while he himself came back to Pitt Street for ovations and fanfare is weighing on Alto's mind.

In front of him, the old computer with the missing keys shows the same old reflection. Hunched-over, unfit men and women, lounging in chairs with feet on desks, flicking elastic bands or scribbling notes on files with one hand and eating MSG-rich snacks with the other. Alto normally feels at home here but today something has changed. He feels like a fraud. He knows there are good reasons to keep McAvoy at arm's length and he knows there will be repercussions if anybody finds out that the 'good Samaritan' whom Colonel Deane is so keen to talk about at the press conference is actually a visiting detective from England seeking the killer of Shay Helden.

'You re-running a porno in your head?' comes a familiar voice at his elbow. 'Your mind's so far away you might as well be in Tijuana.'

Alto looks up at the big, fleshy countenance of Detective Hugh Redding. He has jelly on his lower lip and is drinking a mug of coffee brewed so strong that it may well climb over the rim and start heading for the door.

'Long night,' says Alto, pushing a finger under his amber glasses and worrying at his red-seamed eyes.

'Good result though,' says Redding, in a rare moment of sincerity. 'The captain will be tumescent.'

Alto pulls a face. 'You think?'

'Positively engorged. We'll need a syringe to calm him down.'

'Is that why you keep one by your bed? I wasn't sure, and your wife couldn't answer me.'

'No, the ball-gag keeps her quiet. It was a good buy. Thank your mother for the recommendation.'

Alto and Redding have worked together for years. For a short time they were seconded to Homicide South and their clear-up rate rivalled that of the most experienced men on the elite squad. But neither man had the right connections to make the move permanent. Neither shared a rabbi or a priest with a senior officer or were willing to spend their weekends mowing the captain's lawn in return for the nod of approval. They were rotated back to the Seventh and have been perfectly at ease here – even if they get an almighty kick out of upstaging the officers in their old squad.

Alto looks up at the big man and decides to confide. 'Can I ask you something?'

'It's perfectly natural. Happens to everybody. It doesn't mean you're a faggot . . .'

'I'm serious, Hugh.'

Redding licks the jelly off his lip and pulls up a chair, which he sits on backwards, saloon style. 'You okay, man?'

Alto rubs his hands together as if brushing away dirt. 'The Feds,' he says quietly. 'They've been running an operation. The Chechens and the first of the Five Families have been getting friendly. The Feds had an agent in Sergey Volotov's organisation. God only knows who they've got in with the Italians.'

Redding retrieves a Twinkie from the inside pocket of his crumpled suit and lovingly reads the ingredients before he starts to unwrap it. 'So?' he asks, between bites. 'That's what they do.'

'The Irish boys who got hurt last week upstate . . .' says Alto.

'The case you got saddled with for no fucking good reason?'

'It came to me on paper but it was never really mine. The Feds had spoken to the bosses and explained it was gang-related. Two Irish boys seem to have made enemies of either the Chechens or the Italians, or both, and we ended up with a bloodbath.'

'The shit just seems to fall like rain sometimes,' says Redding, looking forlornly at the empty Twinkie wrapper and patting himself down for another.

'And the Scottish cop . . .'

'English, you said . . .'

'He's from Scotland, though.'

'Right, what about him?'

'He's got powerful friends. Or enemies, I can't tell. The Brits got him permission to come over and look into the case. And because there was a whiff of politics about it, the bosses agreed. They asked me to make him feel important – give him some bits and pieces and keep him out of harm's way.'

'Right, usual babysitting stuff. We've all done it.'

Alto scratches at his chest, as if something is biting him. 'Last night, he helped me bring down Ellison. Slapped him so hard I thought his head was going to come off. And you know something else? He put himself between my gun and Ellison's head. Wouldn't let me shoot the bastard.'

Redding cocks his head. 'He a pussy?'

'I don't know what he is. But he's found things out, Hugh. Stuff the Feds don't want him to know about. This morning I had to watch as this stuck-up bitch told him he'd outstayed his welcome and had to head home.'

Redding nods, anticipating this. 'And?'

'And I don't think people realise how much this matters. There's a blood feud back in Ireland and his wife's family are in the thick of it. His brother-in-law is missing and it seems like nobody wants him found. And then there's this priest . . .'

'Priest?'

'In Galway. Grew up here. Used to be a priest here. The Irish boys live a stone's throw from his fucking place in Galway. He greased the wheels to get them over here. They went to his old church and met with a man who I know for a fact we have a duty to talk to.'

Redding moves a little closer: his breath sweet on Alto's face.

'I'm always happy to encourage my brother officers to fuck their careers,' says Redding playfully. 'It gives us something to talk about between jobs. But this sounds like it's got trouble spilling out of it on all sides. Maybe you should just enjoy the plaudits and send this Scotsman a case of decent Scotch and try to forget about it.'

Alto looks down morosely.

'There's more, isn't there?' says Redding resignedly. 'You've done something silly out of guilt, I can tell. You know what happens to you when you get dug in, Ron. You know where it led us . . .'

'I had to look. I'm a cop. And I owe him. I blackmailed him into going into that club. I owe him . . .'

'What did you find?'

Alto looks past him, at the red ink on the whiteboard, stuck up on a black wall. The red spells out the names of the recently deceased: the cases unsolved. Alto finds it blurring as he stares.

'Father Whelan has visited the US once a year for the past thirty-one years. I've checked with Rikers – when Paulie Pugliesca did a stretch, Father Whelan came to see him. He's his confessor. Always has been.'

'And?'

'And I don't know. I can't make it fit. But, look . . . you remember the lawyer? The things we found?'

Redding speaks through gritted teeth. 'That went away,' he hisses. 'It nearly cost you everything and we still don't know what you found.'

'That's the link!' says Alto animatedly. 'I can't understand it but it's there. Look! We've always known Molony was valuable to the old man, we just never had more than guesses to go on and we got hauled off it before we even scratched the surface. But I've pushed a little harder, just on the QT. Molony did this to himself in 1976.' He grabs his notebook from the desk. He clicks on an image and the screen floods with a picture that makes his stomach heave.

'Jesus,' says Redding. He lets out an angry sigh; the detective in him and the human being warring for supremacy. 'Thank fuck they told us to stop before we saw that. I'd hate to have nightmares for the rest of my life.'

'A lawyer, important to the Mob, who once hated himself enough to hack his balls off. A priest from the same neighbourhood. A dead man from the priest's town in Ireland . . .'

'Let me think a moment,' says Redding, rubbing a knuckle against his forehead. He takes a breath. 'Molony, the lawyer – he met up with your Irish boys, yeah? The Irish boys who know Father Whelan.'

'They left the church together,' begins Alto. 'It might not be important,' he adds, but his every instinct is telling him that it is.

'You've got the press conference,' says Redding. 'The world's lining up to shake your hand and you worked so damn hard to let the lawyer thing drop.'

'None of that matters,' says Alto, and means it. 'This does.'

'What are you going to do?'

'I'm going to help McAvoy.'

Redding considers him. 'You're taking him into the lion's den,' he says, shaking his head. 'The old man will eat him alive.'

Alto gives a little shrug. 'He might not. You haven't seen him – the way he affects people. It's creepy but in the right way. And what has the old man got to threaten me with anyway? I'm here now. Homicide was long ago. And more than anything else, McAvoy would take the risk. Even if I gave him the option, he'd choose what has to be done.'

'Sounds like you're falling for him,' says Redding, trying to lighten the mood.

'I'd rather know him than be him,' says Alto, with feeling. 'Besides, I'm helping ensure he has a genuine New York tourist experience.'

'With the head of the Mob?'

'It will make an anecdote when he gets home.'

'*If* he gets home.'

'Don't be a buzz-kill,' says Alto, picking up the phone. 'Now, let's shake the tree . . .'

17

Two naked men are hanging from a hook in the ceiling of a dark, dirty cellar on North 6th Street, Brooklyn. They share a pair of handcuffs and the short metal chain that connects them looks shiny and new against the rust and blackness of the unyielding metal. The cuffs are biting into the men's skin; slowly chewing through tissue as their own body weight acts against them. They are perhaps four feet off the floor. One of the men is dead. The other is watching his own blood puddle on the floor beneath him. The blue tattoos on his legs are almost completely obscured with blood and each time his heart beats, a fresh gout of crimson erupts from the wounds in his knee and shoulder.

'Time's marching on,' says Claudio ruefully. He's catching his breath, one hand pressed against the dusty grey wall of the basement. He raises his other hand and wipes the sweat from his forehead onto the back of his brown calfskin gloves; staining the leather a darker shade.

'That's it,' says the man, through gritted teeth. 'That's all. I swear. Christ, I swear.'

Claudio turns to him and gives a little nod of thanks. The living man is called Igor Zavarov, though his friends call him Zav. As of twenty minutes ago, those friends are one fewer in number. The man who hangs beside Zav was called Viktor. He and Zav have been friends for years. Came to America within weeks of one another. Have drunk and danced and fucked and killed together. And Viktor's last, blood-speckled breath is slowly drying on Zav's face.

'I hope you don't think I'm a cruel man,' says Claudio, and it occurs to him how true the sentence is. 'I don't like doing this. I don't believe that pain is worse than death. If I have to kill you, I kill you. That's how it works. But these are changing times. I never thought your people and mine would end up such good friends. When I was a boy, my mother used to say that the Italians are givers and the Russians are takers. I know you're not Russian, not strictly speaking, but that's all politics and it's not my area.'

Zav lets rip with a stream of curses in his native tongue. Claudio grimaces at the ferocity of the attack.

'I needed to be sure,' says Claudio, as if his prisoner had not spoken. 'It's hard to believe what a person tells you unless they're bleeding when they say it, but I can't spend my whole life making people bleed.'

Claudio looks down at the cement floor of the basement. Whoever built the place did a poor job and there are patches where the cement was disturbed before it dried.

'There will be consequences,' says Claudio to himself. 'My employers asked me to kill those Irish boys and they knew I wouldn't ask why. But, like I just spent a pleasant few hours explaining, what we didn't know was what your boy was doing there. Was Luca a target? Was this a hit? Was I being set up and if I was, what the fuck for? I tell you something, you've blown my mind with the shit you've spilled. I'm grateful.'

Claudio wishes he were at home. He would probably have let Belle stay home from school today. He would be reading to her right now, or listening to her read to him. He'd have made her a sandwich with wholemeal bread and she would have spilled her milk as she placed it back on the coffee table too heavily. She would smell of toothpaste and orange juice and she would be pressing her brown fingers against his face and trying to shape his features into something less fearsome.

The details that Zav provided are written on a scrap of paper in the pocket of Claudio's brown suede coat. He could have found the lawyer's address with a phone call home but Zav had spat it out among the safe-house and stash-house locations that he had wept and bled onto the floor. When he has memorised them all, Claudio will eat the paper. He has been doing this his whole life. One day, he expects to shit a telephone directory.

'You can't tell them,' says Zav, gasping. 'Please. You can't say I talked.'

Claudio gives a warm smile. 'You've nothing to be ashamed of, my friend. You're dying. You need medical care. Anybody in your position would have done the same. Not your friend, of course – he chose to die rather than tell me what your boy was doing in that trunk. But you're a pragmatist. I'm sure Sergey will see that.'

Zav gives in to sobs and Claudio feels an urge to put him out of his misery. He has the weapon for it. It was a present from his father and it has never been far from Claudio's grasp. He feels its pleasing weight against his shin. It's a beautiful item. A 'misericorde', they'd said, in the antique shop when he had it valued to satisfy his own curiosity. It is a small dagger with a thin blade and the handle is decorated with the faces of pagan gods; a collage of piercing eyes and twisted mouths. It is a weapon of mercy, carried on the battle-field in more noble times, used to deliver the death-strike to a fallen enemy. Claudio has used it often. He has grown adept at sliding the point into the base of the skull and extinguishing life as if turning a key in a lock. While he has never felt any emotional attachment to the guns he has used in his career, he cannot imagine being parted from the blade. It has witnessed much.

As he watches the heavy-set man swing in the darkness and listens to the sound of the tendons and joints in his elbow beginning to creak, Claudio finds himself oddly unsettled. The image he glimpsed on the computer has brought back memories he has never allowed himself to examine properly before. Claudio is not a man troubled by guilt or regret but he has never felt good about the death of Sal Pugliesca all those years before. He and Sal had a respect for one another. While Sal was a great man's son and destined to become a boss before his thirtieth birthday, Claudio's own lineage was less celebrated. His father wasn't cut out to be a member of a street crew. He had no mean streak. He hated bullies. He couldn't take pincers to a finger joint or a blowtorch to an eye. But he could kill, quickly and efficiently, if the situation called for it. That was the job he did for Angelo Bruno and the Philadelphia Mob for the best part of thirty years. Claudio was a willing and enthusiastic apprentice. He had no desire to make collections or strong-arm shopkeepers into handing over protection payments. He was a good killer. Quiet, methodical and precise. By the time of the Mob wars, Claudio was very much in demand. He never asked questions. Nor did he worry overmuch about loyalty. He did what had to be done. Provided his actions were sanctioned by Philadelphia, he was free to take whatever job he was offered. In January 1981 he detonated the bomb that turned Salvatore Pugliesca into so much meat and grit. The blast killed Sal's friend, too. The dummy who trotted around after Sal like a lapdog and who Sal never tired of pushing around. What was his name? Claudio struggles to remember. He has never liked bringing the dummy to mind. He can picture him now, half dead on the floor of the kitchen; most of his body trapped beneath bricks and wood and falling masonry. He had a cleaver. God only knew where he had picked the thing up. And he was bringing the blade down on his mangled skin like a coyote trying to chew off its own trapped leg.

Claudio showed mercy. He kneeled atop the dummy and watched as his lips moved soundlessly and his eyes sought out something only he could see.

Claudio slipped the blade into the back of the dummy's skull and watched the light go out in his eyes. He can still picture his face; trapped there, in an expression of mild disappointment, as if somebody had prematurely ended the game.

'You should never dwell on the past,' says Claudio conversationally. 'It can lead to madness. I blame you for all this nostalgia. That picture. The priest. *Madonna*, but that brought back some memories. You've got me thinking and I don't know if that's wise.'

Leaning back against the wall, Claudio realises the truth of what he is saying. Life was tolerable a few days back. He had money. Had Belle. Had his reputation and he was pretty confident he was going to go to his grave without doing any more serious time. Then he got the call about the Irish boys. He had little time to react. He set up a pincer operation using the mean young fuck from upstate and trapped the Irishmen on a cold, snow-filled road that scythed into a forest the colour of tar. Then it all went wrong. The Chechen was in the trunk, angry and bleeding and desperate for blood. When the violence began, he ran. So did the big dumb boxer. It all turned to shit and the Chechen ended up impaling a made man on a tree. Claudio is pretty sure he understands what went down in the woods. But the information he has discovered has started eating away at him. The lawyer. The priest. The face from before. His job was to find out why the Chechen was in the trunk. But he suddenly feels an urge to dig deeper – to dig into the events of his own past. He's earned the right to ask a few more questions. Idly, he wonders about the resale value of his information and just how best to profit from telling his Mob associates that the Chechens have been infiltrated by a pretty, hard-faced bitch with purple hair. Claudio feels a little maudlin. This building is only a short walk from the river and he feels an overwhelming urge to go and stare at the waters and hear the traffic trundling across Williamsburg Bridge. He hopes the sound of the gulls and the tankers and the endless procession of wheels will drown out the sound of his own thoughts. Because despite himself, Claudio is putting the pieces together. He is thinking about a fat lawyer and a priest with the voice of a serpent; whispering in quiet corners as the sun shone through stained glass and pitched blue light onto their faces.

Without intending to, Claudio has removed the small leather bag from around his neck. To still be in possession of it breaks many of his own rules, but he does not seem to be able to bring himself to part with it. The pouch is made of soft leather, like Claudio's gloves, and hangs from a length of cord. Several nights ago, Claudio took it from the pocket of Brishen Ayres's coat. While he was happy to ditch the Irishman's wallet, keys and cell phone, Claudio was unable to toss the pouch in the East River along with the rest of the poor bastard's possessions. Claudio made the mistake of looking inside. And what he found had shaken him. He had not seen its like since he was a boy. He had no doubt that what the bag contained was a part of a person; an object fashioned like a lace handkerchief but made up of human tissue.

Claudio takes his hands out of his gloves and slides two digits into the warm silkiness of the bag. He has to suppress a shudder as he traces his calloused fingertips against the delicate mesh. Touching it makes him want to genuflect and he finds himself crossing himself repeatedly, as if seeking the strength to put the strangely powerful object away. He gives himself a little shake, insisting he keep his eye on the job. He is a weapon: a blade wielded by more powerful men. To overthink it can lead to madness. He puts the pouch back around his neck and wonders whose face he is wearing beside his heart.

'I'm going to say ciao,' mutters Claudio. 'I think you'll survive this. What you do with the rest of your life is up to you. I'm not sure your boss will welcome you back. I'd go to the cops if I were you. But I'm not, so I can't offer much better advice.'

Claudio makes a neat pile of the Chechens' clothes and pulls a small tin of lighter fluid from his back pocket. He gives a generous squirt and tosses a lit match onto the pile. He has taken both men's wallets, phones and jewellery.

'Please,' says Zav, wriggling as the light of the flames casts flickering shadows on his bare torso. 'I can't burn. I can't!'

'You don't need to,' says Claudio warmly.

'The key. Please. Get me down!'

Claudio walks to the stairs and pauses with one hand on the wooden rail. He knows that he is only a dozen steps from another world, where cars cruise slowly down icy streets beneath a sky full of snow. Here, just a flight below the level of the road, a man is in hell. Claudio does not like such thoughts. They make him wonder why he has never thought them before.

'Zav, I know you're a bright boy. You'll work this out. You can get free if you really want to.'

The island of flame seems to grow as Claudio watches Zav fight with his mounting terror. Claudio feels a moment's pity and decides to make it easier for him. He nods at the corpse that hangs next to Zav.

'Bite his arm off. Then walk out the door.'

Zav's mouth drops open and the light of the flames dances on his tongue. Claudio is gone before the bellow of horror and rage can reach his ears.

'. . . a detective from England. Well, Scotland, actually. Investigating the killing of an Irishman. In America. I know, I know, it's very multicultural. Might I ask, am I right in thinking you're Mr Molony?'

Molony? That's who's been sitting here? Sitting here talking all that shite about idolatry and repentance and the good deeds that extinguish the burning in the soul. That voice. That whining monotone, page after page, psalm after psalm, Scripture after Scripture . . .

'Might I see your warrant card, Sergeant? I do believe it would serve as much purpose as a MetroCard in terms of your authority to make enquiries in the US, but that is not a matter of any concern to me. Of course, I should be delighted to assist. McAvoy, you say. An Irish name. County Wexford, if I'm not mistaken.'

'You're a student of Irish history?'

'I'm a student of all things, Detective Sergeant. I am a great believer in the importance of continually expanding one's mind.'

Prick! Fucking slimy prick! Hit him, McAvoy. He answers better when you hurt him.

'That's a nasty bruise, Mr Molony. Have you been in the wars?'

'The curse of growing old, Sergeant. I missed my footing and took a tumble.'

'It's kind of you to spend this time with Brishen. Am I right in thinking you met at St Colman's?'

'Indeed. St Colman's has an excellent relationship with the community in Galway of which Mr Ayres is such an important part. He came to light a candle in honour of my friend Father Whelan, who, as I'm sure you are aware, was once a young pastor at the church where I am so honoured to be sacristan. We shared a brief moment of pleasantries and then he and his friend expressed a wish to see the almost-as-splendid St Brigit's, so I showed them the way. The next I heard was that they had met with tragedy. I felt compelled to sit at his bedside and try to bring some comfort.'

Lying bastard. Lying bastard!

'Am I right in thinking you're also a lawyer?'

'Of sorts. I am not a regular in courtrooms but I represent clients whose situations are not always as straightforward as the world would like them to be.'

'Very cryptic. Could you elaborate?'

'Forgive me, Detective, but I wonder whether you have considered the consequences of poking around in a strange country into things that are so very complex. If we were to consider poor Brishen here as an example – his handsome face has been butchered. The lesson would seem clear: some things are best left alone.'

I can hear the copper breathing. He sounds like a big guy. Lungs like a bear. He's leaning over me. I can feel him. Fuck, Brish, wake up. Wake up and tell him what this lying bastard did to you . . .

'I'm here to try to find a young man who was an associate of Brishen and Shay Helden. Valentine Teague. Does the name mean anything to you?'

It does to me! Punch that could shatter your chin but no fucking discipline. No self-control . . .

'I'm afraid not, though I recognise the name. I believe the Teagues are Travellers, as you would call them.'

'Yes. My wife was a Teague, before we married.'

'A Traveller married to a policeman? How delightful.'

That fella! Roisin's man. Valentine's brother-in-law. Took Giuseppe Hamer down like he were made of bread. Fuck, they've sent the cavalry. Wake up, Brish, this one might actually listen . . .

'We're very concerned for Valentine. Look at this picture. Do you recognise him?'

'He has your colouring, Sergeant. But fewer scars.'

'Do you know him?'

'I have not had the pleasure.'

'Might I ask what chapters you are reading to Brishen?'

'I allow the Lord to open the pages at random. He selects what Brishen most needs.'

'And today?'

'I believe this is a private communion, Sergeant McAvoy. You will forgive me if I do not feel compelled to share it with a stranger, however well intentioned he may be.'

Movement. The sound of rustling fabric and the sudden smell of crushed flowers and damp earth.

'Don't go on my account, Mr Molony. I came to see Brishen. I had planned to call at your office to ask you a few questions . . .'

'I work from my home, and I do not enjoy visitors. I apologise if this seems rude but I have learned to enjoy solitude.'

'So when can I see you for a proper discussion?'

'I think it would be best if you did not.'

'Best for whom?'

'Whom? How delightful. Now, if you'll excuse me.'

'Why are you being so evasive?'

'The police and I have differing views. I do not wish to go into any more details.'

Don't let him go, big man. Drag him down to the ground by his fecking jaw.

'I'm here on behalf of friends and family in Galway. Friends and family who are being sustained during this difficult time by Father Whelan – your friend. I would not wish for news to reach him that you are being so obtuse.'

'Goodbye, Sergeant. Do give my regards to your delightful Traveller girl.'

He's gone. The smell's fading. I can hear the temper coming off the Scotsman. He's looking down at me and shaking his head. Muttering, muttering . . .

'What did you learn, Brishen? Why did you need to get out of the city so fast? Where were you going?'

I want to wake up, big man. Christ, I do. I want to tell you the lot. But I'm just a dream, floating between places; a fog of half-remembered things and whispers that cannot be real. I remember arms growing cold against my skin; the taste of dust and dirt and something sour. And the ground shifting: fissures opening up at my ankles as they broke with the shifting ground . . .

'Aector. You didn't listen. You're supposed to be gone.'

Another man. Local, from the sound of him. Smells of last night's whiskey and expensive aftershave.

'Ronny. I couldn't.'

'Shall we talk?'

'Here?'

'No. We don't know what he can hear.'

'You think he can hear anything?'

I can! I fecking can!

'You're redder than usual. You okay?'

McAvoy presses the can of Coke to his forehead and imagines the contents starting to bubble, spit and steam. Molony has angered him. He kept giving little twitches with his nose, as if trying to reposition a pair of spectacles without using his hands. He looked as though he could smell something faintly distasteful.

'Molony,' says McAvoy. 'He spoke to me like I was a fool.'

'He's a lawyer. That's what they're good at.'

'But he had no need to be that way. And why was he even here?' McAvoy considers Alto. 'He looked ill. That yellow look to him. There was a smell coming off him I can't place.' He stops talking and looks at Alto. 'What are you doing here anyway?'

Alto sips at his espresso. They have a seat by the window in the hospital cafeteria but neither man particularly wants the beverages or bag of potato chips on the plastic table in front of them. Outside, despite the hour, the sky is slowly darkening and it looks to McAvoy as if somebody is leaching the colour from the city with a straw.

'I didn't feel I could let you go with so little reward,' says Alto, scratching his hairline. 'I understand that you didn't come here wanting to stir things up or cause trouble. New York must seem like a different world to you. Maybe I'm being naïve here but I get the sense that in your world, you know who the villains are and who the good people are and the villains go to jail.'

McAvoy looks at him with the tiniest flicker of contempt. 'You think that, huh? Believe me, no one place is more rotten than the next. Some places are just bigger.'

Alto is not really listening; stirring a second sugar into his drink. 'You don't think about it,' he says, more to himself. 'Cops, I mean. Cops here. You get used to how things are and then you just become a part of it. It's only when you have to explain it to somebody else you realise how bad it all is.'

'How bad what is?'

'All this,' says Alto bleakly, gesturing with his spoon. 'You tell yourself that if you catch enough bad guys then the streets will be safer but that's so much bullshit. I'm a garbage man but I can only pick up the shit that falls out the top of the trash cans. I can't rummage all the way to the bottom because the stench is too goddamn strong.'

McAvoy considers his companion. Alto looks energised but tired; as if somebody were running a battery through a corpse.

'What is it you want me to know?' asks McAvoy gently.

'The Feds are all about headlines,' says Alto, through a sigh. 'They want to bring down the people that voters have heard of. They want seizures worth a hundred million. They want to be able to say they've smashed a cartel or brought down a corrupt senator, rescued a hostage or saved a little girl's life.'

McAvoy nods. He understands. He's familiar with the same pressures.

'They don't give a damn about Brishen and Helden and it's not their responsibility. It's not even mine. It's a case for the upstate police and they've been told to give it to me and back off. Some of the suits think the Chechens are making a move on the Italians. The rest think it's the other way around. There are some who think the Irishmen were connected to the Boston Mob and that we've got some sort of three-way to look forward to. Then there's the other theory: this was all a gigantic fuck-up and everybody involved is trying to find out if they're being messed with. In among all that, the lives and deaths of the Irish boys kind of get forgotten. Every department head is trying to use the escalation of events as an excuse to get more budget and resources for their departments. That's what this is to the people who authorise the overtime – an opportunity to further their own agenda. Nobody really wants to know what happened to the Irishmen, Aector. Just you.'

'And you too,' says McAvoy hopefully.

Alto smiles ruefully, and finishes his coffee. 'Everything will change inside the next twenty-four hours. Now word is spreading about Luca Savoca's body being found this is all most definitely a Federal case and it will be folded into their investigation into organised crime. Chances are that the Italians will have known for the last two weeks that their boy is dead but now it's common knowledge they can't be seen to do nothing. Things will have been set in motion. They'll already be asking questions in their own way. It's about to get very loud. You don't have long.'

'Long for what?'

'To find out what actually happened before the powers that be concoct a lie that everybody can live with.' Alto sighs, unsure where to start. 'We all tell lies, Aector. That's part of our job. We tell little ones and big ones and they fold into one another and overlap and nobody ever knows the whole truth. I sometimes don't know when I'm keeping a secret. I was asked to assist the Feds on their Chechen investigation because I have some associates who can help. I was asked to look after you because when I'm not drinking I can be relied upon not to cause any trouble. But since you arrived, I swear, my reflection seems to keep telling me that I've got a chance to do something good. There are things you need to know.'

'I don't understand . . .'

'Read this,' says Alto, and he passes a manila folder across the table. 'This is the investigation that got me transferred. The one that was shut down the second I found anything interesting. I wasn't sure it mattered. Now I think it does. Here's the inside track on your new friend, Mr Molony.'

McAvoy does as he is told. He opens the file and acquaints himself with the man who has been sitting praying at Brishen Ayres's bedside, and who has made McAvoy's spine twitch in frustration.

McAvoy looks up, eyes wide. 'He trained as a priest?'

'Thrown out, but ask me why and I'll tell you to spend ten years caught up in legal wrangling, because that's what it would take to get the seminary to open its files.'

'And this offence . . . ?'

Alto nods. 'In 1973. He was arrested for the attempted abduction of an eight-year-old boy from Yonkers. He'd been playing with his friends and Molony started talking to them. Asked them about whether they were good children or bad children. Told them if they were good they would get candy. This little boy, he wanted candy. Went off with him and didn't come home. Molony was caught with him in the back room of a Bible wholesalers in Tribeca. Said he wanted to read the Scriptures together. Case was dropped when the little boy's family encouraged him to withdraw his statement. Molony was still a seminarian at the time. It wouldn't be a leap to suggest the Church leaned on them.'

'This is why he was kicked out?'

'Not long after that he was back living with Mother. Worked in soup kitchens. Joined Catholic charities that would have him. Took a beating that could have killed him. But this lost lamb was picked up by a shepherd. Somebody helped him find a job and find a better use for his brain. Started him on a different road. He never fell out of love with the Church.'

McAvoy purses his lips and stares at the words on the page. He scans the text but finds no physical evidence or witness testimony. 'Do you think he did anything to the boy? Really? I mean, a mistake could be forgiven . . .'

'Absolutely.' Alto nods. 'I'm not huge on forgiveness but I'll accept that he may have done a terrible thing and felt bad enough about it not to do it again. But take a look at what happened to him in 1974.'

McAvoy turns the page. His face falls.

'The ambulance was called by his mother, with whom he was living at that time. She found him in the bathtub. He'd castrated himself. Nearly died from blood loss.'

'There's a statement here. From his mother.'

'Yep. Says that her son had run himself a bath after having been out with his friend Jimmy. Jimmy had said his goodbyes and her boy went about his ablutions.'

'But there's no statement from Jimmy?'

'No. And in the statement that Molony made before he was discharged from hospital, he didn't mention him either. It was only in the psych report that the name came up again.'

'Psych report?'

'Standard practice. You can't just be stitched up and sent home when you've cut your own balls off.'

'And you have the report?'

'I spent a lot of the department's money to get hold of this when I first got interested in him,' says Alto.

'That's what got your superiors asking questions?'

'I've had it in my drawer for a while,' says Alto, looking uncomfortable. 'It was compiled when he was allowed home.'

'Home from?' asks McAvoy.

'A state facility,' says Alto, looking at the backs of his hands. 'I'm sure it was luxury compared to the seminary. Either way, he said that his visits from Jimmy had helped him a lot.'

McAvoy presses the warm can to his head and closes his eyes. 'They've still got visitor records, haven't they? You're going to tell me that Jimmy was James Whelan.'

Alto smiles. 'I am. Father Whelan, then and now. A regular visitor, like you say. But he wasn't just there for Molony.'

'No?'

'You remember we spoke about Paulie Pugliesca? The guy whose son was blown up during the Mob wars in 1981?'

McAvoy nods. 'Salvatore was his son, yes? And his friend died too.'

'The friend was called Tony Blank.'

'Right,' says McAvoy, waiting for more. 'And?'

'And Tony was also a patient at St Loretta's. He was there at the same time as Molony.'

McAvoy considers this, looking for connections. 'So, who's Tony Blank?'

'The godson of Pugliesca.'

'So he's Mafia too?'

Alto produces a piece of paper from a back pocket and hands it to McAvoy as if he is performing a magic trick. It shows the front page of the *Cleveland Plain Dealer*, dated March 1961. The picture is pixelated and hard to make out but there is no mistaking the shape of two human corpses beneath white blankets. Nor can McAvoy take his eyes off the wide, staring eyes of the five-year-old boy being carried from the scene in the arms of a tall police officer, clad in black. The eyes look as though they have watched another person's nightmares.

'This is Tony Blank. He saw it,' says Alto. 'Everything they did to his mother and father.'

McAvoy screws up his face, wishing he were making notes. His head is spinning.

'Somebody killed his parents.'

'And he saw it all.'

'Who did it?'

'Nobody was ever charged. But he was released into the care of his godfather.'

'Paulie Pugliesca?'

'The same.'

'So when Salvatore was killed, it was like Pugliesca lost two sons.'

'I doubt that. I don't think the old man ever did particularly right by the boy. He had him put away without much of a fight – the sort of institution you have nightmares about. He went back to Pugliesca in his teens and things seem to have been happy enough for a couple of years. But Tony ended up at St Loretta's when he attacked a dental assistant during a check-up. Bit two of her fingers off when she pressed on his gums. Pugliesca no doubt used some influence to ensure he went into a facility rather than a prison. Either way he was sent to St Loretta's, which was a holiday home compared to where he'd been before. Molony was there at the same time, for eight months between '74 and '75. St Loretta's had a connection with the Church. They had techniques for helping people deal with their urges, though I think he'd kind of taken care of that himself.'

Alto stops and gives McAvoy an appraising glance. 'I don't know what he'll make of you.'

'Molony? He didn't think much of me at all.'

'No, the old man. Pugliesca.'

'What? What do you mean?'

'He's been asking questions. Doesn't know what to believe. Mean old bastard needs to have his mind put at ease and in this particular matter, you represent the Irish involvement. You're Valentine's family. It can't hurt to answer a question or two and ask some of our own. Finish your drink. Straighten your collar. He likes us smart.'

'Ronny, I don't . . .'

'His driver's outside.'

19

The discovery of Luca Savoca's body is the second item on the news website that Alto shoves under McAvoy's nose as they climb from the back of the Lexus. The press conference trumpeting Murray Ellison's arrest is first.

'Don't start thinking that Luca's father has just found out,' warns Ronny. 'He'll have known about this long before we did.'

McAvoy says nothing. He doesn't want to be here. Doesn't know what to say. They're back on Mulberry Street, Little Italy. The Christmas lights are red and green and white and they sway on a rapidly increasing breeze, sending gaudy shadows across the restaurant awnings and shop fronts and chinking against the walls of the tall buildings. It has begun to snow and only the most hardcore smokers sit outside the oyster bar opposite where Ronny, McAvoy and a fat man who declined to introduce himself now stand. It's only a little after lunchtime but the sky is so dark it could be midnight.

'They barely mention the Irish boys in the article,' says Ronny, taking his phone back. 'Just a passing sentence. Now it's a gangland thing, that's how it will stay.'

McAvoy tries to digest the information. His head is spinning. The bulletin spoke of how a rising star in a ruthless crime family had been found impaled on a tree in woodland in upstate New York. The rest is speculation and a collection of anodyne comments from the authorities. McAvoy ran out of enthusiasm to read on around the time the journalist who wrote it ran out of things to say: padding out the rest of the piece with bland information on the area where Luca Savoca was found. There's a quote from a local woman, saying she's never seen so many cops. 'This way,' says the driver, ushering McAvoy and Ronny through the side door of a pleasant-looking restaurant. 'Down the stairs.'

McAvoy fears that if he hesitates he will never pluck up the courage to get himself moving again, so he does not pause. He follows Alto down a wide, dog-leg staircase. Pictures of the Roman Coliseum and the Trevi Fountain stare down from butter-coloured walls.

They emerge in a large function room. It's a tasteful space with a high ceiling and round wooden tables and chairs. A bar runs the full length of one wall, stocked with a dazzling array of spirits. Large Art Deco adverts for Italian staples like limoncello and Vespas take up the space between the tops of the crushed red velvet booths and the wooden panels in the ceiling. Busts of various Roman emperors scowl out from the alcoves, garlanded with laurel wreaths and Italian flags.

There are three men in the restaurant. Two are seated together at a round table beneath a black and white image of a large tenor, caught in full operatic warble. To their left is a bust of Caesar. The third man sits at the bar sipping water.

'Go on, they don't bite.'

McAvoy's footsteps sound loud in the silence of the almost-empty restaurant. He follows Ronny around the tables towards the two seated men. They come into focus as he does so.

Nicky Savoca and Paulie Pugliesca are the right age to be father and son, but the two most senior figures in their crime family share no physical similarities. Old man Pugliesca lives up to his moniker. He looks as though he has spent every day of his eighty years engaged in a fight with enemies only marginally less tough than himself. He is a small man, and in a different life his features may have been thought of as delicate. Originally, he had high cheekbones and an aquiline nose; a slender jaw and dainty fingers. Now he looks the way a mannequin would look after being hit with a hammer for a few days. What's left of his hair is slicked back from his head and pushed behind ears that both carry hearing aids. He's wearing a black sweater over a button-down shirt. A pair of spectacles hang on a chain around his neck. He is staring intently at something on the table in front of him, his hands busy. It looks as though he is doing a jigsaw puzzle.

Beside him, Nicky Savoca looks huge. He's pushing 300 pounds and his jowelly face looks like orange peel. His hair is dyed the same black as his leather jacket. He's sipping from a crystal glass half full of amber liquid. A long, thin cigarette is burning in the ashtray at his elbow.

McAvoy operates without thinking. He offers a smile and his hand. 'Mr Savoca. I'm so dreadfully sorry about your son.'

Savoca looks up into McAvoy's eyes with a fierceness that could shatter glass. For a moment he does nothing. Just stares into him, hard. McAvoy feels as though the inside of his skull is being stirred with a finger. Then Savoca extends his hand and takes McAvoy's. The grip is strong; the flesh warm.

'I appreciate that,' says Savoca, still looking hard at McAvoy. 'You're the first cop to say that.'

McAvoy senses Ronny shuffle beside him. 'We appreciate you giving this time,' he says.

Pugliesca raises his head from the task that has been distracting him. He squints at McAvoy, then Alto.

'Fucking phones,' he says, nodding at the shattered cell phone in front of him. 'Used to be that when you threw a phone at the wall, you bought another fucking phone. Now it's all so complicated. I've never liked the damn things but you have to move with the times, or at least, that's what they tell me.'

'I think that one's broken, Mr Pugliesca,' says Alto tactfully.

Pugliesca sucks on his lower lip. 'I think you're right. But I'm enjoying thinking I'm fixing it. This one belongs to a friend of a friend. It wasn't mine to break. At least when he gets it back, he'll know I tried. I don't want to use my own phone. I got a sense people are listening.'

'That's kind,' says McAvoy.

Pugliesca swivels his eyes from Alto to McAvoy. 'You look like fucking Shrek. Sound like him too. I'll be guessing you're the Scotsman.'

'I am.'

'And your new best friend here says that if we give you a little of our time, you can vouch for the Irishmen.'

'That's the hope,' says McAvoy.

Pugliesca looks at his number two. 'You hear that, Nicky? That's the hope.'

'I'm full of hope,' says Savoca, taking a drag on his cigarette. 'Hope sustains me.'

'Faith, hope and charity,' says Pugliesca thoughtfully. 'It's how I try to live my life.'

'There are worse ways,' says McAvoy, forcing himself not to look away.

'Sit down,' says Savoca, pushing a chair across with his boot. 'You too, Ronny.'

McAvoy lowers himself onto the wooden chair. Alto does the same.

'Drink?'

'I'm fine,' says McAvoy.

'You're not. Drink?'

'I'll take a Coke,' says McAvoy.

'You won't,' says Savoca. He speaks to the man at the bar without looking at him. 'Vinny. Get our friends here something they'll like.'

At the table, Pugliesca has returned to his task, trying to fit tiny fragments of glass back into the smashed screen. It is clear that it is his consigliere who will be doing the talking.

'The press have it,' says Alto. 'You're going to be in the eye of the storm for a while. They'll be digging things up, pulling things out of the archives. I'm sorry.'

'I bet you fucking are,' says Savoca.

McAvoy considers the large man. McAvoy has known many grieving parents. He knows the taste of the air in the rooms where they mourn, has grown accustomed to that numbness, that stillness, which comes over men and women whose loved ones have been taken before their time. He catches a whiff of that in the man before him. He does not strike McAvoy as the sort who will give in to tears but there is no doubt that this is a man who is gripped by pain. He would die before letting it consume him.

'I don't want to make you any false promises,' says McAvoy quietly. 'I'm a visitor here. I'm not particularly welcome and I'm horribly out of my depth. I'm looking for a family member who has got caught up in something much bigger than him or me. It seems we're all as confused as one another about what happened out in the woods but I can promise you that as far as anybody back home is aware, the lads came out here for a boxing try-out. Somehow, they got caught up in an underground bout and that led to blood. People are keeping a lot of secrets and I can't go home without knowing the truth . . .'

'He always talk like this?' Savoca asks Alto. 'Why you think you're here, you prick? You're here to make a promise, that's all. A promise that whatever you find out, if you find out anything at all, you tell it to Ronny here before anybody else. We've got people asking our own questions. I just wanted you to know how things work, and Ronny here said you were a man with talents. Talents should be rewarded. And it would take a talented man to find out anything I don't already know. So, if you get the opportunity to impress me, don't think it would go unrewarded.'

A glass of rust-coloured liquid is placed in front of McAvoy; a beer with a foaming top in front of Alto. 'Thank you,' says McAvoy automatically, and the corner of Savoca's mouth twitches.

'You seem all right,' says Savoca, and he takes his glass and raises it in McAvoy's direction.

McAvoy takes a sip of his own drink. It's a bourbon, but tastes sufficiently of toffee apples for him not to shudder. He looks at Alto, who is studying a poster on the far wall: a curvy dark-haired woman on a Vespa, grinning as she glides past a group of wolf-whistling men.

'I don't think we should talk like that,' says McAvoy quietly. 'I don't really like it.'

'You don't?' Savoca grins.

'No. That's not a conversation we ever need to have again.'

Savoca glares into McAvoy's eyes. McAvoy refuses to look away. His pulse is racing and there is sweat soaking into his clothes but his glare is a statue's and Savoca is the one who nods, blinks, and settles back in his chair.

'Valentine Teague,' says McAvoy, a little breathlessly. As he reaches into his pocket, he notices Savoca give the tiniest of hand gestures, telling Vinny to stand easy. McAvoy tries not to blush or get himself flustered as he shows him the picture. 'This is the man I'm looking for. He came here with Brishen Ayres and Shay Helden. Different flight but it seems they were due to meet up. At some point, there was an underground boxing bout. The following day, Brishen and Helden stole a car and headed upstate. They were found soon after. Brishen is still in a coma. Somebody put his nose in his pocket around the time they shot him in the head. Your son was found not very far away. You can understand why I need to ask some questions.'

Savoca looks right through him. 'You're saying my boy was with them? Or are you saying he did this to them?'

'Yeah, Shrek, what is it you're saying?' asks Pugliesca, not looking up.

'I'm not saying. I'm asking. I'm asking if you know Valentine. Because if he was involved in something that led to the death of your son, it's possible that you discovered that information before anybody else did. And perhaps . . .'

'Perhaps what?'

McAvoy leaves it there. In his chest, his heart feels as though it is three times too large.

Savoca sucks his cheek, staring at McAvoy. 'Perhaps I found the motherfucker and fed him to the dogs, is that what you're asking me?'

McAvoy stays silent. Takes another sip of his drink.

After a moment, Savoca turns to Alto and nods in McAvoy's direction. 'You believe this guy? You believe the balls on him?'

'It's a question you'll be asked by the Feds,' says Alto soothingly. 'They'll ask it soon.'

'But I won't be fucking answering,' says Savoca, his voice rising. 'Do you know how long the Feds have had a hard-on for me, Ronny? You know how many hoops they have to jump through just to get a minute of my time? Do you know how many lawyers I have at work keeping them from messing with me? Do you know how fucking excited they are that they've got a reason to get close to me now? Using my own dead son against me? Those fucking mutts!'

Savoca's hand comes down hard on the table. McAvoy glances at Pugliesca. The old man picked up the broken pieces of cell phone the moment his associate's voice started to rise. He places it back on the tablecloth and continues with his work.

'Why did you agree to speak to us?' asks McAvoy.

'Ronny and me go back,' says Savoca, running his hand through his hair and moving himself in a way that suggests he is trying to rein in his temper. 'When he was in Homicide South we came to an agreement. If he wanted to talk to me, I'd talk to him, so long as he never came to the house or made me look like a fucking idiot in front of the people who matter to me. He kept the shit from my doorstep and I respect him for that – even if he did get a little fucking impolite towards the end. It's been a while, though, Ronny. And favours don't last for ever.'

McAvoy turns to Alto. He wonders how much more Alto has to tell him. How many secrets his brain holds.

'So . . .' begins McAvoy.

'I ain't heard of no Valentine Teague,' says Savoca, slowly and clearly. 'Unless Teague is some Chechen name I ain't familiar with, I don't know shit about him.'

'You believe this was the Chechens?' asks McAvoy. 'Chechens killed Shay? Killed your son?'

'Who the fuck else? I knew them bastards wasn't to be trusted. They got us cosy and now they're sending a message. We should never have showed weakness!'

Pugliesca raises his head and looks at his associate. 'Finish your drink, Nicky. Calm yourself.'

'Sorry, Paulie,' says Savoca, breathing hard. 'I'm all wound up.'

'Of course you are, my friend. But these gentlemen might start to feel uncomfortable.'

'You're safe to say what you like,' says Alto. 'McAvoy has no authority. And anything you say to me is unofficial.'

'Safe?' asks Pugliesca, and his voice is suddenly ice. 'I don't believe my safety is something that rests in your hands, Ronny. I don't wake in the morning hoping to God that some detective from the Seventh will be there to make sure nothing bad happens to me.'

'I didn't mean to offend . . .'

'But you managed it anyways.'

McAvoy throws himself into the awkward silence by putting his drink down too heavily on the table and spilling a splash of his drink.

'Fucking klutz,' says Savoca, checking his clothes for splashes but looking at McAvoy for just long enough to betray a modicum of respect for the interruption.

'I'm so sorry,' says McAvoy, dabbing at the tablecloth. 'Was that expensive?'

'Everything worth having is expensive,' says Pugliesca, turning away from Alto and considering McAvoy as if for the first time. 'People talk about the simple things in life being what matters. Family. Peace. Love. I've lost all of that and the only thing I have to keep me warm at night is money. But if you've got enough money, you can be warmer than you ever thought a man could be.'

McAvoy holds the old man's gaze. 'You lost your son,' he says softly. 'Salvatore.'

Pugliesca waves a hand idly. 'There's not a day goes by I wouldn't change places with him. He was my eldest boy. A good boy. And those motherfuckers killed him to get to me. Turned that beautiful boy inside out. We couldn't even have an open casket. It destroyed his mother. His sisters too.'

McAvoy scratches the back of his head. He realises that the fear inside him is slowly dissipating. The more he feels like a policeman the less he feels like he is about to have his head blown off.

'It must be frustrating, knowing that nobody was ever caught,' says McAvoy.

Savoca gives a tiny bark of a laugh and Pugliesca's mouth splits in a grin. 'Nobody caught?'

'It remains an unsolved murder, is what I mean.'

'Maybe it does in your books,' says Savoca, hard. 'We have our own.'

McAvoy feels himself begin to colour. 'I understand there was another victim. Tony Blank.'

'The fucking dummy,' says Savoca dismissively. 'Creepy bastard.'

'Lay off,' says Pugliesca, snapping his head in Savoca's direction. 'He was my godson. He was Sal's friend. He was no dummy.'

'Kid didn't speak, Paulie.'

'Some people don't listen, Nicky. And they're a lot more of a dummy than somebody who keeps their mouth shut. The kid saw things. Things it's hard to come back from. He could have been okay.'

Savoca gives a little nod of his head. If he were a simian, he would be extending an upturned palm in supplication.

'There's not a lot of information about Tony,' says McAvoy.

'Draw a blank, did you?' asks Savoca, and laughs at his own joke.

'But I understand he spent some time in some specialist hospitals.'

'He was no retard,' says Pugliesca. He mimes slapping his own wrist, his smile a hard, humourless line. 'Oh, sorry, I know we're not allowed to say that word these days. He had problems. I did my best by him. But he was wired wrong. You know what happened to his parents?'

McAvoy doesn't know if it will help his own agenda in the slightest but is not about to start making enemies by telling the Mob boss that he's not interested. 'Tell me,' he says encouragingly.

Pugliesca shrugs. 'Jewish family. His dad was a friend of mine. We did some business together. He was a tough fuck. Didn't take shit. People believed he knew more than he did. They went to his house. Hung him from the light in his living room. Went to work on him with cleavers. He still didn't say shit. So they started on his wife. By then I think they'd forgotten what they were there for. Left Tony's father dead and his mother not so far off. They didn't know Tony was hiding in the crawl space under the house. He heard it all. Sat with his mother's corpse for three days before anybody raised the alarm. He didn't speak again after that.'

'But you took him in?'

'His dad was a friend.'

'He was your godson, you said.'

'Easiest way to describe it. His dad was a Jew, I'm Sicilian. Stuff gets lost in translation.'

'Tony and your son were close?'

'Sal loved him. I'm not saying he was always kind. Kids can be mean. But he saw him as a brother.'

'The bomb that killed them both . . .'

Pugliesca gives a tiny shake of his head. He doesn't want to think about it. 'Cowards,' he mutters. 'If Sal was gonna die he deserved to see it coming. And it was me they wanted. I said to them, go after me like a man, not my boys. They broke their word.'

McAvoy gives him a moment to compose himself before continuing to probe.

'The facility where he spent time. St Loretta's. There was another inmate. A Peter Molony. Mr Molony is sacristan of St Colman's Church and a close friend of Father Whelan, with whom I believe you are well acquainted, Mr Pugliesca.'

Savoca's body language changes. Pugliesca's does not.

'Ronny, what the fuck is this shit?' asks Savoca. 'Why's he asking this bullshit?'

Pugliesca has not taken his eyes off McAvoy. After a moment's pause, he lifts the cell phone and shakes all the fragments of broken glass back onto the pristine fabric.

'Father Whelan is a good man. He's from the neighbourhood. We go back a ways. This Molony? I don't know if I know the name. I wasn't around so much when Tony was away. I was doing time. But St Loretta's was better than where he'd been. He got better there. Got well enough to look after himself and breathe the air of a free man.'

'When you were in Rikers between 1988 and 1993, Father Whelan visited you once a year.'

'He's my priest.'

'He's Brishen's priest too. And he secured the letter that got Valentine Teague into the country.'

'He's a good man. Good men do the right thing.'

'And you're saying you don't know Molony?'

'You got something wrong with your ears?' asks Savoca, his whole tone and posture changing. His temper is a fiery thing.

'Why was Luca so far from home?' asks McAvoy, turning his attention to the bigger man. 'What was he doing in those woods?'

Savoca puts both hands on the table. He looks like he wants to push it over and smash McAvoy's head with his ashtray.

'I think that we'll leave it there,' says Alto, putting a hand on McAvoy's arm.

McAvoy does not move. Suddenly, he is sick of being lied to. He is sick of not understanding. He is far from home and feels completely adrift. What he wants more than anything else is to wrap his arms around Roisin and the children and tell them that everything's okay because he's home. And all that stands between this moment and the one he seeks is shaking some truths out of the mouths of accomplished liars.

'Somebody sent Luca to that little stretch of road,' says McAvoy, staring hard into Savoca's eyes. 'We know from ballistics that he fired his gun. He put a bullet in Brishen. He cut his nose off. He maybe even slid a short, sharp blade into the back of Shay Helden's head. And then somebody skewered him on a tree.'

Savoca turns to Pugliesca, his face red. 'Paulie, what the fuck?'

Pugliesca clears his throat. He has begun placing the pieces of glass back in the shattered screen. He does not look as though the outburst has affected his pulse.

'I think we've probably been about as helpful as we're going to be,' says Pugliesca slowly. 'Thank you for your time.'

McAvoy feels pressure on his arm as Alto begins to pull him upright. Half crouched, half standing, McAvoy's face betrays his frustration.

'You look uncertain, Shrek,' says Pugliesca. 'I understand that. You're struggling with a whole new set of ideals. You want things to make sense. You want answers. You probably want to go home.

The thing is, life isn't as neat as all that. Sometimes, things happen and there is no good explanation. In '96 I had the misfortune of spending eight months in a prison run by spics and blacks in California. Hell of a place. The Feds were fucking with me, working up some bullshit charge out of state so I would do time far away from my wife and girls. I did the time. There weren't many white faces down there. There were spic Nazis running the place. You believe that? Spic Nazis! And while I was inside, word came down that there was a contract out on me. You imagine that? You're living in hell, 120-degree heat, food that tastes like somebody's already eaten it, an hour's exercise in the fucking dog-run they call a yard. And now my life's in danger. So what do I do, Shrek? What's my solution? I ain't got no weapons. I ain't got no friends. All I got is my brains. So I keep my ears open. I learn who's going to do the hit. Do I whack him first? Shit, I can't get close. So I do the next best thing. I'm good with my hands. I can make anything. I can take an envelope and roll it tight and I can chew the gum from the flap and I can make a catapult hard as wood. I can unpick the elastic on my shorts and come up with a drawstring. I can whisper in the ear of low-life degenerates who will do anything to get their hands on a little meth. Which guards are dirty, which ones need a little pocket change. I find my guy. One of the guards opens the hatch to the guy's cell and tells me I have thirty seconds. And I take my shot. The inside of a bic goes through the grille and into his chest like a fucking arrow. And nobody fucked with me any more.'

McAvoy looks at the old man with the hearing aids and the glasses and wonders how much blood is on his hands. He looks as though he is floating in a wine vat full of it.

'You want me to know you're dangerous?' asks McAvoy. 'I already know that. What I want to know is what's between you and Father Whelan.'

'He's my friend. An old friend.'

'And I bet he knows all your secrets,' says McAvoy.

'I can think of no safer place for them,' says Pugliesca, and he drops his head back to the task at hand.

'That's your lot, Ronny,' says Savoca, nodding in the direction of the stairs.

'I'm sorry about all this,' says Alto, and it isn't clear to whom he's speaking.

McAvoy stands. His whole body is rigid and his hands are clenched. Alto has to tug at his sleeve before he starts to move. He crosses the restaurant, stamping towards the stairs. Before he leaves he glances back over his shoulder and catches a last glimpse of Savoca. He's staring into space, one eye closed in concentration.

'You're fucking dangerous,' whispers Alto as they climb the stairs and begin to accelerate. 'Fuck, we don't talk to them that way.'

'I was polite,' says McAvoy. And then, with a tiny smile, 'You should meet my boss.'

'She's tougher than you?'

'She's tougher than Pugliesca.' He stops, halfway up the stairs. 'You believe that, about the catapult?'

'Sure. It's one of the stories people tell about him. Why? You don't believe him?'

'How do you believe a liar about anything?' asks McAvoy.

'I'd love to visit your planet,' says Alto, shaking his head. 'Are they all like you?'

McAvoy smiles and breathes out; releasing a breath he has been holding for half an hour. 'No,' he says. 'Not a soul.'

'That's a relief.' Alto smiles. 'Anyways, how was all that for you? Feel like you've had a genuine New York moment?'

McAvoy says nothing for a while, chewing on his thoughts. He cocks his head at Alto. 'You're very cosy with them,' he says flatly. 'And he offered to reward me. Was that what you promised him? Is that what you think I am?'

They emerge onto the street and Alto leans back against the wall of the restaurant. His breath gathers on the grey air. 'No,' he says. 'Not for one second. But it makes him feel like a somebody to make those kind of offers and if playing to his ego gets us some of his time, I'm willing to use that. I've never taken a cent from him. For all his talk about our friendship, who do you think it was who leaned on the suits to get me sent back to the Seventh? The second I got close to anything useful, it didn't matter how respectful I'd been.'

McAvoy rubs his jaw with a noise like a match being struck. 'Did we actually learn anything?' he asks quietly.

'Savoca knows nothing,' says Alto, puffing out his cheeks and sighing. 'He's all muscle. All anger. If Pugliesca sent Luca up there to kill your Irish boys, he might have done so without telling his father. The question is, why? And why use the son of your closest ally? He might be playing a game we can't even fathom.'

'But Molony. Father Whelan.' McAvoy looks so frustrated he seems about to stamp his foot like a giant in a nursery rhyme. 'I'm more confused than before I went in.'

Alto gives a tired laugh and pushes off from the wall, deliberately walking in front of a Korean couple who are taking photographs of the building's front; immortalising its glass and neon, all vibrant green and red.

'Welcome to my world,' says Alto, disappearing onto Broome Street with the air of a man who does not know which burden will break him first.

McAvoy stands still for a moment. He doesn't really know what to do next. Doesn't know which of his fears to concentrate on.

He follows Alto like a man with nowhere else to go.

20

Since meeting Trish Pharaoh, McAvoy has got good at standing behind smaller people and looking menacing. He finds it easiest simply to clear his mind and look a little confused and somehow, this translates itself into an intimidating posture and daunting expression. He does it now, staring at the small Latin-American woman behind the counter of the deli and feeling like a hundred different types of shit for doing so.

'I don't want to cause you trouble,' says Alto, looking as reasonable as he can. He's leaning on the counter, hands squashing the candies and cookies in front of the cash register. 'You're the last person whose day we want to spoil. You're good people. You're the sort we need more of. Hell, we're all immigrants originally, right? But there are people who'll make all kinds of fuss and I want to spare you that, I really do. And all you have to do to avoid that is give me the keys.'

'I can't,' says the lady fiercely. 'He's an angry man. He shout at me before.'

McAvoy senses that there are people behind him, watching the exchange from between the towering shelves of produce. His skin is prickling.

'This man here,' says Alto, gesturing at McAvoy. 'He's come a long way. He's looking for somebody important in his country. There may even be a reward.'

McAvoy can see the old lady weighing it up. She's plump, with shiny skin and large brown eyes. He imagines she has a nice smile, though he has yet to see it. She doesn't deserve this. The deli she runs with her husband is the gateway to a squat brown apartment building that can only be accessed through the store's delivery bay, or the locked door tucked discreetly beside the tattoo parlour next door.

'I'm very sorry to do this to you,' says McAvoy, breaking character and gently moving Alto out of the way. 'I wouldn't ask if it wasn't important. Perhaps if you left the keys on the counter and then when you looked again they were gone . . .'

McAvoy can feel bile rising in his mouth. He hates breaking the rules. Feels like his nose is going to bleed every time he goes against regulations.

The lady closes her eyes and a moment later she leans over. 'One, two, five, nine. That's on the keypad.' She looks at Alto. 'You got lucky, understand.'

McAvoy gives her a look of genuine thanks and Alto winks at her as they leave the deli and emerge back onto Avenue B. They are within spitting distance of St Colman's; not far from where Brishen and Shay were seen with Molony. They are about to let themselves into Molony's home.

'You sure you want to do this?' asks Alto, ducking into the alcove that houses the doorway to Molony's apartment block.

McAvoy's mouth drops open in surprise. 'You're asking? It was you who suggested it!'

Alto grins. He seems to be coming to life.

McAvoy leans his back on the door, taking a deep breath. Above, the sun is losing its battle with the mounting grey clouds and the first soft flurries of snow are beginning to fall in large, fat flakes. They evaporate upon touching the ground but it will not be long before an inch or two of fresh snow ornaments the gutters and sidewalks and further buries the cars that have been stuck in pack-ice since last week's blizzard.

'One, two, five, nine,' says McAvoy, as if in prayer. He presses the buttons on the small keypad and there is a click as the mechanism gives. McAvoy pulls the door open and steps into the soft yellow light of the corridor.

McAvoy was sitting in the passenger seat of Alto's police-issue Honda when his friend Redding called him back to confirm that nothing had changed about Molony's domestic arrangements since he had last looked into his life and been transferred for his pains. Molony still lived in an apartment building off Avenue B. He owned the whole thing and let out three of the four apartments. He lived in the penthouse, which was also registered as a workspace and the administration address for four different charities with Catholic affiliations. The other apartments were also registered as charitable organisations, administering funds for the needy in far-flung places like El Salvador, Belize and Namibia. McAvoy had expected to find a gleaming apartment building, bustling with well-meaning types in cardigans and sensible shoes, instead of a dilapidated building without a single nameplate by the door. Nobody answered when he and Alto rang the buzzers. Alto had tried the deli next door on a hunch; confident that Molony would have given his neighbours a key in case of emergencies.

'This look like a charity HQ to you?' asks Alto, indicating a plain white door.

McAvoy looks back and realises he has left muddy bootprints on the hardwood floor. Something tells him he would be wise to wipe his feet. He turns and walks back to the front door and scrubs the soles of his boots on the rough rectangle of carpet. It moves as he does so and underneath he finds a small ring of keys, hanging on a key-ring bearing the legend 'St Anthony Saved Me' and a tiny sketch of an old church.

'You've got the luck of the Irish,' says Alto, grinning, as McAvoy holds them up.

'That's been said before. Let's hope it lasts.'

McAvoy selects a key at random and slips it into the lock of the first door. When it fails to turn he tries again and the second key is a perfect fit. McAvoy opens the door to an empty apartment, containing nothing more than grey air. A telephone and answerphone sit on the dark cord carpet, red light twinkling.

Alto looks at his notes. 'Looks like St Francis's Blessed Relief of Nepalese Orphans is going through a quiet spell,' he says, shaking his head.

McAvoy closes and locks the door behind them. They climb to the first floor and find the same set-up in two further apartments.

McAvoy is growing increasingly uneasy. He half entertained the hope that in one of these rooms he would find answers. Without being able to explain the thought as anything other than wishful thinking, he had even imagined finding Valentine, tied up and bruised but alive, grateful and ready to go home. Instead, McAvoy senses he and Alto have stumbled onto something else entirely.

'This is the one,' says Alto needlessly, indicating the door at the end of the corridor on the third floor. The door is more opulent than the others; a lavish creation of old wood painted a deep red. As he peers at it, McAvoy notices the subtle crucifix motif that has been artfully incorporated into the twisted wood. This is a work of art.

'In for a penny, in for a pound,' says McAvoy, and picks a solid brass key from the ring. It slips into the lock and turns without effort.

'NYPD. We heard shots. We're coming in!' says Alto quietly, and when McAvoy looks at him quizzically, he shrugs. 'It pays to be able to say that you said it.'

McAvoy opens the door and has to force himself not to make a sound. He steps onto a solid marble floor that glitters as if carpeted with crushed diamonds. A Moroccan rug covers the expensive stone, perfectly matching the North African batiks that hang on the wall. The apartment is a colossal, open-plan space and no expense has been spared in making it look fit for a photoshoot in a style magazine. The lounge area is a splendid concoction of oxblood Chesterfield sofas, chairs and footstools, all set around a wood-burning stove mounted in a fireplace that matches the old timbers of the door. A wicker basket full of pine cones stands on the tiled surround. Above, twisted chocolate-coloured railway sleepers give the ceiling the air of a mock-Tudor mansion. A grandfather clock stands by the mahogany writing desk at the rear of the room, the colours clashing slightly with the patterned mauve rug that covers the floor. A large architectural blueprint of an old church hangs in a gold rococo frame. The living room leads into a kitchen that puts McAvoy in mind of a stately home: all wrought-iron hooks, hanging brass pans and a huge black stove against red tiles. The place is spotless.

'No TV,' says Alto, looking around for something to criticise. 'And his books are all different shapes.'

McAvoy follows Alto's nod and looks in awe at the full wall of hardback books. They are the only things that have not been arranged obsessively. They are a pleasing jumble, piled higgledy-piggledy onto units that carry the same subtle crucifix motif as the door.

'Eclectic mix,' says McAvoy, examining the spines of the books. '*The Dictionary of Saints*; *Wicked Plants*; *The Complete Herbalist*; *Breverton's Phantasmagoria*; *Harrap's Illustrated Dictionary of Art and Artists*; *1000 Home Remedies*; *Stargazing for Beginners*; *Practical Homicide Investigation* . . .'

McAvoy picks this last, weighty tome from the shelf. The cover shows yellow letters on a black background, partially obscuring a headless corpse wrapped in crime-scene tape. It falls open on a picture of a man who has suffered a self-inflicted shotgun wound and whose features look the way a watermelon would if it had been driven over. McAvoy puts it back and pulls a face.

'Interesting character,' says Alto, trying the drawers in the writing desk. 'Writes with pen and ink. I reckon with a few candles he could see himself as a monk.'

McAvoy crosses to the window. The Venetian blinds are closed and he peers between them. The snow has started coming down in earnest, billowing in off the river like a plague of butterflies. The city looks as though it has been ripped into fragments and then scattered on the wind.

'You can see St Colman's from here,' says Alto, joining him.

'And he's been here how long?'

'Bought the building in '87. Been here ever since.'

'He came into some serious money, then.'

'Or discovered a way to make it.'

McAvoy nods, looking around again. Something troubles him. He stands in the centre of the room and moves his head slowly from side to side, as if running his finger across a smooth surface and trying to find the crack.

'Migraine?' asks Alto, playing with his phone. 'I know a great girl for massages.' He stops talking and scowls at his surroundings. 'Damn, if they'd just let me push. This guy is crooked as they come. Look at this place. What do you think? You think I was right? Aector, you think I was right?'

'Just a second, please.'

McAvoy holds up a hand to ask, as politely as he can, for silence. He sucks on his lower lip, reading the room. Everything about the environment is tasteful: all perfectly matched. The entire space is organised to complement and flow. He crosses back to the rear of the room and squats down, looking at the mauve rug. Then he slides to the floor and looks at it from a fresh angle.

'Listening for a train?' asks Alto.

'Look,' says McAvoy. 'The pattern isn't symmetrical. And it's fluffier here. It's been scrubbed.'

Alto lies down next to McAvoy. He lifts his amber glasses and looks closely at the floor.

'That spray,' says McAvoy. He reaches out and rolls back the rug, looking at the reverse of the area that has caught his attention. 'Blood,' he says.

Both men stand, and without exchanging a word, they begin to consider scenarios. McAvoy pulls out his cell phone and starts taking pictures. In moments he thinks he understands. He walks back to the doorway and lifts the Moroccan rug. It, too, shows discolouration to the underside.

'He was bleeding when he came in. Dripping, but not spraying. And here,' says McAvoy, standing by the armchair. 'Around here, they – the victim – were struck.'

McAvoy paces around the living room, wishing there were more. Concentrating, he is unaware that he is pulling his hair hard enough to hurt. He follows the path of the spray; looks for the final patch of discolouration on the reverse of the rug.

'There,' says Alto, and he indicates the basket of pine cones. McAvoy nods and begins, carefully, to lift them out one by one, examining each in turn.

'You're fucking joking,' says Alto, marvelling, as something catches the light towards the bottom of the basket.

McAvoy feels a cold weight settling in his gut. He takes the latex gloves offered by Alto and slips them on. He reaches into the basket and closes his finger and thumb around the nugget of gold.

'Fuck,' says Alto, and this seems to cover his feelings on the subject.

'Valentine,' says McAvoy, looking at the tooth that should be glinting in the upper row of his brother-in-law's mouth.

'You sure?'

'I saw his dad knock the real one out,' says McAvoy, without thinking. 'He wasn't even out of his teens.'

'Fuck,' says Alto again.

'I'm putting it back,' says McAvoy, and sweat begins to seep into his hairline and soak his back and shoulders. He is trying not to shiver. 'You've got to do this right now, Ronny. Come back with a proper warrant. Question him. Find out what happened – why Valentine was here and what he came for. Most importantly, where he is now . . .'

Alto is nodding, his face colouring with the sudden burst of adrenalin. He pushes his fair hair back from his face.

'This is bigger than I ever imagined. I don't want any part of this. I'm just going to mess it up for you. But if you do it right . . .'

McAvoy stops talking. He is staring hard at Alto's slicked-back fringe. It is waving, as if on a breeze.

'Do you have a lighter?' he asks quietly.

'Sorry?'

'A lighter.'

Alto nods and pulls out a Zippo, emblazoned with a Jack Daniel's logo. He hands it to McAvoy, who spins the wheel. The flame stands erect for a moment, and then drifts lazily to the right, like Alto's errant strands of hair.

McAvoy raises the lighter and begins to pace the room, looking at the flame as if it contains answers. Slowly, he moves closer to the bookcase.

Alto watches, fascinated. He pulls a face as McAvoy begins pushing at shelves and pulling books from the wall.

'You're not serious,' he says, just as McAvoy reaches the grand-father clock and peers at the face.

'Fifty minutes late,' says McAvoy, checking his watch. He reaches forward and takes the gleaming pendulum in his left hand. He tugs, and there is a satisfying click as one whole section of the bookcase glides slowly away from the wall.

'Fuck,' says Alto, who appears to have downsized his vocabulary.

McAvoy slides himself between the bookcase and the wall and into the open space behind. The space is perhaps six feet by six feet. There is no carpet, and dirt crunches beneath McAvoy's boots as he steps inside, lowering his head as he does so. A metal ladder is fixed to one wall.

'Christ, this is an old elevator shaft,' says Alto, stepping inside and peering upwards. 'Can you make anything out?'

McAvoy uses the lighter, holding it above his head. He fancies that around twelve feet above his head, there is a darker space.

'After you,' says Alto, pointing at the ladder. His voice has gone quiet. Neither man looks as if he is sure what to do next. Both look nervous.

The ladder makes no protest as it takes McAvoy's considerable bulk. Soundlessly, he climbs into the cool and the dark above him.

'Anything?' asks Alto, from beneath.

McAvoy struggles to make anything out but as he climbs higher, a shape becomes clear. There is a doorway a little above him and a soft light is emanating from within. McAvoy reaches up and his hands touch a length of rope. He lets out a breath; staggered and shallow. Without thinking, he pulls himself up and over the lip, slithering over hard ground. He yelps as his hands brush something soft and organic. He scrambles to his feet, heart beating hard and fast, and takes in the scene before him.

He stands in the huge open loft of the apartment building. It is a chilly, half-dark space. What little light there is comes from the colossal pyramid of candles that flicker and dance amid a pulpy mass of melted wax halfway down the room.

'Jesus,' says McAvoy, as his eyes adjust and he sees what his fingers touched as he emerged into this extraordinary place.

The entire floor of the attic is covered with soil. In places it is mounded up in tiny molehills; elsewhere it is as flat and featureless as glass.

McAvoy takes a breath. He catches the traces of something familiar: an aroma that makes him think of disturbed waters; the stench that rises when the silt and bones and decay at the bottom of a fish pond are stirred with a stick.

McAvoy moves slowly forward, using the lighter to examine the ground beneath him. It shows footprints. Different shapes and sizes. Trainers, smart shoes, bare toes.

McAvoy shudders as his feet crunch over dry earth. A sudden tinkling sound causes him to snap his head to the left and he is unable to stop himself from releasing a long, low groan. There are hundreds of them, stretching away like stepping stones, their smooth, sleek sides reflecting in the flames. Urns. An endless walkway of empty urns, black openings like dead eyes, dead mouths. McAvoy puts his hand over his mouth, suddenly aware of the dust in the air. He finds himself struggling to breathe. The air is full of burned bodies; he is in a place of earth and ash and dust. He feels his feet lose grip on the carpet of earth and as he stumbles, his hand plunges through the grey crust of soil and into the damp loam beneath.

'What the fuck?' asks Alto, as he emerges into the darkness behind him.

'Get back,' says McAvoy. 'We can't be here. This is . . .'

Alto has a flashlight and is swinging it wildly from side to side, illuminating the empty urns and exposing the haze of dust that fills the air. Suddenly, the light stops on the wall next to the candles. McAvoy catches sight of metal; flickering like flame.

He cannot help himself. Every instinct is telling him to leave this terrible place but he cannot bring himself to do so. Slowly he crosses to the wall.

The image is a tree; each individual leaf made of brass and screwed into the bare brick of the wall. McAvoy holds up the lighter. Each leaf bears a name, save for the first. It shows a simple rose, engraved with reverence into gold.

McAvoy has seen such a creation before. In the entrance of St

Colman's, it served as a wall of remembrance; each leaf carrying the name of a soul departed but not forgotten.

The tree on the wall of Peter Molony's hidden place carries many names. Some are Hispanic, others Jewish. Others are mere descriptions: *Blonde, early twenties, 1979.*

Among them, McAvoy sees a name he recognises. *Alejandra Mota Valverda.* It is almost lost among the forest of names.

McAvoy lets the light guide him. Finds the most recent leaf, high to the right of the sinewy trunk. It reads simply: Shay Helden.

McAvoy feels as though he is choking. Feels himself gag on this air suffused with particles of dead, burned skin.

'We have to go,' says Alto, pulling out his cell phone. He stops before he has a chance to make a call. Reads the words on the screen.

'Tell me, Ronny,' says McAvoy softly.

'Uniform have picked up a Chechen, walking around Brooklyn with blood all down his face. He wants to talk. Wants to make a deal.' Alto's eyes gleam in the twitching light. 'He wants to tell us about the Irishmen.'

McAvoy cannot take his eyes off the wall.

'We have to go,' says Alto.

'I can't,' says McAvoy quietly. 'I can't just leave this.'

'But he has information. We can come back. Do things properly.'

'You go. I'll take photographs. Try to understand . . .'

'He could be back any moment.'

'I want that,' says McAvoy, his jaw set. 'I really want that to happen.'

'Aector, you came here for your brother-in-law. This isn't your responsibility.'

McAvoy looks at the names. Sees girl after girl after girl. Sees the aberration that is Shay. His mind fills with the sad eyes of the lady at the church, lighting candles for her daughter thirty-five years after she disappeared on her way home from church.

'I just need to understand. You go. Call me if it's genuine.'

'I'll come back,' says Alto, looking desperate to get away from this bleak place with its rank stench and its clouds of human dust.

'I'll come back and we'll do things right. I need to think. We both need to think.'

Alto is already descending the ladder, almost falling in his hurry to get away.

McAvoy sits down on the carpet of earth and dust and reaches over for the nearest urn. He holds it in his lap like a bear with a honey-pot, looking into its depths as if it contains answers.

He wants to call home. Wants to ring Pharaoh. Wants to be told what to do.

Instead, he lifts his cell phone and begins snapping pictures of the names on the tree, the urns at his feet, and the candles that burn like dying suns.

And all the while he yearns to be disturbed; to be interrupted by a creature whose actions reek of evil and despair.

21

The Pink Pug, Ludlow Street, 6.18 p.m.

McAvoy has taken care to position himself as far away from the large mirror on the bare brick wall as he can. He is horribly aware that he looks as though he has been recently excavated. Dirt and dust cling to his clothes and despite washing his hands and face rigorously in the restroom, he feels that a miasma of soil and pulverised bone still encases his skin. He has found a table at the rear of the small, stylish bar and wedged himself into the angle created by two walls. Nobody can approach him from behind. From where he sits, peering over his laptop, he can see the entirety of the Pink Pug. The vantage point offers him some comfort. He hates the thought of people laughing behind his back but at least from here he can see their sniggers unimpeded. He does not begrudge them their smiles. He knows how he looks; this huge, dirt-streaked, red-haired behemoth who whispers into his computer and sips a cocktail from a coconut shell packed so full with straws, umbrellas and sparklers that it is less of a beverage and more of a cry for help.

McAvoy stares at the screen and listens to the sounds of the dozen or so drinkers and diners who are knocking back tequila slammers or nibbling on olives, cheeses and meats presented on planks of wood. It's a fun bar and painfully cool. The barman flips bottles and shakes cocktails with the grace of a circus juggler. He wears a stripy shirt without a collar, round glasses and a bowler hat. The ends of his moustache have been waxed into little tips. Here, on the Lower East Side, he is the absolute pinnacle of sophistication. McAvoy cannot help but think that back home, in Hull, he would be found in a wheelie bin with a cocktail shaker wedged somewhere invasive.

'It's never simple with you, is it?' says Pharaoh, suddenly filling the screen. 'A few days off, that's what you said. Going to see if I can track down my brother-in-law, you said. I've checked my notes, Hector, and there was absolutely no mention of cremated remains in swanky loft apartments or lawyers cutting their balls off. I'd remember that sort of thing. I've got a good memory for balls.'

Pharaoh drops her head and then gives him a little smile that means the world to him. He can tell she wishes she were with him, that she knows what he is going through and would give anything to help him feel less alone.

'I didn't want any of this,' says McAvoy quietly.

'Shush. Sip your coconut and be quiet while I read through this lot.'

McAvoy does as he is told and watches as Pharaoh leafs through a sheaf of documents. Her dark hair falls forward like curtains and he knows it will only be a second or two until she pushes it behind her ears. It will slip forward again in moments and she will blow it out of her eyes without thinking about it. Behind her is the familiar sight of the Serious and Organised Unit at Courtland Road Police Station in Hull. The computer that Pharaoh is using to talk to him is on McAvoy's own desk and he is experiencing the surreal and disembodied sensation of staring out from the screen at a location where he usually sits. When Pharaoh disappeared to go and pick up some documents from the printer, he had given Detective Constable Andy Daniells a nasty scare – walking past and seeing his sergeant's motionless head and shoulders looming out from the screen. When McAvoy had muttered a 'Hello, Andy', the pleasant, corpulent young detective who had elected to stay late and catch up on paperwork had made a noise that McAvoy had previously associated with mating foxes.

'I think the Yanks expect me to eat this when I'm finished with it,' says Pharaoh, looking up. 'I thought we were all supposed to be friends these days. Special relationship, isn't that what Blair called it?'

'They're worried about jeopardising an undercover operation,' says McAvoy, even though he has already told her this several times. 'We'd be just the same.'

Pharaoh shrugs. 'He seemed okay, this Redding bloke. Sounded very New York.'

'Of course he did,' says McAvoy. 'He's from New York. He probably thinks you sound very Mexborough.'

'What did he make of your accent?'

'I haven't spoken to him,' says McAvoy.

'And yet he's calling your colleagues in little old Hull and risking his neck to share information with us,' says Pharaoh accusingly. 'You do have a way with people. Why is he doing that, by the way? Just asking, you understand.'

'Like I said, he's friends with Ronny Alto – the detective who's been helping me. Alto and his colonel were the only ones at the Seventh who knew the Feds had an operative in the Chechen organisation. Alto has a good relationship with the Italians and he was brought into the circle of trust when Brishen and Shay were attacked to see if he had anything he could share. When I turned up, he was the poor sod tasked with keeping me out of it and then making me go home. He feels bad at not telling me the truth. So he's sticking his neck out and sharing information with me. Or at least, with you.'

Pharaoh shakes her head, licking her lips. 'We're all quite enjoying this, anyway. Ben has got a twenty-quid bet with Sophie Kirkland that you're going to get deported by Monday afternoon.'

'What does Sophie say?'

'Monday morning,' says Pharaoh distractedly, as she looks again at the information Detective Hugh Redding sent her at Alto's request. She looks up at him and her expression softens. 'I know that a big part of you wanted to keep this all to yourself. I appreciate the fact you asked for help.'

'Keep it to myself?' asks McAvoy.

'Not for the glory, Hector, not anything like that. I just know you'd want to shoulder it all, like it's all your responsibility. It's not. You were right to share.'

McAvoy looks away. She knows him too well. As he stood at the lip of the loft and stared at that landscape of earth and ash, something inside him felt a personal connection to the scene. It evoked something intangible; some hazy sense that it had been laid out just for him. It was a vista that held an undeniable power. Almost an allure. McAvoy wanted to thrust his hand into that damp soil. The desire had been close to overwhelming. It took self-control not to disturb the scene more than he had to. He wanted to lift each of the urns and the cardboard boxes and examine each for identifiers that could help him make sense of his discovery. But such action would be detected. So McAvoy did what he could. He took pictures from the doorway, examined the urns within his reach, and then scurried back down the ladder and out into the light. He made sure not to leave footprints and as he closed the door behind him, he felt as though he were shutting something inside. It was only as he emerged onto the cold, snow-blown street that he realised he had been sweating so profusely that his clothes were clinging to his skin. The cold air caused the perspiration to turn to ice and he was soon shivering so badly that he struggled to key in the right buttons on his cell phone. Any thoughts he had of keeping his discovery secret disappeared the moment he heard Pharaoh's voice. He told her what he had found. She listened, and told him what to do. He did as he was ordered. Got himself something to eat and sent her all the images from his phone. He sent a text message to Alto and received two letters back in response: ok.

For the past couple of hours McAvoy has been trying to make sense of his thoughts while back home, Pharaoh and Ben Neilsen have been ignoring the lateness of the hour to sift through the pictures and try to find a pattern amid the different names. Half an hour ago, Redding emailed Molony's psychiatric history to Pharaoh and told her that McAvoy had helped his buddy catch a serial date rapist and would never have to buy a drink in his town ever again. McAvoy would have taken more comfort in the prediction if he had not been spending twelve dollars on a Tropical Scream.

'You've got that look on your face,' says McAvoy, turning his attention back to the screen. 'You look like you've got the scent in your nostrils.'

'Are you calling me a hunting dog?'

'No, you know what I mean. You've got something.'

'Hector, if I handed this report to one of the ladies in the canteen they would be able to see that this is not a guy you would want babysitting. It's interesting reading, that's for sure.'

'Well?'

Pharaoh looks at the paperwork again. 'We've got a lot of stuff here. It worries me how much stuff we've got, if I'm honest. I don't even know if these records would have been digitised as a matter of course. Alto was right when he said he'd only scratched the surface. How much do you trust him, Hector? He got close to this guy and then the next minute he was ordered off and the whole thing was dropped. And then next thing he's trying to tie your own bumbling investigation into something that's been eating away at him. Sounds fucking fishy, my lad. I know they do things differently but you don't become a cop unless you want to lock up bad people. Am I being horribly naïve?' She stops, and appears to file the thought away for further analysis when she has the time. 'Point is, Molony might be a corrupt lawyer or a money-launderer but this is something else. Why's he got a room of ashes in his loft? Why is Ronny not there right now with squad cars raiding the damn place?'

McAvoy massages his hands. He has a headache at his temples and his eyes are stinging.

'He's using you,' says Pharaoh tactfully. 'The Feds – and I warn you, I feel like a prick just saying the phrase "the Feds" – are going to go bananas at him for getting in the way of a bigger investigation so he's letting you be the fall-guy. I thought it was all too easy, the way they agreed to help, the way they let you wander around like a bear at a model village. You heard what that cow said in the restaurant; the daft bitch with the purple hair and the tramp-stamp on her arse. They're letting you shake the tree to see what falls out. None of this feels right and I can't make up my mind whether to drag you home or buy a bucket of popcorn.'

McAvoy sighs. He shares her misgivings but he knows that he has come too far to give up.

'Whatever,' says Pharaoh, waving a hand. 'But I warn you, there will be repercussions and I only have so many aces up my sleeve.'

She looks at her documents again and huffs her hair out of her eyes. She and Ben have only been digging for a short time but already they have fleshed out the file that Alto had first shown McAvoy at the hospital. With his mind a whirl of different and conflicting theories, he is grateful to hear her read the details afresh.

'Peter Molony,' she says musically, in her best nursery rhyme voice. 'Born October 1952. Only son of Orla and Conor Molony, who emigrated to the States from County Wexford in 1949. Dad was thirty years older than Mum. Already in his fifties by the time Peter came along. They lived in an area called Hell's Kitchen, which is a place I've definitely heard of and which, from a marketing perspective, I've always thought of as a poor choice of name. Anyway, Dad worked as a delivery driver for a brewery, Mum looked after her boy at home. Dad died in 1966, leaving Orla and Peter without a great deal of money. Death certificate said he suffered complications following a car accident. Mum remarried within eight months. Gianluca Bucco. I'm only guessing, but he sounds Italian . . .'

'Come on, Trish,' says McAvoy.

'Right, right. Molony started serving as an altar boy at St Colman's Church when he was ten years old. Mum was a regular at Mass. The school he attended was a mix of Irish and Italian. I've looked it up on Google Maps and it was a bit of a jaunt from where he was living to get to St Colman's so I'm guessing he went there because it was popular with the Irish crowd. The priest at the time was a Father O'Flaherty, who, y'know, sounds a bit Irish.'

'Trish . . .'

'He showed interest in joining the priesthood. Went on residential courses upstate. Went on a Catholic retreat with Father O'Flaherty and a group of other boys. In 1972 he entered a seminary on Father O'Flaherty's recommendation.'

'And?'

'He left in 1973.'

'What does his report say about that?'

'Unsurprisingly, not a lot. They can be a bit of a closed book, these religious institutions. Anyway, the next thing we know, he was committed to the state hospital for evaluation having performed a fairly severe act of self-harm.'

'The auto-castration,' says McAvoy with a shudder.

'That's only the half of it. They found evidence of scarring all over his body. It seems Daddy was a bit free with his temper. Liked to lash his son with a home-made cat-o'-nine-tails. Stuck pins in his legs.'

'Pins?'

'He told this to his psychiatrist on admission and they didn't believe him until they X-rayed him. Found twenty-seven pins in his thighs.'

McAvoy pushes his drink away, feeling tired and cold.

'Did he tell the psychiatrist why he did it? Cut himself?'

'Atonement. That was the word. According to the report, Molony was a relatively model patient at St Loretta's. He was good at talking with the other inmates, and was especially close to a patient who had previously spent time at a different state facility and was completely mute.'

McAvoy nods, his pulse quickening. 'Is he named?'

'No. It says he was a patient at a facility on Staten Island and had been for several years prior to his being released to the care of his family. I'm thinking it wouldn't be a terrible guess to assume this was Tony Blank.' She scans her notes and nods. 'Aye, he was committed afresh after biting off a dental nurse's fingers. St Loretta's was good for him, as was his relationship with Molony. They spent a lot of time in the hospital chapel. Within a year, Molony was permitted to leave. There's no mention of Blank. Like Alto told you, Jimmy Whelan was a regular visitor. Came in plain clothes, not his dog-collar. Would pray with Molony and his mute friend. Helped him find himself again. Helped him become the person he became.'

'And then what? Molony becomes a regular model citizen?'

'Released to his mother's address. Did his degree at night school. Passed the bar in 1981 . . .'

'Quick study.'

'And got a job as a junior at Dash and Spadaro – a legal firm that got itself a dishonourable mention during the Mob trials of the 1980s. They were hooked up to at least one of the crime families that the FBI tried to bring down at that time. The two senior partners retired and Molony set up a very specialist practice. He was a relatively young man but he got a reputation specialising in wills, probate and charitable donations. He was very good at setting up charitable funds that circumnavigated a lot of the death duties payable on estates. He also helped rich Catholics establish benevolent organisations for giving to good causes.'

'Sounds like a good man,' says McAvoy cautiously.

'Indeed. He's been investigated only twice over allegations he persuaded two very elderly Catholic ladies to give their estates to one of his charitable organisations instead of to their families, but both times the investigations petered out.'

'And now?'

'Wealthy man, very successful. Sacristan at St Colman's Church and pillar of society.'

McAvoy chews on his lower lip. 'Father Jimmy Whelan?'

Pharaoh smiles. 'Same seminary, different years. That's how they met. Been associates ever since.'

McAvoy strokes his jaw. As he inspects his hands he expects to see dust and bone upon his skin.

'His mother. His stepfather . . .'

'Mum passed away in 1988. Cancer. Stepfather the following year. Seems a decent enough sort. Left his money to the Open Hands Missionary Association, which provides help for victims of abuse in the Philippines and Cebu. I'm sure it was a cause close to his heart.'

McAvoy scratches at his head and looks over the top of the computer. The other drinkers have drifted away from him. Through the mass of bodies he can make out the scaffolding that wraps the tall apartment building on the opposite side of Ludlow Street. The fat flakes of snow that billow across the darkened glass look like shredded white feathers.

'The names,' says McAvoy. 'On the tree.'

'You'll never make a photographer,' says Pharaoh. 'They're blurry as hell. But Ben worked his mojo and we've got a few names. *Alejandra Mota Valverda*. You know about her.'

'Only the basics.'

'That's all there is. Disappeared walking back from St Colman's. Never seen again.'

'Was Molony ever questioned?'

'Only as a witness, not as a suspect. He was working for the legal firm at that time, becoming the respectable lawyer, devoting his time to St Colman's.'

'Shay's name was on the wall. I saw it.'

'Yes, you did. What that means, we can't say. His body's being flown home so there're no ashes. Perhaps it's a wall of connections; people he's encountered whose lives have been lost, but then there's no obvious connection to the majority of the names. Of course, there are others we can say with some certainty he had a link to.'

'Such as?'

'Salvatore Pugliesca,' says Pharaoh, twitching her face into a smile. 'I thought I'd tell you that one first.'

'And Tony Blank?'

Pharaoh shakes her head. 'If his name's up there, it's not clear on the photographs.'

'What about strangers? People with no obvious link?'

Pharaoh consults her notes. 'Laura Prime,' she says. 'Reported missing in 1978. Last seen leaving a party in Philipstown, New York. She was nineteen years old. Red hair, freckled skin, gap in her front teeth. She was a trainee beautician and lived with her large family. Prior to her disappearance she had reported that she felt as if she were being followed, but made no complaint to police.'

'Irish family?'

'Yes. Roman Catholic and good church-going types, before you ask.'

McAvoy pinches the bridge of his nose between forefinger and thumb. 'There's more?'

'Paulette Obasi. Twenty-four. Student at Columbus University. Nigerian origins but she was studying there on one of these adorable Christian benevolent grants. Shy, church-going girl, according to the reports. Last seen leaving the library to head for the evening Mass at the university chapel. April 1979. She didn't arrive. No sign since.'

McAvoy stirs the dregs of liquid at the base of his ridiculous drink. 'What have we found?' he asks, shaking his head.

'Maybe nothing,' says Pharaoh. 'This guy may be a good Catholic chap who has made his own memorial to the lost. These cases made a few headlines but they weren't front-page news. Maybe they mattered to him and he's chiselled their names into his own private church because he feels a connection to them. He wants to atone and it's clear he takes that stuff seriously.'

The door of the bar bangs open and a swirl of snow follows two girls in their early twenties into the welcoming warmth. They giggle and high-five, pulling themselves out of thick padded coats, scarves and hats. There is something somehow delightful about them, with their wide eyes and white teeth, their zeal and their sparkle. McAvoy wonders what their lives consist of. Wonders what they will become. Finds himself growing smaller in his chair as he thinks about the way strangers ricochet off one another, colliding and intersecting, missing one another or slamming together based on the tiniest ministrations of moments and chance.

'The tooth,' says McAvoy quietly.

'Oh, there's no doubt that's fucking odd,' says Pharaoh brightly. 'He needs to be questioned on that, though how your friend Alto will explain his presence in the apartment is for him to decide. It seems pretty damn clear that Valentine was there at some point – unless there was a bare-knuckle bout that Molony attended and he took himself a souvenir. My advice to Redding was to come up with a good cover story, but Molony needs to be questioned. Don't forget, Valentine is what you're there for.'

McAvoy considers this. His head drops to his hand. 'I don't know what I'm doing.'

'You never do.' Pharaoh smiles. 'Anyway, this might cheer you up. Ben's blown up your terrible photos and managed to make out a name on the lip of one of the urns in Molony's creepy loft. It's for a funeral home in Baltimore.'

McAvoy looks at his boss and enjoys the little frisson of devilment that crosses her face. 'You called them?' he asks.

'Not me. Ben. Played the deferential English detective part perfectly. Spoke to the funeral director himself. Described it in all its glory, including the silver flower that's etched into the side of the urn. He said it was from their Sacred Chalice range, and that it had been discontinued in the early eighties. Only sold a handful of them because the price was prohibitive.'

McAvoy waits for more. 'And?'

'Went through his records and called us back with a list. We didn't recognise any of the names but we've passed them on to your friend Redding.'

McAvoy frowns at the screen. 'I know there's more . . .'

Pharaoh grins. 'Of course there's more. The funeral director warmed to Ben. Explained that two years ago he published an article in the *Baltimore Sun* warning that the funeral parlour had reached critical mass in terms of unclaimed remains and they were going to be disposed of. Turns out it's a real problem. Funeral parlours the world over end up with a mountain of unclaimed ashes. They've recently agreed a feasible amount of time that they should keep them for before they are respectfully disposed of.'

'And this urn was among those unclaimed?'

'Shush,' says Pharaoh testily. 'The funeral director remembers receiving a telephone call from a Christian organisation that said it would be happy to take the ashes so that they could be scattered on holy ground. The Christian organisation said they would make a sizeable donation to the funeral parlour's outreach programmes – and I'd say that's code for a bribe – if they would send the remains to a postal box.'

'Where was the postal box?'

'Cairo,' says Pharaoh, looking at him intently. 'The one upstate, not the one with the sphinx.'

'Where Brishen, Shay and Savoca were found?'

'I do wonder whether our American cousins have ever considered joined-up thinking,' muses Pharaoh. 'They might actually be good at it, if they gave it a shot.'

McAvoy's head is reeling. He wants to run outside into the snow and let the cold caress of each snowflake lift the ash and dirt from his skin. He did not ask to be involved in any of this. He closes his eyes as he talks, rubbing his hands together softly and wishing the skin that stroked his belonged to somebody who loved him.

'Trish, I'm so lost. I don't even know what to do next.'

'You tell all this to Alto,' she says firmly. 'You let him bring in Molony. If you're lucky, he'll spill his guts and tell you he knows where Valentine is. If you're very lucky he'll also cough to being a serial killer and money-launderer and you and me will be invited Stateside to receive medals from George Clooney. Until then, you need to get some rest, change your clothes and tell Roisin she's fabulous. Don't let all this stuff climb inside your head. You know how you get . . .'

The door bangs and McAvoy stops listening. Ronny Alto pushes his way through the crowd, brushing snow from his hair and moisture from his amber glasses. He looks tired and old.

'I have to go,' says McAvoy. 'Thank you. Thank you so much.'

'Hector, hang on, I've got to—'

McAvoy closes the lid on the laptop and looks up at the detective. 'I've so much to tell you,' he says.

'Likewise,' says Alto, removing his glasses.

McAvoy looks into his eyes, as if searching for answers. 'Valentine,' he says, and his voice cracks as his lips form his name. 'You're going to tell me he's dead.'

Ronny shakes his head, taking a breath, as if preparing to run.

'He's not dead,' he says at last. 'But he wishes he were. And in a moment, you'll wish that for him too.'

Spring 1980: The Fifth Absolution

They're waiting for Father Whelan as he steps out of the vestry. He didn't hear them come in. They have that way about them, men like this. Their personalities are huge but they can move with absolute silence when they need to.

'You gave me a start,' says Father Whelan. He's taken off his robes. His dog-collar is barely visible under his black sweater. It is less conspicuous than the blizzard of dandruff that coats his shoulders. He has aged a lot these last few years. His hair is thinning and he has red spots on his nose and chin. The doctor recently gave him a cream for them and asked if there was anything troubling him. He'd found it as easy to lie to the physician as he does to himself. He has found himself unable to pray privately in recent months. He can recite Mass and deliver a sermon but when he kneels at his bedside and talks to God, the words die upon his tongue. He thought for a time about asking his bishop for guidance. Instead he has chosen simply to stop praying.

'Don't like frightening you, Father,' says Salvatore Pugliesca. 'Hot and sweaty as a stripper's ass-crack out there. And look at you, dressed for winter. You should poke your head out the door some time. Girls walking by in not much more than a stitch. Boys too. Sinful times, Father. Good times, if you know how to live the right way.'

Sal is leaning against one of the great marble columns that stretches up to the ornate roof. He looks like he should be lounging against the wall in a nightclub. He's a handsome man with the same dark hair and dark eyes and slim fingers as his father. He has

218

recently shaved off his moustache, having been told by his father that it made him look like 'some sort of fucking spic trumpet player'. His recently denuded top lip is now less tanned than the rest of his face and in the low light of the empty church the strip of pale skin blends with the hollows of his cheeks to make his handsome countenance seem oddly cartoonish.

'I was about to lock up,' says Whelan. He makes no attempt to smile. He doesn't fear Salvatore. But seeing him here, in the majesty of St Colman's, always turns his stomach. His very presence in a house of God is thanks to a deal Father Whelan made with the devil. The knowledge has already given him a stomach ulcer. He rarely sleeps and when he manages to wrestle himself into unconsciousness, his dreams are peopled with innocents in pain; their bones being shattered by the clubs and bullets, blades and boots of the men to whom he gives absolution.

'I need to confess,' says Salvatore with a shrug. 'Dad says.'

Whelan glances around him. It is a little after 9 p.m. The church is supposed to be closed. Peter said his goodnights half an hour ago. He has seen less of him in recent weeks. His legal practice is going well and he has proven invaluable to his new employers. He has established several worthwhile charities for the church and has a keen eye for new opportunities. His zeal and efficiency have repaid his benefactors several times over. He is ambitious, too. He is constantly approaching Whelan with new ideas, new stratagems; new revenue streams that will ensure the diocese accounts have never looked healthier. He approaches his profession with the same obsessive love with which he serves his God. Whelan has never seen a man take so much pride in holding a chalice containing the blood of the Lord. Whelan does not even think of the liquid as the blood of Christ any longer. He simply sees wine; as cheap and tasteless as the communion wafer which sticks to the roof of his mouth and clogs his throat.

'It has to be now?' asks Whelan.

Salvatore is accompanied by two of his crew. They have both styled themselves after their young captain, in flared jeans and patterned shirts; their hair pushed back from slim, handsome faces.

'I got places to be,' sniffs Salvatore. He reaches into his jacket for a smoke and then remembers himself. 'You gonna listen?' he asks, jerking his head at the confessional.

'Is Tony with you?' asks Father Whelan, looking past the three men. 'I'd hoped we could talk.'

'Tony don't talk,' says Sal with a laugh.

'But he listens,' snaps Father Whelan. 'I heard he was living quite comfortably, quite independently. I had hoped to see him to tell him how proud I am of his journey.'

'Pride's a sin, Father,' says Salvatore. 'And if you want to see him so bad we can arrange it. He don't like surprises. Neither does Dad. But I'll give him your best wishes. He'll be pleased.'

Whelan pauses, wondering if he can delay the moment. Resignation settles upon him like snow. He nods his head and follows Salvatore to the confessional. He opens the ornate wooden door and steps inside. The old wood of the ancient booth seems to be suffused with the sins of countless decades. He feels as though he can taste the accumulated misdeeds; the pitiful pleas; the cold, dispassionate words of so many priests . . . he feels them climb inside his mouth and into his throat.

'Bless me, Father, for I have sinned,' mutters Salvatore beyond the wrought-iron grille. 'It has been eleven months and two weeks since my last confession.'

'Confess your sins and feel God's love,' replies Father Whelan, and his whisper sounds pained.

'I've had impure thoughts,' says Salvatore, sounding bored. 'Had a fucking lot of them.'

'Have you acted on these thoughts, my son?' asks Whelan, and already knows what is to come.

'She was pretty. Tits like melons. She shoved them in my face like they were for sale. I thought the school uniform was for show, like she was a dancer or something. She looked older than her age.'

Whelan closes his eyes. He has heard much worse. He is already full to bursting with the horrors for which he has become a repository. He knows he should ask Salvatore to unburden himself further – to give details and to vouchsafe his true and sincere regret. But Whelan has learned that Pugliesca's men do not come for him to save their souls. They come because Pugliesca tells them to. All they want is a blessing and an Amen.

'This girl,' asks Whelan cautiously. 'Is she . . . harmed?'

'Couldn't say, Father.' Sal sighs, with an audible shrug. 'I told Dad about it. It's taken care of.'

'Her family,' says Whelan. 'There will be those desperate for answers . . .'

'Better they never find them, eh, Father? I don't think she had the kind of family to worry about her. She was sitting on a bench at the bus stop, looking lost. I was just friendly with her. Gave her some money for food. She knew what I was buying. I didn't mean for what happened to happen.'

'Where did you leave her?' asks Whelan, and his voice is little more than a breath.

'Fuck should I know?' asks Sal sharply. 'Woods somewhere. She'd have made her way back to the city when she got herself together. Few leaves in her hair and a bruise or two but she had more money in her pocket than she did when I found her. I only told Dad because the fucking Feds are watching so close. You hear about Henry? Got lifted for supplying drugs, the dumb Irish fuck. That's why they're never made, y'know? You got to be Sicilian. Got to be pure.'

Across the grille, Whelan finds his throat closing. His mind is filling with pictures of a young, bewildered girl: brutalised, tormented and abandoned.

'Are you truly sorry for your sins?' asks Whelan, and he feels a tear trickle down into his collar. He has stopped trying to reconcile himself to the good that he did through his pact with Pugliesca: the closure of the Staten Island facility; the bright new dawn for Tony Blank, the fresh start for Peter.

'Dad says I have to be,' says Sal petulantly.

Whelan screws up his eyes and drops his head. 'God the Father of mercies, through the death and resurrection of your son, you have reconciled the world to yourself and sent the Holy Spirit among us for the forgiveness of sins. Through the ministry of the Church, may God grant you pardon and peace. And I absolve you of your sins, in the name of the Father, and of the Son and of the Holy Spirit. Amen.'

'Amen,' says Sal breezily. 'We done? Stinks in here.'

Whelan hears the neighbouring door open. He angrily swats away a tear as he pushes open his own door and steps back into the church.

In the central aisle, Salvatore is standing with his legs apart, hands in his pockets. He is looking past Father Whelan, past the entrance to the vestry and sacristy, towards the great double doors. Ali is standing there, pretty, dark-skinned and plump. She wears her school blazer over a tight white blouse. She is looking at Father Whelan nervously.

'I brought the sauce that Mama promised,' she says in her pleasant, accented voice. 'Mama said you hadn't eaten anything. Asked me to bring you a plate.'

Her voice echoes in the great empty space. Salvatore looks at her as if she were a character in a nursery rhyme, skipping through the woods with a basket over her arm.

'That's fine, Ali,' says Father Whelan. 'I'm just with some associates. Could you leave it there and thank your mother for me?'

'No rush, Ali,' says Salvatore. He has pulled out his cigarettes and is making a great show of lighting one. 'I'm hungry myself. You got enough for all of us?'

Whelan turns to Sal. 'You've been absolved,' he hisses. 'Go on. I have work . . .'

Salvatore licks his lips. Then he nods. 'I'll tell Tony you were asking after him,' he says with a wink. 'He's proving a good boy, like you promised. Reads his Bible. Draws his pictures. Sometimes he comes into the city and helps Dad and me with little bits of work. He's stronger than he looks. Knows how to dig.'

Whelan stares at the younger man and wishes him dead. Wishes them all dead. He feels no reason to bless himself for the sin of his desire.

'Your father said he would take care of him. Keep him away from influences.'

'And he does, Father. He keeps him away from you.'

Whelan reaches out and rests his weight on the hard, warm wood of the pew. The men file out past him, making half-hearted signs of the cross. He stares at the floor. He wants to lie down on the cool flagstones and puddle into the ground. When he finally drags his eyes upwards, he is alone in the church.

22

The Penitent has not taken his medicine in over a week. It has been many years since he last endeavoured to live his life without the complex cocktail of prescription pills that have helped him become the person that he allows the world to see. This time, he is unsure whether the absence of drugs has had any effect upon him. He feels weak and dizzy and there is a sound in his head like the far-off jingling of keys, but he is aware that he has lost a lot of blood and has barely eaten or drunk for many days. Perhaps the strange colours and shapes in his vision are a direct result of the physical abuses visited upon his body, and not a resurgence of the condition that left him unsure of what was real and what was not. It is taking an effort of will to differentiate between the men he has taught himself to be. This morning, while ordering his morning coffee and bagel, he saw tiny scampering beetles erupt from beneath the fingernails of the waitress who served him. She acted as though there were nothing there, even as the tiny dots flooded over her fingers and wrist and scurried over her dark skin. He recoiled in his chair as if struck and tore open the wounds upon his back. A wave of nausea engulfed him and he vomited all over the yellow floor of the diner, spattering the girl's legs and shoes with a mixture of bile and blood. He stumbled into the snow, reeking of foulness; tasting his own rotting insides. And then his head made a noise like an aeroplane taking off and he was back in the restaurant, sipping iced water, talking to the waitress about the book she had been reading and listening to her thoughts on what she planned to do when she graduated.

Here, now, the Penitent cannot be sure that he is talking with the right voice. He can hear himself and the conversation he is having with the man who has made him rich, but he knows that the words could be an auditory hallucination, masking the true conversation taking place beneath.

He listens, like an eavesdropper, to the words he is muttering into the telephone.

'There may be hope. If he wakes, the surgeon doubts he will ever be the man he was and his memory may be so incapacitated as to be harmless. He takes comfort in the words. I wish only that it had not been so. I know this is my doing. I was tempted. I went against your instructions and it cost us all something too dear to calculate. I know your pain equals my own. Believe me, I fought to stop this. But I was weak. It was beaten from my disloyal lips. My consciousness floated above as he tore the truth from my bleeding body. We had no choice. You had no choice. With the Lord's help we can make his sacrifice a thing of beauty. Forgive me . . .'

The Penitent hears someone begin to cough and is surprised to feel wetness upon his own chin. Has the man sprayed blood and phlegm upon him? Or were the words his own? He feels faint as he considers the question. Feels himself falling, tumbling through floor after floor of his own insides like an angel tumbling from heaven; watching the perfect lights of paradise grow faint and the heat of hell begin to cook the tenderised meat upon his back.

He forces himself to stand and realises he is already upright. There is a candle, burning, inches from his face. People are looking at him. He can feel a cool breeze upon his face. He looks at the stone floor and the multicoloured lights that shimmer like goldfish upon its hardness. And he sees the blood; the blood he dripped and knelt in as he stooped to take the body of Christ into his mouth.

'Are you hurt, my son?'

And he is falling again: falling for real, tumbling over backwards to clatter onto the blood-speckled stone; his stench erupting in his nostrils.

The last thing he sees before the blackness takes him is the faceless child. He sees that tiny, shrivelled entity encased in darkness and lace; sucking on the brown nipple of its dead mother in that place of cobwebs, dirt and rose petals. He sees the child, and sees what he became.

When he wakes, the Penitent is still sitting in the chair at the foot of Brishen Ayres's bed. He is still holding his Bible and stroking the soft leather of its spine. The room smells of flowers and surgical wipes. He can taste red wine and there is a crumb of communion wafer wedged into a back molar.

He removes it with his tongue and swallows it, body and soul.

23

'Orange juice,' says Alto, turning to the barkeep. He has his NYPD shield in his right hand, in case the cocktail virtuoso thinks about making him wait. The badge has the desired effect and the elaborately moustachioed bartender pauses in his twirling of a silver shaker for long enough to pour a good-sized glug of freshly squeezed orange juice into a tall glass. He adds two straws, a spray of mint and a paper umbrella, places the creation on a plastic tray and brings it over to where Alto has slumped down in the chair opposite McAvoy.

'On the house,' says the barkeep, smiling. He reveals teeth that are no strangers to hand-rolled cigarettes.

'Kind of you,' says Alto.

'And you, sir? Another?'

McAvoy looks at his coconut shell and for a moment it makes him think of a hollowed-out skull. He is unaccustomed to such grisly imaginings and shakes the thought away before he visibly shudders. 'I'm fine, thanks.'

'I love your accent,' says the barkeep, taking the empty shell. 'I went to Edinburgh once. Wonderful city though it's all uphill. What is it they call New Year? Hogmanay? Best party of my life . . .'

McAvoy feels a sudden urge to take the man's face in his fist and close his mouth. He wants him to go away. Wants to shake Alto by the ankles until everything he knows comes tumbling out of his mouth like coins from a pocket.

'Really? I went to university there for a while. Beautiful city and very welcoming. Do you think you'll go back?'

McAvoy hears himself speaking and hates himself more with every word. Just once, he would like to find the strength of character to be rude.

Alto comes to his rescue. 'We'll catch up later, sir. For now, my friend and I need some privacy.'

The barkeep gives a nod. He understands. He's seen it all before. He walks away without another word.

'Why do you indulge them?' asks Alto, removing the flamboyant additions to his drink and dropping them on the tabletop. 'It's okay to tell people to fuck off.'

'Courtesy,' says McAvoy, without thinking about it. 'Manners. Basic niceness. I don't like being rude. Boarding school put the varnish on the lessons of my father.'

'You'll never get any peace.'

'Okay, I'll be rude now. What the fuck is going on?'

'I'm sorry?'

'The files Trish is going through. That's some proper police work. People have investigated Molony before and you've given them to a virtual stranger. And why aren't you raiding Molony's house? How did you get me a sit-down with the leader of the Mob? I might be a stranger but I didn't come down the river on a water biscuit, my friend. Who's got their hands on my steering wheel?'

Alto looks as though he is about to protest then stops himself. He removes his spectacles and polishes them on his napkin. When he puts them back on his eyes look crisp and clear.

'I haven't been totally honest,' says Alto, and gives in to a laugh at the level of understatement. 'Where do I begin, Hector? You know I have a connection to the Italians, that much I've been honest about. But, look, this business works on favours. And when I was in Homicide, Pugliesca and Savoca were good friends to have. We were concerned about who was killing street dealers. We were preoccupied with innocent people getting caught up in the fallout from organised crime. We had a sort of arrangement . . .'

'A deal?'

'Not a deal,' says Alto defensively. 'Not for money or anything like that. But when they could, the Italians slipped us a name or two. They helped make sure that bad people got put away. They didn't inform, never gave evidence, but they were useful.'

'And in return you turned a blind eye,' says McAvoy quietly.

Alto shakes his head. 'You don't get it,' he says. 'Making a case stick – it's years of manpower. It's wiretaps and warrants and so much money you could weep. You don't turn a blind eye – you just prioritise differently. And that's what I did at Homicide South. The Feds were responsible for bringing down the Mob and I was just a detective who had some good contacts. Hell, I was invited to Mobsters' weddings and baptisms. And you hear things. If people get drunk enough and relaxed enough, they talk. And that's when I heard about the man who helped them hide their money. Some lawyer. Some ex-priest who'd sold his soul to the Mob. That was it, I swear to you, but when I left Homicide I had no reason not to rock the boat and I did a little digging. Hugh, too. We thought he would be a good collar. Everybody loves taking down a lawyer, don't they? We unearthed something that we didn't know what to do with. Seminary records, psychiatric reports, medical files. We got down a few layers and found a name.'

Alto looks McAvoy in the face. 'I got warned off. It was subtle, nothing you could point to and call a threat, but I would get home and my wife would tell me she had heard noises, or that she felt she'd been followed on her drive to work. Files saved on my computer just vanished. I started getting all the shittiest jobs. Detectives I'd never met before were suddenly getting partnered up with me and they had accounts at racetracks and bars all over the city where there was always good credit for a man with a badge. I started drinking. I drank a lot. And after that I didn't care much about a lawyer who was helping the Mob hide their cash because my wife had left me and I was a drunk who nobody listened to anyway.

'It took me a long time to get myself together and then suddenly I've got you in front of me with stories about dead Irishmen and devious priests. I used you for Murray Ellison. I got the collar that mattered. So I wanted to repay you by helping out and as soon as I did any digging I found the arrows pointing to Peter Molony. The same Peter Molony who had almost undone me when I first started digging. I didn't know whether to tell Hugh or Pugliesca or the Feds. In the end I decided to nudge things along. I asked Hugh to contact your boss – help out a little. I've bumbled along, hoping you would do it all for me and I've had everything I could sent to your boss because she seems strong enough to make the decisions I can't.'

Alto's shoulders slump. His lips become a tight line.

'She will,' says McAvoy quietly. 'So will I. And if you ask me honestly, I couldn't tell you whether I think you've done good or bad. But I know that there's a way to do something important and I think you want to help me.'

Alto looks at him. Manages a flash of a smile.

'You need to pick up Molony,' says McAvoy decisively.

Alto shakes his head. He sits back in his chair. 'Forget that a moment. Listen to me, Aector. I'm going to tell you something and I'm going to trust you to do nothing stupid with the information, okay. I think we know where Valentine is.'

McAvoy spreads his hands. His skin is prickling. He feels as though it is snowing inside the bar; as if everything has turned and switched and he is sitting in the middle of the street at a metal table, chatting with a friend in the face of onrushing traffic.

'Tell me.'

'He was never there,' says Alto, sighing. 'Cairo, I mean. Never with Brishen and Shay at the scene of the attack.'

McAvoy cocks his head. He doesn't know what to do with his hands so just sits on them, like a schoolboy frightened of getting into trouble for picking his nose.

'The man we picked up . . .' says Alto. 'His name is Zav. He's Chechen. A soldier for Sergey Volotov. The Chechens and the Ukrainians are all part of the same lovely party at the moment. Things are peaceful out at Brighton Beach. We don't even know what to call most of the motherfuckers who run that part of town. Just think of it as Russian Mob, and you'll get halfway there. Anyway, this afternoon Zav succeeded in chewing through the arm of a friend with whom he had been tortured in a Brooklyn basement. Zav was also the passenger in the car that picked you up last night. The description he gave of his captor matches what Polina said: an older, Italian male with poor teeth and bad skin. He shot Zav full of holes and asked him a lot of questions about the night

Shay was killed. Zav held out for a time but eventually he broke. And now Zav can't go back to Volotov. So he's come to us. The Feds have arrived and I don't think I'm going to get a chance to talk to him again. But I had him alone for long enough to ask about that night. He's holding back until he gets the right deal from the Feds but he's in a fragile state and he responded to a bit of pressure.'

McAvoy scratches at his beard. Grey dust spirals down like snow.

'There was a fight,' says Alto. 'An underground boxing match between Helden and Byki. High stakes, big purse.'

McAvoy starts to shake his head, refusing to believe Brishen Ayres would allow his protégé to involve himself in the brutality of the underground circuit. Then he stops himself, knowing his own preconceptions to be self-erected barriers between himself and the truth.

'It went the distance,' says Alto. 'It wasn't as open and shut as everybody expected. After fifteen rounds the crowd started getting bored. There were complaints. The organisers decided to spice things up. They told Ayres his man had to take the gloves off. It was going to be bare-knuckle. Ayres said no but Helden didn't want to let his coach down and he pulled the gloves off. Went after Byki like a madman. Some of the crowd started getting involved. That's when Valentine stepped in.'

McAvoy looks at the tabletop. The drips of spilled drink look at him like a melted face; ghoulish and dead-eyed.

'Valentine laid out two of the Chechen boys in the crowd. The whole thing broke down. Ayres, Helden and Valentine had to run for their fucking lives.'

McAvoy can picture it. Can scent the whole damn scene, with its sweat and blood and smelling salts; its reek of male skin and beer.

'Zav watched it all,' says Alto. 'They'd enjoyed every moment of it, even if there was no clear winner. There were no plans to take out Ayres. Helden had fought well.'

'Until . . . ?'

Alto gives a half-hearted laugh. 'Valentine came back a while later. Walked straight in, bold as you like. He was bleeding from the mouth. He was high on something. And he demanded the prize money.'

McAvoy feels his heart beat faster, as though it is swelling in his chest. He can picture his brother-in-law so clearly. Wishes he could not.

'One of the Russian captains told Valentine he admired him for having balls of solid rock, but warned him he had better fuck off. Valentine didn't do as he was told. He pulled a gun.'

'A gun? Where did he get a gun?'

'Zav claims that he must have taken it from one of the Chechens during the bout. Either way, he put his gun to the head of one of the men present and threatened to blow his brains out if he wasn't paid.'

'Did they care?' asks McAvoy, shocked.

'They wouldn't have, but the guy he happened to be threatening was Chebworz Khamzateyev,' says Alto resignedly.

McAvoy looks blank. 'I'm sorry . . .'

'His father is about as high up in the Obschina as you can get.'

'The what?'

'The fucking Chechen Mafia,' says Alto testily. 'He's important, yeah? He's the son of an important man and he's pretty ruthless himself. And Valentine put a gun to his head.'

'Christ.'

'Christ indeed. These fucking Irish! They're just not scared.'

'Ronny, tell me the rest.'

'Valentine must have realised he was onto something because the mobsters dropped their guns. Zav saw his captain throw an envelope of money at Valentine's feet. But Chebworz wasn't frightened of him. Called him an Irish pussy. Told him to shoot him if he had the balls. Valentine slapped him in the mouth with the gun. He picked up the money and ran.'

McAvoy realises he is bouncing on the balls of his feet beneath the table. He feels as though he is watching the whole thing unfold before him.

'And?'

'They went after him,' says Alto. 'Chebworz in the lead, threatening all sorts. That's when Brishen and Shay Helden arrived.'

231

McAvoy puts his head in his hands.

'Zav saw them shouting for Valentine to jump in the car. Chebworz shot him.'

'Shot Val?'

'Clipped him, Zav says. Valentine fell and Chebworz's men grabbed him. So Brishen drove straight at them. Chebworz took the brunt of it. Helden jumped out, grabbed Chebworz and threw him in the car. Valentine made a run for it but then the bullets started flying and Brishen drove out of there like the tail-pipe was on fire.'

'With Chebworz in the car?'

Alto nods. 'It got messy very quickly. The Chechens picked up Valentine within the hour, limping and bleeding and still threatening them with all kinds of hell.'

'And the others?'

'The Chechens rallied the troops. They were all set to unleash unholy hell on the Irishmen. Then Brishen got in touch with his contact – the man who had set up the fight. He told him to get the message to the Chechens that they wanted Valentine returned unharmed and all the money he was owed.'

'And what did the Chechens say?'

'They said yes. Culturally, they admire that kind of thing, if you'll forgive the generalisation.'

'So what happened?'

'They arranged a meet that same night. Neutral place in the Village. The Chechens showed, the Irishmen didn't.'

'This was the evening of the shootings? The night Shay died?'

'By the time they were due to meet the Chechens, we know for certain that Brishen and Shay were already miles upstate, being shot to pieces by whoever did this to them.'

McAvoy is breathing heavily. He gives in to a fit of coughing as he aggravates his wounded throat.

'Next morning, Chebworz phoned his father from a rest-stop about eight miles from where all this shit went down. He'd got himself free. He demanded they come and pick him up. He'd been thrown in the trunk and driven upstate. Been gagged and tied.

Next thing he's hearing curses and shots and the trunk is thrown open by a young Italian male who must have been Luca Savoca. From the way he tells it, the Italians had no fucking clue he was there. Luca dragged him out on some forest road. Blackness and snow and trees and two Italians pointing guns in his face. Brishen and Shay were on their knees, hands behind their backs, battered and bleeding. Brishen's face was a mess – a hole where his nose should be. Chebworz saw it all. When they pulled the gag free he started cursing the Italians – telling them he was important and that if this was a set-up, there would be war. Luca just laughed. Started hitting him. Showed him the blade he had used on the bleeding Irishmen. Stuck his gun behind Brishen's head and pulled the trigger just as Shay ran. Chebworz ran too. Shots were fired. They went after him. He got the upper hand and rammed Luca onto a tree. Left the other guy bleeding. Then he ran. Ran until he reached a rest-stop and called his men.'

'And the people he left behind?' asks McAvoy softly.

'The older Italian must have tidied up as best he could,' says Alto.

McAvoy takes a moment to digest it all. 'So they still have him. Valentine.'

'If they haven't cut off his hands, face and feet and dumped him in the river,' says Alto, who suddenly looks apologetic. 'That's their MO. That's what they do.'

'But they could still have him,' says McAvoy, hardly moving his jaw.

'Zav says that as of last night, Valentine was still alive, but who knows what's happened since then. It's clear that whatever relationship was blossoming between the Chechens and the Italians, something has gone horribly wrong.'

'How much can we trust what your witness is saying? Maybe the whole thing was a set-up. If Brishen was short of money they could have found a way to lure the Italians to the middle of nowhere and then Cheb could have killed them. Or Brishen took some money from the Italians to grab Chebworz. The Irishmen may just have been collateral damage.' He locks his jaw. 'Why won't people just stop lying?'

Alto smiles contritely. 'Either way, we no longer have an inform-ant in the organisation. The Feds may have moles in the Italian Mob but if they do, they're not sharing that information with NYPD. This whole thing will be bundled up into an organised crime investigation and you and I will have nothing more to do with it. If we raid Molony's place we may find nothing but a lot of dust and some name-tags.'

'And Valentine . . .' protests McAvoy.

'Could be anywhere,' says Alto kindly. 'Or nowhere. All we have is the word of one Chechen soldier who will do and say anything to save his own life.'

McAvoy rocks in his chair, trying to find the words to express himself. His face flushes. 'Where was the fight?' he asks, and his accent becomes more pronounced He sounds like a Scottish chieftain wanting to know who raided his clan's land. 'Where does Chebworz hang out? All we have to do is put some pressure on him. They have no need for Valentine. If we could guarantee there would be no prosecution . . .'

Alto gives a harsh laugh. 'No prosecution? This is the Chechen Mob. They're not scared of anything. There's no benefit to them admitting they've got him. There's nothing in it for them.'

McAvoy looks long and hard at Alto.

'You've already helped me a lot,' says McAvoy. 'I can't ask you for any more. So I won't ask you to tell me where I should go to find Chebworz. I'll just blunder around, asking people who look vaguely Russian, and eventually, somebody will tell somebody else and I'm sure they'll come and find me. That way, your conscience will be clear.'

Alto shakes his head. 'Don't be stupid.'

'It's not stupid. There are a dozen ways to get an address. My colleagues at home have a special relationship with some of your colleagues. So don't trouble yourself.'

Alto looks pained. 'You can't just go and ask them if they've killed him.'

McAvoy finds himself smiling, even as his heart races and he feels fear wrap around his insides. 'He's my wife's brother,' says

McAvoy. 'He's why I'm here. Everything else is none of my business, however much I feel the urge to make it so. If there's a chance of taking him home with me, I'll take it.'

'They'll kill you,' says Alto flatly.

'Why? I'm no threat. I don't want to arrest anybody. I just want to clear up a misunderstanding.'

Alto looks at his glass, clearly wishing it was full to the brim with something that would pitch him into a coma.

'What about Molony?' says Alto. 'Everything we saw there this afternoon. Valentine's tooth. This is so much bigger than a fight gone wrong.'

'Yes it is,' says McAvoy. 'And you can investigate all of it. I'll help, if you want me to. But right now, Valentine is what matters. In fact, no, my wife is what matters. Valentine is an angry little rat without a redeeming feature, but bringing him home will make Roisin happy and that's all I bloody live for, so that's what I'm going to try to do.'

Alto takes a notebook from his pocket and scribbles an address. 'Don't do it,' he says, standing up and looking at McAvoy as if he were saying goodbye to a prisoner. 'There are better ways.'

McAvoy folds the paper and puts it in his pocket. 'The apartment,' he says. 'Molony's. There's enough to pick him up. Somebody shot Brishen and Shay. Whether any of it is to do with Molony is something I can't answer but I don't think we'd be particularly good police officers if we didn't ask questions about the names, the ashes and his link to Brishen. My boss reckons you're using me. I hope not. Either way, I can't just wash my hands of all this blood and dirt. Neither can you.'

Alto gives a curt nod. He leaves without another word. As the door bangs behind him, another flurry of shredded angel wings fills the bar.

McAvoy unearths the piece of paper. Gives the tiniest nod. He knows, for a fraction of a second, who he is, and what he is for.

A minute later, he leaves the warm embrace of the Pink Pug and steps into blackness and snow, yellow lights and swirling trash.

He turns to face the gale, feeling the last of the ash and bone lift from his skin to tumble away upon the screeching wind.

24

Claudio stands by the large windows of Molony's living room and looks out upon the city. He is not a New Yorker by birth but it is a vista in which he feels an odd kind of pride. There is certainly a beauty to it. Claudio has always preferred paintings and photographs of natural scenes to anything man-made. He likes rolling fields or woodland, moonlit lakes or flower meadows. But in this moment, the view beyond the glass seems to be an equally organic thing. This city has grown like mould. It is the vision of endless different planners, architects, politicians and developers, the product of a billion warring desires. It has been fettered by bureaucracy and chiselled into unexpected shapes by artless hands. Its buildings have grown, forest-like, from tiny acorns of inspiration and then been felled by violence, poverty and hate. And yet it is beautiful, viewed from afar. Up close, he knows the city to be different. Its inhabitants are ticks, buried deep in the fetid skin of a half-rotten dog: growing fat on its blood until they risk bursting. He counts himself among their number. He wishes this view belonged to him, and not to the pitiful specimen who first wriggled into his life three decades ago, and with whom he has never exchanged a word.

Claudio did not need to intimidate or charm the elderly lady at the nearby deli. He gained entry into Molony's apartment building the old-fashioned way. He picked the lock on the subterranean garage and made his way to the ground floor along a grey, sloping hallway, holding his gun in his right hand and his shoes in his left. He did as McAvoy and Alto had done; checking the empty apartments and forming his own conclusions about the scam being perpetrated by the landlord. And then he reached the red door. He picked the lock in eight seconds. Allowed himself a whistle of appreciation at the luxurious living space enjoyed by the lawyer. Then he got to work. He has checked the entire apartment for surveillance equipment and hidden cameras and been mildly gratified to discover motion sensors in the living room and kitchen. He idly wondered who was monitoring the alarm, and how long he had before it caused him difficulties. An hour later, he has begun to feel secure. Nobody is coming. Whoever Molony is paying for security should offer the shmuck his money back.

He has surprised himself with his actions. When he was finished with the Chechen he should have telephoned his employer and told him that the whole thing had been a clusterfuck. Wrong place, wrong time. Cheb may have killed Luca Savoca but what was the poor bastard supposed to have done? There was no need to go to war. No need to disturb the peace. Instead, Claudio is indulging himself. It was the Chechen who told him what the owner of this apartment had been doing for Pugliesca for so many years. He was soon going to be doing it for the Chechens too and, in return, Pugliesca was going to get new territory and a new line of supply on his heroin business. In payment, they wanted his system for cleaning up their millions. Claudio is unsure how much of the information has been passed on to the other New York crime families. Nor does he know why he was sent into the woods in the middle of the night to go and kill two Irishmen. A job for New York – that's what he'd been told. That order could only have come from Pugliesca or Savoca. And Luca hadn't mentioned his father as Claudio outlined his hasty plan. If Pugliesca wanted the Irishmen dead, he would need a good reason. Claudio knows the old man and knows that money and power are his favourite mistresses. Could the Irishmen be fucking with his lucrative new deal, perhaps? A deal to which Molony was central? The more Claudio considered it, the more he began to feel that Molony held the answers. He wants to poke around a little. Wants to burrow beneath the veneer and see how many answers will spill out if he were to split the lawyer open. He is following his initiative, even as he knows the risks. If this man is important to Pugliesca, Claudio's presence here is a grave mistake. He just can't seem to persuade himself to leave without knowing more.

The Venetian blinds protest a little as Claudio adjusts them. There is a tiny discolouration upon their surface, as though they have never been opened, and Claudio wonders what kind of man would live in a place like this and not enjoy the view.

As he watches the snow blow like so much ripped tissue across the rooftops of Manhattan, Claudio finds himself overcome by memory. He has felt this way all day. He is not a man who feels much in the way of regret. He thinks of guilt as an indulgence. He has made his confessions and pays a handsome contribution to his neighbourhood church in Philly each year as recompense for any misdeed he felt uncomfortable about sharing with his confessor. He is not haunted by the faces of men he has killed. But were he to admit to feeling the presence of any of the men he has dispatched, Sal Pugliesca's face would fill his mind.

Claudio has a sudden memory of a basement room in Brooklyn. He and Sal, dressed to the nines in wing-tips and gleaming suits. He remembers the tiny sting of the needle as it punctured his skin, the acrid smell as the picture of the saint curled to ash before him. Remembers the slaps to his back and the bill-folds being stuffed in his pocket. They were two of the youngest men ever to be made by the Mob. Sure, Sal's father had greased the wheels for his boy but there was no arguing that he was a good earner. He was loyal and fearless. Claudio was there on merit too. He already had three hits on his record and he had done his brief stint in Rikers like a stand-up guy. He was a good earner and he respected the hierarchy. He was good at keeping his mouth shut. He deserved this. Deserved his moment in the sun. Even smiled through it as the older guys busted his balls for being a member of the Philly outfit. 'A jumped-up crew,' they called it, and Claudio did not point out how much more money his 'crew' were bringing to the table than the NY family to which they were affiliated.

It was a damn awful winter, Claudio recalls. Snow in Miami, slush in Alaska, as if the world had turned on its head. The drifts were six feet deep in Buffalo. The Salvation Army had volunteers clambering over snowdrifts to bring groceries to people who couldn't open their front doors for the ice around the frames. He and Sal spent the night in a pizzeria, crammed in with dozens of other New Yorkers who warmed themselves on the wood-fired ovens and ate free slices like they were refugees from a war. The dummy was there too, looking at Sal with those big baby eyes. He was like a dog that followed his master. Occasionally, Sal would turn and ask him if he was okay, or to check if he was warm enough or wanted something else to eat. The dummy would look down and shake his head and it seemed like it was all Sal could do not to tickle him behind the ear. Claudio had been too embarrassed to acknowledge the presence of the pale-skinned mute who followed them from bar to bar as they celebrated their new status as made men. He just trudged behind them through the snow, uncomplaining; stepping in the footsteps left by the man who called him 'brother'.

It was a grim surprise when Claudio received his instructions that night in 1981. A hit had been authorised. Sal was informing. He had to go. Claudio had earned his reputation by doing as he was told and though he felt a flicker of distaste at killing a man he thought of as a friend, he didn't utter a word of protest. He built the device himself. Didn't say any kind of Hail Mary or apology as he flicked the switch and blew Salvatore Pugliesca's body into strips of meat. The cops found parts of him six houses away. They didn't speak much about the mute. Tony Blank – that was his name. The dummy, to everybody else. Tony was collateral damage – merely 'an associate' of the deceased. Claudio expected there to be questions asked about the extra corpse on his ledger, but not long after Sal's death the Philly Mob was once more engulfed in one of the power struggles that erupted every few years. Claudio was kept busy, staying alive and stopping hearts. He was never asked a single question about how the poor dumb bastard had ended up caught in the blast. Claudio wouldn't have had an answer even if he had been interrogated. He simply didn't know that Tony was there. Sal had driven into the driveway of his Philadelphia home. He had climbed out of the car and approached his door. He paused on the step to find his keys. His shoulders sagged for a moment, as if he had just remembered something he couldn't be bothered to do. And then Claudio flicked the switch and Sal disappeared in a cloud of red and grey.

Claudio should have driven away. There was no doubting that his target was dead. But then he heard the noise. Even above the sound of falling timbers and crackling flame, he heard something rhythmic and unfathomable.

He stepped over what was left of Sal Pugliesca. And he saw the dummy, laid out beneath wood and brick. Tony was pinned by his left hand. There was a dark stain spreading across his chest. Blood was dripping into his wide eyes from a wound to his skull. And in his hand, he held a cleaver; its blade already gory with his own blood. As Claudio watched, Tony hacked down again at the spot just above his right elbow. His lips moved not in pain but in silent prayer. Claudio stood still until he heard the sirens. Then he knelt down and softly skewered the dummy's skull on the gleaming blade. He prayed as he did it and has never understood why. Then he walked away. He put his memory of Sal in the little box in his head and kept it shut. He had done his job and nobody ever criticised him for it. Claudio closes his eyes before the snow makes him feel too morose. It is not that he regrets Sal's death. But he is feeling unsettled. He has been troubled ever since that almighty clusterfuck upstate.

And now he is having to confront his memory of the Glow-worm.

That's what they called him, back in the day. Claudio used to see him around at bars and restaurants where the different crews hung out. He was always on his way to or from somewhere; always carrying books and sweating, whatever the weather. He wore big round glasses that made his eyes look twice the size. He was around Claudio's age. Big round head and already balding. Stuttered when he talked and always looked like he was about to cry. Good at the books though, that's what everybody said. He wasn't to be picked on. Did something important for *our friends* in the city. Leave him alone . . .

How many years ago had it been? Some time after Sal's death. Maybe '82? Claudio had attended a baptism in the city. Half the mobsters from New York and Philly were there. Flashbulbs and champagne, squeezed cheeks, kissed lips and endless bill-folds stuffed in a silk purse. The Glow-worm was there, though Claudio had to stare for an age before he realised who he was looking at. He was unrecognisable from the stumbling, fat-faced fuck who used to cook the books for the city mob. This man had poise. He had self-belief. He wore a white gown and held the silver chalice as if it really did contain the blood of Christ. He looked radiant. Self-assured.

Claudio saw little of him after that day. Sometimes they would pass on the court steps or they would both be present at the same wedding or funeral, but over the years Claudio gradually became more of a background figure. He was no street-hustler or stick-up artist. He was a killer and that was what he got paid to do. He gave the Glow-worm little or no thought. And then this morning, he saw his big fat face staring out at him from a computer screen. A Scottish cop was looking into his background; the same Scottish cop who was piecing together what went wrong out at Cairo. Claudio is a clever man. He is already a few steps ahead. He is also a realist. He knows that whatever service Molony performs for his New York associates is valuable. Molony cannot be harmed without the action being cleared from on high. Clicking his tongue, Claudio closes the blinds and looks around him. He checks his watch. Wherever Molony is, he should be home soon. Claudio is not completely sure how he will proceed. For the fifth time in an hour, he tries to call the number currently being used by Giuliano Pagano back in Philly. Old habits are threatening his resolve. He wants to call Pagano and have him sanction his actions. But he knows Pagano is too much of a pussy to move without New York's say-so, and he doubts Pugliesca would be pleased to learn that Claudio knows so much.

Bored, twitching a little, Claudio walks through to Molony's bedroom. He has removed his shoes and makes no sound as he crosses the floor. He has already been through the lawyer's possessions and found little of interest. The Glow-worm's clothes are all ordered from the same online supplier. Most still carry labels that show they have not been worn. There is no laundry hamper. His drawers are neatly kept. Packets of unopened socks in one drawer; pristine vests and T-shirts in another. Claudio wonders if Molony has the obsessive condition that he has read about. Perhaps he

241

can't bring himself to wear the same thing twice. On impulse, he enters the en-suite bathroom and opens the cabinet next to the wooden medicine cabinet. It is stacked with bars of soap like bricks in a wall.

Claudio returns to the bedroom. He examines the books on Molony's bedside table. There is a hardback with the word 'Unsolved' emblazoned down the spine that Claudio recognises. It covers dozens of cases from the past fifty years where justice was never served. Claudio has briefly flicked through it himself, leafing through the speculation and conclusions like a professor examining a teenager's essay. The book shares space on the bedside table with a ceramic flask, in which a single yellow rose has been placed. It gives off no scent but looks fresh. Claudio opens the bedside drawer. There are pill-boxes inside, their lids showing pictures of noted churches and cathedrals from around the world. Claudio opens one of the ornate little boxes at random. The pills inside are loose. Pink. They are the size of .22 bullets and look damn hard to swallow. Claudio puts them back.

At length, he sits down on the bed and just as quickly stands up again, rubbing the seat of his trousers. Carefully, he pulls back the thick red and gold throw that covers the sheets. The sheets of Molony's bed are stained brown, red and rust by dried blood. It looks as though somebody has been split open and left to bleed out. The coppery tang fills Claudio's nostrils but he does not recoil. He considers the sheets as if he were a forensics expert. The blood is not all fresh. And the sheets themselves are yellowed with age. They are mildewed at the edges and, in places, the cotton has become so threadbare that Claudio can see the stains on the mattress beneath. He can also see the needles. They stick up through the mattress like the quills of a porcupine; each tip silver and gleaming and flecked with blood.

Hunkering down, Claudio looks under the bed. The floor is spotless. Where does the man keep his shoes? His pornography? This place feels false, somehow. It feels like a veneer that caps a rotten tooth. It contains no true traces of the person that Claudio saw so many years ago with his face turned towards the heavens as if witnessing the rapture. Where is his cross? His Bible? Claudio returns to the living room and considers the art upon the walls. He is drawn to the blueprint of the church. It is a classy piece of work, drawn with fine black ink on pale blue paper. There is no name on the drawing and he has no way of knowing whether it is a recent build or the plans for something centuries old. The sketch occupies the prime location on the walls. Claudio leans forward and examines the smudges around the edges of the gold frame. He is a man familiar with the patina of blood. He sees the faintest traces of discolouration upon the glass around the bottom edges, where a man would place his hands to lift the image off the wall.

Claudio does so now. He lifts the whole frame from the hook and places it behind the sofa. Set in the wall behind is a small metal grille; a latticework in wrought iron that reminds him of the old confessional booths. There is a small brass handle on one side and hinges on the other. Claudio pulls the handle and the door slides open without a sound.

The object within is a little larger than a shoe-box. Claudio retrieves it and moves into the kitchen, where there is a marble-topped preparation area in the centre of the wooden floor. Claudio places the case down upon its cold, hard surface. It is a small suit-case, bound in a soft brown leather and with two buckles at the front. Grimy, rust-coloured fingermarks pattern the sides, the handle and the straps.

Claudio remembers these devices. Had one himself when he was a young man.

He opens it up and looks at the Super 8 sound recorder, all black and silver and strangely futuristic despite being a relic of the past.

He settles his hands on the counter. Breathes deep. Presses 'play'. The voice that emerges is flat and monotonous; the words emerging from throat and mouth that sound pained and dry. 'Forgive me, Father, for I have sinned. It has been eight months since my last confession. I have allowed the devil to seduce me on four occasions when I was unable to stop myself from touching my skin in a way that would displease the Lord. I have harboured many impure thoughts. I have thought disrespectfully about the man who calls himself my father. I am grateful for his kindness and yet when he speaks to me I feel a great rage inside me – a hunger for something I can't describe. I have imagined myself stealing into his room at night and smashing his brains in with a hammer – perhaps driving a nail into his skull as if it were the wrists or feet of our Lord. I do sincerely repent . . . *Shush, please, no more* . . . I repent of these sins and ask for the strength not to repeat such offences. Forgive me, Father, for my actions in making this confession. The girl I took had kind eyes and spoke kindly to me. Please allow her torture to cease. She suffers and screams and cries and her skin has begun to repel me. Please intercede with our Lord and pray for her agonies to cease so she may rest with Jesus and her sinful flesh can be consumed by this sacred earth. Bless me, Father. Amen.'

The recording is interrupted midway by the sound of a female voice cracking and breaking around a scream.

Claudio feels a lump in his throat. There is something so animal about the noise; so primal. A plea for mercy that requires no words.

He is so engrossed in the sounds that it takes him a moment to register the smell. The air has changed hue; taken on a milky, rotten foulness.

He turns just in time to see him. The Glow-worm.

He's wearing his white robes and his face shines with the radiance that unnerved Claudio so many years ago.

Before Claudio can move, the Glow-worm thrusts his hand into the black urn beneath his left arm. His face impassive, his eyes unblinking, he pulls free a handful of ash and flings it in Claudio's face like confetti.

As Claudio raises his hands to his face he realises too late he has left himself exposed.

The urn smashes into the side of Claudio's head and as he crumples to the floor he only has time to notice that the man has bare feet and pleasant, pink toes, before the blackness closes around him like a mouth, and swallows him down.

PART FOUR

1974: Forgiveness: The Sacrament of Penance

White sheets and yellow light, smooth green floors and the smell of antiseptic; tears dripping onto black cloth and rust-coloured bandages . . .

'I'm sorry, my friend. Please, Peter. Peter, listen to me. This is all my fault. This was not what I wanted. I am so very sorry. Forgive me . . .'

The figure in the hospital bed smiles up at him, all jowls and sweat. There is a waxiness to his skin that puts Father Whelan in mind of church candles.

'I had to remove temptation,' says Peter Molony. 'You told me we could atone through pain. This is my penance.'

There are tears in Father Whelan's eyes. He had not meant for any of this to happen but knows that the road beneath his feet is chiselled with the best of intentions. It was just a chat between friends; a drink between priest and parishioner. They had history. They had known each other for some time. Something existed between them that was not friendship, but which meant they enjoyed one another's company and each understood a little of the other. Perhaps each saw in the other what they themselves could have been.

'I forgave you,' says Father Whelan. 'God forgave you your transgressions. This was not necessary.'

'The pain cleanses me. I learned that long ago.'

Father Whelan wipes the heel of his hand across his eyes.

'You nearly died,' he says. 'Blood loss. They said you had been hurting yourself for some time.'

'That was for everyday sin. Something greater was needed to demonstrate my repentance for my baser nature.'

'We were getting somewhere,' says Father Whelan, anger in his voice and tears in his eyes. 'You were doing so much better. You didn't have to do this. They will send you away. I will do what I can to set you free but you could end up in places so much worse than the hell you thought you were living.'

'I couldn't risk sinning again, Father.'

'You would have been a good priest five hundred years ago,' mutters Father Whelan angrily. 'Your Bible and mine are different books. You wanted human contact, Peter. That I can forgive. That the devil leads you in the direction of young men . . . you are to be pitied and prayed for, not shunned and scorned. You would not have given in to temptation. You have me. You have my prayers. I told you to read your Bible. You pushed and pushed until I spoke of penance leading to absolution. How good deeds and sincere repentance could wipe away the past. Your mind is ill. You have already missed out on that which you truly desired . . .'

'I would have been a poor priest,' says Molony. He looks different without his glasses. 'You know that. My mind is different. My needs are different.'

'I had made arrangements,' says Father Whelan, frustrated. 'A future. A use for a man with your skills. Please, Peter, do not give up hope. When you are well, there is so much to look forward to.'

The man in the bed smiles up, serene and perfect. He does not look like a man who nearly died.

'I have faith in you,' says Father Whelan, kneeling by the bed and taking the man's hand in his own. 'I know you will live the right life. I absolve you of all sin, my son.'

'I could yet sin again.'

'You will not. And even if temptation struck, your sacrifice absolves you. You cannot sin again. The gates of heaven will never be closed to you. Please, just try to get well.'

Father Whelan finds himself too overcome to remain by the bedside. He pulls himself up, tears dripping onto his black sweater.

He leaves without looking further at the man who castrated himself to atone for his desires.

He does not see the look of perfect happiness that passes over the man's face as he feels the fires of hell cool at his back, and the glory of paradise welcome him inside.

Peter Molony suddenly feels the grace of God.

He has a true chance to repent.

A true chance to atone.

A chance to save sinners like himself.

25

There's still no answer from Roisin's phone. It's a little after 1 a.m. in Ireland but he knows she will be desperate to hear what he has learned. McAvoy has been trying her number throughout the long cab ride from the Village, growing steadily more anxious with each failed call. He's been in the yellow taxi for almost an hour, watching as the snow flurries turned into the blizzard that now assaults the glass. The roads have grown steadily quieter the further they get from Manhattan and as they enter the area known locally as Little Odessa, McAvoy finds himself looking out on a neighbourhood that seems somehow more Soviet than the area after which it was originally named.

'Brighton Beach?' the cab driver asked incredulously, as McAvoy had hailed him on the corner of Delancey and Essex. 'You fancying a swim?'

McAvoy promised a generous tip. He has repeated the pledge each time the driver has threatened to turn back in the face of the snowstorm. McAvoy fed him some lies about needing to reach a family member in trouble and the cab driver has, through sheer bloody-mindedness, managed to get them near enough to their destination. The vehicle is idling by the kerb; snow turning to mush beneath the wheels and steam rising from the hood. The meter says that he owes seventy-six dollars but McAvoy hands over two fifties and tells the driver to keep the change.

'How you getting back?' asks the driver, as McAvoy opens the door and disentangles himself. The tails of his coat are whipped by the gale and as they sting his skin, the snowflakes feel more like needles than angel wings.

'I'll hail a cab,' says McAvoy.

The driver considers him. He's a young guy. Maybe not yet thirty. He's got some Hispanic in him and has done some wonderfully geometric things with his facial hair.

'I can wait,' says the driver. 'I've got to go back to the city myself, man. I can hang on for half an hour, if you ain't gonna be long.'

McAvoy feels a sudden surge of affection towards this virtual stranger. 'You're sure?'

'There's a diner on the boardwalk,' says the driver. 'I'll go get something to eat. Meet me there if you and your friend need to get back to the city. Otherwise you're stuck out here and this is no place for a tourist to be on a night like this.'

McAvoy wishes he'd spent more of the journey talking to the man. Instead he has been glued to his phone, cursing the quality of the cab's vaunted complimentary Wi-Fi service and trying to piece together the two stories becoming increasingly linked in his mind. He knows that Brishen, Shay and Valentine came here for an underground fight. It was talked up into a grudge match; spiced with a little national pride. Those in the backyard fight game would have been bristling for a chance to see the two countries clash. The try-out at Dezzie Estrada's was little more than a cover. Marcel was the man in the middle.

McAvoy pauses, trying to channel his thoughts into a shape. What happened next? The fight occurred. There was no winner. Valentine demanded money. He ended up hurt and in the hands of the Chechens and the other Irishmen took Chebworz away in a car. At some point before, all three Irishmen visited Peter Molony's apartment. In that apartment is a wall containing the names of the dead and a carpet of ashes and earth. Molony spent time in the same seminary as James Whelan – the man who helped secure Valentine's entrance visa to the States. McAvoy can see all the pieces of the puzzle but cannot make sense of the picture.

'I'm Rey,' says the cab driver. 'Hope to see you later.'

McAvoy stands on the kerb until Rey has pulled away. He watches as the vehicle moves slowly over the gathering snow and turns left past a blue warehouse and disappears from view. Then

McAvoy turns and walks in the opposite direction. The snow is blowing against his back and the streetlights turn his shadow into a Gothic vision: all flapping wings and elongated limbs. To distract himself he tries Roisin again. He has left her four messages and texted her half a dozen times. She's not answering and the fear that rests in his stomach is for her safety and not his own.

'Hey you,' he says, trying to sound bright. 'No problems. Just wanted you to know I've got some information. And, y'know . . . I love you.'

Despite the chill he finds himself blushing. He wonders how he looks with his pink face and his red hair and his dirty clothes. And then he doesn't have time to worry about anything any more because he is across the road from the address that Alto so reluctantly gave him.

McAvoy stands in front of a chain-link fence at the corner of Neptune Avenue and Brighton 3rd Street. It is a mostly residential neighbourhood with wooden-fronted houses and squat apartment blocks. The signs on the handful of shops he has passed are written with a Cyrillic font and the company working on the abandoned building across the street advertises the services of Khlebnikov Construction.

This is the building that has McAvoy's attention. It is a long, single-storey block painted an unpleasant shade of cream and devoid of any writing or graffiti save the wooden sign of the construction crew. From his vantage point, squinting against the darkness and the snow, McAvoy fancies that the warehouse looks like a trio of trailers, parked at the kerb and then uncoupled from the wagons that pulled them. The architect who designed this place had clearly done his work in a hurry. Either that, or the client had a fondness for rectangles.

Without giving himself time to change his mind, McAvoy crosses the road. The door to the premises is painted green and as he approaches he hears noises inside. He strains his ears and makes out heavy rock music. He slips his phone into his pocket and bangs hard on the wood. When nobody answers he kicks it several times. Then he takes a step back.

Moments pass. McAvoy looks around him at the deserted street. The vehicles at the kerb are largely nondescript Hyundais or Fords, dotted here and there with a ten-year-old Lexus. Snow is piling up on their hoods and roofs to make perfect white canvases that McAvoy has a fervent desire to go and write his name in. He feels his heart thump. He counts out the seconds as he waits . . .

'The fuck you want?'

McAvoy spins back to the door and looks into the face of a white man with a shaved head and broad flat face. He is looking at McAvoy without malice and despite the profanity he seems genuinely interested to know what he wants.

'I'm McAvoy,' he says flatly. 'I'd like to talk to somebody but I don't really know whom.'

The man at the door looks at him like he's a little slow. 'What you want? You a Mormon? We don't want Mormons, man, but you're brave if you are . . .'

McAvoy shakes his head and says the name he does not think it is really wise to use. 'Chebworz Khamzateyev,' he says. 'I'd like to talk to him.'

The doorman looks at McAvoy with renewed interest. 'You're lost, man. You should go home. It's a cold night.'

McAvoy stands his ground. 'Please,' he says. 'It's important. Look, this is me . . .'

As McAvoy puts his hand in his coat to remove his warrant card the doorman raises the silver handgun he has been holding by his side.

'Easy, big man. No quick moves, yeah? I don't like people moving too quick. Makes me jittery. That's the word, yes? Jittery?'

McAvoy stands perfectly still, hand inside his coat. 'Can I?' he asks.

'Slowly.'

McAvoy retrieves his warrant card and hands it over to the doorman, who keeps the gun on McAvoy while he examines it. Then he shrugs. 'What's this, man?'

'Like it says. I'm a detective. A policeman.'

'No shield,' says the doorman. 'This is shit, brother.'

'No, please, if you'd just listen . . .'

As McAvoy speaks, the music emanating from behind the door suddenly comes to a stop. The street sounds eerily silent in its absence.

'*Tomasz! Staye kholodno. U nas ye biznes. Vin povynen prohrity-sya do. Pozbud'sya nykh . . .*'

McAvoy hears authority in the voice of the man calling from behind the gatekeeper. He cannot help himself. He begins to shout.

'Chebworz Khamzateyev. I need to speak to you. Please! Chebworz!'

'You got a death wish, man?' asks Tomasz, sticking the gun under McAvoy's jaw. He seems to be looking at McAvoy's hair quizzically. 'You fucking Irish?'

'Scottish. I'm here for the Irishman.'

'Fuck,' spits the doorman, and he pulls McAvoy inside.

McAvoy finds himself in a corridor painted the same colour cream as the outside of the building. The man called Tomasz has pushed him up against the wall and is checking his pockets. 'You just walk up and bang on the door, eh? Some balls, you Irish. Some balls . . .'

'Tomasz?'

McAvoy looks down the hall to where a short, stocky figure is standing with his hands on his hips. He's in his late twenties and wears running trousers and white trainers, a wife-beater vest and fur-lined leather jacket. There are thick black tiger-stripe tattoos on his chest and a chunky gold necklace hangs between his well-defined pectoral muscles. He has a round head, shaved down to the skin.

'Who's this fuck?' asks the man.

'Looks Irish,' says Tomasz. 'Says he's here for you.'

'For me? I don't know him.' Chebworz sneers at the newcomer and reveals the space in his bottom row of teeth where three incisors have been dislodged. He speaks directly to McAvoy. 'Who are you?'

'Says he's a cop but he got no shield,' says Tomasz. 'Here,' he spits, tossing the warrant card to Chebworz.

Chebworz picks it up and considers it. 'McAvoy,' he says. 'You're the Englishman, yes? The *mussor*?'

McAvoy nods, letting out a nervous breath. His palms are sweating. 'I'm not English but yes, I'm from England. I'm here to find somebody who matters to my family. I don't care about anything but getting him back.'

Chebworz's face changes and he barks a laugh at McAvoy.

'Two friends of mine had a chat with you last night,' he says, showing the gap in his teeth and poking his tongue through. 'You were told to go home. My father made that very clear. We're drinking to the memory of a good man and saying good-bye to another who we are going to have to hurt for becoming a rat motherfucker. So yes, I know you, and I know what you want and I think you should get the fuck out of here before I lose my shit.'

'This is him?' asks Tomasz, looking at McAvoy like a doctor inspecting a cadaver. 'He doesn't look tough.'

'Slapped down some bitch in the Village,' says Chebworz.

McAvoy tries hard not to speak. But he wants to explain himself, to try to make these men understand reason.

'I want Valentine,' he blurts. 'If he's alive, I want him back. Whatever's happened, that will be the end of it.'

'The end of it?' asks Chebworz. He strides towards McAvoy. 'Look at this, man,' he hisses, pointing at his missing teeth. 'Gun to my head, blood in my mouth. They shoved me in their piece of shit car. They drove me out to Buttfuck County. And then some Sicilian piece of shit smashes me in the mouth with his gun. Shows me this poor bastard with his nose sliced off. I had to walk through snow and mud up to my fucking balls, man.'

'I'm sorry,' says McAvoy, forcing himself to meet the smaller man's stare. 'I don't know what happened . . .'

'The Wop fucks tried to kill me is what happened,' says Chebworz. Up close, he smells of paprika and meat.

'Kill you? But you got away.'

'Too fucking right I did,' says Chebworz. 'I ran. Kept running. You think this country's cold? I'm Chechen. This is fucking summer for me.'

'Who was the Italian?' asks McAvoy, unable to help himself.

'You hear this guy?' asks Tomasz, grinning. 'Gun to his balls and he's still asking questions.'

McAvoy looks down and sees the weapon. He does his best to ignore it.

'You know all this,' says Chebworz. 'Cops know it all, don't they? That's what they think. Putting that bitch in our crew and thinking we wouldn't sniff her out.'

'You knew?'

'We kept her busy. A few errands. Let her feel like she was part of the team. Even let her exercise a little muscle with you. Seems she was a good distraction because when the Wops tried to hit us last night, all they got was two soldiers and a Fed.'

'I thought the Italians and yourselves had come to an arrangement . . .'

'They're greasy lying fucks and they're going to pay the price,' says Chebworz. Then he hits McAvoy in the stomach with a perfectly executed right hand.

For a moment, McAvoy feels nothing. And then it seems like he is folding in on himself. He feels as though he has been punctured; as though a hole has been stamped through his guts. He locks his jaw around the pain and refuses to let himself slide down the wall the way his body is telling him to.

'Tough bastard,' says Chebworz, nodding. 'Tomasz, bring him.'

McAvoy finds himself being dragged down the corridor which emerges into a large storage area. There are no windows and the floor is bare concrete. The supporting columns that hold up the roof have been stripped down to their metal skeleton. Only two of the ceiling lights are switched on and they spill a lurid yellow light onto a boxing ring with sagging ropes and a stained canvas floor. In the ring, a man McAvoy recognises from his YouTube video is pounding right hand after right hand into the body of an elderly man protected by thick brown padding. Each time the boxer lands a right the older man grunts, but whether in admonishment or praise, McAvoy could not say.

'Byki,' says Chebworz, and Tomasz drags him forward. In the shadows of the warehouse McAvoy sees dozens of folding chairs, stacked neatly against the wall. He looks down. Broken glass, cigarette butts and rubbish litter the floor.

Chebworz takes McAvoy's arm from Tomasz. 'This is the English cop,' he says, to the two men in the ring. 'Came for the Irishman. Thinks it's that easy.'

In the ring, the grey-haired man considers McAvoy. 'You must want him bad,' he says, smiling slightly. The voice sounds familiar to McAvoy. His thoughts are a blur but he remembers his helplessness in the car just twenty-four hours ago. Was this the man who told him to leave things alone? He is shorter than Chebworz and his short grey hair is brushed forward to hide his bald patch. He wears blue sweats beneath the padding.

'He's family,' says McAvoy breathlessly.

'He said we owed him money. Money for a fight he ruined. He embarrassed us.'

McAvoy shakes his head. 'He has a temper. He made a mistake. Everything got out of his control. Please, don't make it worse.'

'Worse for who?' asks the man, and his tongue flicks out like a snake tasting the air. 'I have no problems.'

'The Italians,' says McAvoy. 'I don't think they wanted Chebworz at all.'

The old man twitches a smile. 'They wanted the Irishmen and Cheb was just an unlucky fuck? Maybe. But things happened. A boss's son was killed. Peace will be expensive, one way or another.'

'None of that is anything to do with Valentine. Or me. Whatever he's done, he's paid for.'

'Has he?'

'In the car,' says McAvoy, thinking aloud, 'you said you wanted to talk to him. But you had him already.'

'An act of kindness,' he says, shrugging. 'If you'd known he was with me you would have kept pushing. Kept being an irritant. I would have had no choice but to harm you in some way and I do not embrace violence when there is an alternative. I preferred to let you blunder around. Is that the right word? Blunder? Yes. But you have blundered your way here, my friend. Perhaps I was wrong to be so kind.'

McAvoy looks around, him, desperate for an ally. Then the old man gives a wide grin. 'Tomasz. A warm-down for our boy.'

McAvoy feels Tomasz's hands pulling his coat from his shoulders. As he turns, Tomasz rips the buttons from his shirt. Instinctively, McAvoy grabs at his clothes but then Chebworz drags them from his back. He protests, turning, but the two men have done this before. He changes his stance, ready to lash out, and then he hears the 'snick' of a switchblade.

'Easy, *mussor*,' says Tomasz, and he slices McAvoy's T-shirt from waist to neck.

McAvoy hears himself protest but there is nobody in the room who gives a damn. Panic sets in as he realises he is standing in this cold, lonely place with men stripping him down to his bare skin. His instinct is to run. To hit and move and sprint back into the blizzard and the anonymity of the street beyond.

'Tomasz, show me.'

McAvoy finds himself being pushed forward. The cold blade is against his cheek. The old man leans down from the ring and peers at McAvoy's many scars.

'That one,' says the old man, pointing at the ugly trench in McAvoy's shoulder. 'A knife. A big one. Chopping down, yes? And there. That was fire, am I right? These little ones. A small blade? These scratches. You have suffered.'

McAvoy looks away as the man reads his life story on his ruined skin.

'Maybe you can help me and then I will help you, yes? My man here. He makes me a lot of money. He fights people who are strong. He beats them. Then he fights again. He fought with your countryman. It was a good fight but Byki got no satisfaction. It was stopped short. And it is many days until he fights again. He is hungry. I hear you can fight. I see you know pain. So my contract with you is this – survive a round with Byki and

258

I will give you your friend. Fall down, and so will he. Can I be fairer?'

McAvoy's insides feel as though they are burning and it takes him a moment to understand the offer being placed before him. Wild-eyed, he looks at the bearded colossus in the ring, who looks back at him with eyes like a dead fish. He is so hairy he puts McAvoy in mind of a barbarian.

'I can't . . .'

'One round, my friend. You came all this way and now you have the chance to make everything right. One round.'

McAvoy's skin prickles as he feels the knife dig a little deeper into his cheek.

'In the ring,' says Chebworz. 'Now.'

McAvoy finds himself moving forward. He puts up a hand and grabs the bottom rope, pulling himself onto the dirty canvas. It smells of blood and spilled beer.

'He is family, yes? This boy who causes you so many problems. Is he worth this? You can go. You can return home. You have done enough, have you not?'

McAvoy does not answer. He watches as Tomasz pulls the huge man's gloves off to reveal massive hands beneath. He flexes his taped fingers and looks at McAvoy like he is a fly to be stepped on. McAvoy forces himself to concentrate. He looks at Byki. The hair disguises the fact that his muscles are not particularly well defined. He is big, but some of his muscle runs to fat. And there is something about his face, beneath that great beard. The way his jaw sits . . .

'One round,' says the old man, unburdening himself of the padding and climbing through the ring ropes to lean against the side. 'And then your world is your own again.'

McAvoy stares at him. Realises how pitiful he looks. Turns to the brute bouncing on his toes and making the whole damn ring shake.

'Ding fucking Ding,' says Chebworz.

McAvoy barely has time to get his hands up. Byki pushes him backwards with the strength of a bull and in moments McAvoy feels the rope against his back as the huge man starts raining down left hooks that thud into his forearms. He hears the three spectators shout words of encouragement and tries to remember the things he was taught so many years ago. Without thinking, his posture changes. He rises onto the balls of his feet and as Byki swings a wild right, McAvoy slips inside it and spins off the ropes to a chorus of appreciative cheers.

Byki follows McAvoy across the ring, lunging with left and then right as he manages to stay just out of reach. Experimentally, he slips out a left hand and is surprised to see it connect with Byki's chin. He seems almost as surprised as McAvoy but if it pains him he does not show it. Instead he stamps forward, closing the distance and snapping out a barrage of right hands that slam through McAvoy's guard and catch him just above the ear. His head spins and he feels his hands drop and then Byki is backing him onto the ropes and thumping big left hands into his ribs. McAvoy tucks his arms in, trying to protect himself but he simply leaves himself exposed. Byki hits him below his left eye with such precision and power that McAvoy's feet are the last things to hit the floor. He lands on his shoulders and rolls to his side; vision blurred and his whole self spinning as if disappearing down a drain.

'Up, my friend,' comes a voice, above the cheers. 'One round. One whole round.'

McAvoy sees Roisin's face. Imagines her watching. He pictures her in her parents' caravan – wet-eyed and red-faced, listening to the sounds of violence as her family and the Heldens do bloody war outside the flimsy confines of her sanctuary. He sees Valentine. Remembers, for a moment, the child he once was. Eight years old and a cheeky little bastard; twinkly-eyed and full of mischief and trying to steal McAvoy's pen as he took notes at the damn halting site in Cumbria where he and Roisin embarked on the road that would lead to love.

He drags himself up. Sniffs, noisily, and spits blood on the floor.

'He looks pissed off, Byki,' says Chebworz mockingly. 'Easy now.'

McAvoy thinks. What was it Dezzie said? He could make people hate. McAvoy feels a frisson of that now. He feels a sudden, white-hot desire to go home, and the only thing standing between himself and his wife's arms is this colossal hairy bastard who wants to smash his face in.

McAvoy looks at the big man. There is not much going on in his eyes. He has the dazed look of a steroid user. And while he hits hard and he hits fast, McAvoy has been hit harder and got back up.

'One round,' says McAvoy, and moves forward, flicking out left hands that catch Byki on his shoulders and arms.

'Go on,' shouts Tomasz.

Byki swings and McAvoy is staggered as the blow catches him in the chest. He grabs hold of Byki and feels a moment's revulsion as his face slides against the sweaty mass of the fighter's huge chest. Byki pushes him off and swings again.

McAvoy ducks the blow and hits Byki hard in the stomach. It feels like hitting a wall wrapped in a blanket.

'Finish him,' says Chebworz, followed by a stream of his native language.

Byki swings the punch from his knees and McAvoy sees it coming. He lashes out with his right hand and connects with Byki's bicep. It is a good shot and something changes in the big man's eyes.

'Cover up, cover up,' comes the shout from behind him.

McAvoy realises he has hurt the bigger man. Surely one round could not take much longer, could it? But who would call for the bell? Who would end it?

Byki is jabbing with the left now but McAvoy has got inside the blows and is pounding on the big man's stomach, hitting him with good shots that seem to have no effect. McAvoy finds himself remembering two decades before when his boxing coach would scream at him that he had his opponent beat and should damn well finish him off. McAvoy never could. He was frightened of hurting somebody.

McAvoy looks at Byki. He glances at the three men who lounge by the steps. Chebworz and Tomasz look victorious. The old man does not. He sees what McAvoy suddenly sees: the slight dislocation of the big man's jaw, the spot of weakness that his beard cannot conceal . . .

The shot is perfect. McAvoy has thrown harder punches but never one more perfectly placed. His bare right crunches into the hinge of the huge man's jaw and he watches his head snap back. Later, he will fancy that he heard the soft wet splat as Byki's brain hit the inside of his own skull. But in this moment, he simply hears the soft, almost feminine moan as Byki's eyes roll back in his head and he topples to the canvas like a tree.

McAvoy stands perfectly still, arm still outstretched; somehow unable to move.

It takes a moment, and then he hears the soft *clap-clap-clap*. McAvoy turns to look at the three men. The old man is smiling ruefully. Tomasz and Chebworz have their mouths open.

'I'm sorry . . .' says McAvoy, and will never know why he says it.

The old man stops clapping but the sound continues. There is somebody else watching. McAvoy squints into the darkness and sees the shadows take shape.

Valentine Teague walks out of the shadows. He looks clean and well fed. He wears a black leather jacket, like Chebworz, and has gelled his red hair into spikes.

'Valentine?' asks McAvoy, turning to the older man as if for confirmation.

'I never said he was a prisoner.' The man shrugs. 'He's been helping train our beast here. But I think he has some way to go.'

'You're a nasty bastard, Sergey,' says Valentine brightly. He grins, revealing the gap in his top row of teeth. 'You send that video to Marcel and I swear he'll book a fight to make a million. Not that this big bastard will want any of it. I told you, Byki's a pussy. He just got beat by a cop, for fuck's sake. You fucking Russians.'

'You see the respect he gives me?' asks the head of the Chechen Mob, but he looks at Valentine with some whiff of affection.

'I don't understand,' says McAvoy, and his knees begin to give way.

'No,' says Sergey. 'But you can go. Both of you.'

'I wasn't waiting for fucking permission,' snarls Valentine, and he shrugs out of the leather jacket. 'Smells like cabbage anyway,' he says, throwing it at Chebworz's feet.

Valentine looks at McAvoy, leaning against the ropes. His face is already swelling.

'Jesus,' says Valentine. 'Roisin's going to kill me. Let's get you home.'

McAvoy slithers through the ropes. Valentine comes forward and puts an arm under McAvoy's shoulder. It is a tender gesture and McAvoy feels his brother-in-law's warm hands on his anguished skin.

'Shirt. Jacket. Anything else?' mutters Valentine, looking around. 'Well, that'll be us then, lads. Shame it didn't work out but that's the business, eh? I'll bid you go fuck yourself, and good night.'

Valentine keeps his eyes on the Chechens as he moves them towards the door but none of the trio seems intent on stopping them.

'You didn't leave,' says McAvoy, head spinning. 'Do you know what's been happening at home? You have to call . . .'

'Shush, big man. It's all taken care of,' says Valentine.

'I had to fight him. I had to stay up for a round . . .'

'No,' says Valentine, grinning. 'No, you didn't. They called me down the second they spotted you on the monitors. I just wanted to know if you were willing to do it.'

'You bastard,' says McAvoy, and it seems to trigger a sudden flood of relief into his system that threatens to take the strength from him.

'It meant a lot.'

'I can't see out of this eye.'

'You were ugly to start with.'

'Your sister likes me.'

'Aye,' says Valentine, and he kicks open the door to the snowstorm beyond. 'You're not such a cunt. For a cop.'

26

'Some brown stuff and some purple stuff and some bread. Two beers. Vodka. Leave the bottle.'

McAvoy lolls in the wooden chair and listens as Valentine places his food order with the waitress. She's middle-aged with dark hair and poor skin and the kind of earrings that grandchildren buy for special occasions. If she is disturbed by McAvoy's bruised appearance she doesn't show it.

'You want me to hang your coats up above the radiator?' she asks.

Valentine grins and looks at McAvoy. 'You want to take your coat off, Aector?'

'I'm fine,' manages McAvoy, who is bare-chested beneath his jacket.

'I'll bring you *solyanka*. *Ukha*. Maybe some *vareniki*? Your friend enjoyed his.'

Valentine and McAvoy shoot a glance at Rey, who has his back to the wall and looks like somebody who is feeling rattled but is damned if they are going to show it in front of strangers.

'Did you?' asks Valentine.

'It was great,' says Rey, the taxi driver whose gesture of generosity has backfired spectacularly. He has positioned himself in a way that allows him easy access to the cutlery if the two crazy Celts suddenly decide to start trouble.

'That's great,' says Valentine, and he shrugs out of his coat and hands it to the waitress. She disappears through a set of saloon doors into the kitchen.

McAvoy looks around him. His left eye is swelling and he can see the risen flesh, squatting like a sand-dune at the bottom of his vision. His head hurts and his arms feel heavy. He only remembers brief snatches of the journey here. He came to as they entered the pleasant restaurant on Brighton Beach Avenue. Two waiters were playing cards at a table but they hustled out the back when McAvoy and Valentine entered. Rey was the only other customer but he didn't react with much alarm at the sight of his most recent fare appearing so badly bruised. He has been a cab driver in New York City for nine years. He has seen it all before.

'So you found your friend,' says Rey. 'Did he not want to come along?'

Valentine slaps McAvoy on the back. He has his feet on one of the other chairs and is pushing himself back, rocking his seat on two legs. He looks at ease with the world; all testosterone and loose-limbed assurance. He reminds McAvoy of the sort of teen who would terrify teachers with their cocksure certainty that none of this shit matters.

'Came to my rescue, so he did,' says Valentine, and he removes an electronic cigarette from his coat pocket and takes three quick puffs. 'Fought a bear for me. Now that's family, my friend, that's family. I'm Valentine Teague, by the way. Val, if you know me, which you do now.'

'I'm Rey,' he says, extending a hand.

'We're not doing anything complicated with the handshake, are we?' asks Valentine, smiling. 'I'm not good at all that crap.'

'Just a handshake.'

'I can do that,' says Valentine, and does so. 'You'll be Mexican, then.'

Rey cocks his head. 'Honduran,' he says.

'Don't know that one,' says Valentine, shrugging. 'It's like Mexican though, yeah?'

Rey looks to McAvoy. He is unaccustomed to being insulted by somebody who does not seem to realise they are doing it.

'Leave it, Valentine,' says McAvoy, pressing the back of his hand to his face and wincing.

'I'm just asking . . .'

'Well, stop it.'

Valentine puts his hands up in surrender, grinning widely. 'I tried Da again,' he says. 'Used your phone. No answer.'

McAvoy notices that his cell phone is not in his pocket. 'Can I have it back?'

Val hands it over. 'Try her again,' he suggests. 'No answer from Ma neither.'

McAvoy pulls himself upright in his chair, hot and sore. It's too warm in the pleasant little restaurant with its red and black tiles and flickering, battery-operated imitation candles.

'Why haven't you been in touch with anybody?' asks McAvoy, looking hard at his brother-in-law. 'A phone call. Just a call . . .'

'Why do you fucking think?' asks Valentine, rolling his eyes. 'Brishen in hospital? Shay dead? Bullets flying everywhere and me trying to make the best of it with those Russian lads who would have chopped my face off soon as look at it if there was anything to be gained. I only stayed alive by bullshitting and making them think I might be important. It wasn't like I was free to go send an email.'

'You're suddenly telling me you were a prisoner?' asks McAvoy angrily. 'You just walked out with me! There's not a mark on you.'

'It's sorted, Aector. Just relax. I don't even think they believed me when I said you were a big deal. They just sorted other stuff out first and waited for everything to play out.'

McAvoy wipes his nose. There is a smear of blood on the napkin. The sight of it angers him and he turns on the younger man.

'Do you know what I've been through trying to find you? Do you know what's going on at home? The Heldens are gunning for your whole family. They think you're the one who killed Shay. If you don't show your face and smooth things over there'll be blood.'

Valentine has the good grace to look away. When he turns back to McAvoy his features are pink.

'It was a good fucking plan,' he says. 'If Shay hadn't got killed . . .'

'What happened, Valentine?'

266

The tension is broken by the return of the waitress. She places the tall bottles of beer on the table and a frosted bottle of vodka with three glasses. Rey seems unsure whether to take a drink or continue studying the wall.

'Put your feet down,' says the waitress to Valentine, who does as he is told. She smiles and returns to the kitchen.

'They're okay, the Russians,' says Valentine, watching her go. 'Easy to deal with. They're not all that different from us. Just want a few home comforts, a bit of respect and the chance to be left alone.'

'I saw what you put on the YouTube video,' says McAvoy. 'You started all this . . .'

'Just be quiet a second,' says Valentine, taking another puff on his cigarette. He looks at Rey. 'You a trustworthy guy?'

Rey shrugs. 'I'm not even here.'

Valentine accepts this. He pours himself a shot of vodka and follows it up with another. He pours one for McAvoy and slides it across the table. For once, McAvoy does not say no. He downs it in a pleasing, burning swallow and immediately feels the pain in his face begin to lift.

'Brishen's struggling,' says Valentine, shaking his head. 'Back home, I mean. Money troubles. He's made some bad decisions. Put money into things he didn't have the money for. He's had a hard few months. He's a proud man and it was a difficult thing for him to admit it but he opened up after a night on the beer and told Shay and me how bad things had got. He needed money. Needed it quickly. First thing we did was offer to get it for him. A couple of armed robberies and he'd be home free. But that went against his principles. So Shay said he would take a few unsanctioned fights. Again, Brish said no. Didn't want Shay straying from the path. Those were his words, man. The "path".'

Valentine shakes his head and starts looking at the condensation as it turns to dribbles on the side of the vodka bottle. He watches as the flickering light is refracted into a broken rainbow in the tiny droplet.

'It was Shay and me who came up with the idea to do it abroad,' says Valentine, clearing his throat. 'We'd heard about the bare-knuckle fighters in the US. Big business. Some of the lads who win in the backyard matches get UFC contracts off the back of them. Shay had no interest in that but he knew there was money to be made. So we spoke to the lads who organise the bare-knuckle matches in Belfast and they hooked us up with Marcel, and he hooked us up with Chebworz. He fancies himself as a trainer. Reckoned his boy Byki was the real thing. He'd heard of Shay. We sent him some videos and he liked what he saw. Reckoned he could make money out of a scrap between Shay and his man.'

McAvoy pours himself another vodka. Downs it and wishes he hadn't. He starts to shiver beneath his coat but forces himself not to show it.

'Chebworz is a good salesman. He needed an angle for the fight to be a money-maker. So we came up with this idea of making it a grudge match. My people versus his people. It was piss-easy to provoke it. A couple of comments on YouTube and the thing took on a life of its own. All the marketing was underground – posters in boxing clubs, whispers on closed internet groups. It became a big thing. A prize fight. Cheb was good as his word. Got the news out on all these weird Russian sites and we got the lads at home to tell their kin in America and soon there were people paying good money for a fight that hadn't even been agreed on.'

'Brishen . . .' says McAvoy woozily.

'We felt shit for having to play him the way we did but it was for his own good. We told him all about the shit on YouTube and the things people were saying about Shay. Got his patriotism riled up. But he wasn't about to agree to let it happen without a push. But Marcel, the big fucker at the boxing club – he knew how to play things. Had a word in his boss's ear and we did the same with Brish and soon Dezzie and Brish thought it was all their idea for Shay to go over for a try-out. It wasn't a total lie. Shay was in with a chance. Brishen was so excited it was like Shay was his son, or something. And then I told him how easy it would be to kill two birds with one stone if he would just look the other way and let Shay fight Byki. The purse for the fight was going to be enough to cover Brishen's debts. He was tempted. Prayed for guidance, spoke to his priest. We sold him on it when Chebworz spoke to him direct. He promised it would be a proper bout, properly refereed, corner-men, twelve rounds. Gloves and wraps. Brishen agreed.'

McAvoy reaches for the beer. Presses the bottle to his forehead and puts it down again.

'Your passports and visas . . .'

Valentine mimes slapping himself in the head. 'Hadn't fucking occurred to us. Brish and Shay had passports but mine was years out of date. And there was no fucking way I was being left behind. Brish is friends with Father Whelan. They've done charity stuff together. Go way back. So the bishop did him a favour and wrote a letter on my behalf. It was good of Whelan to sort it, considering he didn't think we should be going. He'd advised Brishen against it and it pained Brishen not to listen. But being a good Catholic doesn't always pay the bills.'

'You flew out separately . . .'

'I was shitting myself.' Valentine laughs and takes another shot. 'Never flown before and those bastards were a day ahead of me. I was on my own. Drank half a bottle of Jameson before I even got on board. Was all I could do not to scream when it took off. Woke up at JFK. My phone wouldn't let me make calls because I was in a new time zone and every time I tried to call Brish on a pay-phone it wouldn't connect. I was hung over as shit. All I could remember was the address of Dezzie Estrada's gym, so I got a taxi there. I was feeling awful so the driver dropped me at a bar and I had a few drinks to get myself in the mood for the fight. I went to Dezzie's place, thinking that was where the bout was gonna be. I thought Shay would be there. Dezzie was there – the man himself. Told me Shay had already had his try-out and they'd gone to look at some church. I was getting pissed off. Thought it was going to happen without me. Then Marcel came and found me on the street and told me where I needed to be. We got a cab together, out to this shit-hole.'

The waitress emerges from the kitchen carrying a tray laden with soups, breads and little dishes of spiced cabbage and potato dumplings. She frowns at Valentine.

'What did you say about my restaurant?'

'Sorry, love,' says Valentine, looking at her with eyes that put McAvoy in mind of a baby spaniel who is sincerely sorry to have eaten their owner's favourite shoes. 'Not this place. This place shines, love. This is somewhere that's first-date material. I love your place. No, I mean some crappy area a few blocks over. You wouldn't like it. You've got class.'

The waitress knows she is being charmed but it does not stop her smiling at the young man and forgiving him his slander.

A waft of spiced meat engulfs McAvoy and it is all he can do not to let his mouth begin to water. He sits forward in his chair and rips a piece of bread from the pie-sliced hunk in the centre of the table.

'My sister's married somebody who doesn't pray?' asks Valentine, shaking his head disapprovingly. 'We'll be having words.'

Valentine mutters a quick blessing under his breath and McAvoy, red-faced, mumbles an Amen. When he dips the bread in the *solyanka* he feels an overwhelming urge to text Roisin and enquire whether she knows how to make it. He tastes beef, tomatoes, onions and a dozen different herbs and spices. The dish is so addictive that if the waitress admitted that it contained a mild trace of cocaine, he would not be in the least surprised.

'We got to Cheb's gym and there was a good crowd,' says Valentine, between mouthfuls. 'You wouldn't know it from the street because there was barely a car parked there but that was because all these massive great 4x4s and limos were dropping so many rich Russians you'd think it was a pay-per-view in Vegas. All these blonde women with diamonds and furs and pearls. All these men with tailored suits and shiny shoes and red faces, like they were trying not to fart. Place was packed. Cheb had these gorgeous lasses in cocktail dresses waltzing about with trays of champagne and caviar. Place looked awesome. Had a real big fight feel. I found Shay and Brish and it was clear something was wrong.'

'Brishen didn't want the fight to go ahead?' asks McAvoy.

'The plan had changed,' says Valentine, more quietly than before. 'Cheb had suddenly offered Shay twice the money to fall in the tenth.'

'And Shay refused?'

'Shay was fine about it. It was Brishen who wasn't going to let his man take a dive.'

'Pride?' asks McAvoy.

Valentine waves his arms dismissively, splattering the tablecloth with gravy from his spoon. 'He wasn't himself. He and Shay had been out seeing churches all day, making new friends. He'd got himself all confused. Didn't know what was right and what wasn't. Either way, he wasn't agreeing to take the fall. And that pissed Cheb off. He said that if Shay put his man down there was likely to be a fucking riot. Brish didn't budge. I tried to talk sense into him and he just kept saying that he was a Rom, a Traveller, and that's the only thing that mattered. So the fight went on. Good bout too. Evenly matched. It got to the tenth and Shay kept looking at Brishen, hoping he'd let him go down but Brish was having none of it. The crowd got nasty. So Cheb got in the ring and said the rules were changing.'

'Bare-knuckle . . .'

'Too right. Brish looked like he was going to pass out and Shay was getting frightened. I did what I had to.'

'You started a riot, Valentine . . .'

'It was going to happen anyways and the way the crowd turned I don't think we'd have got out of there without somebody getting hurt.'

'You made a run for it?'

'Sure did. One of those Russian bitches had a gun in her handbag. Pretty little thing. I smacked a couple of lads and we got the fuck out of there.'

'All three of you?'

'Yeah, man. The rules had changed. We ran like there was no tomorrow – Shay still in his shorts. Brishen was in a state. Never seen him like that. We jumped in a taxi and headed back for the city. Brishen had an address in his pocket for some old bloke that he and Shay had met earlier in the day. Cab dropped us off at the apartment block. Old bloke buzzed us up. No bugger else lived there and he had this swanky apartment on the top floor. Gorgeous, it was.'

'Molony,' says McAvoy, closing his eyes and pushing away the last of his meal.

'Yeah. Creepy-looking fuck. Looked like Friar Tuck, or a mole, or something. Fat. Round glasses. Baldy head. But he was okay, man. Invited us in like we were family. Soon as we got in Brishen went for me. Hit me so hard I was seeing stars. Knocked out my fucking goldie.' Valentine pulls up his lip to show the hole in his smile. 'Told me it was all my fault and I'd let him down. Said Shay had been cheated and now they were going home for nothing. He cheapened his soul for nothing, that was what he said. Starts banging on about the honour of the Gypsies, about being part of a noble people who were above things like this. Said he knew that I'd set him up and manipulated him. He'd gone against the wishes of a priest. Said I was a devil, tempting him. I've got to be honest, he hurt my feelings. I love Brish, man. I'd never do that to him.'

'So you decided to make things right.'

'I had tears in my eyes,' says Valentine, and doesn't look ashamed to say it. 'I wanted to make it up to him. I still had the gun and I figured Cheb would see sense once it had all calmed down. I told them to go fuck themselves and headed straight back to Brooklyn.'

'But Cheb didn't see sense?'

Valentine shrugs. 'I played it wrong. I went in there angry. There were still a load of them there, drinking and joking and cleaning up. I went in with the gun in my hand. They laughed at me, man. Made me feel like a kid. I was already bleeding from the smack Brish had given me and Cheb said I would be lucky if he paid a cent after what I'd done. So I stuck a gun in his face. I wasn't thinking. Da says I never do.'

'What happened?'

Valentine finishes eating and takes another hit of vodka. 'I didn't have much of a plan. Just grabbed Cheb and headed for the door. Gave him a couple of slaps to show I wasn't kidding.'

'And?'

'Brish and Shay showed up like the cavalry,' says Valentine, letting a warm smile flash across his face. Just as quickly it fades. 'It all kicked off. It was like something from a cowboy movie. People shooting and shouting and making a break for it. Somehow, Brishen and Shay grabbed Cheb.'

'And you?'

'Nearly made it. Then I got nicked.' Valentine rolls up the leg of his track pants to show an ugly scab surrounded by purple-yellow bruising. 'Went down like a sack of shit.'

McAvoy drops his head to his hand. He can see it all.

'They took you? The Russians?'

'Yeah. Put a few kicks in. Slapped me about. Tied me to the fucking wall and said they were going to cut my head off if I didn't tell them where Brish had taken Cheb.'

'And did you?'

'I had no fucking idea,' says Valentine. 'I didn't know the fat bloke's address and Brishen didn't know anybody else in the city. They kept me there for ages. Pissed my pants,' he adds ruefully, and it sounds like he is making a confession for a grave sin.

'But when I got there tonight . . .'

'Things all changed the next day,' says Valentine, and he reaches for his e-cig. 'They moved me to an apartment. Stank of cigs and meat and women. Not a very nice place. Left me in a room with the door locked. Only a mattress and a chest of drawers full of condoms and lube. It was grim.'

'How long were you there?'

'Day or so. Somebody brought me some food. Some vodka. This thing,' he says, indicating the e-cig. 'Day or so later, Cheb walks in to my room, bold as brass. He's had a few slaps and he's pissed off but he's gentle in the way he tells me what happened. About Brish. About Shay. I appreciated that.'

'He told you what had gone on?'

Valentine nods. 'They'd tied him up and thrown him in the boot. It had all got out of hand. Brish wanted me back and was willing to make a swap for Cheb. That was the plan. They parked this car they'd stolen in some garage underground. Left Cheb in the boot with a bottle of water. He was there for hours.' Valentine gives a quick smile. 'Bet *he* pissed himself.'

'Valentine, what happened?'

'Next thing they were driving like the devil was on their tail. Cheb says he was in there for an age. Then they stopped, he heard voices and, to use his words, some greasy wop motherfucker was pulling him out and slapping him around. They were in the woods, somewhere dark and full of snow. Brish and Shay were on their knees beside him. Brish's face was all blood. There were two Italians pointing guns at their heads. The young one was a nasty motherfucker. Enjoying himself, putting the boot in.'

'Chebworz ran,' says McAvoy.

'The way he told it he was the hero of the hour but you could see in his eyes he'd got lucky. He took the older one down with a branch and shoved the young one out of his way. Shoved him harder than he intended. Skewered him like a pencil through a muffin. Ran like fuck. His boys came to pick him up. They've got contacts everywhere and they got the news almost as soon as the cops did. Shay was dead. They reckoned Brish was too. They were crossing themselves like proper Catholics when they heard he'd risen from the ground.'

Valentine looks like he wants to hit something. His eyes fill with tears. 'Cheb was okay about it all. Gave me a drink. Said it was going to be hot for me for a few days. Invited me to stay with him.'

'Invited?'

'He didn't look like he was going to take no for an answer. And I didn't know what the fuck to do. I was in a different country and my only two friends were either dead or dying. I didn't even know who to wish bloody death on.'

McAvoy sees genuine pain in the young man's eyes. He wants to reach over and put a hand on his shoulder but is in too much pain to risk moving. As he looks into his tear-filled eyes, he sees something of Roisin in her brother's features. While she is dark and tanned, Val is red-haired and pale, but they have the same grey-blue eyes and they are both capable of looking at him in a way that suggests their problems should become his.

'You stayed at the gym?'

'Brought me there from the apartment yesterday. They told me some English cop had arrived, asking questions and looking for me. They described you. I told them you weren't English. They didn't seem to care. They had a lot of discussions about what to do with me. With you. I don't doubt there were people saying it would be easier if I was out of the picture. Last night they had a little chat with you. Two of the big lads and some pretty lass with purple hair. I saw them leave from the gym. Byki and me were doing some pad work. Sounds mental, doesn't it? But they thought they might as well make use of me. And besides, I'd told a fib or two. Said the Teagues had the money to make their lives wonderful or terrible. They were sending over their problem-solver. They didn't exactly seem scared. But when I came up with the idea of a grudge re-match, they could see the value to it. I said I could set that up. Bring over a fucking terror of a man from Ireland. I think they still hadn't decided whether or not to kill me about an hour ago but then Sergey took a call from one of his connections and suddenly it was all smiles. Suddenly I wasn't really important so they said I could go. Then you turned up.'

'Did you hear what happened?' asks McAvoy. 'After they let me go last night?'

'This same greasy wop bastard blew up their car and took two of Cheb's men. You've been busy, eh?'

McAvoy looks away. His gaze takes in Rey, whose knuckles are now white around his Coke bottle. He looks undecided about whether he is enjoying this, or wishing to God he'd never picked up tonight's fare.

'Is it bad?' asks Valentine, without bravado. 'At home? Is Ro there? The little ones? The Heldens don't really think I'd kill Shay, do they? He's my friend. He was, I mean. Here, pass the phone, I'll try again.'

McAvoy looks at his brother-in-law and suddenly feels bone-tired. He wants to ring Alto and tell him that he has Valentine. He wants Alto to accept the lad's story and let them go. Then he wants to fly home, hug his wife and children, and pull the familiarity of Hull over his head like a blanket. But even as he sits here he knows that there is still work to be done. He has been here for two days and has unearthed something that smells of blood and soil and secrets. He cannot forget the names on Molony's wall or the link between Father Whelan and this city. His head swims with names and connections. Tony Blank. Sal Pugliesca. Luca Savoca. Paulie Pugliesca. Peter Molony. He scrunches up his eyes and hopes that when he opens them, the answers will be written on the wall. When he does, all he sees is Rey, looking at him with concern. McAvoy feels dampness on his face and wipes the blood from his top lip as it dribbles from his nose. He picks up his phone and tries Roisin again, praying under his breath that this time she will answer. He fears the call will go straight to her voicemail and then suddenly the call is answered by a male voice.

'Hello, Ro's phone,' says the quiet, Irish-tinged voice.

'Hello?' says McAvoy, startled. 'I'm looking for Roisin. My wife . . .'

'You must be Aector,' whispers the man pleasantly. He pronounces his name perfectly. 'I'm sorry, Roisin's snoring her wee head off with her little girl right now. Away with the fairies, so she is. Slept right through every time the phone rang and when I saw it was yourself I thought it was less of a crime to answer it than to leave you worrying. I'm not much of a sleeper so it's no drama to me.'

McAvoy's face burns. He cannot feel his heart. Who is answering his wife's phone?

'Who is this?' he asks, trying not to let his voice betray him.

'I'm sorry, this is Father Jimmy Whelan. If you're worried I'm a threat on the romance front, even if I weren't a man of the cloth I'd be too old for that carry-on now.'

'Father Whelan,' says McAvoy wheezily. He tries to get hold of his thoughts. 'What's happening? The Heldens. The Teagues . . .'

'Temporary ceasefire,' says Whelan brightly. 'I'm staying with the Teagues for a couple of days. The hope is that the Heldens won't risk any sort of nastiness while I'm here. Roisin has been a diamond, God bless her. Talking you up. Reckons you'll be bringing Valentine home any day now, poor lass. She fought her eyelids for hours but she dropped where she sat. I'll wake her if you insist but if you'll take an old man's advice, sometimes it's as well to let people be.'

McAvoy is about to blurt out the truth when something makes him pause. He reaches out and takes the shot of vodka from Val's hand. He downs it and enjoys the burn.

'Father Whelan, where precisely is Roisin?'

'In her mother's caravan, my son.'

'And where are you?'

'Same caravan. Her da's on the step, holding a jug and a shotgun but she won't do as I've asked and go into the village where she's safe. All I can do is stay here – put a bit of holy fire between the innocents and the danger.'

'My colleagues at Humberside Police have been in touch with your office, I think,' says McAvoy, getting hold of himself. His voice becomes more official. 'It's regarding your association with Paulie Pugliesca. Also, with Peter Molony.'

'Peter's an old friend,' says Father Whelan in the same soft but cheery tone. 'As for Paulie, I do wish the various authorities would accept that all men deserve spiritual counsel. I visit him because I believe him to be a man whose soul is worth saving.'

'You're a priest,' says McAvoy.

'And I'm a New Yorker who does not give up on his friends or his flock. Might I ask why you want to know?'

'Brishen,' says McAvoy. 'I understand he met up with Mr Molony at your old church. He also visited him at his home. Has Mr Molony informed you of this, or the fact he has been a regular visitor at Brishen's hospital bedside?'

There is a pause. At the other end of the line, McAvoy hears the other man take a sip of something and then give a polite cough.

'When Brishen told me of the trip he was planning with Shay and Valentine I was happy to help,' says Whelan. 'He knows about my link to St Colman's. I asked him to light a candle there for me. Peter was aware that somebody dear to me was coming to Manhattan. They met at the church. No doubt they shared stories about myself, though I would not wish to have been a fly on the wall during that conversation. Peter told me they had hit it off, as it were. I am sure he has been great consolation to Brishen as he lies in his hospital bed. It pains me that I cannot be there myself and I pray that this situation can be resolved. For now, he is in my prayers. He is my friend, Aector, and I feel responsible in some way for what has occurred.'

'You asked the bishop to write a letter for Valentine,' says McAvoy.

'Indeed.'

'It was an unsanctioned bout . . .'

'What is said in confession is sacred,' says Whelan. 'I cannot discuss our philosophical differences. Now, may I enquire if there have been any positive developments regarding Valentine?'

McAvoy wants to tell him the truth. But there is something a little oily, a little slick, about the man who holds his wife's phone. He finds it hard to imagine that a respected man of the Church would go and sleep in a humble caravan to prevent bloodshed between two warring Gypsy clans, and then realises how terrible an indictment on the clergy this actually is. Of course that's where he should be. Of course he should make a sacrifice in order to help secure peace.

'I'm putting the pieces together,' says McAvoy cautiously. 'It would be a big help to speak to Mr Molony. We had a very brief chat at Brishen's bedside and he seemed rather reluctant to talk to me.'

'Peter can be querulous,' says Whelan, and it sounds like he is smiling. 'He has not always been treated with kindness by the police.'

'I'm aware that his past is intriguing,' says McAvoy.

'Intriguing, Aector? Painful, certainly. Hard. But he is a good man who has done good things in his life.'

'Perhaps he would have made a good priest,' says McAvoy softly.

'Perhaps,' says Whelan, not rising to it.

'You were a regular visitor to the seminary where he studied . . .'

'This is beginning to feel like an interview, Aector. Should I tell Roisin you called?'

'Should I give Mr Molony your regards?' responds McAvoy. 'I saw another of your friends earlier today. Paulie Pugliesca. He spoke well of you. Will you be offering long-distance counsel to Nicky Savoca? He has lost a son, you understand. Or are you focused only on Mr Molony? I'm on my way to his apartment now, actually. I'm hoping he will be more helpful when we chat. I have some questions that trouble me.'

'Really?' asks Father Whelan. 'He has answered all such questions before, I'm sure. Are you not there to find Valentine Teague? Is that not what you are for, in this matter?'

There is silence on the line. It stretches out, becoming uncomfortable. McAvoy feels an urge to speak; to drag something else out of the man who sits in the same quiet space as his wife and children. But it is Father Whelan who breaks the silence.

'Is it arrogance, do you think?' His tone of voice has changed and he seems to be talking as much to himself, or to God, as he is to McAvoy.

'Father?'

'Arrogance to believe you can change things. Arrogance to believe your decisions are blessed. Is that how it feels for you, Aector? Do you believe yourself to be divinely chosen? Picked out to fight on the side of the angels? You trust yourself, yes? Know yourself to be a good man. You love your family and you want to do what is right. You believe that a man who feels such things must by definition be able to make decisions that please God.'

'I don't know what I believe,' says McAvoy, uncertain where the priest is leading him.

'Do you know what it is to make a decision that you believe to be God's will, only to learn that it is not His design? Nor is it the work of the devil. It is the wish of your own accursed self. Can you imagine what it is to know that your acts of decency have caused so much pain and suffering? How does one atone for such a thing? Is there a penance great enough? God forgives all, but to forgive ourselves? That is where prayer falls short.'

McAvoy listens to the priest's breathing. He doesn't know whether to push or stay silent.

'If life were a scale, I would be able to weigh my good deeds against my unforeseen consequences and not be found wanting. My life, on balance, has served God. And so I tell myself that I am still blessed. Still welcome at His side. Yet I still fear Judgement Day. I fear what I will learn at that great and terrible time. I will accept God's decisions about my deeds.'

Father Whelan coughs. It sounds dry and painful. It seems to put some steel back into his voice.

'God may judge me, Aector, but I do not know any man who could say in good conscience whether my life has been one of goodness and charity or of terrible sin. I do not wish to hear either case. Could you understand that, do you think? Could you allow yourself to leave things be? To leave my fate in the hands of God? I have never prayed for myself. For the sake of all that will crumble if you kick at my foundations, I would ask you to leave things be.'

McAvoy rubs at the bruise below his eye. The pain sings in his cheek.

'Father, it doesn't work like that. I'm not accusing you of anything. We all make mistakes. Talk to me. Talk to Roisin, if it's easier. I'm not a policeman right now – just a man lost and far from home. I know you can help me. I know you want to. I can hear the conflict in you.'

'We are all conflicted, Aector.'

'You asked me if I thought myself a good man,' says McAvoy urgently. 'The truth is, I don't know. How do we know such a thing? Any of us? You have your religion, your God, to tell you what it is to live a good life. But what of those with different codes? What is it to be a good man when you have no notion of an after-life or judgement? Would you stop praying if you learned there

280

was no heaven? We all pray to our souls, our own selves – we pray to find out who we are, and that prayer can be words, or song, or the thoughts that creep up on us as we hold the ones we love. Nobody has answers. Not really. Please, Father, I can hear the weight upon your conscience. Unburden yourself.'

Father Whelan doesn't speak for a long time. When he does, there is a tremble in his voice.

'Bless you, my son.'

McAvoy stares at the dead phone. It feels as though his ribs are slowly opening like wings. His face is flushed and the sweat has turned cool upon his forehead.

'You were fucking rude,' says Valentine. 'Was that Whelan? Why's he got Ro's phone? Why didn't you tell them I was safe and this was nowt to do with me?'

'We have somebody to visit,' says McAvoy, teeth clamped together. 'Molony.'

'The monk-looking bloke with the nice house? Why?'

'He's involved. Involved in what happened to Brishen and Shay.'

'Nah, he was okay. Really took to Brish. Gave him a good-luck charm, for all the good it did him.'

'A good-luck charm?'

Valentine smiles. 'Yeah, Brish was holding it like it was the crucifix when we were waiting for the fight. Said Molony had given him it.'

'What was it?'

'Leather pouch on a string. I don't know what was inside it. Brish told me but I must have misheard. It didn't make sense.'

McAvoy looks at him. Watches the lights flicker in the jewels of water on the side of the vodka bottle. Out on the street the snow blows in with the same relentlessness with which McAvoy pursues the truth.

'He said it was his face,' says Valentine, and he is not smiling as he says it.

'Whose face?'

Valentine shrugs. He seems to be running out of energy, the bravado that has been sustaining him draining away.

'Let's ask him,' says Valentine, setting his jaw. 'Let's knock on the prick's door.'

Both men turn to look at Rey, who has not spoken in half an hour.

'Is it always like this with you?' he asks McAvoy, eyes wide.

McAvoy gives a weary nod. 'You don't know the half of it.'

27

A pleasant room on the sixth floor of the Wade-Christie
Presbyterian Hospital: 1.04 a.m.

A well-built, chestnut-skinned man with dark hair and a swathe
of bandages where his nose used to be; split to allow the breathing
tube into his lungs.

His eyelids flicker. His fingers twitch.

A petal falls from the roses that stand in a crystal vase on the
table by the window. As it tumbles downwards it is caught by the
breeze that billows gently from the air-conditioning unit, and the
pinkish petal pinwheels across the air to land on the perfect white
sheets that swaddle the comatose man's body.

Though there is no way for him to be able to smell the bloom,
perhaps he senses it. Perhaps he can taste a change in the air. As
the petal lands, the rapidity of his eye movements increases. His
finger jerks. He can see something, in the darkness behind his
eyelids. In his private world between life and death, he can sense
himself being tugged between two tomorrows; racked and
stretched by the hands that drag him between waking up, or drift-
ing away . . . *Come on, Brish. Think. Think!* You were pissed off,
you know that much. Pissed off and scared. You'd fucked up. Val
had played you and you'd lost your temper with him. You went
after him and it all turned to shit. You had some Russian prick in
the boot of the car and nowhere to go with him. What did you do?
You'd been at the fat man's place. Swanky gaff, like something out
of a magazine. He'd been welcoming. Friendly, like he had been at
church. All the love in the world for Father Whelan and who could
blame him. Made you welcome, didn't he? Even when you turned
up with Shay and Valentine and smacked the little prick in the

mouth so hard his tooth came out. He didn't judge. Still the same kind eyes and happy smile, even though you could see the poor bastard was suffering. Smelled like sour milk. Needed all the luck he could get and still he didn't ask for the charm back. He'd handed it over like it was a lock of Mother Mary's hair. Kept this safe for you, he said. You need it back. What is it? you asked. He said it was your face, Brish. And you were too polite to ask for an explanation. Felt right though, didn't it? Little soft leather pouch, dangling there on your chest. Don't look inside, he said, as if it were Pandora's fucking Box. And you didn't, did you? Just held it and let it take the edge off the pain in your gut . . .

Was different when you came back though, wasn't it? Different when you parked up in his garage with Chebworz in the boot. Molony had been drinking. Had taken his pills. And the way he moved, you could see he was hurting. There was blood showing through his pyjamas but he said it didn't matter. You tried to be kind, Brish. Put him to bed and said you would be out of his hair as soon as you could. Fixed yourself a drink and watched the view while Shay slept in the armchair and you wondered if Valentine was dead or alive.

You shouldn't have listened, should you? Shouldn't have snooped around in another man's home or cased his house like some burglar. Shouldn't have leaned on the picture or looked behind it when it moved. Shouldn't have played with his little old tape recorder. But you did. Listened to a man with a voice like a quiet scream, talking about the people he had hurt and the lives he had taken and begging, begging, begging for forgiveness in the name of the Father, the Son . . .

He heard, of course. Woke up. And you went mad, didn't you, Brish? Wanted answers. Who the fuck did the voice belong to? Was it real? Who was the sick fuck who was talking about sacrifice? Penance? Atonement? And who was the girl, screaming and begging for water as he confessed and confessed and confessed . . .

He showed you, didn't he? Showed you the wounds on his skin. And you wanted to puke. You wanted to puke even before he started talking. And once he started, you wanted him to stop. So you hit him. Knocked him down and laid the boots in and all the while he looked at you with big sad eyes; so full of disappointment and confusion.

What did he tell you, Brish? Why did you get your arse in that car and drive to those fucking woods? Where were you going? It cost Shay his life, you silly bollocks. Next thing it was all blue lights and that bumpy road and the trees getting thicker and darker and the snow beneath your knees as that bastard put his gun to your head and told you that this was what happened to people who stuck their noses in where they didn't belong . . .

Remember, Brish. Remember . . .

On the monitor at his bedside, the read-out begins to fluctuate, beeping more swiftly, frenziedly, as a tortured soul tries to find a way back into its body, trying the locked entrances and exits like a burglar: growing more frantic in its desire to live.

28

'It's always like this, is it? Being a copper? I thought it would be more boring, like. More paperwork. More staring at computers and giving people speeding tickets. Not so many fights with Russians or breaking into serial killers' houses . . .'

Valentine is enjoying himself. He's grinning, showing off the gap in his top row of teeth but still managing to look handsome in a bad-boy kind of way.

'We're not breaking in. And we don't know what he's done,' says McAvoy, keying in the code and pushing open the door to Molony's apartment building. 'There are unanswered questions, that's all.'

The door closes behind them as they enter the warm, ground-floor hallway. Outside, the roads are practically deserted and the snow continues to fall. Some of the streets Rey had used to shave some time off their journey back were virtually impassable for snowdrifts or the vehicles that had skidded and been abandoned. Rey had used all of his experience to thrive where others had failed. He drove most of the way in low gear but still made good time. When he dropped them off he had refused their offer of staying in touch.

'You think he's home?' asks Val.

'He didn't answer his buzzer,' says McAvoy as they begin to climb the stairs.

'Maybe he wears ear-plugs. Or he's got company. Or he doesn't answer the door in the middle of the night. Or maybe he's de-limbing a prostitute with a pair of nail scissors.'

'Don't make jokes,' says McAvoy. He's in a lot of pain. His ribs and face are agony and his chat with Father Whelan has left him feeling as though he is walking two inches below the surface of the road. He feels disconnected; holding onto home by a fraying rope.

'I've met this bloke. He was nice. Friendly.'

'I'm sure he is. I'm not making any assumptions. Grab the keys, they're under that rug.'

Valentine does as he is told and they walk in silence to the red front door. Taking a breath, McAvoy gives a policeman's knock and starts to count down from twenty in his head. When he gets to three he knocks again.

'Ear-plugs,' mutters Valentine.

'Police,' shouts McAvoy. 'Open up.'

'Are you?' asks Val.

'What?'

'Police. Here, I mean.'

'I'm doing my best, Valentine.'

Valentine raises his hands in surrender, grinning at his brother-in-law. 'Wait until I tell Roisin.'

McAvoy ignores him, fumbling with the keys. 'Here, hold this.' He hands his phone to Valentine. A red light is flashing. 'I need you to record this.'

'Yeah? Why?'

'I want to show I did things properly.'

'If nothing else it will be popular on YouTube. Especially if he's waiting behind the door with a golf club.'

'Shush,' says McAvoy, and turns the handle. He leads the way into Molony's apartment and at once something feels different. He was here just a few hours ago and though it had felt anodyne and far from homely, it had at least felt as though it could be turned into a comfortable abode with a change of furniture and some drawings stuck to the fridge. It feels cold now. Empty. McAvoy knows at once that there is nobody at home. Even so, he calls out as he walks down the corridor, stating his name and rank and calling Molony's name.

There are no lights on in the apartment and McAvoy raises his hand to shield his eyes when Valentine blithely flicks on a light switch and floods the living room with a yellow glare. It reveals a scene of chaos. The luxurious space has been ransacked. Drawers have been pulled free and their contents spilled across the floor. Papers, some pristine white and others yellowing with age, carpet the floor. The drawers themselves have been tossed aside and the paintings pulled down from the walls to lay among the smashed glass and spilled pages. This place has seen violence.

'Christ,' says Valentine.

McAvoy spots a splatter of blood, running across a stack of spilled tri-fold leaflets advertising a Catholic retreat. He bends down and spots another, further away, towards the kitchen. He follows the trail. Turns on the light.

There is a mound of ash upon the floor. A discarded urn, lying on its side by the cooker.

Blood.

'Well, the cleaner's taking a day off,' says Valentine behind him.

McAvoy takes the phone and slowly films everything around him. He zooms in on the blood. Against the tiles and the ash it looks like a lot but McAvoy has seen enough murders to know that a person can lose this amount and live. He has lost twice this much himself and walked away.

'Molony, you think?' asks Valentine.

'It's his house.'

'Is there somebody after him?'

McAvoy stops recording and closes his eyes for a moment. There is a thudding in his head. He feels Valentine's arm on his shoulder and a moment later he is sitting down in one of the sumptuous red armchairs and Valentine is handing him a glass of water.

'We're contaminating the crime scene,' says McAvoy.

'Don't talk shite. Just drink.'

McAvoy does as he is told and then puts his head back against the comfortable leather. He would love to sleep. He'd like to be found here by NYPD uniforms. He'd like to be told off, cautioned and told to leave the country. He'd like to take Valentine back to Galway, pick up his family, give Father Whelan a knowing look and bugger off back to Hull. He simply can't let himself.

'What now?' asks Valentine. 'You want me to go and film the shit in the loft that you told me about? Sounds creepy as fuck. And I'm good at not leaving footprints.'

McAvoy shakes his head. He feels inert. Clueless. He looks at his phone for a moment and wishes that the screen would light up with advice. For something to do, he calls Alto again. The policeman still isn't picking up. He's either interviewing Zav or has gone home to bed.

'You want to try Ro again?' asks Valentine gently. 'You've nowt to worry about. The Heldens are all talk. They'll make a lot of noise but it won't come to anything. And they won't come in all guns blazing with Whelan there. You're acting like she's with another man. He's a priest, Aector. That's almost the same as a eunuch.'

McAvoy considers this. 'You really think that? You don't think that priests are just men in funny uniforms? Men with the same needs and hungers and wants as the rest of us?'

'The Church has had a lot of shit,' says Valentine. 'All that paedophile stuff. It's horrible. Sick. Evil, even. But they're just a tiny few, mate. Priests I know are good blokes. Like their whiskey and give good advice. They want us to be nice to each other.'

'Really? What about if you're different? If you're not Catholic? Or if you're gay? Or if you can't afford to bring your new baby into the world . . .'

'Would you want to be the one making up the rules? At least they know what they stand for.'

McAvoy bites his cheek. He feels irritated. Feels unsure of his opinions or even his suspicions.

'I'm going to call this in,' he says, making up his mind. 'I'll just phone 911 and tell them there're signs of disturbance. They can take over. I've got no bloody idea what I was even thinking.'

Valentine looks at him kindly. 'Don't start feeling sorry for yourself. You're doing a grand job. You got me away from those Russian wankers.'

'You could have walked whenever you liked.'

'I don't know,' says Valentine thoughtfully. 'Maybe. Maybe not. When I tell Roisin I'll make you sound like Johnny Big-Bollocks.'

McAvoy smiles, despite himself. 'I should really use a pay-phone,' he muses, looking at his phone. 'I'm going to forward this video clip to Alto, then that's us done.'

'Really?' asks Valentine, disappointed. 'Shall we go see Brish at the hospital, then? Maybe Molony's there. He might just have cut himself and gone to the hospital. Maybe all the mud and ash in the loft is for a herb garden. Shay's name on the wall . . . a face in a bag . . . I'll grant you, it's creepy, but . . .'

McAvoy is about to respond when his phone lights up. He recognises the number of Courtland Road Police Station in Hull and it has the same effect on his spirits as the sight of a giggling baby. He smiles as he answers.

'Now then,' says Pharaoh breathlessly. She sounds as if she has been running, which McAvoy finds unlikely. Pharaoh believes that people should only run when being pursued by psychopaths or if the prize for a first-across-the-line dash is a bottle of Nero d'Avola.

'It's good to hear from you,' says McAvoy.

'I'm sure it is,' says Pharaoh, and starts coughing. 'Those bloody stairs. Took them two at a time.'

'How did you manage that?'

'My legs aren't that short,' says Pharaoh. 'I'm still quite bendy.'

'Why were you running?' asks McAvoy, refusing to consider Pharaoh's alleged suppleness.

'I had a Skype chat with a contact at the NBCI. Had to take it in the ACC's office as he's the only one with clearance.'

'Was he there?'

'Of course not. He's got his password written in his contacts file. Calls him Mr Password.'

'Really?'

'Really. If you're interested I've also got the digits for Mr Account Number, Mr Sort Code and Mr Long Number Across the Middle of the Card.'

Sitting in a house he has no right to be inside, surrounded by paper, glass, ash and blood, McAvoy finds himself grinning. He would give anything to have her here.

'What have you got?' he asks. 'I'm at Molony's place. It's been ransacked. There's blood on the floor.'

'His blood?'

'I presume so.'

'Chances are high,' says Pharaoh. 'From what I've just found out, he's been making enemies out of powerful friends.'

'Father Whelan?' asks McAvoy. 'The Italians?'

'Just hang on. Let me sort my brain out.'

McAvoy waits. He hears the familiar soft crackle as she pulls on her cigarette. He imagines the tip glowing red, the smoke trickling from her lips as she talks.

'Molony's not a well man,' says Pharaoh. 'Cancer. Started in his pancreas and has spread to his liver, bones and brain. He hasn't got long.'

'This from the NBCI?' asks McAvoy. 'Where did they hear it? And what's it to do with them?'

'Alto's been busy on your behalf. A lot of old files have been dusted off. It seems questions have been asked about some of the so-called "charitable" institutions that have been benefiting from donations at the churches where Father Whelan has any influence. Charities that might not be totally legit. The paper-trails are a labyrinth but we're getting there and I tell you this much – if anybody leans on me and tells me to stop they'll be going home with their bollocks in their pockets. Anyway, don't fret on it. We're getting help for you on all sides right now, even if nobody is saying anything official. And the simple fact is, Molony's dying.'

'Poor man,' says McAvoy, without thinking.

'Aye, maybe. I'm not going to start blubbing for him just yet. The Feds have a recording of him, made earlier this year. They've got informants all the way through Pugliesca's crew. They've got a wiretap on Paulie's personal mobile phone. Normally it's just chats with his mistress, his wife, his kids and grandkids. There's nothing relates to business. But a while back he took a call from Peter Molony.'

'Go on.'

There is a rustle of paper and Trish reads from the transcript. *'It's Peter. Why you calling this number? Give me a moment I'll call you back. No, I need to say this now. I can't do it. The tests have come back. It's all through my body. I'm rotting. I'm dying. I need to put things right and that means I have to stop doing what I've been doing. I know it leaves you in trouble and I wish there was another way but I have to say no.'*

'That's all on tape?' asks McAvoy.

'That, and Pugliesca's response. He tells him to stop talking and to listen to him. He'll pay for the best doctors. He won't let him die. He's too important. He tells him to think things through clearly. Then Molony hangs up.'

'What did the Feds make of it?'

'That's when they started looking into him properly. And they found that a certain Detective Alto had been trying to make connections long before, only for him to be warned off by people with powerful allies. Whatever. You were right in your hunch. Molony's been laundering Pugliesca's money for years. Benzano too – the old boss in jail. Fraudulent charities. Dozens of them. Some exist for real and provide help for orphans and widows and all manner of good and deserving people. Others just exist on paper. There's a trail of false accounts and false addresses and made-up trust funds and it's damn complex. The Feds have been trying to disentangle it all so they can fold the whole lot into one big RICO indictment against Pugliesca. If they can prove the connection they'll be able to seize millions but to do that they risk having to ask for money back from some legitimate charities so you can imagine why they've been cautious.'

'But they know this? They know he's been doing it?'

'There's more,' says Pharaoh, ignoring him. 'The information they have concerning the Chechens and the Ukrainians and the Russians and every bugger coming out of the old Eastern bloc – it seems that as part of their new arrangement with Pugliesca, Sergey's men want access to their money-laundering operation. Molony's been asked to expand.'

'And that's what he's said no to?'

'That's the assumption.'

McAvoy frowns. He looks at Valentine, who has crossed to the window and is looking out across the rooftops of Manhattan at the darkness and the snow.

'This is the same Molony who trained as a priest? The same Molony who is sacristan of St Colman's? The one who's best friends with Father Whelan? The one who castrated himself and spent time in a mental hospital?'

'He's led a colourful life,' says Pharaoh. 'Feds have his medical records too. Doctors treating him for the cancer made a note in his file about the extensive scarring to his body. Evidence of continued self-harm.'

'From years back?'

'No, continued self-harm right up to the present day. They wanted to photograph his injuries. Were sufficiently concerned to ask for a psych consultation. He refused.'

'Can he do that?'

'We get the impression somebody leaned on somebody else because nothing more came of it. Like I said, powerful friends.'

'And you think Pugliesca may be trying to persuade him to carry on cooking the books?'

'If the friendship with the Russian Mob is at risk, Pugliesca may need to have all his aces in play. The Italians get all sorts of muscle and resources out of their partnership with the Russians. If the Russians want a money-launderer in return, you have to hope that he's willing to do the job.'

McAvoy lets out a long deep breath. 'So what had Brishen done to warrant getting killed? Why were they sent?'

Pharaoh gives a little growl. 'Maybe they saw his dirty secret? Maybe he gets precious about his urns. Called his paymaster and asked him to step in. Chebworz got in the way and it turned to shit.'

McAvoy gives a grunt of assent. 'I was just about to call 911 and report the disturbance at the apartment. The place has been turned over. It looks like somebody has lost their mind in here – like a whirlwind has come through. There's blood . . .'

'Don't call it in,' says Pharaoh immediately. 'I can tell our friends at the NBCI. They can tell the Feds. That way, you get the credit for helping rather than the flak for interfering.'

McAvoy nods at the sense of this. She is far better at the politics of being a police officer. It has helped her rise to the rank she wears like both sword and shield.

'Molony could be in danger,' says McAvoy.

'He might, yes. But they can make a decision on how to play things.'

McAvoy bites his cheek again. He looks down at the tattered paper and discarded pictures. He looks at the blood on the fold-out leaflet. Squinting, he makes out the words. It advertises the St Anthony House of Prayer. On the front is a sketch of a pleasant woodland property, all wooden panels, ornate eaves and attractive windowsills.

'What about his connection with Whelan?'

'The nice sergeant at the Guards said Whelan's currently stay-ing with the Teagues at the site in Galway. He's arbitrating the dispute. We knew that already.'

'Valentine's with me,' says McAvoy in a rush.

'You got him? Bloody hell. Bet Roisin's relieved.'

'I haven't told her yet. I tried to ring and Whelan answered her phone.'

'Yeah? So you told him, then.'

McAvoy clears his throat, colouring. 'Not yet. I thought I'd wait until I knew more.'

Pharaoh stays silent for a moment. 'You wanted to hear her voice, you mean,' she says, and some ice enters her voice. 'You wanted to hear her tell you how great you'd done.'

'No, that's not it . . .'

'Yes, it is,' says Pharaoh. 'I don't blame you. You've done incred-ibly. But there are people at risk. Your own family, for God's sake. They need to know.'

'But just because he's safe doesn't mean the Heldens will believe he didn't kill Shay.'

'Hector, I'm going to phone Roisin myself if you don't do it.'

McAvoy feels chastened. His cheeks burn. What the hell had he been thinking? He pulls himself out of the chair and runs his hands through his hair. It stays sticking up.

'I thought I was doing things right,' says McAvoy, and his voice has gone small.

'You are. You have. Look, don't beat yourself up. It will all work out. You're going to be getting back-slaps on two sides of the Atlantic. And the stuff you found in his loft? Who knows where that will lead?'

McAvoy concentrates on his breathing as he paces back and forth on the square of floor not covered in paperwork and glass. He starts shuffling the documents into some kind of order. Last wills and testaments. Architectural plans. Deeds of transfer. Minutes of committee meetings from fraudulent charities. He looks up to see if Valentine is still listening and sees the square hole in the wall. He crosses the room and peers into the empty space. Angling his head he notices the larger rectangle of discolouration around it. A picture hung here until recently.

McAvoy looks around him, trying to work out which one of the discarded frames seems the right size.

'What are you doing?' asks Pharaoh. 'You're rustling.'

McAvoy finds the gold-edged frame propped behind the sofa. The picture faces away from him and the back is bare wood. He turns it around and looks at the image. It is a blueprint, an architectural sketch of a church, created in blue ink on quality paper. The dimensions of the building are inscribed in a neat hand. A cross-section of the nave and cloisters has been sketched in the upper left-hand square of the plan. The image suggests something medieval in origin. Something European. McAvoy wishes he knew more about church design; whether it is Gothic or Norman or Saxon in style. He just knows that it looks like something from home. He leans in closer. The numbers showing the width and breadth of the central aisle must be measured in some archaic unit. The digits make no sense.

He looks down at the papers on the floor around him. Molony's neat handwriting is a match for the words on the blueprint. He looks at them more closely.

Transept.

Cloisters.

Sacristy.

Crypt.

McAvoy focuses on this last. The crypt has been sectioned off on the plan. A dozen neat lines divide the floor-space. In eight of them, a tiny **x** has been placed in the bottom right-hand corner. In the ninth is a faint symbol, faded to almost nothing. It is a delicate pencil sketch of a rose.

'Hector?'

McAvoy takes a step back and holds up the frame. He tilts it to see the glass better. With the light at a certain slant he stares at the writing, inscribed in such tiny, perfect lettering that it could only have been written using a magnifying glass.

He reads the words aloud, squinting so hard his face hurts.

'Now I rejoice in my sufferings for your sake, and in my flesh I complete what is lacking in Christ's affliction for the sake of his body, that is, the church.'

'Cheery,' says Valentine, nodding.

'This matters to him,' says McAvoy quietly. 'Centre of the room, covering his safe; his secrets. The digits don't make sense. They aren't the right measurements . . .' He peers again. 'Dates!' he says sharply. 'Look. Along the boundary wall. 110176110976. Split it down the middle. They're dates . . .'

He fumbles with his phone. Hears Pharaoh protest at the beeping in her ear. Brings up the information Ben sent him. Missing girls. Names on the wall of gold leaves in Molony's loft of atonement. The dates of disappearances. Dates of deaths. He looks again at the image and the tiny crosses in the crypt.

'I've found something,' says McAvoy. 'Can I call you back?'

'Hector . . .'

He ends the call.

'What you found?' asks Valentine. He takes the frame from McAvoy and turns it over. 'Pretty church. Galway, is it?'

'Why do you ask that?'

'That looks like the church outside Tuam. We fixed the roof

296

there, years back. Father Whelan was priest there for a time. St Anthony's. That's where Siobhan's baptism is. The one we missed. That Ro went over for . . .'

'St Anthony's?' asks McAvoy, scratching the crown of his head. He clicks his tongue against the roof of his mouth. He's tired. Wrung-out. But he can sense the tail of something vile and slippery scuttling away from him and he reaches out in his mind to haul it back.

'You okay, Aector?' asks Valentine, concerned.

McAvoy crosses to where the leaflets have been tossed to the floor in a chaotic pile of loose papers. He bends down and looks at the hand-drawn image on the front. It shows a pleasant, decent-sized cottage in a quiet wooded copse; a stream running through the grounds and a simple cross hanging from the quaint eaves above the doorway. McAvoy turns it over. Scans the contents: '. . . a place of healing . . . quiet Christian reflection . . . an opportunity to heal the soul . . .'

McAvoy flicks to the back page. Alongside the request for charitable donations is an address for the charity that runs it. The address is Molony's own.

'St Anthony's,' he says to himself. He closes his eyes and begins to see the connections. The poor bastard from the institution who spent time with Father Whelan and Peter Molony up at St Loretta's. The lad who got caught in the blast that took out Sal Pugliesca. Molony was the family lawyer? He would have taken care of Sal's estate after the blast in '81. Molony, who has been setting up fake charities and bogus religious institutions for years to help launder the Mob's cash. Would he have printed leaflets for a place that didn't exist?

'Arrogance or pride?' mutters McAvoy, opening up a search page on his phone. He keys in the name of the retreat and finds no relevant hits. The only suggestion that there is a Catholic retreat near where Shay was killed is on the leaflet he holds in his other hand.

McAvoy rummages on the floor, looking for deeds of title. He grabs for a yellowing document: black typewritten ink. The sale of

Molly's Farm in Crow, Schoharie County, to SP Holdings Ltd in 1976. He begins picking up pieces of paper and scanning them. His movements are jerky and frantic, as though he is afraid that if he rests the thoughts will slip away.

'SP,' he mutters to himself. 'SP Ltd. No, no. Yes!'

He brandishes the paper as if having discovered gold. 'SP Ltd. Company established in 1976. Joint partners, Salvatore Pugliesca and Tony Blank.'

McAvoy looks again at the picture of the peaceful cottage. Compares the frontage to the blueprint of the farmhouse on the deeds. He sees the similarities at once.

McAvoy calls up a map on his phone. Crow is an hour further on from Cairo, not far from the Interstate that Brishen took on his desperate drive north. Could that be where they were going? Could Molony have told him something that made him risk everything in a frantic drive into the wilderness on the night Shay Helden was killed?

'What are you thinking?' asks Valentine, looking at the leaflet.

'Everything points to reverence,' says McAvoy manically. 'He's venerating St Anthony and his deeds.'

'St Anthony? What's he . . . ?'

McAvoy shakes his head. 'Not a real saint. Not a true martyr. He's venerating somebody. Somebody he has spent a lifetime idolising and revering.'

'Father Whelan?' asks Valentine, surprised.

McAvoy shakes his head. 'The rose on the first gold leaf. The place it all started. In the attic and on the wall of his church. There was no name on the first leaf. He left it Blank.'

'What?'

'Tony. St Tony. The martyr who saved souls at his quiet little retreat in the middle of nowhere. The mute who found a way to be understood. How many souls, Valentine? How many did he take?'

McAvoy is not in pain any more. He's not tired or frustrated. He thinks he understands. He thinks he has made the connections that will allow him to go home.

Like Brishen Ayres before him, Aector McAvoy feels he may have stumbled onto an evil that has lain undetected for decades – festering beneath the cold ground. Festering in a place that all the holy water that has passed through the sacristan's hands will never be able to make clean.

He turns to Valentine. 'You can steal a car, right?'

The younger man smiles, eyes sparkling. 'Yes, Officer.'

January 1981: The Final Absolution

Father Whelan feels as if his heart is going to come apart. He sees it as a clockwork mechanism, all cogs and coils, and as he slides down the wall of the church he pictures it bursting into its component pieces in a maelstrom of jagged metal and crooked springs.

'It was you who got into his head,' spits Salvatore. He has a hand on Whelan's throat and is pushing him back against the wall.

'Sal,' he hisses. 'Sal, I can't breathe.'

'He seen bad things, yeah. Done bad things. But fuck, I never . . . I never . . . !'

Sal releases his hold on Whelan's neck. He collapses back onto a pew. His face is white. The hems of his flared jeans are soaked with snow and there is blood upon his knuckles.

Whelan stays where he fell, barely moving in the shadow of the column beside the vestry.

'I wasn't supposed to be visiting,' mutters Sal, pushing a hand through his hair. 'But I got a delivery. Just some powder from another supplier but Dad doesn't like it when I do things my own way so I figured I'd keep it safe and out the way. He wasn't expecting me. I walked in and there he was. In his rocking chair, talking like he'd always had a voice. Talking to you about the things he'd done. The girls he'd buried alive. Said he could only talk to the dying. His throat would close if he tried to speak to the living. He said he'd found a way to confess. And the voice, all crackly and low, like it was coming straight out of hell. I know I done things, Father. I'm no saint. But fuck!'

Whelan rubs at his throat. There are dots dancing in his vision. He cannot tell what is candlelight and what is stained glass and what is hallucination brought on by the horrors that fill him like too much wine.

'You seek absolution?' he wheezes. 'You seek forgiveness?'

'I don't know what I fucking seek!' bellows Sal. 'I came here for something . . . something I thought you had. Some answers. Some explanation. But look at you, all busted up and sorry for yourself. You're just a man, ain't you? Not some bouncer for God, not some wizard with an eraser who can take all the bad shit from your soul. You're a snivelling Mick bastard and you're going to burn. We're all going to burn. I put a hurting on him but he still won't say a word. I need to think. Need somewhere I can take him. I need to think . . .'

Whelan tries to speak but finds his tongue sticking to his mouth. Through the tears he sees Salvatore stand. He reaches into his coat. Whelan recoils, shuddering. He is suddenly terrified of death. He has fallen so far; plunged himself into such darkness. He cannot meet God like this. He suddenly yearns for redemption with a hunger that threatens to overwhelm him.

'Please,' sobs Whelan. 'I can make things right. There can be absolution . . .'

Sal spits on the flagstones and pulls out an envelope from his jacket pocket.

'For you, Father,' he says coldly. 'They were all for you. I got to think. I don't know what to do. Fuck. Got to think . . .'

He drops the envelope on the pew and turns his back, stalking towards the door without looking back towards the altar or the fallen priest. His shadows lengthen and then shrink and he steps back into the darkness beyond the great double doors without making the sign of the cross.

It takes Whelan several moments to find the strength to open the package. He closes his shaking fingers around the reel for a tape recorder. Written on the centre, as if scrawled by a child, he can make out his own name.

When he plays the recording in the solitude of his bedchamber, he wishes he were back against the wall. Wishes Salvatore had put a bullet in him rather than give him this.

As he listens to the mumbled words and the desperate screams, he stops being Father Whelan. He becomes Jimmy, from Hell's Kitchen. And his heart and soul speak to him in the voice of a devil. Jimmy knows he can never be a good man again. But he knows how to save a little piece of himself. He knows that for all his bullshit, Salvatore has hurt as many people as the 'brother' whose actions have so appalled him. Was that why he reacted so angrily? He saw something of himself in the actions of the emotionally scarred Tony? Jimmy begins to think. Starts to work out a way to remove an impure soul from the world. Two, if he plays it right. At no point does he remember to pray.

An hour later, he is sitting in a bar on Mulberry, drinking brandy with hands that shake. Paulie Pugliesca is sitting opposite him, his face as cold and stony as that of a corpse. A cigarette has burned itself out at his lips and a column of curling ash hangs in front of his face.

'You'll go to hell for this, Father,' says Nicky Savoca, seated at the smaller man's elbow. 'The seal of the confessional is sacred.'

Whelan shakes his head, huddling in on himself, teeth chattering against the glass. 'It wasn't in confession, I told you. He hadn't said the prayers.' He forces himself to look up at the big man and show a little fight. 'And I know more about the soul of man than any of you.'

At last, Pugliesca takes the cigarette from his mouth and grinds it out on the ashtray that sits on the red and white tablecloth beside an empty bottle of quality Sicilian red.

'You know what I have to do,' he says, teeth locked. 'By telling me this, you know what I have to do?'

'God forgives all,' says Whelan, and blesses the man across the table.

'My own son,' says Pugliesca, half to himself. 'A fucking rat. A fucking rat!'

He turns away and clicks his fingers. From the darkness, a tall, pot-bellied man emerges, hands clasped loosely at the wrist in front of him like a choirboy.

'We never speak of this,' he says. 'Fucking never. And you absolve me, Father. This shit gets wiped, you hear?'

Father Whelan nods.

'Claudio,' says Pugliesca, thinking aloud. 'Wake him up, Giulio. He's good. Quiet. It doesn't have to hurt.'

He turns back to Whelan. 'I don't want to be damned for this,' he says, and the black in his eyes devours the white.

'God forgives all,' says Whelan, and drains his drink. It ignites a fire in him. And as he sits in the quiet and the cool of the little Italian restaurant, he smells the burning of another man's soul, and the resurrection of his own.

29

If there were still any teenagers left in the village of Crow, the creepy house at the end of Euclid Creek Road would be the kind of place they would dare one another to enter after dark. With its sagging roof and rotting timbers, its litter-strewn stoop and flaking paint, it could earn a place in local legends. It could serve as an initiation ceremony, of sorts. You weren't a man, you weren't ready for the big wide world, until you'd set foot inside Molly's Farm and counted to ten.

It would have happened in any other village. Not Crow. There aren't enough people in this community to produce enough teenagers for adventures. This is a farming community; fields and forests, creeks and rock-pools, straggled out at the foot of the Catskills. Economically, times have never been as bad. Today's residents are incomers who have moved out of the city looking for a different kind of life. They mow their grass with ride-on mowers and maybe buy themselves a few chickens and a goat and tell themselves they are farmers while the yield from their orchard of apple trees turns to mulch upon the ground. Most don't last more than a few winters. The dark months are vicious up here; as if the wind and the snow are possessed of a malicious spirit.

Those residents whose roots go back further have no more affection for the area than those who have been attracted by the falling prices of property and land. There are those who can trace their kin back through the centuries and whose ancestors are buried out the back of their timber homes; headstones bearing names that have cropped up again and again through the generations and which serve as daily reminders to the current householders that their problems will not last for ever. In such homes are serious, hard-working men and women. The grind of their existence shows in their hands and in their faces. Each line in their foreheads tells of a bereavement, a foreclosure, a bad harvest or a stillborn calf. Such people have little time for daring one another to enter a spooky house.

There are even those in Crow who remember when Molly owned Molly's Farm. She sold up in '76. Went to live in Florida with a great-nephew who had taken one look at the rundown house where she was living and did the Christian thing by inviting her to live with him. He sold her house to some city folk for a decent price. Nobody brought over a housewarming basket or a peach cobbler for the newcomer. Nobody was even sure when he took possession, or whether he lived there full-time, or used the place as a vacation home. And nobody questioned him about the state of the overgrown lawn or the peeling paint. Only a couple of locals saw him and when he failed to return their waves, they put him down as an ignorant city slicker. They carried on with their lives, even as the woods closed in around the house and the bumpy, potholed road leading to his front door became more and more difficult to drive down.

Over the years, a few lost motorists knocked on the door in the hope of using the telephone or the gift of a glass of water. A handful of walkers in their hiking boots and waterproofs rapped their knuckles on the rotting wood of the squat, two-storey property. Nobody ever answered. And nobody went inside. The windows held firm and the front door was locked and bolted. Sun-bleached curtains still hung at the window and those who peered through the dusty glass could make out a few sticks of furniture and the signs of habitation. This was not an abandoned property – just an unloved one.

The next town over from Crow is called Summit, and in the bars of that quiet, pretty town, the talk would occasionally stray to the occupant of the old house by the river. On the occasions that the subject came up, people instinctively lowered their voices. Old anecdotes were regurgitated. Even as recently as this winter, old George Severn re-told the story of the time he saw the owner back in '81. *Pale, he was,* said George, when asked how he looked. *Almost see-through. I swear to God I thought he were a ghost. No prettier than his house.*

And soon the others would chip in. They would tell and re-tell their yarns about the occasional pilgrims who have knocked on their doors, asking for directions to St Anthony. They had heard tell of a place of healing. Some had even displayed leaflets, glorifying the saint's name and illustrated with a picture of the old cottage.

The Penitent, Peter Molony, knows it was folly to print the leaflets. He had never intended to show them to anybody. But he had journeyed, in his quiet moments, into a world behind his eyes in which Tony Blank was revered by all as a saint. He had imagined how it would be if the world knew the truth about his actions and his sacrifice. He had indulged his whim and incorporated the fantasy into the list of fake charities set up to help launder Pugliesca's money. To do so was a mistake, and in the moments after he knocked Claudio unconscious, he had allowed his rage at himself to lead him into a bout of violence and destruction. He had smashed up his beautiful home. Torn at his papers as he liked to lash at his skin; spilled precious ashes among the blood and the broken glass.

Here, now, Molony is again at peace. This is his church; his occasional sanctuary. He knows that nobody has set foot inside the house on Euclid Creek Road because behind the rotting façade is a state-of-the-art alarm system. The last time he came here was in August, when he discovered that the hole in the roof had grown so bad that rain had found a way through the rafters and fertilised grass seeds that had blown in to the holes on the moth-eaten couch. The grass has grown tall now. The sofa looks as though it is being swallowed up by nature. So, too, does the man who lies upon it, blood on his face, hands bound tightly at the wrists. He woke up on the drive here and Molony was forced to pull over and hit him afresh. There is blood on the lens of his eyeball now and more trickles from his ear, as if something is broken in the man's head.

Molony feels the same sense of calm he has always enjoyed when visiting this place. He finds it almost remarkable that so many years have elapsed since he drove out here to assess Sal Pugliesca's estate the day after the poor man was blown apart. Sal was very clear in his instructions. If anything happened to him, this property was to be Molony's priority. Tony needed taking care of. He deserved the lawyer's attentions. Molony had made it here within twenty-four hours of the mobster's death: arriving with a briefcase full of documents which only made sense to a man with Molony's ordered mind and which divided up the dead man's assets.

The different companies set up by the murdered Mafioso had interests in two refuse businesses and owned a property on South Street in Philly. He also had a part share in a nightclub and owned half a condo in the Keys. The house was a gift for his brother, Tony, when he was released from St Loretta Hospital in 1976, having been declared sane enough to live alone. It was at once a kind gesture and a selfish one. It ensured that Tony had a place to call his own, and also that Sal had somewhere to hide the occasional shipment of contraband.

Molony had not yet passed the bar exams but he was already proving an invaluable asset to the law firm that Paulie Pugliesca had set him up with. The partners knew he was the future. He had a gift for numbers; a flair for creativity. Sure, he was a peculiar piece of work but he was efficient and he made money. Who cared about the sweat patches and the little round glasses, the fleshy face or the perfectly bald head? He was a lawyer, not a pin-up, and if their Mob clients wanted him to look after their assets, the senior partners were happy to hand off to him.

The day after Sal and Tony were blown up at Sal's house in Philadelphia, Molony drove to Crow to assess the value of the property and to ensure that any possessions of questionable origin could be matched to fictional bills of sale should there be any difficult questions. Molony remembers weeping for Tony, his old friend from St Loretta's, the martyr he has spent a lifetime revering; though the tears were not of grief. He envied the boy who had suffered so much and who had now been granted his place in heaven.

Here, now, Molony remembers the sight that greeted him. The house was in a poor state of repair. The roof sagged, the wood panels were splitting around the rusting nails. And yet Molony liked it. Tony's living room was spartan but not uncomfortable. There was a sofa and a rocking chair, books and magazines. The floor was dirty and the sills needed the dust wiping away but for a young man who had spent time in so many dreadful institutions, this was a place of luxury.

It was only when Molony sat in the rocking chair that he felt the breeze coming up from the floor. It caused goose-pimples to rise upon his arms. His investigations led him to the basement. And in the basement, he made the discovery that changed everything.

Molony finds himself smiling as he remembers that day.

Now would be a good time, he thinks. *I am ready. This is right.*

Molony looks at his watch. It has a blue face and a gold band. It was expensive. A gift from Sal Pugliesca. He wore one himself, like his father. Like Tony Blank. Molony had not been sure about taking it but Sal had been so pleased with the work he had done in laundering a huge score from a hijacking, that Molony had felt it would be wrong to refuse it. He has worn it ever since. It is as much a part of him now as his cross and his scars.

It is almost 7 a.m. The sun has yet to rise but Molony feels no sadness at the thought he will die by moonlight. It seems right, somehow. He has never been one for sunshine. He burns.

'Wake up,' says Molony softly, and shakes the man on the sofa by the arm. He has to do it quite forcefully. Claudio coughs and retches as he wakes and Molony can see how much pain he is in. When he pulls the gag from his mouth it is with regret that he rips off with the tape some pieces of skin.

'Are you quite well?' asks Molony, peering at him. Claudio recoils a little. 'Can you smell me?' he says apologetically. 'I'm very sorry. My skin is ulcerous in places and parts of my stomach are rotting away. Cancer, I'm afraid. It has consumed me from the inside out. Would you like some water?'

Claudio nods. He scrunches up his eyes and a drip of blood runs out of his tear duct. Molony produces a ceramic chalice and brings it to the man's lips. Gently, he pours some into his mouth.

'It does not matter if you spill it,' says Molony, smiling warmly. 'The ground here is sacred.'

'Where the fuck am I?' asks Claudio, looking around at the threadbare room.

'I would ask you not to curse,' says Molony politely. 'This is God's house, as well as my own.'

Molony reaches into his white robe and removes the other man's wallet.

'Claudio,' says Molony. 'A nice name. More French than Italian. I am surprised Mr Pugliesca would utilise somebody whose credentials are not entirely Sicilian.'

'I am Sicilian,' says Claudio, and his voice sounds thick and slurred.

'And you work for Mr Pugliesca.'

'I work for nobody.'

'I believe I know you,' says Molony.

'I'm Philadelphia. I've seen you places. You've seen me. You're the lawyer. The fucking Glow-worm.'

'Indeed.' Molony smiles. 'Sensible, I suppose, to use somebody from out of the city. You are the man Mr Pugliesca uses for complex matters. I have heard about you. It seems quite neat you should be the one to do me this kindness.'

On the sofa, Claudio screws up his face again. He seems only half awake and the left-hand side of his body does not seem to be responding to his commands.

'It is not your fault,' says Molony, shaking his head. 'It is mine. I never dared hope for a second miracle and yet I was wrong to doubt.'

'. . . the fuck you talking about?' slurs Claudio.

'Was it you who shot Brishen or your excitable colleague?' asks Whelan.

'The Irishmen? I did my job. Made the best of it. You can tell Mr Pugliesca I won't say a word . . .'

Molony holds up a hand to quieten him. 'This place belonged to Salvatore Pugliesca,' he says. 'You remember him?'

'It was orders,' protests Claudio, whose nose is running with blood. He seems as though he is talking to somebody that only he can see. 'He was turning rat.'

Molony pauses a moment. Then he grins. 'Truly, all things are connected,' he says, clapping his fleshy hands. 'The bomb that killed Sal. That killed Anthony. That was your work?'

'You know it was,' protests Claudio. 'I did as I was told. Sal was my friend but he had to die. His dumb brother just got in the way. But he was going to inform . . .'

'Sal would not have informed,' says Molony, shaking his head. 'He had few qualities but he was loyal. His father should have had more faith.'

Claudio mumbles something and then begins to cough.

Molony sighs.

'Truly, the Lord sees all. We close the circle here today. My sin becomes yours as the sins of others have become mine. You, who defaced a miracle because of my weakness. I asked Paulie to stop them, that was all. Told him I would do what he wanted for the Russians if he would only stop Brishen and his young friend from coming here and seeing things they could not understand. I did not know what I meant to ask of him but I believe he read my disloyal heart. He despatched death. He despatched you.' Molony angles his head, suddenly puzzled. 'I called Paulie as soon as they left. How did you stop them so swiftly? How were they intercepted?'

Claudio's eyes roll back and there is blood in his words. 'Giulio told me New York had a man upstate we could use. He played the traffic cop. Set up the roadblock. I was driving like all hell from Philly. It was close. A matter of minutes. So perfect it would be enough to make you believe in a higher power . . .'

Molony gives a shake of his head. He has no wish to further expose himself to the details of Brishen's torment.

'Enough,' he says, abruptly. 'You will do me the honour of ending my entrapment, as God has so decreed. With this act, I save Father Whelan's soul. Those who know of the miracle are no more and he can walk at last in peace.'

Claudio rubs a hand across his mouth. There is fear in his eyes.

'I was a young man when I first came here,' says Molony, rubbing at the concentric keloids upon his skin. 'It was only a day after the deaths of Sal and Anthony, as Sal had decreed. I did grieve but not for their deaths. My friend, Father Whelan – he had put such effort into Tony's salvation and it had been for naught. I was soon to be shown that such doubts were the work of the devil. I, too, should have believed more fervently in the plan the Lord has for us all.'

'What plan?' says Claudio and blood pools in his lap.

Molony lifts the cord from around his neck and looks in wonder at the leather pouch.

'This was in your possession,' says Molony. 'I found it in your pocket. I had not expected to see it again. I felt its absence to my bones. For a time I feared I had been punished for idolatry but is it idolatry to venerate a holy relic? Would the bones of the saints be considered idols?'

'Saints? Fuck you talking about?'

'Beneath us,' says Molony, simply. 'Anthony found a way to achieve salvation. His sacrifice was greater than any I have ever known.'

'Anthony?' Claudio's eyes roll. 'Tony . . . the dummy . . .'

'He was mute, yes,' says Molony. 'He witnessed terrible things as a child. He wished so very fervently to be able to speak but he could not force himself. I witnessed that frustration. His eyes would pop, his bones and tendons would stretch and crack and yet he could make no sound save this pitiable mewling. He longed so desperately to hear his own voice in prayer. When he received the Word from Father Whelan he could not even say "amen". It pleased me to imagine he found this new life, a new home, a place to call his own for however short a time. And only when I opened the door to this sacred place did I learn the lengths he had gone to in order to make his confessions.'

'Untie me,' drools Claudio. 'I can't breathe . . .'

'The man you shot. The man called Brishen. He was my blessing and my temptation.'

Molony stops talking as he remembers that day. The floorboards in the cellar were pulled up like a storm-hatch. In the dark of the basement he found the girl, with her dark skin and her almond eyes. He knew her from church. She was a kind person; helpful and honest. She had been plump enough to conceal the child. The perfect, spotless child. And now she was dead beneath Tony's floor, with a newborn child clutched to her breast. Molony felt his strength leave him. He collapsed to his knees at the magnitude of Tony's sin. And then the child cried and everything changed.

'He was a miracle,' says Molony, eyes shining. 'He came to life in my sight. Truly, at that moment, I thought terrible things of Anthony. I felt lost and alone and yet I knew myself to be in the presence of something wondrous that was too colossal for just one man. I needed counsel. I drove to Summit and called Father Whelan. I told him where I was and what I had found. I drove back to the house and waited. Eventually, to silence his cries, I lifted the child from his mother's grasp. How hard he clung to me, Claudio. How desperate he was to live and be loved. And yet his face was hidden from view. A thick web encased his features. He had found his mother's breast through the tiniest hole in the mesh that smothered him. I peeled it from him. I helped him to breathe and to see. I was the first thing he saw. I still held him as Father Whelan arrived. The weight upon Father Whelan's soul was a terrible thing to behold. He spoke of what he knew. Perhaps it was confession but we were both men of God and together we shared truths. He had cemented them in, Claudio. Runaways. Vagrants. Prostitutes. Poor unfortunates. In their company, Anthony found his voice. He could not bring himself to speak in the company of the living. Anthony had spoken his last words as he clutched his dying mother when he was still a child. And in that doorway between life and death he found himself able to speak. As these girls slipped away, in that place between life and death, he gave them his prayers. He made his confession. He recorded his words of confession for Father Whelan.'

Molony smiles up at the sky and moves to where he placed the tape recorder that has been his spiritual nourishment for so many years. This is where the recordings were made – the recordings that have been his companion in his brutal prayers. He selects a reel at random and plays it back in the silence of the room.

'Forgive me, Father, for I have sinned. It has been five months since my last confession. In that time I have wished harm upon the men who slayed my mother and father and I have prayed for your help in learning their names. I have behaved jealously towards my brother, whom I have envied for his possessions and for the many women he has lain with. Last month I helped my brother to dump parts of a man in woodland on Staten Island, near the place where you saved me and set me on the path of righteousness. In order to make this confession I have been forced to take a girl called Nadina. She is a prostitute and curses when I ask her to pray with me. She will be at your side and beseeching you for mercy before the dawn, Father. Please help her to know that her sacrifice is your will. In her company I can hear my voice. In her company I can seek absolution. Thank you, Lord. Amen.'

Molony smiles beatifically. 'Father Whelan seemed to stagger for a time under the weight of Anthony's sacrifice. It took me time to make him see. After all, how else could Anthony make confession? He could not speak. He could not write. Only in the presence of the dying could he find his tongue. Father Whelan saved us both in St Loretta's. He told us of God's love and set us on the right path. I made my sacrifice and removed temptation with one swift slice of the knife. Anthony was the most lost of God's lambs but Father Whelan set us on the road to righteousness.'

'The baby,' says Claudio, eyes wide.

'Father Whelan was willing to make a sacrifice to continue his good works far from home. Two nuns from Ireland carried the child overseas. He spent time in their care in Tuam. Soon afterwards Father Whelan was moved to a neighbouring parish. It surprised me when word reached me that the child had been adopted by a Gypsy family but Father Whelan said they were good people. He always remained close by the child. He witnessed the child become a man and a good man too. He never denied me comfort or friendship. He would return home often with photographs and news of how the boy called Brishen was maturing. I felt almost as a father towards him, despite the distance.'

'Brishen,' says Claudio and sniffs back blood. 'The one who came back to life . . .'

'Last year I discovered I was dying. I knew the time had come to make my peace. I have done things that I am not proud of. I have helped men of questionable virtue to conceal their funds and not as much of it as I had promised myself has gone to do God's work. I made my own self comfortable when better men lay dead. And I was under instruction to do even more for new associates of Paulie Pugliesca. For much of my life I have been sacristan of St Colman's. I have been responsible for disposal of the water in which we wash the plates and chalices onto which the body and blood of Christ are poured. I have felt God's love and seen His miracles. Despite my sacrifices I know I have strayed from His path and though Father Whelan has absolved me of all future sin I know in my heart that I can only truly atone through pain.'

Moving slowly, as if the act pains him, Molony strips himself of his vestments. He stands naked before Claudio. Upon his chest is a mass of scarred flesh; concentric circles of ridged purple scar tissue.

'There are sinners within me,' he says, pointing at the scars. 'Those who have died unforgiven. I am their intercessor. I who am absolved. I take their mortal remains and make them one with me so through my sacrifice they too may be absolved. And through my penitence, I am moved closer to God. I have helped so many sinners through the gates of heaven.'

'You're insane,' says Claudio.

'In the secret places in my home you will find many wonders. Human remains. Blessed ground. There is a splendid golden tree containing the names of all those touched by Anthony's sacrifice: from those he placed beneath the ground on which we stand, to those who have found heaven through my own intercession. You say I am insane. No. I was found to be a good and clever man. My sin was to doubt the Lord. My sin was to indulge my earthly

314

pleasures and close the gates of heaven to myself. But through Father Whelan's counsel I found a way to become a good man, if not a whole one. Yes, my friend . . . I have made a room of wonders. That room contains the earth onto which I drain the holy water of St Colman's. I nourish it with the ashes of the unforgiven — ashes that it has been my privilege to acquire and use for a higher purpose. Through my perfect blood I help them know their way to heaven. I ask, now, for forgiveness once more.'

Swiftly, his skin rippling obscenely, Molony crosses to Claudio. From the case containing the tape recorder he retrieves a knife and gun.

'These are yours, yes? You cut off Brishen's nose the way I cut free his caul. You used this gun to put a bullet in his head.'

'It was Luca Savoca,' says Claudio, urgently. 'He wanted to show off. Enjoyed the blood and the cries. I ended the Irishman's suffering. I buried him. Left Luca on the tree and tended to him. I thought he was dead. I didn't know anything other than the fact that New York wanted them dead. Paulie is New York and, I swear, Paulie would kill Christ himself.'

Molony stands in front of him. He cocks his head, waiting for more.

'The Irishmen were the targets,' says Claudio, and his eyes seem to darken. 'I didn't know why, I just got the call. I had to get upstate and stop these two men. Paulie was the one who ordered the hit. Luca came down from the hills and set off towards the city. I was heading upstate, not far behind the Irish boys. I told Luca how to run the job. A diversion off the Interstate and a quiet road in the forest. He did as he was told. Couple of traffic signs and a blue light and next thing he's got them down Silver Spur Road and he's got his gun on them both and he's waiting for me. But he's a sick fuck. By the time I got there he'd been drinking and getting himself high. He was slapping them around. And there was some fucking Russian in the trunk. Luca said he wanted to send a message that he was still a player, still a Savoca. He cut Brishen's nose off, not me. And then the Russian ran. So did Helden. Luca went after them. Helden fell and I finished him as

315

gently as I could. Chebworz – the Chechen – he came back. Got me from my blind side. Skewered Luca. It was chaos and I was all blood and blindness. I tidied up best I could and got the hell out of there. New York and the Chechens have been asking questions ever since.' Claudio gives a tight smile. 'It was nothing to do with turf, or territory, or war. I was sent to kill the men who were a threat to you and Pugliesca. They were going to learn the truth . . .'

'Brishen,' says Molony, fascinated. 'You left him dead. And yet he rose again.'

'I thought he was dead. He should be dead.'

'He was not your sin,' says Molony, thoughtfully. 'He was mine. I prayed to see him again. I prayed to be allowed to gaze into eyes that had first gazed upon me. And when I fell ill my prayers were answered. Father Whelan told me that despite his attempts to persuade him not to, Brishen was coming to New York. He told me the importance of not telling him of his origins. But as a kindness to me he did what he could to facilitate the trip. When I saw him he was all I had hoped. He was kind, strong and warm. I even gave him this pouch, which has been my constant companion.'

Molony strokes the pouch and presses it to his heart. 'He came to my home later that night. There had been trouble. Violence. He even struck one of his friends in my living room. There was blood upon his hand and upon his face. Even then I saw the repentance in him. But I was in such pain. I took my medication and I drank the wine and thanked the Lord for His mercy in allowing Brishen to enter my life once more. And then he came back.'

Molony looks at his naked feet. He smiles at his plump, pink toes.

'May God forgive me but he found my secrets. Played Tony's confessions. And through fear and regret and weakness I told him all. I told him he was a living miracle. He crumpled under the weight of it. And then the devil whispered in his ear and he hurt me. He beat me and demanded to know the truth. About his mother's name. About his father. About where this had all taken place. In my weakness I told him all. Told them of his father. I saw Sal in him. Saw the girl too – the girl Salvatore took the way that other men

316

would take a cookie from a jar. Father Whelan, in his weakness, explained all. He told me of the way Salvatore looked at Alejandra. Perhaps Tony saw in her an even greater sacrifice. Perhaps that was why he chose her to hear his confession and allow him some form of absolution. God forgives, but in His absence, there is only Father Whelan. Ask for redemption and it shall be yours. And God helps those who help themselves. They left me bleeding and I was alone with my regrets and my sins. They had to be stopped. I could not expect Brishen to understand the nature of Anthony's sacrifice.'

'You called Pugliesca,' mutters Claudio. 'They sent me.'

'And now you are here to complete the circle.'

Molony cuts through the bonds that hold Claudio's wrists. He sags.

'I have made my confession,' says Molony, nodding at the tape recorder. 'I am ready.'

He picks up the gun and hands it to Claudio.

'Please,' he says. 'Suicide is a sin. I need your help.'

Uncertainly, Claudio takes the gun. His hand wavers. He seems at first to be trying to grab the air next to the weapon.

Molony steps back. He stretches his arms wide. Claudio gulps, drowsily, and wipes the blood from his chin with the back of his hand.

'I killed him too,' says Claudio, slowly, standing up. 'Tony.'

'The explosion, I know.'

'He was still alive afterwards. Tried to cut his arm off with a cleaver. Didn't say a word.'

'He died . . .'

'I know. Mine was the last face he saw. And the next one was never going to be St Peter's. He was going straight to hell.'

'No,' says Molony, shaking his head. 'He made his confession. He met God with a clear conscience.'

'And so will you, yes?'

Molony smiles, wide and happy. 'Please.'

Claudio raises the gun. Molony raises his eyes skywards.

The door comes off its hinges as McAvoy throws himself against the wood. A huge figure in a dirty black coat, he slithers onto the grimy floor in a shower of splinters. Without a word, Claudio turns. Fires. The bullet thumps into the smaller, red-haired man who stands in the open doorway.

Molony lets out a screech of frustration and grabs for the knife.

On the floor, clutching his arm, McAvoy tries to get to his feet. He slips on the snow that billows in through the open doorway. Behind him he hears Valentine crying out in pain. Red pours from the wound in his shoulder like spilled communion wine.

McAvoy scans the room. Sees Molony, naked and horrifically scarred. Swivels his gaze to the other man. Old. Tanned. Blood dripping from a head wound and a gun in his hand.

McAvoy pushes himself upright as Claudio pulls the trigger. The bullet whistles under his arm and through the tails of his coat. McAvoy hurls himself sideways as Molony slashes at him with the knife. McAvoy lashes out with a boot, and something snaps in the Penitent's knee. He howls and falls back.

Claudio catches the stumbling Molony by the wrist. He spins him, takes the hand that holds the knife and turns it back upon Molony.

Close enough to kiss, close enough to see one another's souls, Claudio forces Molony's hand back. The blade enters his heart in slow increments. His soul does not leave his body until the hilt touches skin.

In his dying moments, Molony sees his own hand holding the blade. He knows himself a sinner. His last vision is of Claudio, face emotionless. His last thought is the absolute certainty of his damnation.

Claudio lets body and blade drop to the floor and turns to where McAvoy lies in a carpet of leaves and snow.

'Amen,' says Claudio, and slips to the ground.

Epilogue

'He didn't cry,' says Roisin. 'Walked out of his church the way people do in the films when they're walking to the gallows and want to show they're not afraid. I don't know I'd have been so brave – not with all the cameras and Guards.'

McAvoy listens to her voice. There is a sadness to her words. It sounds as if she is describing a funeral.

'I don't know how much of what he did is a crime,' says McAvoy, just as solemnly. 'How do you charge a priest for absolving sins?'

Roisin stays quiet. McAvoy is pressing the phone into his face so hard that it is leaving an impression upon his cheek. All he wants is her closeness.

'They said he had helped set up fake charities. He'd been complicit in money-laundering. Is that the right word? Complicit?'

McAvoy nods. He can't find any words.

'You're coming home,' says Roisin suddenly. 'Right away. I can get a flight to Humberside, even if it means going via fecking North Korea. I need you. My skin isn't my own, Aector. It's yours. And you need to press yourself against it.'

McAvoy rubs a hand across his nose. 'It was dumb luck,' he says quietly. 'Don't go thinking I did anything impressive. I just blundered around. That's all I did. I bumbled into a situation . . .'

'Shush your bollocks,' says Roisin, and there's a smile in her voice. 'Valentine's coming home. The Teagues and the Heldens are drinking together and my husband is the king of all of it. When I see you, it's going to take a team of firemen to peel me off you.'

McAvoy finds himself grinning. 'A team of firemen? You had to spice the pot, eh?'

Roisin laughs, and when she speaks again, he can hear tears in her words.

'I love you so fucking much I think I could fly,' she says.

'I love you back,' says McAvoy, and he realises he is shaking. 'Always.'

He ends the call and turns back into the hospital room. Ronny Alto has the good grace to pretend he has only just arrived.

'Would have been nice if he'd woken up,' says Alto, looking down at Brishen. 'Doctor says there are good indications in his brain patterns, whatever that means.'

Leaning by the wall, McAvoy gives a nod. 'Travellers are clubbing together to have him flown home. Private facility. The Church is going to contribute.'

'I bet it is,' says Alto, turning away from Brishen. Two days on from the incident at Crow, Alto looks exhausted. He has had to write a lot of reports and tell a lot of lies. In Trish Pharaoh he has found an excellent tutor. Over the course of several Skype chats they have nailed down a plausible story for what happened. In it, McAvoy's role is diminished to little more than an observer but the bosses at both the FBI and the Seventh Precinct are sufficiently impressed with him to allow him to fly home without the need for handcuffs. Valentine is unlikely to be extended the same courtesy until he has finished debriefing the Feds on the size and scale of the underground fight scene and the role of the Russian mob within it. He seems to be enjoying the attention and intends to have the bullet that lodged in his left shoulder turned into a replacement tooth for his upper row.

'You got the results,' says McAvoy quietly. 'I know you did.'

'An unauthorised blood test? Without his permission? That would be a disciplinary matter.'

'Please,' says McAvoy. 'I'm too tired to argue.'

'He's Sal Pugliesca's,' says Alto, nodding at Brishen. 'And Alejandra Mota Valverda's. She was fourteen. Sal liked them young. Whether she thought he was her boyfriend or whether he raped her without preamble, we don't know. Best we can surmise is she was six or seven months pregnant when Tony took her. She gave birth prematurely in that hole. Died there too. True miracle that the baby lived. That place was something out of hell, Aector. It was a madman's vision. We're only just scratching the surface and we've found enough bones to convince you there's true evil in the world. Alejandra must have seen and felt things in those last days that you wouldn't wish on a monster.'

McAvoy swallows. He shakes his head.

'Did Tony take her because of Sal?' asks McAvoy.

Alto shrugs. 'The things that poor bastard went through I don't think we can ever make sense of his motivations. He could only talk among the dying so he took people and made his confessions while they breathed their last. Kept all his confessions in a box for Father Whelan. Maybe he thought he was helping Sal – maybe he thought he was giving his god a more perfect sacrifice. Maybe he was fucking nuts.'

'And Claudio?'

'Your testimony will see him go down for killing Sal Pugliesca and Tony Blank in 1981.'

'For killing a rapist and a serial killer,' mutters McAvoy. 'What about Paulie Pugliesca?'

'Doubt we'll get him but we can get his money. Molony kept detailed accounts. We've got some very clever people with glasses and questionable personal hygiene poring over old manuscripts and church passages trying to make sense of the code he used to hide the different account numbers. They've never been happier. Pugliesca's not showing it but he'll be breaking his heart over this. People will start to doubt the power, after a while. We're already hearing whispers. And Claudio might just cough to killing Sal and Tony on the old man's orders.'

'I can't make sense of Claudio,' says McAvoy gloomily. 'You said he had a stepdaughter?'

'Don't get hung up on it,' says Alto tiredly. 'He's a very bad man, Aector. He's killed so many people.'

'He saved my life.'

'Not really,' says Alto. 'You saved his. How would he have gotten away and got medical attention if he shot Molony? He'd be dead.'

'I thought I'd left it too long. I needed to know, even if it cost him his life.'

Alto shakes his head. 'You did everything right.'

McAvoy closes his eyes. Even after endless showers, a change of clothes and a shave he still looks as though he has been dragged behind a truck. The bruise beneath his eye is the colour of over-ripe bananas.

'Whelan,' says McAvoy. 'How much did he know?'

'Your NBCI are having some interesting conversations with him. He seems quite relieved. He's been confessor to the Mob for decades and his soul sounds like it weighs more than his church.'

'I can't work him out either,' says McAvoy.

'I think he was like any of us. Thought of himself as a good man and then didn't know how to save himself when he realised he'd made mistakes. He certainly seems to have done his best by Brishen. But even thousands of miles away he couldn't really get free. He was valuable to Pugliesca. Valuable to all of them. He thought he was saving souls and he was just giving them a get-out-of-jail-free card.'

McAvoy swallows. It hurts to do so but looking at the miracle man in the hospital bed, he refuses to feel sorry for himself.

'The problems at home are sorted, yeah? No blood feuds? No warring Gypsies?'

McAvoy smiles tiredly. 'All best friends again. Valentine phoned from the ambulance. They'll all be laughing about it over Guinness before Shay's body's in the ground. I don't mean that in a bad way – it's just how they are.'

'And you?'

McAvoy looks away before his blush betrays him. 'She's pleased. She's happy.'

'I'd love to meet her, your Roisin.'

'She'd have been happy even if I'd failed,' says McAvoy, and coughs when he hears his voice crack. 'I don't know who I'd be without her.'

'Or her without you, my friend.'

McAvoy feels too embarrassed to say anything else. He changes the subject.

'Do you think he did it?'

'Who?'

'Paulie Pugliesca? Do you think he ordered his own son to be murdered for informing?'

Alto takes his glasses off and rubs them on his shirt. 'We have to ask Whelan about that. If Whelan knew what Sal was . . . if he knew about Tony Blank. If he'd received those tapes of confession . . . you think he might have broken the seal of the confessional?'

McAvoy shakes his head. Sometimes it seems as though the darkness is like cold water and today it is reaching past his neck.

'How many bodies?'

'Eight. Ali was the last one. Starved to death like the others. We're piecing together Tony's movements over those last days. He told everything to Father Whelan in confession.'

'How? He didn't speak.'

'He could speak in the presence of the dying.'

'Psychologically, is that possible?'

Alto sighs. 'Elective mutism, or selective mutism, or whatever you want to call it – it takes funny shapes. We've got a profiler who says she knew a kid who could speak really lucidly while being beaten but couldn't utter a word at other times. Tony's parents were killed within earshot of where he cowered. He heard his father beaten with golf clubs and chopped into bloody chunks. Saw his mum raped and chopped up with a bloody hatchet. Who are we to say how that would affect somebody?'

'Why did Pugliesca take him in?'

'Guilty conscience?' Alto laughs. 'There are a few old inform-ants reckon he was to blame for the death of Tony's parents in the first place.'

'And he just dumped him in that place on Staten Island.'

'Wherever his soul is now it's no worse than that place,' says Alto, arching his back. 'All the evil involved in this investigation and that's the worst of it by far. The way those kids were treated . . .'

323

'Who do you think he'd have been if he'd just lived a normal life?' asks McAvoy as he crosses to the window. There has been no snow for the past two days and a blue sky is doing battle with the last remaining storm cloud. As he watches the parking lot, a van with a Christmas tree on the roof pulls up. Moments later, McAvoy sees the driver start walking a quartet of reindeer down a ramp from the back of the van. Alto joins him by the window.

'Christmas,' he says. 'They bring them for the sick kids.'

'Sick as in ill? They pet them, not stab them, yes?'

'Jesus,' says Alto. 'Must be rough in Hull.'

'It's never dull,' says McAvoy.

His plane leaves tonight. He's flying back to Galway. Roisin and the children will be there to meet him. He can already taste her kisses. Can summon the smell of his children's skin. He feels as though he lost himself somewhere. He wants to find himself again and knows he cannot do so without them at his side.

'Give Trish my best,' says Alto, and they shake hands by Brishen's bedside. 'She's an impressive woman.'

'She's something,' says McAvoy.

'It's been interesting,' adds Alto, and stares at the bigger man with a look halfway between bemusement and admiration. 'If you're going to come back, let us know in advance. We'll call out the army.'

McAvoy watches him leave. Only when he knows himself to be alone does he cross to Brishen's bedside and look down upon the man born decades ago in a pit in the ground.

'We're more than the sum of our parts,' whispers McAvoy. 'We're more than just our blood. You're a survivor. A fighter. Don't let go, Brishen. Get up. Don't ever stop swinging.'

McAvoy pulls up a chair and sits by the bed.

He has been asleep for only twenty minutes when the bleeping of the monitor changes its rhythm.

On the bed, Brishen's hand becomes a fist . . .

. . . and his eyes open like the gates of heaven.

Acknowledgements

As a lad from Cumbria who lives in Lincolnshire and writes about Hull, I'm perhaps a little under-qualified to pen a crime novel set in New York. Thankfully, there are nice people everywhere who were willing to overlook this fact and help me out with the extraordinary amounts of research needed to make *Cruel Mercy* come to life.

Some, I can name. Others, who spend a lot of their time punching people in underground boxing gyms and pulling people's teeth out with pliers, I had probably better leave in the shadows.

But I think I'm relatively safe to say thanks to the following.

Jack the limo driver from Hong Kong; Fiz on reception at the Comfort Inn; Justin from Melbourne at Lucky Jack's; Genaro and Richie at Church Street Gym; Luis at Oficina Latina for a cocktail that made my ears ring; Shamar from Jamaica and Brandon from Brixton at Bowlmor off Times Square; and at the awesome restaurant Balthazar, I'd like to apologise to Lorraine the waitress for the jokes about your Fanny Bay oysters. Your tolerance was impressive.

As ever, my thanks also go to the team at Mulholland. Ruth, you are an editing wizard and you make the whole process so painless I'm almost sad when you tell me the book is ready to be left alone. Cicely, Rosie, Fleur, Naomi – thanks for putting up with my weirdness. Kerry, you are just the most fabulous firecracker in the box.

Oli, friend and agent, you actually persuaded people to publish a McAvoy novel set in America. Go light a cigar.

Sam Taylor – you brought literally nothing to the writing process and didn't even offer cash. But you asked to be acknowledged and now you have been. You're awesome.

And thanks again to the fellow authors who have supported, cajoled and admonished me in equal measure during a trying time. I'll always appreciate you. Susi Holliday, you're a true friend. Neil White, thanks for, well, you know what. Alexandra, Steph, Helen ... thanks for just being who you are. Val, Peter and Peter – thanks for throwing a kindly word my way and allowing me to think that one day I might be as good as you. Mari, Danielle, Sarah, I love the lot of you.

Finally, thanks to my safety net. The people who catch me when I fall and who put up with more nonsense than anybody should have to endure. George and Elora. I'll never deserve you, but I will always know what love looks and feels like thanks to you.

And once again, here's to you dear reader. Love you, you sick lot.

You've turned the last page.

But it doesn't have to end there . . .

If you're looking for more first-class, action-packed, nail-biting suspense, join us at **Facebook.com/ MulhollandUncovered** for news, competitions, and behind-the-scenes access to Mulholland Books.

For regular updates about our books and authors as well as what's going on in the world of crime and thrillers, follow us on **Twitter@MulhollandUK**.

There are many more twists to come.

MULHOLLAND:
You never know what's coming around the curve.

HODDE